KU-430-006

CONTENTS

THE MAN UPSTAIRS

There were three distinct stages in the evolution of Annette Brougham's attitude towards the knocking in the room above. In the beginning it had been merely a vague discomfort. Absorbed in the composition of her waltz, she had heard it almost subconsciously. The second stage set in when it became a physical pain like red-hot pincers wrenching her mind from her music. Finally, with a thrill in indignation, she knew it for what it was—an insult. The unseen brute disliked her playing, and was intimating his views with a boot-heel.

Defiantly, with her foot on the loud pedal, she struck—almost slapped—the keys once more.

'Bang!' from the room above. 'Bang! Bang!'

Annette rose. Her face was pink, her chin tilted. Her eyes sparkled with the light of battle. She left the room and started to mount the stairs. No spectator, however just, could have helped feeling a pang of pity for the wretched man who stood unconscious of imminent doom, possibly even triumphant, behind the door at which she was on the point of tapping.

'Come in!' cried the voice, rather a pleasant voice; but what is a pleasant voice if the soul be vile?

Annette went in. The room was a typical Chelsea studio, scantily furnished and lacking a carpet. In the centre was an easel, behind which were visible a pair of trousered legs. A cloud of grey smoke was curling up over the top of the easel.

'I beg your pardon,' began Annette.

'I don't want any models at present,' said the Brute. 'Leave your card on the table.'

'I am not a model,' said Annette, coldly. 'I merely came—'

At this the Brute emerged from his fortifications and, removing his pipe from his mouth, jerked his chair out into the open.

'I beg your pardon,' he said. 'Won't you sit down?'

How reckless is Nature in the distribution of her gifts! Not only had this black-hearted knocker on floors a pleasant voice, but, in addition, a pleasing exterior. He was slightly dishevelled at the moment, and his hair stood up in a disordered mop; but in spite of these drawbacks, he was quite passably good-looking. Annette admitted this. Though wrathful, she was fair.

'I thought it was another model,' he explained. 'They've been coming in at the rate of ten an hour ever since I settled here. I didn't object at first, but after about the eightieth child of sunny Italy had shown up it began to get on my nerves.'

Annette waited coldly till he had finished.

'I am sorry,' she said, in a this-is-where-you-get-yours voice, 'if my playing disturbed you.'

One would have thought nobody but an Eskimo wearing his furs and winter under-clothing could have withstood the iciness of her manner; but the Brute did not freeze.

'I am sorry,' repeated Annette, well below zero, 'if my playing disturbed you. I live in the room below, and I heard you knocking.'

'No, no,' protested the young man, affably; 'I like it. Really I do.'

'Then why knock on the floor?' said Annette, turning to go. 'It is so bad for my ceiling,' she said over shoulder. 'I thought you would not mind my mentioning it. Good afternoon.'

'No; but one moment. Don't go.'

She stopped. He was surveying her with a friendly smile. She noticed most reluctantly that he had a nice smile. His composure began to enrage her more and more. Long ere this he should have been writhing at her feet in the dust, crushed and abject.

'You see,' he said, 'I'm awfully sorry, but it's like this. I love music, but what I mean is, you weren't playing a *tune*. It was just the same bit over and over again.'

'I was trying to get a phrase,' said Annette, with dignity, but less coldly. In spite of herself she was beginning to thaw. There was something singularly attractive about this shock-headed youth.

'A phrase?'

'Of music. For my waltz. I am composing a waltz.'

A look of such unqualified admiration overspread the young man's face that the last remnants of the ice-pack melted. For the first time since they had met Annette found herself positively liking this blackguardly floor-smiter.

'Can you compose music?' he said, impressed.

'I have written one or two songs.'

'It must be great to be able to do things—artistic things, I mean, like composing.'

'Well, you do, don't you? You paint.'

The young man shook his head with a cheerful grin.

'I fancy,' he said, 'I should make a pretty good house-painter. I want scope. Canvas seems to cramp me.'

It seemed to cause him no discomfort. He appeared rather amused than otherwise.

'Let me look.'

She crossed over to the easel.

'I shouldn't,' he warned her. 'You really want to? Is this not mere recklessness? Very well, then.'

To the eye of an experienced critic the picture would certainly have seemed crude. It was a study of a dark-eyed child holding a large black cat. Statisticians estimate that there is no moment during the day when one or more young artists somewhere on the face of the globe are not painting pictures of children holding cats.

'I call it "Child and Cat",' said the young man. 'Rather a neat title, don't you think? Gives you the main idea of the thing right away. That,' he explained, pointing obligingly with the stem of his pipe, 'is the cat.'

Annette belonged to that large section of the public which likes or dislikes a picture according to whether its subject happens to please or displease them. Probably there was not one of the million or so child-and-cat eyesores at present in existence which she would not have liked. Besides, he had been very nice about her music.

'I think it's splendid,' she announced.

The young man's face displayed almost more surprise than joy.

'Do you really?' he said. 'Then I can die happy—that is, if you'll let me come down and listen to those songs of yours first.'

'You would only knock on the floor,' objected Annette.

'I'll never knock on another floor as long as I live,' said the ex-brute, reassuringly. 'I hate knocking on floors. I don't see what people want to knock on floors *for*, anyway.'

Friendships ripen quickly in Chelsea. Within the space of an hour and a quarter Annette had learned that the young man's name was Alan Beverley (for which Family Heraldic affliction she pitied rather than despised him), that he did not depend entirely on his work for a living, having a little money of his own, and that he considered this a fortunate thing. From the very beginning of their talk he pleased her. She found him an absolutely new and original variety of the unsuccessful painter. Unlike Reginald Sellers, who had a studio in the same building, and sometimes dropped in to drink her coffee and pour out his troubles, he did not attribute his non-success to any malice or stupidity on the part of the public. She was so used to hearing Sellers lash the Philistine and hold forth on unappreciated merit that she could hardly believe the miracle when, in answer to a sympathetic bromide on the popular lack of taste in Art, Beverley replied that, as far as he was concerned, the public showed strong good sense. If he had been striving with every nerve to win her esteem, he could not have done it more surely than with that one remark. Though she invariably listened with a sweet patience which encouraged them to continue long after the point at which she had begun in spirit to throw things at them, Annette had no sympathy with men who whined. She herself was a fighter. She hated as much as anyone the sickening blows which Fate hands out to the struggling and ambitious; but she never made them the basis of a monologue act. Often, after a dreary trip round the offices of the music-publishers, she would howl bitterly in secret, and even gnaw her pillow in the watches of the night; but in public her pride kept her unvaryingly bright and cheerful.

Today, for the first time, she revealed something of her woes. There was that about the mop-headed young man which invited confidences. She told him of the stony-heartedness of music-publishers, of the difficulty of getting songs printed unless you paid for them, of their wretched sales.

'But those songs you've been playing,' said Beverley, 'they've been published?'

'Yes, those three. But they are the only ones.'

'And didn't they sell?'

'Hardly at all. You see, a song doesn't sell unless somebody well known sings it. And people promise to sing them, and then don't keep their word. You can't depend on what they say.'

'Give me their names,' said Beverley, 'and I'll go round tomorrow and shoot the whole lot. But can't you do anything?'

'Only keep on keeping on.'

'I wish,' he said, 'that any time you're feeling blue about things you would come up and pour out the poison on me. It's no good bottling it up. Come up and tell me about it, and you'll feel ever so much better. Or let me come down. Any time things aren't going right just knock on the ceiling.'

She laughed.

'Don't rub it in,' pleaded Beverley. 'It isn't fair. There's nobody so sensitive as a reformed floor-knocker. You will come up or let me come down, won't you? Whenever I have that sad, depressed feeling, I go out and kill a policeman. But you wouldn't care for that. So the only thing for you to do is to knock on the ceiling. Then I'll come charging down and see if there's anything I can do to help.'

'You'll be sorry you ever said this.'

'I won't,' he said stoutly.

'If you really mean it, it *would* be a relief,' she admitted. 'Sometimes I'd give all the money I'm ever likely to make for someone to shriek my grievances at. I always think it must have been so nice for the people in the old novels, when they used to say: "Sit down and I will tell you the story of my life." Mustn't it have been heavenly?'

'Well,' said Beverley, rising, 'you know where I am if I'm wanted. Right up there where the knocking came from.'

'Knocking?' said Annette. 'I remember no knocking.'

'Would you mind shaking hands?' said Beverley.

A particularly maddening hour with one of her pupils drove her up the very next day. Her pupils were at once her salvation and her despair. They gave her the means of supporting life, but they made life hardly worth supporting. Some of them were learning the piano. Others thought they sang. All had solid ivory skulls. There was about a teaspoonful of grey matter distributed among the entire squad, and the pupil Annette had been teaching that afternoon had come in at the tail-end of the division.

In the studio with Beverley she found Reginald Sellers, standing in a critical attitude before the easel. She was not very fond of him. He was a long, offensive, patronizing person, with a moustache that looked like a smear of charcoal, and a habit of addressing her as 'Ah, little one!'

Beverley looked up.

'Have you brought your hatchet, Miss Brougham? If you have, you're just in time to join in the massacre of the innocents. Sellers has been smiting my child and cat hip and thigh. Look at his eye. There! Did you see it flash then? He's on the warpath again.'

'My dear Beverley,' said Sellers, rather stiffly, 'I am merely endeavouring to give you my idea of the picture's defects. I am sorry if my criticism has to be a little harsh.'

'Go right on,' said Beverley, cordially. 'Don't mind me; it's all for my good.'

'Well, in a word, then, it is lifeless. Neither the child nor the cat lives.'

He stepped back a pace and made a frame of his hands.

'The cat now,' he said. 'It is—how shall I put it? It has no—no—er—'

'That kind of cat wouldn't,' said Beverley. 'It isn't that breed.'

'I think it's a dear cat,' said Annette. She felt her temper, always quick, getting the better of her. She knew just how incompetent Sellers was, and it irritated her beyond endurance to see Beverley's good-humoured acceptance of his patronage.

'At any rate,' said Beverley, with a grin, 'you both seem to recognize that it is a cat. You're solid on that point, and that's something, seeing I'm only a beginner.'

'I know, my dear fellow; I know,' said Sellers, graciously. 'You mustn't let my criticism discourage you. Don't think that your work lacks promise. Far from it. I am sure that in time you will do very well indeed. Quite well.'

A cold glitter might have been observed in Annette's eyes.

'Mr Sellers,' she said, smoothly, 'had to work very hard himself before he reached his present position. You know his work, of course?'

For the first time Beverley seemed somewhat confused.

'I—er—why—' he began.

'Oh, but of course you do,' she went on, sweetly. 'It's in all the magazines.'

Beverley looked at the great man with admiration, and saw that he had flushed uncomfortably. He put this down to the modesty of genius.

'In the advertisement pages,' said Annette. 'Mr Sellers drew that picture of the Waukeesy Shoe and the Restawhile Settee and the tin of sardines in the Little Gem Sardine advertisement. He is very good at still life.'

There was a tense silence. Beverley could almost hear the voice of the referee uttering the count.

'Miss Brougham,' said Sellers at last, spitting out the words, 'has confined herself to the purely commercial side of my work. There is another.'

'Why, of course there is. You sold a landscape for five pounds only eight months ago, didn't you? And another three months before that.'

It was enough. Sellers bowed stiffly and stalked from the room.

Beverley picked up a duster and began slowly to sweep the floor with it.

'What are you doing?' demanded Annette, in a choking voice.

'The fragments of the wretched man,' whispered Beverley. 'They must be swept up and decently interred. You certainly have got the punch, Miss Brougham.'

He dropped the duster with a startled exclamation, for Annette had suddenly burst into a flood of tears. With her face buried in her hands she sat in her chair and sobbed desperately.

'Good Lord!' said Beverley, blankly.

'I'm a cat! I'm a beast! I hate myself!'

'Good Lord!' said Beverley, blankly.

'I'm a pig! I'm a fiend!'

'Good Lord!' said Beverley, blankly.

'We're all struggling and trying to get on and having hard luck, and instead of doing what I can to help, I go and t-t-taunt him with not being able to sell his pictures! I'm not fit to live! *Oh!*'

'Good Lord!' said Beverley, blankly.

A series of gulping sobs followed, diminishing by degrees into silence. Presently she looked up and smiled, a moist and pathetic smile.

'I'm sorry,' she said, 'for being so stupid. But he was so horrid and patronizing to you, I couldn't help scratching. I believe I'm the worst cat in London.'

'No, this is,' said Beverley, pointing to the canvas. 'At least, according to the late Sellers. But, I say, tell me, isn't the deceased a great artist, then? He came curveting in here with his chest out and started to slate my masterpiece, so I naturally said, "What-ho! 'Tis a genius!" Isn't he?'

'He can't sell his pictures anywhere. He lives on the little he can get from illustrating advertisements. And I t-taunt—'

'*Please!*' said Beverley, apprehensively.

She recovered herself with a gulp.

'I can't help it,' she said, miserably. 'I rubbed it in. Oh, it was hateful of me! But I was all on edge from teaching one of my awful pupils, and when he started to patronize you—'

She blinked.

'Poor devil!' said Beverley. 'I never guessed. Good Lord!'

Annette rose.

'I must go and tell him I'm sorry,' she said. 'He'll snub me horribly, but I must.'

She went out. Beverley lit a pipe and stood at the window looking thoughtfully down into the street.

It is a good rule in life never to apologize. The right sort of people do not want apologies, and the wrong sort take a mean advantage of them. Sellers belonged to the latter class. When Annette, meek, penitent, with all her claws sheathed, came to him and grovelled, he forgave her with a repulsive magnanimity which in a less subdued mood would have stung her to renewed pugnacity. As it was, she allowed herself to be forgiven, and retired with a dismal conviction that from now on he would be more insufferable than ever.

Her surmise proved absolutely correct. His visits to the newcomer's studio began again, and Beverley's picture, now nearing completion, came in for criticism enough to have filled a volume. The good humour with which he received it amazed Annette. She had no proprietary interest in the painting beyond what she acquired from a growing regard for its parent (which disturbed her a good deal when she had time to think of it); but there were moments when only the recollection of her remorse for her previous outbreak kept her from rending the critic. Beverley, however, appeared to have no artistic sensitiveness whatsoever. When Sellers savaged the cat in a manner which should have brought the S.P.C.A.

down upon him, Beverley merely beamed. His long-sufferingness was beyond Annette's comprehension.

She began to admire him for it.

To make his position as critic still more impregnable, Sellers was now able to speak as one having authority. After years of floundering, his luck seemed at last to have turned. His pictures, which for months had lain at an agent's, careened like crippled battleships, had at length begun to find a market. Within the past two weeks three landscapes and an allegorical painting had sold for good prices; and under the influence of success he expanded like an opening floweret. When Epstein, the agent, wrote to say that the allegory had been purchased by a Glasgow plutocrat of the name of Bates for one hundred and sixty guineas, Sellers' views on Philistines and their crass materialism and lack of taste underwent a marked modification. He spoke with some friendliness of the man Bates.

'To me,' said Beverley, when informed of the event by Annette, 'the matter has a deeper significance. It proves that Glasgow has at last produced a sober man. No drinker would have dared face that allegory. The whole business is very gratifying.'

Beverley himself was progressing slowly in the field of Art. He had finished the 'Child and Cat', and had taken it to Epstein together with a letter of introduction from Sellers. Sellers' habitual attitude now was that of the kindly celebrity who has arrived and wishes to give the youngsters a chance.

Since its departure Beverley had not done much in the way of actual execution. Whenever Annette came to his studio he was either sitting in a chair with his feet on the window-sill, smoking, or in the same attitude listening to Sellers' views on art. Sellers being on the upgrade, a man with many pounds to his credit in the bank, had more leisure now. He had given up his advertisement work, and was planning a great canvas—another allegorical work. This left him free to devote a good deal of time to Beverley, and he did so. Beverley sat and smoked through his harangues. He may have been listening, or he may not. Annette listened once or twice, and the experience had the effect of sending her to Beverley, quivering with indignation.

'Why do you *let* him patronize you like that?' she demanded. 'If anybody came and talked to me like that about my music, I'd—I'd—I don't know what I'd do. Yes, even if he were really a great musician.'

'Don't you consider Sellers a great artist, then, even now?'

'He seems to be able to sell his pictures, so I suppose they must be good; but nothing could give him the right to patronize you as he does.'

'"My learned friend's manner would be intolerable in an emperor to a black-beetle,"' quoted Beverley. 'Well, what are we going to do about it?'

'If only you could sell a picture, too!'

'Ah! Well, I've done my part of the contract. I've delivered the goods. There the thing is at Epstein's. The public can't blame me if it doesn't sell. All they've got to do is to waltz in in their thousands and fight for it. And, by the way, talking of waltzes—'

'Oh, it's finished,' said Annette, dispiritedly. 'Published too, for that matter.'

'Published! What's the matter, then? Why this drooping sadness? Why aren't you running around the square, singing like a bird?'

'Because,' said Annette, 'unfortunately, I had to pay the expenses of publication. It was only five pounds, but the sales haven't caught up with that yet. If they ever do, perhaps there'll be a new edition.'

'And will you have to pay for that?'

'No. The publishers would.'

'Who are they?'

'Grusczinsky and Buchterkirch.'

'Heavens, then what are you worrying about? The thing's a cert. A man with a name like Grusczinsky could sell a dozen editions by himself. Helped and inspired by Buchterkirch, he will make the waltz the talk of the country. Infants will croon it in their cots.'

'He didn't seem to think so when I saw him last.'

'Of course not. He doesn't know his own power. Grusczinsky's shrinking diffidence is a by-word in musical circles. He is the genuine Human Violet. You must give him time.'

'I'll give him anything if he'll only sell an edition or two,' said Annette.

The outstanding thing was that he did. There seemed no particular reason why the sale of that waltz should not have been as small and as slow as that of any other waltz by an unknown composer. But almost without warning it expanded from a trickle into a flood. Grusczinsky, beaming paternally whenever Annette entered the shop—which was often—announced two new editions in a week. Beverley, his artistic growth still under a watchful eye of Sellers, said he had never had any doubts as to the success of the thing from the moment when a single phrase in it had so carried him away that he had compelled to stamp his applause enthusiastically on the floor. Even Sellers forgot his own triumphs long enough to allow him to offer affable congratulations. And money came rolling in, smoothing the path of life.

Those were great days. There was a hat ...

Life, in short, was very full and splendid. There was, indeed, but one thing which kept it from being perfect. The usual drawback to success is that it annoys one's friends so; but in Annette's case this drawback was absent. Sellers' demeanour towards her was that of an old-established inmate welcoming a novice into the Hall of Fame. Her pupils—worthy souls, though bone-headed—fawned upon her. Beverley seemed more pleased than anyone. Yet it was Beverley who prevented her paradise from being complete. Successful herself, she wanted all her friends to be successful; but Beverley, to her discomfort, remained a cheery failure, and worse, absolutely refused to snub Sellers. It was not as if Sellers' advice and comments were disinterested. Beverley was simply the instrument on which he played his songs of triumph. It distressed Annette to such an extent that now, if she went upstairs and heard Sellers' voice in the studio, she came down again without knocking.

One afternoon, sitting in her room, she heard the telephone-bell ring.

The telephone was on the stairs, just outside her door. She went out and took up the receiver.

'Halloa!' said a querulous voice. 'Is Mr Beverley there?'

Annette remembered having heard him go out. She could always tell his footstep.

'He is out,' she said. 'Is there any message?'

'Yes,' said the voice, emphatically. 'Tell him that Rupert Morrison rang up to ask what he was to do with all this great stack of music that's arrived. Does he want it forwarded on to him, or what?' The voice was growing high and excited. Evidently Mr Morrison was in a state of nervous tension when a man does not care particularly who hears his troubles so long as he unburdens himself of them to someone.

'Music?' said Annette.

'Music!' shrilled Mr Morrison. 'Stacks and stacks and stacks of it. Is he playing a practical joke on me, or what?' he demanded, hysterically. Plainly he had now come to regard Annette as a legitimate confidante. She was listening. That was the main point. He wanted someone—he did not care whom—who would listen. 'He lends me his rooms,' wailed Mr Morrison, 'so that I can be perfectly quiet and undisturbed while I write my novel, and, first thing I know, this music starts to arrive. How can I be quiet and undisturbed when the floor's littered two yards high with great parcels of music, and more coming every day?'

Annette clung weakly to the telephone box. Her mind was in a whirl, but she was beginning to see many things.

'Are you there?' called Mr Morrison.

'Yes. What—what firm does the music come from?'

'What's that?'

'Who are the publishers who send the music?'

'I can't remember. Some long name. Yes, I've got it. Gruszcinsky and someone.'

'I'll tell Mr Beverley,' said Annette, quietly. A great weight seemed to have settled on her head.

'Halloa! Halloa! Are you there?' came Mr Morrison's voice.

'Yes?'

'And tell him there are some pictures, too.'

'Pictures?'

'Four great beastly pictures. The size of elephants. I tell you, there isn't room to move. And—'

Annette hung up the receiver.

Mr Beverley, returned from his walk, was racing up the stairs three at a time in his energetic way, when, as he arrived at Annette's door, it opened.

'Have you a minute to spare?' said Annette.

'Of course. What's the trouble? Have they sold another edition of the waltz?'

'I have not heard, Mr—Bates.'

For once she looked to see the cheerful composure of the man upstairs become ruffled; but he received the blow without agitation.

'You know my name?' he said.

'I know a good deal more than your name. You are a Glasgow millionaire.'

'It's true,' he admitted, 'but it's hereditary. My father was one before me.'

'And you use your money,' said Annette, bitterly, 'creating fools' paradises for your friends, which last, I suppose, until you grow tired of the amusement and destroy them. Doesn't it ever strike you, Mr Bates, that it's a little cruel? Do you think Mr Sellers will settle down again cheerfully to hack-work when you stop buying his pictures, and he finds out that—that—'

'I shan't stop,' said the young man. 'If a Glasgow millionaire mayn't buy Sellers' allegorical pictures, whose allegorical pictures may he buy? Sellers will never find out. He'll go on painting and I'll go on buying, and all will be joy and peace.'

'Indeed! And what future have you arranged for me?'

'You?' he said, reflectively. 'I want to marry you.'

Annette stiffened from head to foot. He met her blazing eyes with a look of quiet devotion.

'Marry me?'

'I know what you are thinking,' he said. 'Your mind is dwelling on the prospect of living in a house decorated throughout with Sellers' allegorical pictures. But it won't be. We'll store them in the attic.'

She began to speak, but he interrupted her.

'Listen!' he said. 'Sit down and I will tell you the story of my life. We'll skip the first twenty-eight years and three months, merely mentioning that for the greater part of that time I was looking for somebody just like you. A month and nine days ago I found you. You were crossing the Embankment. I was also on the Embankment. In a taxi. I stopped the taxi, got out, and observed you just stepping into the Charing Cross Underground. I sprang—'

'This does not interest me,' said Annette.

'The plot thickens,' he assured her. 'We left our hero springing, I think. Just so. Well, you took the West End train and got off at Sloane Square. So did I. You crossed Sloane Square, turned up King's Road, and finally arrived here. I followed. I saw a notice up, "Studio to Let". I reflected that, having done a little painting in an amateur way, I could pose as an artist all right; so I took the studio. Also the name of Alan Beverley. My own is Bill Bates. I had often wondered what it would feel like to be called by some name like Alan Beverley or Cyril Trevelyan. It was simply the spin of the coin which decided me in favour of the former. Once in, the problem was how to get to know you. When I heard you playing I knew it was all right. I had only to keep knocking on the floor long enough—'

'Do—you—mean—to—tell—me'—Annette's voice trembled 'do you mean to tell me that you knocked that time simply to make me come up?'

'That was it. Rather a scheme, don't you think? And now, would you mind telling me how you found out that I had been buying your waltz? Those remarks of yours about fools' paradises were not inspired solely by the affairs of Sellers. But it beats me how you did it. I swore Rozinsky, or whatever his name is, to secrecy.'

'A Mr Morrison,' sad Annette, indifferently, 'rang up on the telephone and asked me to tell you that he was greatly worried by the piles of music which were littering the rooms you lent him.'

The young man burst into a roar of laughter.

'Poor old Morrison! I forgot all about him. I lent him my rooms at the Albany. He's writing a novel, and he can't work if the slightest thing goes wrong. It just shows—'

'Mr Bates!'

'Yes?'

'Perhaps you didn't intend to hurt me. I dare say you meant only to be kind. But—but—oh, can't you see how you have humiliated me? You have treated me like a child, giving me a make-believe success just to—just to keep me quiet, I suppose. You—'

He was fumbling in his pocket.

'May I read you a letter?' he said.

'A letter?'

'Quite a short one. It is from Epstein, the picture-dealer. This is what he says. "Sir," meaning me, not "Dear Bill," mind you—just "Sir." "I am glad to be able to inform you that I have this morning received an offer of ten guineas for your picture, 'Child and Cat'. Kindly let me know if I am to dispose of it at this price."'

'Well?' said Annette, in a small voice.

'I have just been to Epstein's. It seems that the purchaser is a Miss Brown. She gave an address in Bayswater. I called at the address. No Miss Brown lives there, but one of your pupils does. I asked her if she was expecting a parcel for Miss Brown, and she said that she had had your letter and quite understood and would take it in when it arrived.'

Annette was hiding her face in her hands.

'Go away!' she said, faintly.

Mr Bates moved a step nearer.

'Do you remember that story of the people on the island who eked out a precarious livelihood by taking in one another's washing?' he asked, casually.

'Go away!' cried Annette.

'I've always thought,' he said, 'that it must have drawn them very close together—made them feel rather attached to each other. Don't you?'

'Go away!'

'I don't want to go away. I want to stay and hear you say you'll marry me.'

'*Please* go away! I want to think.'

She heard him moving towards the door. He stopped, then went on again. The door closed quietly. Presently from the room above came the sound of footsteps—footsteps pacing monotonously to and fro like those of an animal in a cage.

Annette sat listening. There was no break in the footsteps.

Suddenly she got up. In one corner of the room was a long pole used for raising and lowering the window-sash. She took it, and for a moment stood irresolute. Then with a quick movement, she lifted it and stabbed three times at the ceiling.

SOMETHING TO WORRY ABOUT

A girl stood on the shingle that fringes Millbourne Bay, gazing at the red roofs of the little village across the water. She was a pretty girl, small and trim. Just now some secret sorrow seemed to be troubling her, for on her forehead were wrinkles and in her eyes a look of wistfulness. She had, in fact, all the distinguishing marks of one who is thinking of her sailor lover.

But she was not. She had no sailor lover. What she was thinking of was that at about this time they would be lighting up the shop-windows in London, and that of all the deadly, depressing spots she had ever visited this village of Millbourne was the deadliest.

The evening shadows deepened. The incoming tide glistened oilily as it rolled over the mud flats. She rose and shivered.

'Goo! What a hole!' she said, eyeing the unconscious village morosely. '*What* a hole!'

This was Sally Preston's first evening in Millbourne. She had arrived by the afternoon train from London—not of her own free will. Left to herself, she would not have come within sixty miles of the place. London supplied all that she demanded from life. She had been born in London; she had lived there ever since—she hoped to die there. She liked fogs, motor-buses, noise, policemen, paper-boys, shops, taxi-cabs, artificial light, stone pavements, houses in long, grey rows, mud, banana-skins, and moving-picture exhibitions. Especially moving-picture exhibitions. It was, indeed, her taste for these that had caused her banishment to Millbourne.

The great public is not yet unanimous on the subject of moving-picture exhibitions. Sally, as I have said, approved of them. Her father, on the other hand, did not. An austere ex-butler, who let lodgings in Ebury Street and preached on Sundays in Hyde Park, he looked askance at the 'movies'. It was his boast that he had never been inside a theatre in his life, and he classed cinema palaces with theatres as wiles of the devil. Sally, suddenly unmasked as an habitual frequenter of these abandoned places, sprang with one bound into prominence as the Bad Girl of the Family. Instant removal from the range of temptation being the only possible plan, it seemed to Mr Preston that a trip to the country was indicated.

He selected Millbourne because he had been butler at the Hall there, and because his sister Jane, who had been a parlour-maid at the Rectory, was now married and living in the village.

Certainly he could not have chosen a more promising reformatory for Sally. Here, if anywhere, might she forget the heady joys of the cinema. Tucked away in the corner of its little bay, which an accommodating island converts into a still lagoon, Millbourne lies dozing. In all sleepy Hampshire there is no sleepier spot. It is a place of calm-eyed men and drowsy dogs. Things crumble away and are not replaced. Tradesmen book orders, and then lose interest and forget to deliver the goods. Only centenarians die, and nobody worries about anything—or did not until Sally came and gave them something to worry about.

Next door to Sally's Aunt Jane, in a cosy little cottage with a wonderful little garden, lived Thomas Kitchener, a large, grave, self-sufficing young man, who, by sheer application to work, had become already, though only twenty-five, second gardener at the Hall. Gardening absorbed him. When he was not working at the Hall he was working at home. On the morning following Sally's arrival, it being a Thursday and his day off, he was crouching in a constrained attitude in his garden, every fibre of his being concentrated on the interment of a plump young bulb. Consequently, when a chunk of mud came sailing over the fence, he did not notice it.

A second, however, compelled attention by bursting like a shell on the back of his neck. He looked up, startled. Nobody was in sight. He was puzzled. It could hardly be raining mud. Yet the alternative theory, that someone in the next garden was throwing it, was hardly less bizarre. The nature of his friendship with Sally's Aunt Jane and old Mr Williams, her husband, was comfortable rather than rollicking. It was inconceivable that they should be flinging clods at him.

As he stood wondering whether he should go to the fence and look over, or simply accept the phenomenon as one of those things which no fellow can understand, there popped up before him the head and shoulders of a girl. Poised in her right hand was a third clod, which, seeing that there was now no need for its services, she allowed to fall to the ground.

'Halloa!' she said. 'Good morning.'

She was a pretty girl, small and trim. Tom was by way of being the strong, silent man with a career to think of and no time for bothering about girls, but he saw that. There was, moreover, a certain alertness in her expression rarely found in the feminine population of Millbourne, who were apt to be slightly bovine.

'What do you think *you're* messing about at?' she said, affably.

Tom was a slow-minded young man, who liked to have his thoughts well under control before he spoke. He was not one of your gay rattlers. Besides, there was something about this girl which confused him to an extraordinary extent. He was conscious of new and strange emotions. He stood staring silently.

'What's your name, anyway?'

He could answer that. He did so.

'Oh! Mine's Sally Preston. Mrs Williams is my aunt. I've come from London.'

Tom had no remarks to make about London.

'Have you lived here all your life?'

'Yes,' said Tom.

'My goodness! Don't you ever feel fed up? Don't you want a change?'

Tom considered the point.

'No,' he said.

'Well, *I* do. I want one now.'

'It's a nice place,' hazarded Tom.

'It's nothing of the sort. It's the beastliest hole in existence. It's absolutely chronic. Perhaps you wonder why I'm here. Don't think I *wanted* to come here. Not me! I was sent. It was like this.' She gave him a rapid summary of her troubles. 'There! Don't you call it a bit thick?' she concluded.

Tom considered this point, too.

'You must make the best of it,' he said, at length.

'I won't! I'll make father take me back.'

Tom considered this point also. Rarely, if ever, had he been given so many things to think about in one morning.

'How?' he inquired, at length.

'I don't know. I'll find some way. You see if I don't. I'll get away from here jolly quick, I give you *my* word.'

Tom bent low over a rose-bush. His face was hidden, but the brown of his neck seemed to take on a richer hue, and his ears were undeniably crimson. His feet moved restlessly, and from his unseen mouth there proceeded the first gallant speech his lips had ever framed. Merely considered as a speech, it was, perhaps, nothing wonderful; but from Tom it was a miracle of chivalry and polish.

What he said was: 'I hope not.'

And instinct telling him that he had made his supreme effort, and that anything further must be bathos, he turned abruptly and stalked into his cottage, where he drank tea and ate bacon and thought chaotic thoughts. And when his appetite declined to carry him more than half-way through the third rasher, he understood. He was in love.

These strong, silent men who mean to be head-gardeners before they are thirty, and eliminate woman from their lives as a dangerous obstacle to the successful career, pay a heavy penalty when they do fall in love. The average irresponsible young man who has hung about North Street on Saturday nights, walked through the meadows and round by the mill and back home past the creek on Sunday afternoons, taken his seat in the brake for the annual outing, shuffled his way through the polka at the tradesmen's ball, and generally seized all legitimate opportunities for sporting with Amaryllis in the shade, has a hundred advantages which your successful careerer lacks. There was hardly a moment during the days which followed when Tom did not regret his neglected education.

For he was not Sally's only victim in Millbourne. That was the trouble. Her beauty was not of that elusive type which steals imperceptibly into the vision of the rare connoisseur. It was sudden and compelling. It hit you. Bright brown eyes beneath a mass of fair hair, a determined little chin, a slim figure—these are disturbing things; and the youths of peaceful Millbourne sat up and took notice as one youth. Throw your mind back to the last musical comedy you saw. Recall the leading lady's song with chorus of young men, all proffering devotion simultaneously in a neat row. Well, that was how the lads of the village comported themselves towards Sally.

Mr and Mrs Williams, till then a highly-esteemed but little-frequented couple, were astonished at the sudden influx of visitors. The cottage became practically a *salon*. There was not an evening when the little sitting-room looking out on the garden was not packed. It is true that the conversation lacked some of the sparkle generally found in the better class of *salon*. To be absolutely accurate, there was hardly any conversation. The youths of Melbourne were sturdy and honest. They were the backbone of England. England, in her hour of need, could have called upon them with the comfortable certainty that, unless they happened to be otherwise engaged, they would leap to her aid.

But they did not shine at small-talk. Conversationally they were a spent force after they had asked Mr Williams how his rheumatism was. Thereafter they contented themselves with sitting massively about in corners, glowering at each other. Still, it was all very jolly and sociable, and helped to pass the long evenings. And, as Mrs Williams pointed out, in reply to some rather strong remarks from Mr Williams on the subject of packs of young fools who made it impossible for a man to get a quiet smoke in his own home, it kept them out of the public-houses.

Tom Kitchener, meanwhile, observed the invasion with growing dismay. Shyness barred him from the evening gatherings, and what was going on in that house, with young bloods like Ted Pringle, Albert Parsons, Arthur Brown, and Joe Blossom (to name four of the most assiduous) exercising their fascinations at close range, he did not like to think. Again and again he strove to brace himself up to join the feasts of reason and flows of soul which he knew were taking place nightly around the object of his devotions, but every time he failed. Habit is a terrible thing; it shackles the strongest, and Tom had fallen into the habit of inquiring after Mr Williams' rheumatism over the garden fence first thing in the morning.

It was a civil, neighbourly thing to do, but it annihilated the only excuse he could think of for looking in at night. He could not help himself. It was like some frightful scourge—the morphine habit, or something of that sort. Every morning he swore to himself that nothing would induce him to mention the subject of rheumatism, but no sooner had the stricken old gentleman's head appeared above the fence than out it came.

'Morning, Mr Williams.'

'Morning, Tom.'

Pause, indicative of a strong man struggling with himself; then:

'How's the rheumatism, Mr Williams?'

'Better, thank'ee, Tom.'

And there he was, with his guns spiked.

However, he did not give up. He brought to his wooing the same determination which had made him second gardener at the Hall at twenty-five. He was a novice at the game, but instinct told him that a good line of action was to shower gifts. He did so. All he had to shower was vegetables, and he showered them in a way that would have caused the goddess Ceres to be talked about. His garden became a perfect crater, erupting vegetables. Why vegetables? I think I hear some heckler cry. Why not flowers—fresh, fair, fragrant flowers? You can do a lot with flowers. Girls love them. There is poetry in them. And, what is more, there is a recognized language of flowers. Shoot in a rose, or a calceolaria, or an herbaceous border, or something, I gather, and you have made a formal proposal of marriage without any of the trouble of rehearsing a long speech and practising appropriate gestures in front of your bedroom looking-glass. Why, then, did not Thomas Kitchener give Sally Preston flowers? Well, you see, unfortunately, it was now late autumn, and there were no flowers. Nature had temporarily exhausted her floral blessings, and was jogging along with potatoes and artichokes and things. Love is like that. It invariably comes just at the wrong time. A few months before there had been enough roses in Tom Kitchener's garden to win the hearts of a dozen girls. Now there were only vegetables, 'Twas ever thus.

It was not to be expected that a devotion so practically displayed should escape comment. This was supplied by that shrewd observer, old Mr Williams. He spoke seriously to Tom across the fence on the subject of his passion.

'Young Tom,' he said, 'drop it.'

Tom muttered unintelligibly. Mr Williams adjusted the top-hat without which he never stirred abroad, even into his garden. He blinked benevolently at Tom.

'You're making up to that young gal of Jane's,' he proceeded. 'You can't deceive *me*. All these p'taties, and what not. *I* seen your game fast enough. Just you drop it, young Tom.'

'Why?' muttered Tom, rebelliously. A sudden distaste for old Mr Williams blazed within him.

'Why? 'Cos you'll only burn your fingers if you don't, that's why. I been watching this young gal of Jane's, and I seen what sort of a young gal she be. She's a flipperty piece, that's what she be. You marry that young gal, Tom, and you'll never have no more quiet and happiness. She'd just take and turn the place upsy-down on you. The man as marries that young gal has got to be master in his own home. He's got to show her what's what. Now, you ain't got the devil in you to do that, Tom. You're what I might call a sort of a sheep. I admires it in you, Tom. I like to see a young man steady and quiet, same as what you be. So that's how it is, you see. Just you drop this foolishness, young Tom, and leave that young gal be, else you'll burn your fingers, same as what I say.'

And, giving his top-hat a rakish tilt, the old gentleman ambled indoors, satisfied that he had dropped a guarded hint in a pleasant and tactful manner.

It is to be supposed that this interview stung Tom to swift action. Otherwise, one cannot explain why he should not have been just as reticent on the subject nearest his heart when bestowing on Sally the twenty-seventh cabbage as he had been when administering the hundred and sixtieth potato. At any rate, the fact remains that, as that fateful vegetable changed hands across the fence, something resembling a proposal of marriage did actually proceed from him. As a sustained piece of emotional prose it fell short of the highest standard. Most of it was lost at the back of his throat, and what did emerge was mainly inaudible. However, as she distinctly caught the word 'love' twice, and as Tom was shuffling his feet and streaming with perspiration, and looking everywhere at once except at her, Sally grasped the situation. Whereupon, without any visible emotion, she accepted him.

Tom had to ask her to repeat her remark. He could not believe his luck. It is singular how diffident a normally self-confident man can become, once he is in love. When Colonel Milvery, of the Hall, had informed him of his promotion to the post of second gardener, Tom had demanded no *encore*. He knew his worth. He was perfectly aware that he was a good gardener, and official recognition of the fact left him gratified, but unperturbed. But this affair of Sally was quite another matter. It had revolutionized his standards of value—forced him to consider himself as a man, entirely apart from his skill as a gardener. And until this moment he had had grave doubt as to whether, apart from his skill as a gardener, he amounted to much.

He was overwhelmed. He kissed Sally across the fence humbly. Sally, for her part, seemed very unconcerned about it all. A more critical man than Thomas Kitchener might have said that, to all appearances, the thing rather bored Sally.

'Don't tell anybody just yet,' she stipulated.

Tom would have given much to be allowed to announce his triumph defiantly to old Mr Williams, to say nothing of making a considerable noise about it in the village; but her wish was law, and he reluctantly agreed.

There are moments in a man's life when, however enthusiastic a gardener he may be, his soul soars above vegetables. Tom's shot with a jerk into the animal kingdom. The first present he gave Sally in his capacity of fiance was a dog.

It was a half-grown puppy with long legs and a long tail, belonging to no one species, but generously distributing itself among about six. Sally loved it, and took it with her wherever she went. And on one of these rambles down swooped Constable Cobb, the village policeman, pointing out that, contrary to regulations, the puppy had no collar.

It is possible that a judicious meekness on Sally's part might have averted disaster. Mr Cobb was human, and Sally was looking particularly attractive that morning. Meekness, however, did not come easily to Sally. In a speech which began as argument and ended (Mr Cobb proving solid and unyielding) as pure cheek, she utterly routed the constable. But her victory was only a moral one, for as she turned to go Mr Cobb, dull red and puffing slightly, was already entering particulars of the affair in his note-book, and Sally knew that the last word was with him.

On her way back she met Tom Kitchener. He was looking very tough and strong, and at the sight of him a half-formed idea, which she had regretfully dismissed as impracticable, of assaulting Constable Cobb, returned to her in an amended form. Tom did not know it, but the reason why she smiled so radiantly upon him at that moment was that she had just elected him to the post of hired assassin. While she did not want Constable Cobb actually assassinated, she earnestly desired him to have his helmet smashed down over his eyes; and it seemed to her that Tom was the man to do it.

She poured out her grievance to him and suggested her scheme. She even elaborated it.

'Why shouldn't you wait for him one night and throw him into the creek? It isn't deep, and it's jolly muddy.'

'Um!' said Tom, doubtfully.

'It would just teach him,' she pointed out.

But the prospect of undertaking the higher education of the police did not seem to appeal to Tom. In his heart he rather sympathized with Constable Cobb. He saw the policeman's point of view. It is all very well to talk, but when you are stationed in a sleepy village where no one ever murders, or robs, or commits arson, or even gets drunk and disorderly in the street, a puppy without a collar is simply a godsend. A man must look out for himself.

He tried to make this side of the question clear to Sally, but failed signally. She took a deplorable view of his attitude.

'I might have known you'd have been afraid,' she said, with a contemptuous jerk of her chin. 'Good morning.'

Tom flushed. He knew he had never been afraid of anything in his life, except her; but nevertheless the accusation stung. And as he was still afraid of her he stammered as he began to deny the charge.

'Oh, leave off!' said Sally, irritably. 'Suck a lozenge.'

'I'm not afraid,' said Tom, condensing his remarks to their minimum as his only chance of being intelligible.

'You are.'

'I'm not. It's just that I—'

A nasty gleam came into Sally's eyes. Her manner was haughty.

'It doesn't matter.' She paused. 'I've no doubt Ted Pringle will do what I want.'

For all her contempt, she could not keep a touch of uneasiness from her eyes as she prepared to make her next remark. There was a look about Tom's set jaw which made her hesitate. But her temper had run away with her, and she went on.

'I am sure he will,' she said. 'When we became engaged he said that he would do anything for me.'

There are some speeches that are such conversational knockout blows that one can hardly believe that life will ever pick itself up and go on again after them. Yet it does. The dramatist brings down the curtain on such speeches. The novelist blocks his reader's path with a zareba of stars. But in life there are no curtains, no stars, nothing final and definite—only ragged pauses and discomfort. There was such a pause now.

'What do you mean?' said Tom at last. 'You promised to marry me.'

'I know I did—and I promised to marry Ted Pringle!'

That touch of panic which she could not wholly repress, the panic that comes to everyone when a situation has run away with them like a strange, unmanageable machine, infused a shade too much of the defiant into Sally's manner. She had wished to be cool, even casual, but she was beginning to be afraid. Why, she could not have said. Certainly she did not anticipate violence on

Tom's part. Perhaps that was it. Perhaps it was just because he was so quiet that she was afraid. She had always looked on him contemptuously as an amiable, transparent lout, and now he was puzzling her. She got an impression of something formidable behind his stolidity, something that made her feel mean and insignificant.

She fought against the feeling, but it gripped her; and, in spite of herself, she found her voice growing shrill and out of control.

'I promised to marry Ted Pringle, and I promised to marry Joe Blossom, and I promised to marry Albert Parsons. And I was going to promise to marry Arthur Brown and anybody else who asked me. So now you know! I told you I'd make father take me back to London. Well, when he hears that I've promised to marry four different men, I bet he'll have me home by the first train.'

She stopped. She had more to say, but she could not say it. She stood looking at him. And he looked at her. His face was grey and his mouth oddly twisted. Silence seemed to fall on the whole universe.

Sally was really afraid now, and she knew it. She was feeling very small and defenceless in an extremely alarming world. She could not have said what it was that had happened to her. She only knew that life had become of a sudden very vivid, and that her ideas as to what was amusing had undergone a striking change. A man's development is a slow and steady process of the years—a woman's a thing of an instant. In the silence which followed her words Sally had grown up.

Tom broke the silence.

'Is that true?' he said.

His voice made her start. He had spoken quietly, but there was a new note in it, strange to her. Just as she could not have said what it was that had happened to her, so now she could not have said what had happened to Tom. He, too, had changed, but how she did not know. Yet the explanation was simple. He also had, in a sense, grown up. He was no longer afraid of her.

He stood thinking. Hours seemed to pass.

'Come along!' he said, at last, and he began to move off down the road.

Sally followed. The possibility of refusing did not enter her mind.

'Where are you going?' she asked. It was unbearable, this silence.

He did not answer.

In this fashion, he leading, she following, they went down the road into a lane, and through a gate into a field. They passed into a second field, and as they did so Sally's heart gave a leap. Ted Pringle was there.

Ted Pringle was a big young man, bigger even than Tom Kitchener, and, like Tom, he was of silent habit. He eyed the little procession inquiringly, but spoke no word. There was a pause.

'Ted,' said Tom, 'there's been a mistake.'

He stepped quickly to Sally's side, and the next moment he had swung her off her feet and kissed her.

To the type of mind that Millbourne breeds, actions speak louder than words, and Ted Pringle, who had gaped, gaped no more. He sprang forward, and Tom, pushing Sally aside, turned to meet him.

I cannot help feeling a little sorry for Ted Pringle. In the light of what happened, I could wish that it were possible to portray him as a hulking brute of evil appearance and worse morals—the sort of person concerning whom one could reflect comfortably that he deserved all he got. I should like to make him an unsympathetic character, over whose downfall the reader would gloat. But honesty compels me to own that Ted was a thoroughly decent young man in every way. He was a good citizen, a dutiful son, and would certainly have made an excellent husband. Furthermore, in the dispute on hand he had right on his side fully as much as Tom. The whole affair was one of those elemental clashings of man and man where the historian cannot sympathize with either side at the expense of the other, but must confine himself to a mere statement of what occurred. And, briefly, what occurred was that Tom, bringing to the fray a pent-up fury which his adversary had had no time to generate, fought Ted to a complete standstill in the space of two minutes and a half.

Sally had watched the proceedings, sick and horrified. She had never seen men fight before, and the terror of it overwhelmed her. Her vanity received no pleasant stimulation from the thought that it was for her sake that this storm had been let loose. For the moment her vanity was dead, stunned by collision with the realities. She found herself watching in a dream. She saw Ted fall, rise, fall again, and lie where he had fallen; and then she was aware that Tom was speaking.

'Come along!'

She hung back. Ted was lying very still. Gruesome ideas presented themselves. She had just accepted them as truth when Ted wriggled. He wriggled again. Then he sat up suddenly, looked at her with unseeing eyes, and said something in a thick voice. She gave a little sob of relief. It was ghastly, but not so ghastly as what she had been imagining.

Somebody touched her arm. Tom was by her side, grim and formidable. He was wiping blood from his face.

'Come along!'

She followed him without a word. And presently, behold, in another field, whistling meditatively and regardless of impending ill, Albert Parsons.

In everything that he did Tom was a man of method. He did not depart from his chosen formula.

'Albert,' he said, 'there's been a mistake.'

And Albert gaped, as Ted had gaped.

Tom kissed Sally with the gravity of one performing a ritual.

The uglinesses of life, as we grow accustomed to them, lose their power to shock, and there is no doubt that Sally looked with a different eye upon this second struggle. She was conscious of a thrill of excitement, very different from the shrinking horror which had seized her before. Her stunned vanity began to tingle into life again. The fight was raging furiously over the trampled turf, and quite suddenly, as she watched, she was aware that her heart was with Tom.

It was no longer two strange brutes fighting in a field. It was her man battling for her sake.

She desired overwhelmingly that he should win, that he should not be hurt, that he should sweep triumphantly over Albert Parsons as he had swept over Ted Pringle.

Unfortunately, it was evident, even to her, that he was being hurt, and that he was very far from sweeping triumphantly over Albert Parsons. He had not allowed himself time to recover from his first battle, and his blows were slow and weary. Albert, moreover, was made of sterner stuff than Ted. Though now a peaceful tender of cows, there had been a time in his hot youth when, travelling with a circus, he had fought, week in, week out, relays of just such rustic warriors as Tom. He knew their methods—their headlong rushes, their swinging blows. They were the merest commonplaces of life to him. He slipped Tom, he side-stepped Tom, he jabbed Tom; he did everything to Tom that a trained boxer can do to a reckless novice, except knock the fight out of him, until presently, through the sheer labour of hitting, he, too, grew weary.

Now, in the days when Albert Parsons had fought whole families of Toms in an evening, he had fought in rounds, with the boss holding the watch, and half-minute rests, and water to refresh him, and all orderly and proper. Today there were no rounds, no rests, no water, and the peaceful tending of cows had caused flesh to grow where there had been only muscle. Tom's headlong rushes became less easy to side-step, his swinging blows more difficult than the scientific counter that shot out to check them. As he tired Tom seemed to regain strength. The tide of the battle began to ebb. He clinched, and Tom threw him off. He feinted, and while he was feinting Tom was on him. It was the climax of the battle—the last rally. Down went Albert, and stayed down. Physically, he was not finished; but in his mind a question had framed itself—the question. 'Was it worth it?'—and he was answering, 'No.' There were other girls in the world. No girl was worth all this trouble.

He did not rise.

'Come along!' said Tom.

He spoke thickly. His breath was coming in gasps. He was a terrible spectacle, but Sally was past the weaker emotions. She was back in the Stone Age, and her only feeling was one of passionate pride. She tried to speak. She struggled to put all she felt into words, but something kept her dumb, and she followed him in silence.

In the lane outside his cottage, down by the creek, Joe Blossom was clipping a hedge. The sound of footsteps made him turn.

He did not recognize Tom till he spoke.

'Joe, there's been a mistake,' said Tom.

'Been a gunpowder explosion, more like,' said Joe, a simple, practical man. 'What you been doin' to your face?'

'She's going to marry me, Joe.'

Joe eyed Sally inquiringly.

'Eh? You promised to marry *me*.'

'She promised to marry all of us. You, me, Ted Pringle, and Albert Parsons.'

'Promised—to—marry—all—of—us!'

'That's where the mistake was. She's only going to marry me. I—I've arranged it with Ted and Albert, and now I've come to explain to you, Joe.'

'You promised to marry—!'

The colossal nature of Sally's deceit was plainly troubling Joe Blossom. He expelled his breath in a long note of amazement. Then he summed up.

'Why you're nothing more nor less than a Joshua!'

The years that had passed since Joe had attended the village Sunday-school had weakened his once easy familiarity with the characters of the Old Testament. It is possible that he had somebody else in his mind.

Tom stuck doggedly to his point.

'You can't marry her, Joe.'

Joe Blossom raised his shears and clipped a protruding branch. The point under discussion seemed to have ceased to interest him.

'Who wants to?' he said. 'Good riddance!'

They went down the lane. Silence still brooded over them. The words she wanted continued to evade her.

They came to a grassy bank. Tom sat down. He was feeling unutterably tired.

'Tom!'

He looked up. His mind was working dizzily.

'You're going to marry me,' he muttered.

She sat down beside him.

'I know,' she said. 'Tom, dear, lay your head on my lap and go to sleep.'

If this story proves anything (beyond the advantage of being in good training when you fight), it proves that you cannot get away from the moving pictures even in a place like Millbourne; for as Sally sat there, nursing Tom, it suddenly struck her that this was the very situation with which that 'Romance of the Middle Ages' film ended. You know the one I mean. Sir Percival Ye Something (which has slipped my memory for the moment) goes out after the Holy Grail; meets damsel in distress; overcomes her persecutors; rescues her; gets wounded, and is nursed back to life in her arms. Sally had seen it a dozen times. And every time she had reflected that the days of romance are dead, and that that sort of thing can't happen nowadays.

DEEP WATERS

Historians of the social life of the later Roman Empire speak of a certain young man of Ariminum, who would jump into rivers and swim in 'em. When his friends said, 'You fish!' he would answer, 'Oh, pish! Fish can't swim like *me*, they've no vim in 'em.'

Just such another was George Barnert Callender.

On land, in his land clothes, George was a young man who excited little remark. He looked very much like other young men. He was much about the ordinary height. His carriage suggested the possession of an ordinary amount of physical strength. Such was George—on shore. But remove his clothes, drape him in a bathing-suit, and insert him in the water, and instantly, like the gentleman in *The Tempest*, he 'suffered a sea-change into something rich and strange.' Other men puffed, snorted, and splashed. George passed through the ocean with the silent dignity of a torpedo. Other men swallowed water, here a mouthful, there a pint, anon, maybe, a quart or so, and returned to the shore like foundering derelicts. George's mouth had all the exclusiveness of a fashionable club. His breast-stroke was a thing to see and wonder at. When he did the crawl, strong men gasped. When he swam on his back, you felt that that was the only possible method of progression.

George came to Marvis Bay at about five o'clock one evening in July. Marvis Bay has a well-established reputation as a summer resort, and, while not perhaps in every respect the paradise which the excitable writer of the local guide-book asserts it to be, on the whole it earns its reputation. Its sands are smooth and firm, sloping almost imperceptibly into the ocean. There is surf for those who like it, and smoother water beyond for those whose ideals in bathing are not confined to jumping up and down on a given jelly-fish. At the northern end of the beach there is a long pier. It was to this that George made his way on his arrival.

It was pleasant on the pier. Once you had passed the initial zareba of fruit stands, souvenir stands, ice-cream stands, and the lair of the enthusiast whose aim in life it was to sell you picture post-cards, and had won through to the long walk where the seats were, you were practically alone with Nature. At this hour of the day the place was deserted; George had it to himself. He strolled slowly along. The water glittered under the sun-rays, breaking into a flurry of white foam as it reached the beach. A cool breeze blew. The whole scenic arrangements were a great improvement on the stuffy city he had left. Not that George had come to Marvis Bay with the single aim of finding an antidote to metropolitan stuffiness. There was a more important reason. In three days Marvis Bay was to be the scene of the production of *Fate's Footballs*, a comedy in four acts by G. Barnert Callender. For George, though you would not have suspected it from his exterior, was one of those in whose cerebra the grey matter splashes restlessly about, producing strong curtains and crisp dialogue. The company was due at Marvis Bay on the following evening for the last spasm of rehearsals.

George's mind, as he paced the pier, was divided between the beauties of Nature and the forthcoming crisis in his affairs in the ratio of one-eighth to the former and seven-eighths to the latter. At the moment when he had left London, thoroughly disgusted with the entire theatrical world in general and the company which was rehearsing *Fate's Footballs* in particular, rehearsals had just reached that stage of brisk delirium when the author toys with his bottle of poison and the stage-manager becomes icily polite. *The Footpills*—as Arthur Mifflin, the leading juvenile in the great play, insisted upon calling it, much to George's disapproval— was his first piece. Never before had he been in one of those kitchens where many cooks prepare, and sometimes spoil, the theatrical broth. Consequently the chaos seemed to him unique. Had he been a more experienced dramatist, he would have said to himself, 'Twas ever thus.' As it was, what he said to himself— and others—was more forcible.

He was trying to dismiss the whole thing from his mind—a feat which had hitherto proved beyond his powers—when Fate, in an unusually kindly mood, enabled him to do so in a flash by presenting to his jaundiced gaze what, on consideration, he decided was the most beautiful girl he had ever seen. 'When a man's afraid,' shrewdly sings the bard, 'a beautiful maid is a cheering sight to see'. In the present instance the sight acted on George like a tonic. He forgot that the lady to whom an injudicious management had assigned the role of heroine in *Fate's Footballs* invariably—no doubt from the best motives—omitted to give the cynical *roue* his cue for the big speech in Act III His mind no longer dwelt on the fact that Arthur Mifflin, an estimable person in private life, and one who had been a friend of his at Cambridge, preferred to deliver the impassioned lines of the great renunciation scene in a manner suggesting a small boy (and a sufferer from nasal catarrh at that) speaking a piece at a Sunday-school treat. The recollection of the hideous depression and gloom which the leading comedian had radiated in great clouds fled from him like some grisly nightmare before the goddess of day. Every cell in his brain was occupied, to the exclusion of all other thoughts, by the girl swimming in the water below.

She swam well. His practised eye saw that. Her strong, easy strokes carried her swiftly over the swell of the waves. He stared, transfixed. He was a well-brought-up young man, and he knew how ill-bred it was to stare; but this was a special occasion. Ordinary rules of conventional etiquette could not apply to a case like this. He stared. More, he gaped. As the girl passed on into the shadow of the pier he leaned farther over the rail, and his neck extended in joints like a telescope.

At this point the girl turned to swim on her back. Her eyes met his. Hers were deep and clear; his, bulging. For what seemed an eternity to George, she continued to look at him. Then, turning over again, she shot past under the pier.

George's neck was now at its full stretch. No power of will or muscle could add another yard to it. Realizing this, he leaned farther over the rail, and farther still. His hat slid from his hand. He grabbed at it, and, overbalancing, fell with a splash into the water.

Now, in ordinary circumstances, to fall twelve feet into the ocean with all his clothes on would have incommoded George little. He would hardly have noticed it. He would have swum to shore with merely a feeling of amused self-reproach akin to that of the man who absent-mindedly walks into a lamp-post in the street. When, therefore, he came to the surface he prepared without agitation to strike out in his usual bold fashion. At this moment, however, two hands, grasping him beneath the arms, lifted his head still farther from the waves, and a voice in his ear said, 'Keep still; don't struggle. There's no danger.'

George did not struggle. His brain, working with the cool rapidity of a buzz-saw in an ice-box, had planned a line of action. Few things are more difficult in this world for a young man than the securing of an introduction to the right girl under just the right conditions. When he is looking his best he is presented to her in the midst of a crowd, and is swept away after a rapid hand-shake. When there is no crowd he has toothache, or the sun has just begun to make his nose peel. Thousands of young lives have been saddened in this manner.

How different was George's case! By this simple accident, he reflected, as, helping the good work along with an occasional surreptitious leg-stroke, he was towed shorewards, there had been formed an acquaintanceship, if nothing more, which could not lightly be broken. A girl who has saved a man from drowning cannot pass him by next day with a formal bow. And what a girl, too! There had been a time, in extreme youth, when his feminine ideal was the sort of girl who has fuzzy, golden hair, and drops things. Indeed in his first year at the University he had said—and written—as much to one of the type, the episode concluding with a strong little drama, in which a wrathful, cheque-signing father had starred, supported by a subdued, misogynistic son. Which things, aided by the march of time, had turned George's tastes towards the healthy, open-air girl, who did things instead of dropping them.

The pleasantest functions must come to an end sooner or later; and in due season George felt his heels grate on the sand. His preserver loosed her hold. They stood up and faced each other. George began to express his gratitude as best he could—it was not easy to find neat, convincing sentences on the spur of the moment—but she cut him short.

'Of course, it was nothing. Nothing at all,' she said, brushing the sea-water from her eyes. 'It was just lucky I happened to be there.'

'It was splendid,' said the infatuated dramatist. 'It was magnificent. It—'

He saw that she was smiling.

'You're very wet,' she said.

George glanced down at his soaked clothes. It had been a nice suit once.

'Hadn't you better hurry back and change into something dry?'

Looking round about him, George perceived that sundry of the inquisitive were swooping down, with speculation in their eyes. It was time to depart.

'Have you far to go?'

'Not far. I'm staying at the Beach View Hotel.'

'Why, so am I. I hope we shall meet again.'

'We shall,' said George confidently.

'How did you happen to fall in?'

'I was—er—I was looking at something in the water.'

'I thought you were,' said the girl, quietly.

George blushed.

'I know,' he said, 'it was abominably rude of me to stare like that; but—'

'You should learn to swim,' interrupted the girl. 'I can't understand why every boy in the country isn't made to learn to swim before he's ten years old. And it isn't a bit difficult, really. I could teach you in a week.'

The struggle between George and George's conscience was brief. The conscience, weak by nature and flabby from long want of exercise, had no sort of chance from the start.

'I wish you would,' said George. And with those words he realized that he had definitely committed himself to his hypocritical role. Till that moment explanation would have been difficult, but possible. Now it was impossible.

'I will,' said the girl. 'I'll start tomorrow if you like.' She waded into the water.

'We'll talk it over at the hotel,' she said, hastily. 'Here comes a crowd of horrid people. I'm going to swim out again.'

She hurried into deeper water, while George, turning, made his way through a growing throng of goggling spectators. Of the fifteen who got within speaking distance of him, six told him that he was wet. The other nine asked him if he had fallen.

Her name was Vaughan, and she was visiting Marvis Bay in company with an aunt. So much George ascertained from the management of the hotel. Later, after dinner, meeting both ladies on the esplanade, he gleaned further information—to wit, that her first name was Mary, that her aunt was glad to make his acquaintance, liked Marvis Bay but preferred Trouville, and thought it was getting a little chilly and would go indoors.

The elimination of the third factor had a restorative effect upon George's conversation, which had begun to languish. In feminine society as a rule he was apt to be constrained, but with Mary Vaughan it was different. Within a couple of minutes he was pouring out his troubles. The cue-withholding leading lady, the stick-like Mifflin, the funereal comedian—up they all came, and she, gently sympathetic, was endeavouring, not without success, to prove to him that things were not so bad as they seemed.

'It's sure to be all right on the night,' she said.

How rare is the combination of beauty and intelligence! George thought he had never heard such a clear-headed, well-expressed remark.

'I suppose it will,' he said, 'but they were very bad when I left. Mifflin, for instance. He seems to think Nature intended him for a Napoleon of Advertising. He has a bee in his bonnet about booming the piece. Sits up at nights, when he ought to be sleeping or studying his part, thinking out new schemes for advertising the show. And the comedian. His speciality is drawing me aside and asking me to write in new scenes for him. I couldn't stand it any longer. I just came away and left them to fight it out among themselves.'

'I'm sure you have no need to worry. A play with such a good story is certain to succeed.'

George had previously obliged with a brief description of the plot of *The Footpills*.

'Did you like the story?' he said, tenderly.

'I thought it was fine.'

'How sympathetic you are!' cooed George, glutinously, edging a little closer. 'Do you know—'

'Shall we be going back to the hotel?' said the girl.

Those noisome creatures, the hired murderers of *Fate's Footpills*, descended upon Marvis Bay early next afternoon, and George, meeting them at the station, in reluctant pursuance of a promise given to Arthur Mifflin, felt moodily that, if only they could make their acting one-half as full of colour as their clothes, the play would be one of the most pronounced successes of modern times. In the forefront gleamed, like the white plumes of Navarre, the light flannel suit of Arthur Mifflin, the woodenest juvenile in captivity.

His woodenness was, however, confined to stage rehearsals. It may be mentioned that, once the run of a piece had begun, he was sufficiently volatile, and in private life he was almost excessively so—a fact which had been noted at an early date by the keen-eyed authorities of his University, the discovery leading to his tearing himself away from Alma Mater by request with some suddenness. He was a long, slender youth, with green eyes, jet-black hair, and a passionate fondness for the sound of his own voice.

'Well, here we are,' he said, kicking breezily at George's leg with his cane.

'I saw you,' said George, coldly, side-stepping.

'The whole team,' continued Mr Mifflin; 'all bright, bonny, and trained to the minute.'

'What happened after I left?' George asked. 'Has anybody begun to act yet? Or are they waiting till the dress-rehearsal?'

'The rehearsals,' admitted Mr Mifflin, handsomely, 'weren't perfect; but you wait. It'll be all right on the night.'

George thought he had never heard such a futile, vapid remark.

'Besides,' said Mr Mifflin, 'I have an idea which will make the show. Lend me your ear—both ears. You shall have them back. Tell me: what pulls people into a theatre? A good play? Sometimes. But failing that, as in the present case, what? Fine acting by the leading juvenile? We have that, but it is not enough. No, my boy; advertisement is the thing. Look at all these men on the beach. Are they going to roll in of their own free wills to see a play like *The Footpills*? Not on your life. About the time the curtain rises every man of them will be sitting in his own private corner of the beach—'

'How many corners do you think the beach has?'

'Gazing into a girl's eyes, singing, "Shine on, thou harvest moon", and telling her how his boss is practically dependent on his advice. You know.'

'I don't,' said George, coldly.

'Unless,' proceeded Mr Mifflin, 'we advertise. And by advertise, I mean advertise in the right way. We have a Press-agent, but for all the good he does he might be back on the old farm, gathering in the hay. Luckily for us, I am among those present. I have brains, I have resource. What's that?'

'I said nothing.'

'I thought you did. Well, I have an idea which will drag these people like a magnet. I thought it out coming down in the train.'

'What is it?'

'I'll tell you later. There are a few details to be worked upon first. Meanwhile, let us trickle to the sea-front and take a sail in one of those boats. I am at my best in a boat. I rather fancy Nature intended me for a Viking.'

Matters having been arranged with the financier to whom the boat belonged, they set forth. Mr Mifflin, having remarked, 'Yo-ho!' in a meditative voice, seated himself at the helm, somewhat saddened by his failure to borrow a quid of tobacco from the *Ocean Beauty's* proprietor. For, as he justly observed, without properties and make-up, where were you? George, being skilled in the ways of boats, was in charge of the sheet. The summer day had lost its oppressive heat. The sun no longer beat down on the face of the waters. A fresh breeze had sprung up. George, manipulating the sheet automatically, fell into a reverie. A moment comes in the life of every man when an inward voice whispers to him, 'This is The One!' In George's case the voice had not whispered; it had shouted. From now onward there could be but one woman in the world for him. From now onwards—The *Ocean Beauty* gave a sudden plunge. George woke up.

'What the deuce are you doing with that tiller?' he inquired.

'My gentle somnambulist,' said Mr Mifflin, aggrieved, 'I was doing nothing with this tiller. We will now form a commission to inquire into what you were doing with that sheet. Were you asleep?'

'My fault,' said George; 'I was thinking.'

'If you must break the habit of a lifetime,' said Mr Mifflin, complainingly, 'I wish you would wait till we get ashore. You nearly upset us.'

'It shan't happen again. They are tricky, these sailing boats—turn over in a second. Whatever you do, don't get her broadside on. There's more breeze out here than I thought there was.'

Mr Mifflin uttered a startled exclamation.

'What's the matter?' asked George.

'Just like a flash,' said Mr Mifflin, complacently. 'It's always the way with me. Give me time, and the artistic idea is bound to come. Just some little thought, some little, apparently obvious, idea which stamps the man of genius. It beats me why I didn't think of it before. Why, of course, a costume piece with a male star is a hundred times more effective.'

'What are you talking about?'

'I see now,' continued Mr Mifflin, 'that there was a flaw in my original plan. My idea was this. We were talking in the train about the bathing down here, and Jane happened to say she could swim some, and it suddenly came to me.'

Jane was the leading woman, she who omitted to give cues.

'I said to myself, "George is a sportsman. He will be delighted to do a little thing like that".'

'Like to do what?'

'Why, rescue Jane.'

'What!'

'She and you,' said Mr Mifflin, 'were to go in swimming together, while I waited on the sands, holding our bone-headed Press-agent on a leash. About a hundred yards from the shore up go her arms. Piercing scream. Agitated crowds on the beach. What is the matter? What has happened? A touch of cramp. Will she be drowned? No! G. Barnert Callender, author of *Fate's Footballs*, which opens at the Beach Theatre on Monday evening next, at eight-fifteen sharp, will save her. See! He has her. He is bringing her in. She is safe. How pleased her mother will be! And the public, what a bit of luck for them! They will be able to see her act at eight-fifteen sharp on Monday after all. Back you come to the shore. Cheering crowds. Weeping women. Strong situation. I unleash the Press-agent, and off he shoots, in time to get the story into the evening paper. It was a great idea, but I see now there were one or two flaws in it.'

'You do, do you?' said George.

'It occurs to me on reflection that after all you wouldn't have agreed to it. A something, I don't know what, which is lacking in your nature, would have made you reject the scheme.'

'I'm glad that occurred to you.'

'And a far greater flaw was that it was too altruistic. It boomed you and it boomed Jane, but I didn't get a thing out of it. My revised scheme is a thousand times better in every way.'

'Don't say you have another.'

'I have. And,' added Mr Mifflin, with modest pride, 'it is a winner. This time I unhesitatingly assert that I have the goods. In about one minute from now you will hear me exclaim, in a clear musical voice, the single word, "Jump!" That is your cue to leap over the side as quick as you can move, for at that precise moment this spanking craft is going to capsize.'

George spun round in his seat. Mr Mifflin's face was shining with kindly enthusiasm. The shore was at least two hundred yards away, and that morning he had had his first swimming-lesson.

'A movement of the tiller will do it. These accidents are common objects of the seashore. I may mention that I can swim just enough to keep myself afloat; so it's up to you. I wouldn't do this for everyone, but, seeing that we were boys together—Are you ready?'

'Stop!' cried George. 'Don't do it! Listen!'

'Are you ready?'

The *Ocean Beauty* gave a plunge.

'You lunatic! Listen to me. It—'

'Jump!' said Mr Mifflin.

George came to the surface some yards from the overturned boat, and, looking round for Mr Mifflin, discovered that great thinker treading water a few feet away.

'Get to work, George,' he remarked.

It is not easy to shake one's fist at a man when in deep water, but George managed it.

'For twopence,' he cried, 'I'd leave you to look after yourself.'

'You can do better than that,' said Mr Mifflin. 'I'll give you threepence to tow me in. Hurry up. It's cold.'

In gloomy silence George gripped him by the elbows. Mr Mifflin looked over his shoulder.

'We shall have a good house,' he said. 'The stalls are full already, and the dress-circle's filling. Work away, George, you're doing fine. This act is going to be a scream from start to finish.'

With pleasant conversation he endeavoured to while away the monotony of the journey; but George made no reply. He was doing some rapid thinking. With ordinary luck, he felt bitterly, all would have been well. He could have gone on splashing vigorously under his teacher's care for a week, gradually improving till he emerged into a reasonably proficient swimmer. But now! In an age of miracles he might have explained away his present performance; but how was he to—And then there came to him an idea—simple, as all great ideas are, but magnificent.

He stopped and trod water.

'Tired?' said Mr Mifflin. 'Well, take a rest,' he added, kindly, 'take a rest. No need to hurry.'

'Look here,' said George, 'this piece is going to be recast. We're going to exchange parts. You're rescuing me. See? Never mind why. I haven't time to explain it to you now. Do you understand?'

'No,' said Mr Mifflin.

'I'll get behind you and push you; but don't forget, when we get to the shore, that you've done the rescuing.'

Mr Mifflin pondered.

'Is this wise?' he said. 'It is a strong part, the rescuer, but I'm not sure the other wouldn't suit my style better. The silent hand-grip, the catch in the voice. You want a practised actor for that. I don't think you'd be up to it, George.'

'Never mind about me. That's how it's going to be.'

Mr Mifflin pondered once more.

'No,' he said at length, 'it wouldn't do. You mean well, George, but it would kill the show. We'll go on as before.'

'Will we?' said George, unpleasantly. 'Would you like to know what I'm going to do to you, then? I'm going to hit you very hard under the jaw, and I'm going to take hold of your neck and squeeze it till you lose consciousness, and then I'm going to drag you to the beach and tell people I had to hit you because you lost your head and struggled.'

Mr Mifflin pondered for the third time.

'You are?' he said.

'I am,' said George.

'Then,' said Mr Mifflin, cordially, 'say no more. I take your point. My objections are removed. But,' he concluded, 'this is the last time I come bathing with you, George.'

Mr Mifflin's artistic misgivings as to his colleague's ability to handle so subtle a part as that of rescuee were more than justified on their arrival. A large and interested audience had collected by the time they reached the shore, an audience to which any artist should have been glad to play; but George, forcing his way through, hurried to the hotel without attempting to satisfy them. Not a single silent hand-shake did he bestow on his rescuer. There was no catch in his voice as he made the one remark which he did make—to a man with whiskers who asked him if the boat had upset. As an exhibition of rapid footwork his performance was good. In other respects it was poor.

He had just changed his wet clothes—it seemed to him that he had been doing nothing but change his wet clothes since he had come to Marvis Bay— when Mr Mifflin entered in a bathrobe.

'They lent me this downstairs,' he explained, 'while they dried my clothes. They would do anything for me. I'm the popular hero. My boy, you made the mistake of your life when you threw up the rescuer part. It has all the fat. I see that now. The rescuer plays the other man off the stage every time. I've just been interviewed by the fellow on the local newspaper. He's correspondent to a couple of London papers. The country will ring with this thing. I've told them all the parts I've ever played and my favourite breakfast food. There's a man coming up to take my photograph tomorrow. *Footpills* stock has gone up with a run. Wait till Monday and see what sort of a house we shall draw. By the way, the reporter fellow said one funny thing. He asked if you weren't the same man who was rescued yesterday by a girl. I said of course not—that you had only come down yesterday. But he stuck to it that you were.'

'He was quite right.'

'What!'

'I was.'

Mr Mifflin sat down on the bed.

'This fellow fell off the pier, and a girl brought him in.'

George nodded.

'And that was you?'

George nodded.

Mr Mifflin's eyes opened wide.

'It's the heat,' he declared, finally. 'That and the worry of rehearsals. I expect a doctor could give the technical name for it. It's a what-do-you-call-it—an obsession. You often hear of cases. Fellows who are absolutely sane really, but cracked on one particular subject. Some of them think they're teapots and things. You've got a craving for being rescued from drowning. What happens, old man? Do you suddenly get the delusion that you can't swim? No, it can't be that, because you were doing all the swimming for the two of us just now. I don't know, though. Maybe you didn't realize that you were swimming?'

George finished lacing his shoe and looked up.

'Listen,' he said; 'I'll talk slow, so that you can understand. Suppose you fell off a pier, and a girl took a great deal of trouble to get you to the shore, would you say, "Much obliged, but you needn't have been so officious. I can swim perfectly well?"'

Mr Mifflin considered this point. Intelligence began to dawn in his face. 'There is more in this than meets the eye,' he said. 'Tell me all.'

'This morning'—George's voice grew dreamy—'she gave me a swimming-lesson. She thought it was my first. Don't cackle like that. There's nothing to laugh at.'

Mr Mifflin contradicted this assertion.

'There is you,' he said, simply. 'This should be a lesson to you, George. Avoid deceit. In future be simple and straightforward. Take me as your model. You have managed to scrape through this time. Don't risk it again. You are young. There is still time to make a fresh start. It only needs will-power. Meanwhile, lend me something to wear. They are going to take a week drying my clothes.'

There was a rehearsal at the Beach Theatre that evening. George attended it in a spirit of resignation and left it in one of elation. Three days had passed since his last sight of the company at work, and in those three days, apparently, the impossible had been achieved. There was a snap and go about the piece now. The leading lady had at length mastered that cue, and gave it out with bell-like clearness. Arthur Mifflin, as if refreshed and braced by his salt-water bath, was infusing a welcome vigour into his part. And even the comedian, George could not help admitting, showed signs of being on the eve of becoming funny. It was with a light heart and a light step that he made his way back to the hotel.

In the veranda were a number of basket-chairs. Only one was occupied. He recognized the occupant.

'I've just come back from a rehearsal,' he said, seating himself beside her.

'Really?'

'The whole thing is different,' he went on, buoyantly. 'They know their lines. They act as if they meant it. Arthur Mifflin's fine. The comedian's improved till you wouldn't know him. I'm awfully pleased about it.'

'Really?'

George felt damped.

'I thought you might be pleased, too,' he said, lamely.

'Of course I am glad that things are going well. Your accident this afternoon was lucky, too, in a way, was it not? It will interest people in the play.'

'You heard about it?'

'I have been hearing about nothing else.'

'Curious it happening so soon after—'

'And so soon before the production of your play. Most curious.'

There was a silence. George began to feel uneasy. You could never tell with women, of course. It might be nothing; but it looked uncommonly as if—

He changed the subject.

'How is your aunt this evening, Miss Vaughan?'

'Quite well, thank you. She went in. She found it a little chilly.'

George heartily commended her good sense. A little chilly did not begin to express it. If the girl had been like this all the evening, he wondered her aunt had not caught pneumonia. He tried again.

'Will you have time to give me another lesson tomorrow?' he said.

She turned on him.

'Mr Callender, don't you think this farce has gone on long enough?'

Once, in the dear, dead days beyond recall, when but a happy child, George had been smitten unexpectedly by a sportive playmate a bare half-inch below his third waistcoat-button. The resulting emotions were still green in his memory. As he had felt then, so did he feel now.

'Miss Vaughan! I don't understand.'

'Really?'

'What have I done?'

'You have forgotten how to swim.'

A warm and prickly sensation began to manifest itself in the region of George's forehead.

'Forgotten!'

'Forgotten. And in a few months. I thought I had seen you before, and today I remembered. It was just about this time last year that I saw you at Hayling Island swimming perfectly wonderfully, and today you are taking lessons. Can you explain it?'

A frog-like croak was the best George could do in that line.

She went on.

'Business is business, I suppose, and a play has to be advertised somehow. But—'

'You don't think—' croaked George.

'I should have thought it rather beneath the dignity of an author; but, of course, you know your own business best. Only I object to being a conspirator. I am sorry for your sake that yesterday's episode attracted so little attention. Today it was much more satisfactory, wasn't it? I am so glad.'

There was a massive silence for about a hundred years.

'I think I'll go for a short stroll,' said George.

Scarcely had he disappeared when the long form of Mr Mifflin emerged from the shadow beyond the veranda.

'Could you spare me a moment?'

The girl looked up. The man was a stranger. She inclined her head coldly.

'My name is Mifflin,' said the other, dropping comfortably into the chair which had held the remains of George.

The girl inclined her head again more coldly; but it took more than that to embarrass Mr Mifflin. Dynamite might have done it, but not coldness.

'*The* Mifflin,' he explained, crossing his legs. 'I overheard your conversation just now.'

'You were listening?' said the girl, scornfully.

'For all I was worth,' said Mr Mifflin. 'These things are very much a matter of habit. For years I have been playing in pieces where I have had to stand concealed up stage, drinking in the private conversation of other people, and the thing has become a second nature to me. However, leaving that point for a moment, what I wish to say is that I heard you—unknowingly, of course—doing a good man a grave injustice.'

'Mr Callender could have defended himself if he had wished.'

'I was not referring to George. The injustice was to myself.'

'To you?'

'I was the sole author of this afternoon's little drama. I like George, but I cannot permit him to pose in any way as my collaborator. George has old-fashioned ideas. He does not keep abreast of the times. He can write plays, but he needs a man with a big brain to boom them for him. So, far from being entitled to any credit for this afternoon's work, he was actually opposed to it.'

'Then why did he pretend you had saved him?' she demanded.

'George's,' said Mr Mifflin, 'is essentially a chivalrous nature. At any crisis demanding a display of the finer feelings he is there with the goods before you can turn round. His friends frequently wrangle warmly as to whether he is most like Bayard, Lancelot, or Happy Hooligan. Some say one, some the other. It seems that yesterday you saved him from a watery grave without giving him time to explain that he could save himself. What could he do? He said to himself, "She must never know!" and acted accordingly. But let us leave George, and return—'

'Thank you, Mr Mifflin.' There was a break in her laugh. 'I don't think there is any necessity. I think I understand now. It was very clever of you.'

'It was more than cleverness,' said Mr Mifflin, rising. 'It was genius.'

A white form came to meet George as he re-entered the veranda.

'Mr Callender!'

He stopped.

'I'm very sorry I said such horrid things to you just now. I have been talking to Mr Mifflin, and I want to say I think it was ever so nice and thoughtful of you. I understand everything.'

George did not, by a good deal; but he understood sufficient for his needs. He shot forward as if some strong hand were behind him with a needle.

'Miss Vaughan—Mary—I—'

'I think I hear aunt calling,' said she.

But a benevolent Providence has ordained that aunts cannot call for ever; and it is on record that when George entered his box on the two hundredth night of that great London success, *Fate's Footballs*, he did not enter it alone.

WHEN DOCTORS DISAGREE

It is possible that, at about the time at which this story opens, you may have gone into the Hotel Belvoir for a hair-cut. Many people did; for the young man behind the scissors, though of a singularly gloomy countenance, was undoubtedly an artist in his line. He clipped judiciously. He left no ridges. He never talked about the weather. And he allowed you to go away unburdened by any bottle of hair-food.

It is possible, too, that, being there, you decided that you might as well go the whole hog and be manicured at the same time.

It is not unlikely, moreover, that when you had got over the first shock of finding your hands so unexpectedly large and red, you felt disposed to chat with the young lady who looked after that branch of the business. In your genial way you may have permitted a note of gay (but gentlemanly) badinage to creep into your end of the dialogue.

In which case, if you had raised your eyes to the mirror, you would certainly have observed a marked increase of gloom in the demeanour of the young man attending to your apex. He took no official notice of the matter. A quick frown. A tightening of the lips. Nothing more. Jealous as Arthur Welsh was of all who inflicted gay badinage, however gentlemanly, on Maud Peters, he never forgot that he was an artist. Never, even in his blackest moments, had he yielded to the temptation to dig the point of the scissors the merest fraction of an inch into a client's skull.

But Maud, who saw, would understand. And, if the customer was an observant man, he would notice that her replies at that juncture became somewhat absent, her smile a little mechanical.

Jealousy, according to an eminent authority, is the 'hydra of calamities, the sevenfold death'. Arthur Welsh's was all that and a bit over. It was a constant shadow on Maud's happiness. No fair-minded girl objects to a certain tinge of jealousy. Kept within proper bounds, it is a compliment; it makes for piquancy; it is the gin in the ginger-beer of devotion. But it should be a condiment, not a fluid.

It was the unfairness of the thing which hurt Maud. Her conscience was clear. She knew girls—several girls—who gave the young men with whom they walked out ample excuse for being perfect Othellos. If she had ever flirted on the open beach with the baritone of the troupe of pierrots, like Jane Oddy, she could have excused Arthur's attitude. If, like Pauline Dicey, she had roller-skated for a solid hour with a black-moustached stranger while her fiance floundered in Mug's Alley she could have understood his frowning disapprovingly. But she was not like Pauline. She scorned the coquetries of Jane. Arthur was the centre of her world, and he knew it. Ever since the rainy evening when he had sheltered her under his umbrella to her Tube station, he had known perfectly well how things were with her. And yet just because, in a strictly business-like way, she was civil to her customers, he must scowl and bite his lip and behave generally as if it had been brought to his notice that he had been nurturing a serpent in his bosom. It was worse than wicked—it was unprofessional.

She remonstrated with him.

'It isn't fair,' she said, one morning when the rush of customers had ceased and they had the shop to themselves.

Matters had been worse than usual that morning. After days of rain and greyness the weather had turned over a new leaf. The sun glinted among the bottles of Unfailing Lotion in the window, and everything in the world seemed to have relaxed and become cheerful. Unfortunately, everything had included the customers. During the last few days they had taken their seats in moist gloom, and, brooding over the prospect of coming colds in the head, had had little that was pleasant to say to the divinity who was shaping their ends. But today it had been different. Warm and happy, they had bubbled over with gay small-talk.

'It isn't fair,' she repeated.

Arthur, who was stropping a razor and whistling tunelessly, raised his eyebrows. His manner was frosty.

'I fail to understand your meaning,' he said.

'You know what I mean. Do you think I didn't see you frowning when I was doing that gentleman's nails?'

The allusion was to the client who had just left—a jovial individual with a red face, who certainly had made Maud giggle a good deal. And why not? If a gentleman tells really funny stories, what harm is there in giggling? You had to be pleasant to people. If you snubbed customers, what happened? Why, sooner or later, it got round to the boss, and then where were you? Besides, it was not as if the red-faced customer had been rude. Write down on paper what he had said to her, and nobody could object to it. Write down on paper what she had said to him, and you couldn't object to that either. It was just Arthur's silliness.

She tossed her head.

'I am gratified,' said Arthur, ponderously—in happier moments Maud had admired his gift of language; he read a great deal: encyclopedias and papers and things—'I am gratified to find that you had time to bestow a glance on me. You appeared absorbed.'

Maud sniffed unhappily. She had meant to be cold and dignified throughout the conversation, but the sense of her wrongs was beginning to be too much for her. A large tear splashed on to her tray of orange-sticks. She wiped it away with the chamois leather.

'It isn't fair,' she sobbed. 'It isn't. You know I can't help it if gentlemen talk and joke with me. You know it's all in the day's work. I'm expected to be civil to gentlemen who come in to have their hands done. Silly I should look sitting as if I'd swallowed a poker. I *do* think you might understand, Arthur, you being in the profession yourself.'

He coughed.

'It isn't so much that you talk to them as that you seem to like—'

He stopped. Maud's dignity had melted completely. Her face was buried in her arms. She did not care if a million customers came in, all at the same time.

'Maud!'

She heard him moving towards her, but she did not look up. The next moment his arms were round her, and he was babbling.

And a customer, pushing open the door unnoticed two minutes later, retired hurriedly to get shaved elsewhere, doubting whether Arthur's mind was on his job.

For a time this little thunderstorm undoubtedly cleared the air. For a day or two Maud was happier than she ever remembered to have been. Arthur's behaviour was unexceptionable. He bought her a wrist-watch— light brown leather, very smart. He gave her some chocolates to eat in the Tube. He entertained her with amazing statistics, culled from the weekly paper which he bought on Tuesdays. He was, in short, the perfect lover. On the second day the red-faced man came in again. Arthur joined in the laughter at his stories. Everything seemed ideal.

It could not last. Gradually things slipped back into the old routine. Maud, looking up from her work, would see the frown and the bitten lip. She began again to feel uncomfortable and self-conscious as she worked. Sometimes their conversation on the way to the Tube was almost formal.

It was useless to say anything. She had a wholesome horror of being one of those women who nagged; and she felt that to complain again would amount to nagging. She tried to put the thing out of her mind, but it insisted on staying there. In a way she understood his feelings. He loved her so much, she supposed, that he hated the idea of her exchanging a single word with another man. This, in the abstract, was gratifying; but in practice it distressed her. She wished she were some sort of foreigner, so that nobody could talk to her. But then they would look at her, and that probably would produce much the same results. It was a hard world for a girl.

And then the strange thing happened. Arthur reformed. One might almost say that he reformed with a jerk. It was a parallel case to those sudden conversions at Welsh revival meetings. On Monday evening he had been at his worst. On the following morning he was a changed man. Not even after the original thunderstorm had he been more docile. Maud could not believe that first. The lip, once bitten, was stretched in a smile. She looked for the frown. It was not there.

Next day it was the same; and the day after that. When a week had gone by, and still the improvement was maintained, Maud felt that she might now look upon it as permanent. A great load seemed to have been taken off her mind. She revised her views on the world. It was a very good world, quite one of the best, with Arthur beaming upon it like a sun.

A number of eminent poets and essayists, in the course of the last few centuries, have recorded, in their several ways, their opinion that one can have too much of a good thing. The truth applies even to such a good thing as absence of jealousy. Little by little Maud began to grow uneasy. It began to come home to her that she preferred the old Arthur, of the scowl and the gnawed lip. Of him she had at least been sure. Whatever discomfort she may have suffered from his spirited imitations of Othello, at any rate they had proved that he loved her. She would have accepted gladly an equal amount of discomfort now in exchange for the same certainty. She could not read this new Arthur. His thoughts were a closed book. Superficially, he was all that she could have wished. He still continued to escort her to the Tube, to buy her occasional presents, to tap, when conversing, the pleasantly sentimental vein. But now these things were not enough. Her heart was troubled. Her thoughts frightened her. The little black imp at the back of her mind kept whispering and whispering, till at last she was forced to listen. 'He's tired of you. He doesn't love you any more. He's tired of you.'

It is not everybody who, in times of mental stress, can find ready to hand among his or her personal acquaintances an expert counsellor, prepared at a moment's notice to listen with sympathy and advise with tact and skill. Everyone's world is full of friends, relatives, and others, who will give advice on any subject that may be presented to them; but there are crises in life which cannot be left to the amateur. It is the aim of a certain widely read class of paper to fill this void.

Of this class *Fireside Chat* was one of the best-known representatives. In exchange for one penny its five hundred thousand readers received every week a serial story about life in highest circles, a short story packed with heart-interest, articles on the removal of stains and the best method of coping with the cold mutton, anecdotes of Royalty, photographs of peeresses, hints on dress, chats about baby, brief but pointed dialogues between Blogson and Snogson, poems, Great Thoughts from the Dead and Brainy, half-hours in the editor's cosy sanctum, a slab of brown paper, and—the journal's leading feature—Advice on Matters of the Heart. The weekly contribution of the advice specialist of *Fireside Chat*, entitled 'In the Consulting Room, by Dr Cupid', was made up mainly of Answers to Correspondents. He affected the bedside manner of the kind, breezy old physician; and probably gave a good deal of comfort. At any rate, he always seemed to have plenty of cases on his hands.

It was to this expert that Maud took her trouble. She had been a regular reader of the paper for several years; and had, indeed, consulted the great man once before, when he had replied favourably to her query as to whether it would be right for her to accept caramels from Arthur, then almost a stranger. It was only natural that she should go to him now, in an even greater dilemma. The letter was not easy to write, but she finished it at last; and, after an anxious interval, judgement was delivered as follows:

'Well, well, well! Bless my soul, what is all this? M. P. writes me:

'I am a young lady, and until recently was very, very happy, except that my fiance, though truly loving me, was of a very jealous disposition, though I am sure I gave him no cause. He would scowl when I spoke to any other man, and this used to make me unhappy. But for some time now he has quite changed, and does not seem to mind at all, and though at first this made me feel happy, to think that he had got over his jealousy, I now feel unhappy because I am beginning to be afraid that he no longer cares for me. Do you think this is so, and what ought I to do?'

'My dear young lady, I should like to be able to reassure you; but it is kindest sometimes, you know, to be candid, however it may hurt. It has been my experience that, when jealousy flies out of the window, indifference comes in at the door. In the old days a knight would joust for the love of a ladye, risking physical injury rather than permit others to rival him in her affections. I think, M. P., that you should endeavour to discover the true state of your fiance's feelings. I do not, of course, advocate anything in the shape of unwomanly behaviour, of which I am sure, my dear young lady, you are incapable; but I think that you should certainly try to pique your fiance, to test him. At your next ball, for instance, refuse him a certain number of dances, on the plea that your programme is full. At garden-parties, at-homes, and so on, exhibit pleasure in the society and conversation of other gentlemen, and mark his demeanour as you do so. These little tests should serve either to relieve your apprehensions, provided they are groundless, or to show you the truth. And, after all, if it is the truth, it must be faced, must it not, M. P.?'

Before the end of the day Maud knew the whole passage by heart. The more her mind dwelt on it, the more clearly did it seem to express what she had felt but could not put into words. The point about jousting struck her as particularly well taken. She had looked up 'joust' in the dictionary, and it seemed to her that in these few words was contained the kernel of her trouble. In the old days, if any man had attempted to rival him in her affections (outside business hours), Arthur would undoubtedly have jousted—and jousted with the vigour of one who means to make his presence felt. Now, in similar circumstances, he would probably step aside politely, as who should say, 'After you, my dear Alphonse.'

There was no time to lose. An hour after her first perusal of Dr Cupid's advice, Maud had begun to act upon it. By the time the first lull in the morning's work had come, and there was a chance for private conversation, she had invented an imaginary young man, a shadowy Lothario, who, being introduced into her home on the previous Sunday by her brother Horace, had carried on in a way you wouldn't believe, paying all manner of compliments.

'He said I had such white hands,' said Maud.

Arthur nodded, stropping a razor the while. He appeared to be bearing the revelations with complete fortitude. Yet, only a few weeks before, a customer's comment on this same whiteness had stirred him to his depths.

'And this morning—what do you think? Why, he meets me as bold as you please, and gives me a cake of toilet soap. Like his impudence!'

She paused, hopefully.

'Always useful, soap,' said Arthur, politely sententious.

'Lovely it was,' went on Maud, dully conscious of failure, but stippling in like an artist the little touches which give atmosphere and verisimilitude to a story. 'All scented. Horace will tease me about it, I can tell you.'

She paused. Surely he must—Why, a sea-anemone would be torn with jealousy at such a tale.

Arthur did not even wince. He was charming about it. Thought it very kind of the young fellow. Didn't blame him for being struck by the whiteness of her hands. Touched on the history of soap, which he happened to have been reading up in the encyclopedia at the free library. And behaved altogether in such a thoroughly gentlemanly fashion that Maud stayed awake half the night, crying.

If Maud had waited another twenty-four hours there would have been no need for her to have taxed her powers of invention, for on the following day there entered the shop and her life a young man who was not imaginary—a Lothario of flesh and blood. He made his entry with that air of having bought most of the neighbouring property which belongs exclusively to minor actors, men of weight on the Stock Exchange, and American professional pugilists.

Mr 'Skipper' Shute belonged to the last-named of the three classes. He had arrived in England two months previously for the purpose of holding a conference at eight-stone four with one Joseph Edwardes, to settle a question of superiority at that weight which had been vexing the sporting public of two countries for over a year. Having successfully out-argued Mr Edwardes, mainly by means of strenuous work in the clinches, he was now on the eve of starting on a lucrative music-hall tour with his celebrated inaudible monologue. As a result of these things he was feeling very, very pleased with the world in general, and with Mr Skipper Shute in particular. And when Mr Shute was pleased with himself his manner was apt to be of the breeziest.

He breezed into the shop, took a seat, and, having cast an experienced eye at Maud, and found her pleasing, extended both hands, and observed, 'Go the limit, kid.'

At any other time Maud might have resented being addressed as 'kid' by a customer, but now she welcomed it. With the exception of a slight thickening of the lobe of one ear, Mr Shute bore no outward signs of his profession. And being, to use his own phrase, a 'swell dresser', he was really a most presentable young man. Just, in fact, what Maud needed. She saw in him her last hope. If any faint spark of his ancient fire still lingered in Arthur, it was through Mr Shute that it must be fanned.

She smiled upon Mr Shute. She worked on his robust fingers as if it were an artistic treat to be permitted to handle them. So carefully did she toil that she was still busy when Arthur, taking off his apron and putting on his hat, went out for his twenty-minutes' lunch, leaving them alone together.

The door had scarcely shut when Mr Shute bent forward.

'Say!'

He sank his voice to a winning whisper.

'You look good to muh,' he said, gallantly.

'The idea!' said Maud, tossing her head.

'On the level,' Mr Shute assured her.

Maud laid down her orange-sticks.

'Don't be silly,' she said. 'There—I've finished.'

'I've not,' said Mr Shute. 'Not by a mile. Say!'

'Well?'

'What do you do with your evenings?'

'I go home.'

'Sure. But when you don't? It's a poor heart that never rejoices. Don't you ever whoop it up?'

'Whoop it up?'

'The mad whirl,' explained Mr Shute. 'Ice-cream soda and buck-wheat cakes, and a happy evening at lovely Luna Park.'

'I don't know where Luna Park is.'

'What did they teach you at school? It's out in that direction,' said Mr Shute, pointing over his shoulder. 'You go straight on about three thousand miles till you hit little old New York; then you turn to the right. Say, don't you ever get a little treat? Why not come along to the White City some old evening? This evening?'

'Mr Welsh is taking me to the White City tonight.'

'And who is Mr Welsh?'

'The gentleman who has just gone out.'

'Is that so? Well, he doesn't look a live one, but maybe it's just because he's had bad news today. You never can tell.' He rose. 'Farewell, Evelina, fairest of your sex. We shall meet again; so keep a stout heart.'

And, taking up his cane, straw hat, and yellow gloves, Mr Shute departed, leaving Maud to her thoughts.

She was disappointed. She had expected better results. Mr Shute had lowered with ease the record for gay badinage, hitherto held by the red-faced customer; yet to all appearances there had been no change in Arthur's manner. But perhaps he had scowled (or bitten his lip), and she had not noticed it. Apparently he had struck Mr Shute, an unbiased spectator, as gloomy. Perhaps at some moment when her eyes had been on her work—She hoped for the best.

Whatever his feelings may have been during the afternoon, Arthur was undeniably cheerful that evening. He was in excellent spirits. His light-hearted abandon on the Wiggle-Woggle had been noted and commented upon by several lookers-on. Confronted with the Hairy Ainus, he had touched a high level of facetiousness. And now, as he sat with her listening to the band, he was crooning joyously to himself in accompaniment to the music, without, it would appear, a care in the world.

Maud was hurt and anxious. In a mere acquaintance this blithe attitude would have been welcome. It would have helped her to enjoy her evening. But from Arthur at that particular moment she looked for something else. Why was he cheerful? Only a few hours ago she had been—yes, flirting with another man before his very eyes. What right had he to be cheerful? He ought to be heated, full of passionate demands for an explanation—a flushed, throaty thing to be coaxed back into a good temper and then forgiven—all this at great length—for having been in a bad one. Yes, she told herself, she had wanted certainty one way or the other, and here it was. Now she knew. He no longer cared for her.

She trembled.

'Cold?' said Arthur. 'Let's walk. Evenings beginning to draw in now. Lum-da-diddley-ah. That's what I call a good tune. Give me something lively and bright. Dumty-umpty-iddley-ah. Dum tum—'

'Funny thing—' said Maud, deliberately.

'What's a funny thing?'

'The gentleman in the brown suit whose hands I did this afternoon—'

'He was,' agreed Arthur, brightly. 'A very funny thing.'

Maud frowned. Wit at the expense of Hairy Ainus was one thing—at her own another.

'I was about to say,' she went on precisely, 'that it was a funny thing, a coincidence, seeing that I was already engaged, that the gentleman in the brown suit whose hands I did this afternoon should have asked me to come here, to the White City, with him tonight.'

For a moment they walked on in silence. To Maud it seemed a hopeful silence. Surely it must be the prelude to an outburst.

'Oh!' he said, and stopped.

Maud's heart gave a leap. Surely that was the old tone?

A couple of paces, and he spoke again.

'I didn't hear him ask you.'

His voice was disappointingly level.

'He asked me after you had gone out to lunch.'

'It's a nuisance,' said Arthur, cheerily, 'when things clash like that. But perhaps he'll ask you again. Nothing to prevent you coming here twice. Well repays a second visit, I always say. I think—'

'You shouldn't,' said a voice behind him. 'It hurts the head. Well, kid, being shown a good time?'

The possibility of meeting Mr Shute had not occurred to Maud. She had assumed that, being aware that she would be there with another, he would have stayed away. It may, however, be remarked that she did not know Mr Shute. He was not one of your sensitive plants. He smiled pleasantly upon her, looking very dapper in evening dress and a silk hat that, though a size too small for him, shone like a mirror.

Maud hardly knew whether she was glad or sorry to see him. It did not seem to matter much now either way. Nothing seemed to matter much, in fact. Arthur's cheery acceptance of the news that she received invitations from others had been like a blow, leaving her numb and listless.

She made the introductions. The two men eyed each other.

'Pleased to meet you,' said Mr Shute.

'Weather keeps up,' said Arthur.

And from that point onward Mr Shute took command.

It is to be assumed that this was not the first time that Mr Shute had made one of a trio in these circumstances, for the swift dexterity with which he lost Arthur was certainly not that of a novice. So smoothly was it done that it was not until she emerged from the Witching Waves, guided by the pugilist's slim but formidable right arm, that Maud realized that Arthur had gone.

She gave a little cry of dismay. Secretly she was beginning to be somewhat afraid of Mr Shute. He was showing signs of being about to step out of the role she had assigned to him and attempt something on a larger scale. His manner had that extra touch of warmth which makes all the difference.

'Oh! He's gone!' she cried.

'Sure,' said Mr Shute. 'He's got a hurry-call from the Uji Village. The chief's cousin wants a hair-cut.'

'We must find him. We must.'

'Surest thing you know,' said Mr Shute. 'Plenty of time.'

'We must find him.'

Mr Shute regarded her with some displeasure.

'Seems to be ace-high with you, that dub,' he said.

'I don't understand you.'

'My observation was,' explained Mr Shute, coldly, 'that, judging from appearances, that dough-faced lemon was Willie-boy, the first and only love.'

Maud turned on him with flaming cheeks.

'Mr Welsh is nothing to me! Nothing! Nothing!' she cried.

She walked quickly on.

'Then, if there's a vacancy, star-eyes,' said the pugilist at her side, holding on a hat which showed a tendency to wobble, 'count me in. Directly I saw you—see here, what's the idea of this road-work? We aren't racing—'

Maud slowed down.

'That's better. As I was saying, directly I saw you, I said to myself, "That's the one you need. The original candy kid. The—"'

His hat lurched drunkenly as he answered the girl's increase of speed. He cursed it in a brief aside.

'That's what I said. "The original candy kid." So—'

He shot out a restraining hand. 'Arthur!' cried Maud. 'Arthur!'

'It's not my name' breathed Mr Shute, tenderly. 'Call me Clarence.'

Considered as an embrace, it was imperfect. At these moments a silk hat a size too small handicaps a man. The necessity of having to be careful about the nap prevented Mr Shute from doing himself complete justice. But he did enough to induce Arthur Welsh, who, having sighted the missing ones from afar, had been approaching them at a walking pace, to substitute a run for the walk, and arrive just as Maud wrenched herself free.

Mr Shute took off his hat, smoothed it, replaced it with extreme care, and turned his attention to the new-comer.

'Arthur!' said Maud.

Her heart gave a great leap. There was no mistaking the meaning in the eye that met hers. He cared! He cared!

'Arthur!'

He took no notice. His face was pale and working. He strode up to Mr Shute.

'Well?' he said between his teeth.

An eight-stone-four champion of the world has many unusual experiences in his life, but he rarely encounters men who say 'Well?' to him between their teeth. Mr Shute eyed this freak with profound wonder.

'I'll teach you to—to kiss young ladies!'

Mr Shute removed his hat again and gave it another brush. This gave him the necessary time for reflection.

'I don't need it,' he said. 'I've graduated.'

'Put them up!' hissed Arthur.

Almost a shocked look spread itself over the pugilist's face. So might Raphael have looked if requested to draw a pavement-picture.

'You aren't speaking to ME?' he said, incredulously.

'Put them up!'

Maud, trembling from head to foot, was conscious of one overwhelming emotion. She was terrified—yes. But stronger than the terror was the great wave of elation which swept over her. All her doubts had vanished. At last, after weary weeks of uncertainty, Arthur was about to give the supreme proof. He was going to joust for her.

A couple of passers-by had paused, interested, to watch developments. You could never tell, of course. Many an apparently promising row never got any farther than words. But, glancing at Arthur's face, they certainly felt justified in pausing. Mr Shute spoke.

'If it wasn't,' he said, carefully, 'that I don't want trouble with the Society for the Prevention of Cruelty to Animals, I'd—'

He broke off, for, to the accompaniment of a shout of approval from the two spectators, Arthur had swung his right fist, and it had taken him smartly on the side of the head.

Compared with the blows Mr Shute was wont to receive in the exercise of his profession, Arthur's was a gentle tap. But there was one circumstance which gave it a deadliness all its own. Achilles had his heel. Mr Shute's vulnerable point was at the other extremity. Instead of countering, he uttered a cry of agony, and clutched wildly with both hands at his hat.

He was too late. It fell to the ground and bounded away, with its proprietor in passionate chase. Arthur snorted and gently chafed his knuckles.

There was a calm about Mr Shute's demeanour as, having given his treasure a final polish and laid it carefully down, he began to advance on his adversary, which was more than ominous. His lips were a thin line of steel. The muscles stood out over his jaw-bones. Crouching in his professional manner, he moved forward softly, like a cat.

And it was at this precise moment, just as the two spectators, reinforced now by eleven other men of sporting tastes, were congratulating themselves on their acumen in having stopped to watch, that Police-Constable Robert Bryce, intruding fourteen stones of bone and muscle between the combatants, addressed to Mr Shute these memorable words: "Ullo, 'ullo! 'Ullo, 'ullo, 'ul-*lo*!'

Mr Shute appealed to his sense of justice.

'The mutt knocked me hat off.'

'And I'd do it again,' said Arthur, truculently.

'Not while I'm here you wouldn't, young fellow,' said Mr Bryce, with decision. 'I'm surprised at you,' he went on, pained. 'And you look a respectable young chap, too. You pop off.'

A shrill voice from the crowd at this point offered the constable all cinematograph rights if he would allow the contest to proceed.

'And you pop off, too, all of you,' continued Mr Bryce. 'Blest if I know what kids are coming to nowadays. And as for you,' he said, addressing Mr Shute, 'all you've got to do is to keep that face of yours closed. That's what you've got to do. I've got my eye on you, mind, and if I catch you a-follerin' of him'—he jerked his thumb over his shoulder at Arthur's departing figure—'I'll pinch you. Sure as you're alive.' He paused. 'I'd have done it already,' he added, pensively, 'if it wasn't me birthday.'

Arthur Welsh turned sharply. For some time he had been dimly aware that somebody was calling his name.

'Oh, Arthur!'

She was breathing quickly. He could see the tears in her eyes.

'I've been running. You walked so fast.'

He stared down at her gloomily.

'Go away,' he said. 'I've done with you.'

She clutched at his coat.

'Arthur, listen—listen! It's all a mistake. I thought you—you didn't care for me any more, and I was miserable, and I wrote to the paper and asked what should I do, and they said I ought to test you and try and make you jealous, and that that would relieve my apprehensions. And I hated it, but I did it, and you didn't seem to care till now. And you know that there's nobody but you.'

'You—The paper? What?' he stammered.

'Yes, yes, yes. I wrote to *Fireside Chat*, and Dr Cupid said that when jealousy flew out of the window indifference came in at the door, and that I must exhibit pleasure in the society of other gentlemen and mark your demeanour. So I—Oh!'

Arthur, luckier than Mr Shute, was not hampered by a too small silk hat.

It was a few moments later, as they moved slowly towards the Flip-Flap— which had seemed to both of them a fitting climax for the evening's emotions— that Arthur, fumbling in his waist-coat pocket, produced a small slip of paper.

'What's that?' Maud asked.

'Read it,' said Arthur. 'It's from *Home Moments*, in answer to a letter I sent them. And,' he added with heat, 'I'd like to have five minutes alone with the chap who wrote it.'

And under the electric light Maud read

ANSWERS TO CORRESPONDENTS

By the Heart Specialist

Arthur W.—Jealousy, Arthur W., is not only the most wicked, but the most foolish of passions. Shakespeare says:

It is the green-eyed monster, which doth mock
The meat it feeds on.

You admit that you have frequently caused great distress to the young lady of your affections by your exhibition of this weakness. Exactly. There is nothing a girl dislikes or despises more than jealousy. Be a man, Arthur W. Fight against it. You may find it hard at first, but persevere. Keep a smiling face. If she seems to enjoy talking to other men, show no resentment. Be merry and bright. Believe me, it is the only way.

BY ADVICE OF COUNSEL

The traveller champed meditatively at his steak. He paid no attention to the altercation which was in progress between the waiter and the man at the other end of the dingy room. The sounds of strife ceased. The waiter came over to the traveller's table and stood behind his chair. He was ruffled.

'If he meant lamb,' he said, querulously, 'why didn't he say "lamb", so's a feller could hear him? I thought he said "ham", so I brought ham. Now Lord Percy gets all peevish.'

He laughed bitterly. The traveller made no reply.

'If people spoke distinct,' said the waiter, 'there wouldn't be half the trouble there is in the world. Not half the trouble there wouldn't be. I shouldn't be here, for one thing. In this restawrong, I mean.' A sigh escaped him.

'I shouldn't,' he said, 'and that's the truth. I should be getting up when I pleased, eating and drinking all I wanted, and carrying on same as in the good old days. You wouldn't think, to look at me, would you now, that I was once like the lily of the field?'

The waiter was a tall, stringy man, who gave the impression of having no spine. In that he drooped, he might have been said to resemble a flower, but in no other respect. He had sandy hair, weak eyes set close together, and a day's growth of red stubble on his chin. One could not see him in the lily class.

'What I mean to say is, I didn't toil, neither did I spin. Ah, them was happy days! Lying on me back, plenty of tobacco, something cool in a jug—'

He sighed once more.

'Did you ever know a man of the name of Moore? Jerry Moore?'

The traveller applied himself to his steak in silence.

'Nice feller. Simple sort of feller. Big. Quiet. Bit deaf in one ear. Straw-coloured hair. Blue eyes. 'Andsome, rather. Had a 'ouse just outside of Reigate. Has it still. Money of his own. Left him by his pa. Simple sort of feller. Not much to say for himself. I used to know him well in them days. Used to live with him. Nice feller he was. Big. Bit hard of hearing. Got a sleepy kind of grin, like this— something.'

The traveller sipped his beer in thoughtful silence.

'I reckon you never met him,' said the waiter. 'Maybe you never knew Gentleman Bailey, either? We always called him that. He was one of these broken-down Eton or 'Arrer fellers, folks said. We struck up a partnership kind of casual, both being on the tramp together, and after a while we 'appened to be round about Reigate. And the first house we come to was this Jerry Moore's. He come up just as we was sliding to the back door, and grins that sleepy grin. Like this—something. "'Ullo!" he says. Gentleman kind of gives a whoop, and hollers, "If it ain't my old pal, Jerry Moore! Jack," he says to me, "this is my old pal, Mr Jerry Moore, wot I met in 'appier days down at Ramsgate one summer."

'They shakes hands, and Jerry Moore says, "Is this a friend of yours, Bailey?" looking at me. Gentleman introduces me. "We are partners," he says, "partners in misfortune. This is my friend, Mr Roach."

'"Come along in," says Jerry.

'So we went in, and he makes us at home. He's a bachelor, and lives all by himself in this desirable 'ouse.

'Well, I seen pretty quick that Jerry thinks the world of Gentleman. All that evening he's acting as if he's as pleased as Punch to have him there. Couldn't do enough for him. *It* was a bit of *all* right, I said to meself. It was, too.

'Next day we gets up late and has a good breakfast, and sits on the lawn and smokes. The sun was shining, the little birds was singing, and there wasn't a thing, east, west, north, or south, that looked like work. If I had been asked my address at that moment, on oath, I wouldn't have hesitated a second. I should have answered, "No. 1, Easy Street." You see, Jerry Moore was one of these slow, simple fellers, and you could tell in a moment what a lot he thought of Gentleman. Gentleman, you see, had a way with him. Not haughty, he wasn't. More affable, I should call it. He sort of made you feel that all men are born equal, but that it was awful good of him to be talking to you, and that he wouldn't do it for everybody. It went down proper with Jerry Moore. Jerry would sit and listen to him giving his views on things by the hour. By the end of the first day I was having visions of sitting in that garden a white-baked old man, and being laid out, when my time should come, in Jerry's front room.'

He paused, his mind evidently in the past, among the cigars and big breakfasts. Presently he took up his tale.

'This here Jerry Moore was a simple sort of feller. Deafies are like that. Ever noticed? Not that Jerry was a real deafy. His hearing was a bit off, but he could foller you if you spoke to him nice and clear. Well, I was saying, he was kind of simple. Liked to put in his days pottering about the little garden he'd made for himself, looking after his flowers and his fowls, and sit of an evening listening to Gentleman 'olding forth on Life. He was a philosopher, Gentleman was. And Jerry took everything he said as gospel. He didn't want no proofs. 'E and the King of Denmark would have been great pals. He just sat by with his big blue eyes getting rounder every minute and lapped it up.

'Now you'd think a man like that could be counted on, wouldn't you? Would he want anything more? Not he, you'd say. You'd be wrong. Believe me, there isn't a man on earth that's fixed and contented but what a woman can't knock his old Paradise into 'ash with one punch.

'It wasn't long before I begin to notice a change in Jerry. He never had been what you'd call a champion catch-as-catch-can talker, but now he was silenter than ever. And he got a habit of switching Gentleman off from his theories on Life in general to Woman in particular. This suited Gentleman just right. What he didn't know about Woman wasn't knowledge.

'Gentleman was too busy talking to have time to get suspicious, but I wasn't; and one day I draws Gentleman aside and puts it to him straight. "Gentleman," I says, "Jerry Moore is in love!"

'Well, this was a nasty knock, of course, for Gentleman. He knew as well as I did what it would mean if Jerry was to lead home a blushing bride through that front door. It would be outside into the cold, hard world for the bachelor friends.

Gentleman sees that quick, and his jaw drops. I goes on. "All the time," I says, "that you're talking away of an evening, Jerry's seeing visions of a little woman sitting in your chair. And you can bet we don't enter into them visions. He may dream of little feet pattering about the house," I says, "but they aren't ours; and you can 'ave something on that both ways. Look alive, Gentleman," I says, "and think out some plan, or we might as well be padding the hoof now."

'Well, Gentleman did what he could. In his evening discourses he started to give it to Woman all he knew. Began to talk about Delilahs and Jezebels and Fools-there-was and the rest of it, and what a mug a feller was to let a female into 'is cosy home, who'd only make him spend his days hooking her up, and his nights wondering how to get back the blankets without waking her. My, he was crisp! Enough to have given Romeo the jumps, you'd have thought. But, lor! It's no good talking to them when they've got it bad.

'A few days later we caught him with the goods, talking in the road to a girl in a pink dress.

'I couldn't but admit that Jerry had picked one right from the top of the basket. This wasn't one of them languishing sort wot sits about in cosy corners and reads story-books, and don't care what's happening in the home so long as they find out what became of the hero in his duel with the Grand Duke. She was a brown, slim, wiry-looking little thing. *You* know. Held her chin up and looked you up and down with eyes the colour of Scotch whisky, as much as to say, "Well, what *about* it?" You could tell without looking at her, just by the feel of the atmosphere when she was near, that she had as much snap and go in her as Jerry Moore hadn't, which was a good bit. I knew, just as sure as I was standing there on one leg, that this was the sort of girl who would have me and Gentleman out of that house about three seconds after the clergyman had tied the knot.

'Jerry says, "These are my friends, Miss Tuxton—Mr Bailey and Mr Roach. They are staying with me for a visit. This is Miss Jane Tuxton," he says to us. "I was just going to see Miss Tuxton home," he says, sort of wistful. "Excellent," says Gentleman. "We'll come too." And we all goes along. There wasn't much done in the way of conversation. Jerry never was one for pushing out the words; nor was I, when in the presence of the sect; and Miss Jane had her chin in the air, as if she thought me and Gentleman was not needed in any way whatsoever. The only talk before we turned her in at the garden gate was done by Gentleman, who told a pretty long story about a friend of his in Upper Sydenham who had been silly enough to marry, and had had trouble ever since.

'That night, after we had went to bed, I said to Gentleman, "Gentleman," I says, "what's going to be done about this? We've got about as much chance, if Jerry marries that girl," I says, "as a couple of helpless chocolate creams at a school-girls' picnic." "If," says Gentleman. "He ain't married her yet. That is a girl of character, Jack. Trust me. Didn't she strike you as a girl who would like a man with a bit of devil in him, a man with some go in him, a you-be-darned kind of man? Does Jerry fill the bill? He's more like a doormat with 'Welcome' written on it, than anything else."

'Well, we seen a good deal of Miss Jane in the next week or so. We keeps Jerry under—what's it the heroine says in the melodrama? "Oh, cruel, cruel, S.P. something." Espionage, that's it. We keeps Jerry under espionage, and whenever he goes trickling round after the girl, we goes trickling round after him.

'"Things is running our way," says Gentleman to me, after one of these meetings. "That girl is getting cross with Jerry. She wants Reckless Rudolf, not a man who stands and grins when other men butt in on him and his girl. Mark my words, Jack. She'll get tired of Jerry, and go off and marry a soldier, and we'll live happy ever after." "Think so?" I says. "Sure of it," said Gentleman.

'It was the Sunday after this that Jerry Moore announces to us, wriggling, that he had an engagement to take supper with Jane and her folks. He'd have liked to have slipped away secret, but we was keeping him under espionage too crisp for that, so he has to tell us. "Excellent," said Gentleman. "It will be a great treat to Jack and myself to meet the family. We will go along with you." So off we all goes, and pushes our boots in sociable fashion under the Tuxton table. I looked at Miss Jane out of the corner of my eye; and, honest, that chin of hers was sticking out a foot, and Jerry didn't dare look at her. Love's young dream, I muses to myself, how swift it fades when a man has the nature and disposition of a lop-eared rabbit!

'The Tuxtons was four in number, not counting the parrot, and all male. There was Pa Tuxton, an old feller with a beard and glasses; a fat uncle; a big brother, who worked in a bank and was dressed like Moses in all his glory; and a little brother with a snub nose, that cheeky you'd have been surprised. And the parrot in its cage and a fat yellow dog. And they're all making themselves pleasant to Jerry, the wealthy future son-in-law, something awful. It's "How are the fowls, Mr Moore?" and "A little bit of this pie, Mr Moore; Jane made it," and Jerry sitting there with a feeble grin, saying "Yes" and "No" and nothing much more, while Miss Jane's eyes are snapping like Fifth of November fireworks. I could feel Jerry's chances going back a mile a minute. I felt as happy as a little child that evening. I sang going back home.

'Gentleman's pleased, too. "Jack," he says to me when we're in bed, "this is too easy. In my most sanguinary dreams I hardly hoped for this. No girl of spirit's going to love a man who behaves that way to her parents. The way to win the heart of a certain type of girl," he says, beginning on his theories, "the type to which Jane Tuxton belongs, is to be rude to her family. I've got Jane Tuxton sized up and labelled. Her kind wants her folks to dislike her young man. She wants to feel that she's the only one in the family that's got the sense to see the hidden good in Willie. She doesn't want to be one of a crowd hollering out what a nice young man he is. It takes some pluck in a man to stand up to a girl's family, and that's what Jane Tuxton is looking for in Jerry. Take it from one who has studied the sect," says Gentleman, "from John o' Groat's to Land's End, and back again."

'Next day Jerry Moore's looking as if he'd only sixpence in the world and had swallowed it. "What's the matter, Jerry?" says Gentleman. Jerry heaves a sigh. "Bailey," he says, "and you, Mr Roach, I expect you both seen how it is with me. I love Miss Jane Tuxton, and you seen for yourselves what transpires. She don't value me, not tuppence." "Say not so," says Gentleman, sympathetic. "You're doing fine. If you knew the sect as I do you wouldn't go by mere superficial silences and chin-tiltings. I can read a girl's heart, Jerry," he says, patting him on the shoulder, "and I tell you you're doing fine. All you want now is a little rapid work, and you win easy. To make the thing a cert," he says, getting up, "all you have to do is to make a dead set at her folks." He winks at me. "Don't just sit there like you did last night. Show 'em you've got something in you. You know what folks are: they think themselves the most important things on the map. Well, go to work. Consult them all you know. Every opportunity you get. There's nothing like consulting a girl's folks to put you in good with her." And he pats Jerry on the shoulder again and goes indoors to find his pipe.

'Jerry turns to me. "Do you think that's really so?" he says. I says, "I do." "He knows all about girls, I reckon," says Jerry. "You can go by him every time," I says. "Well, well," says Jerry, sort of thoughtful.'

The waiter paused. His eye was sad and dreamy. Then he took up the burden of his tale.

'First thing that happens is that Gentleman has a sore tooth on the next Sunday, so don't feel like coming along with us. He sits at home, dosing it with whisky, and Jerry and me goes off alone.

'So Jerry and me pikes off, and once more we prepares to settle down around the board. I hadn't noticed Jerry particular, but just now I catches sight of his face in the light of the lamp. Ever see one of those fighters when he's sitting in his corner before a fight, waiting for the gong to go? Well, Jerry looks like that; and it surprises me.

'I told you about the fat yellow dog that permeated the Tuxton's house, didn't I? The family thought a lot of that dog, though of all the ugly brutes I ever met he was the worst. Sniffing round and growling all the time. Well, this evening he comes up to Jerry just as he's going to sit down, and starts to growl. Old Pa Tuxton looks over his glasses and licks his tongue. "Rover! Rover!" he says, kind of mild. "Naughty Rover; he don't like strangers, I'm afraid." Jerry looks at Pa Tuxton, and he looks at the dog, and I'm just expecting him to say "No" or "Yes", same as the other night, when he lets out a nasty laugh—one of them bitter laughs. "Ho!" he says. "Ho! don't he? Then perhaps he'd better get further away from them." And he ups with his boot and—well, the dog hit the far wall.

'Jerry sits down and pulls up his chair. "I don't approve," he says, fierce, "of folks keeping great, fat, ugly, bad-tempered yellow dogs that are a nuisance to all. I don't like it."

'There was a silence you could have scooped out with a spoon. Have you ever had a rabbit turn round on you and growl? That's how we all felt when Jerry outs with them crisp words. They took our breath away.

'While we were getting it back again the parrot, which was in its cage, let out a squawk. Honest, I jumped a foot in my chair.

'Jerry gets up very deliberate, and walks over to the parrot. "Is this a menagerie?" he says. "Can't a man have supper in peace without an image like you starting to holler? Go to sleep."

'We was all staring at him surprised, especially Uncle Dick Tuxton, whose particular pet the parrot was. He'd brought him home all the way from some foreign parts.

"'Hello, Billy!" says the bird, shrugging his shoulders and puffing himself up. "R-r-r-r! R-r-r-r! 'lo, Billy! 'lo, 'lo, 'lo! R-r WAH!"

'Jerry gives its cage a bang.

"'Don't talk back at me," he says, "or I'll knock your head off. You think because you've got a green tail you're someone." And he stalks back to his chair and sits glaring at Uncle Dick.

'Well, all this wasn't what you might call promoting an easy flow of conversation. Everyone's looking at Jerry, 'specially me, wondering what next, and trying to get their breath, and Jerry's frowning at the cold beef, and there's a sort of awkward pause. Miss Jane is the first to get busy. She bustles about and gets the food served out, and we begins to eat. But still there's not so much conversation that you'd notice it. This goes on till we reaches the concluding stages, and then Uncle Dick comes up to the scratch.

"'How is the fowls, Mr Moore?" he says.

"'Gimme some more pie," says Jerry. "What?"

'Uncle Dick repeats his remark.

"'Fowls?" says Jerry. "What do you know about fowls? Your notion of a fowl is an ugly bird with a green tail, a Wellington nose, and—gimme a bit of cheese."

'Uncle Dick's fond of the parrot, so he speaks up for him. "Polly's always been reckoned a handsome bird," he says.

"'He wants stuffing," says Jerry.

'And Uncle Dick drops out of the talk.

'Up comes big brother, Ralph his name was. He's the bank-clerk and a dude. He gives his cuffs a flick, and starts in to make things jolly all round by telling a story about a man he knows named Wotherspoon. Jerry fixes him with his eye, and, half-way through, interrupts.

"'That waistcoat of yours is fierce," he says.

"'Pardon?" says Ralph.

"'That waistcoat of yours," says Jerry. "It hurts me eyes. It's like an electric sign."

"'Why, Jerry," I says, but he just scowls at me and I stops.

'Ralph is proud of his clothes, and he isn't going to stand this. He glares at Jerry and Jerry glares at him.

"'Who do you think you are?" says Ralph, breathing hard.

"'Button up your coat," says Jerry.

"'Look 'ere!" says Ralph.

"'Cover it up, I tell you," says Jerry. "Do you want to blind me?" Pa Tuxton interrupts.

"'Why, Mr Moore," he begins, sort of soothing; when the small brother, who's been staring at Jerry, chips in. I told you he was cheeky.

'He says, "Pa, what a funny nose Mr Moore's got!"

'And that did it. Jerry rises, very slow, and leans across the table and clips the kid brother one side of the ear-'ole. And then there's a general imbroglio, everyone standing up and the kid hollering and the dog barking.

"'If you'd brought him up better," says Jerry, severe, to Pa Tuxton, "this wouldn't ever have happened."

'Pa Tuxton gives a sort of howl.

"'Mr Moore," he yells, "what is the meaning of this extraordinary behaviour? You come here and strike me child—"

'Jerry bangs on the table.

"'Yes," he says, "and I'd strike him again. Listen to me," he says. "You think just because I'm quiet I ain't got no spirit. You think all I can do is to sit and smile. You think—Bah! You aren't on to the hidden depths in me character. I'm one of them still waters that runs deep. I'm—Here, you get out of it! Yes, all of you! Except Jane. Jane and me wants this room to have a private talk in. I've got a lot of things to say to Jane. Are you going?"

'I turns to the crowd. I was awful disturbed. "You mustn't take any notice," I says. "He ain't well. He ain't himself." When just then the parrot cuts with another of them squawks. Jerry jumps at it.

"'You first," he says, and flings the cage out of the window. "Now you," he says to the yellow dog, putting him out through the door. And then he folds his arms and scowls at us, and we all notice suddenly that he's very big. We look at one another, and we begins to edge towards the door. All except Jane, who's staring at Jerry as if he's a ghost.

"'Mr Moore," says Pa Tuxton, dignified, "we'll leave you. You're drunk."

"'I'm not drunk," says Jerry. "I'm in love."

"'Jane," says Pa Tuxton, "come with me, and leave this ruffian to himself."

"'Jane," says Jerry, "stop here, and come and lay your head on my shoulder."

"'Jane," says Pa Tuxton, "do you hear me?"

"'Jane," says Jerry, "I'm waiting."

'She looks from one to the other for a spell, and then she moves to where Jerry's standing.

"'I'll stop," she says, sort of quiet.

'And we drifts out.'

The waiter snorted.

'I got back home quick as I could,' he said, 'and relates the proceedings to Gentleman. Gentleman's rattled. "I don't believe it," he says. "Don't stand there and tell me Jerry Moore did them things. Why, it ain't in the man. 'Specially after what I said to him about the way he ought to behave. How could he have done so?" Just then in comes Jerry, beaming all over. "Boys," he shouts, "congratulate me. It's all right. We've fixed it up. She says she hadn't known me properly before. She says she'd always reckoned me a sheep, while all the time I was one of them strong, silent men." He turns to Gentleman—'

The man at the other end of the room was calling for his bill.

'All right, all right,' said the waiter. 'Coming! He turns to Gentleman,' he went on rapidly, 'and he says, "Bailey, I owe it all to you, because if you hadn't told me to insult her folks—"'

He leaned on the traveller's table and fixed him with an eye that pleaded for sympathy.

"Ow about that?' he said. 'Isn't that crisp? "Insult her folks!" Them was his very words. "Insult her folks."'

The traveller looked at him inquiringly.

'Can you beat it?' said the waiter.

'I don't know what you are saying,' said the traveller. 'If it is important, write it on a slip of paper. I am stone-deaf.'

ROUGH-HEW THEM HOW WE WILL

Paul Boielle was a waiter. The word 'waiter' suggests a soft-voiced, deft-handed being, moving swiftly and without noise in an atmosphere of luxury and shaded lamps. At Bredin's Parisian Cafe and Restaurant in Soho, where Paul worked, there were none of these things; and Paul himself, though he certainly moved swiftly, was by no means noiseless. His progress through the room resembled in almost equal proportions the finish of a Marathon race, the star-act of a professional juggler, and a monologue by an Earl's Court side-showman. Constant acquaintance rendered regular habitues callous to the wonder, but to a stranger the sight of Paul tearing over the difficult between-tables course, his hands loaded with two vast pyramids of dishes, shouting as he went the mystic word, 'Comingsarecominginamomentsaresteaksareyessarecomingsare!' was impressive to a degree. For doing far less exacting feats on the stage music-hall performers were being paid fifty pounds a week. Paul got eighteen shillings.

What a blessing is poverty, properly considered. If Paul had received more than eighteen shillings a week he would not have lived in an attic. He would have luxuriated in a bed-sitting-room on the second floor; and would consequently have missed what was practically a genuine north light. The skylight which went with the attic was so arranged that the room was a studio in miniature, and, as Paul was engaged in his spare moments in painting a great picture, nothing could have been more fortunate; for Paul, like so many of our public men, lived two lives. Off duty, the sprinting, barking juggler of Bredin's Parisian Cafe became the quiet follower of Art. Ever since his childhood he had had a passion for drawing and painting. He regretted that Fate had allowed him so little time for such work; but after all, he reflected, all great artists had had their struggles—so why not he? Moreover, they were now nearly at an end. An hour here, an hour there, and every Thursday a whole afternoon, and the great picture was within measurable distance of completion. He had won through. Without models, without leisure, hungry, tired, he had nevertheless triumphed. A few more touches, and the masterpiece would be ready for purchase. And after that all would be plain sailing. Paul could forecast the scene so exactly. The picture would be at the dealer's, possibly—one must not be too sanguine—thrust away in some odd corner. The wealthy connoisseur would come in. At first he would not see the masterpiece; other more prominently displayed works would catch his eye. He would turn from them in weary scorn, and then!... Paul wondered how big the cheque would be.

There were reasons why he wanted the money. Looking at him as he cantered over the linoleum at Bredin's, you would have said that his mind was on his work. But it was not so. He took and executed orders as automatically as the penny-in-the-slot musical-box in the corner took pennies and produced tunes. His thoughts were of Jeanne Le Brocq, his co-worker at Bredin's, and a little cigar shop down Brixton way which he knew was in the market at a reasonable rate. To marry the former and own the latter was Paul's idea of the earthly paradise, and it was the wealthy connoisseur, and he alone, who could open the gates.

Jeanne was a large, slow-moving Norman girl, stolidly handsome. One could picture her in a de Maupassant farmyard. In the clatter and bustle of Bredin's Parisian Cafe she appeared out of place, like a cow in a boiler-factory. To Paul, who worshipped her with all the fervour of a little man for a large woman, her deliberate methods seemed all that was beautiful and dignified. To his mind she lent a tone to the vulgar whirlpool of gorging humanity, as if she had been some goddess mixing in a Homeric battle. The whirlpool had other views—and expressed them. One coarse-fibred brute, indeed, once went so far as to address to her the frightful words, "Urry up, there, Tottie! Look slippy.' It was wrong, of course, for Paul to slip and spill an order of scrambled eggs down the brute's coatsleeve, but who can blame him?

Among those who did not see eye to eye with Paul in his views on deportment in waitresses was M. Bredin himself, the owner of the Parisian Cafe; and it was this circumstance which first gave Paul the opportunity of declaring the passion which was gnawing him with the fierce fury of a Bredin customer gnawing a tough steak against time during the rush hour. He had long worshipped her from afar, but nothing more intimate than a 'Good morning, Miss Jeanne', had escaped him, till one day during a slack spell he came upon her in the little passage leading to the kitchen, her face hidden in her apron, her back jerking with sobs.

Business is business. Paul had a message to deliver to the cook respecting 'two fried, coffee, and one stale'. He delivered it and returned. Jeanne was still sobbing.

'Ah, Miss Jeanne,' cried Paul, stricken, 'what is the matter? What is it? Why do you weep?'

'The *patron*,' sobbed Jeanne. 'He—'

'My angel,' said Paul, 'he is a pig.'

This was perfectly true. No conscientious judge of character could have denied that Paul had hit the bull's eye. Bredin was a pig. He looked like a pig; he ate like a pig; he grunted like a pig. He had the lavish embonpoint of a pig. Also a porcine soul. If you had tied a bit of blue ribbon round his neck you could have won prizes with him at a show.

Paul's eyes flashed with fury. 'I will slap him in the eye,' he roared.

'He called me a tortoise.'

'And kick him in the stomach,' added Paul.

Jeanne's sobs were running on second speed now. The anguish was diminishing. Paul took advantage of the improved conditions to slide an arm part of the way round her waist. In two minutes he had said as much as the ordinary man could have worked off in ten. All good stuff, too. No padding.

Jeanne's face rose from her apron like a full moon. She was too astounded to be angry.

Paul continued to babble. Jeanne looked at him with growing wrath. That she, who received daily the affectionate badinage of gentlemen in bowler hats and check suits, who had once been invited to the White City by a solicitor's clerk, should be addressed in this way by a waiter! It was too much. She threw off his hand.

'Wretched little man!' she cried, stamping angrily.

'My angel!' protested Paul.

Jeanne uttered a scornful laugh.

'You!' she said.

There are few more withering remarks than 'You!' spoken in a certain way. Jeanne spoke it in just that way.

Paul wilted.

'On eighteen shillings a week,' went on Jeanne, satirically, 'you would support a wife, yes? Why—'

Paul recovered himself. He had an opening now, and proceeded to use it.

'Listen,' he said. 'At present, yes, it is true, I earn but eighteen shillings a week, but it will not always be so, no. I am not only a waiter. I am also an artist. I have painted a great picture. For a whole year I have worked, and now it is ready. I will sell it, and then, my angel—?'

Jeanne's face had lost some of its scorn. She was listening with some respect. 'A picture?' she said, thoughtfully. 'There is money in pictures.'

For the first time Paul was glad that his arm was no longer round her waist. To do justice to the great work he needed both hands for purposes of gesticulation.

'There is money in this picture,' he said. 'Oh, it is beautiful. I call it "The Awakening". It is a woodland scene. I come back from my work here, hot and tired, and a mere glance at that wood refreshes me. It is so cool, so green. The sun filters in golden splashes through the foliage. On a mossy bank, between two trees, lies a beautiful girl asleep. Above her, bending fondly over her, just about to kiss that flower-like face, is a young man in the dress of a shepherd. At the last moment he has looked over his shoulder to make sure that there is nobody near to see. He is wearing an expression so happy, so proud, that one's heart goes out to him.'

'Yes, there might be money in that,' cried Jeanne.

'There is, there is!' cried Paul. 'I shall sell it for many francs to a wealthy connoisseur. And then, my angel—'

'You are a good little man,' said the angel, patronizingly. 'Perhaps. We will see.'

Paul caught her hand and kissed it. She smiled indulgently. 'Yes,' she said. 'There might be money. These English pay much money for pictures.'

It is pretty generally admitted that Geoffrey Chaucer, the eminent poet of the fourteenth century, though obsessed with an almost Rooseveltian passion for the new spelling, was there with the goods when it came to profundity of thought. It was Chaucer who wrote the lines:

The lyfe so short, the craft so long to lerne,

Th' assay so hard, so sharpe the conquering.

Which means, broadly, that it is difficult to paint a picture, but a great deal more difficult to sell it.

Across the centuries Paul Boielle shook hands with Geoffrey Chaucer. 'So sharpe the conquering' put his case in a nutshell.

The full story of his wanderings with the masterpiece would read like an Odyssey and be about as long. It shall be condensed.

There was an artist who dined at intervals at Bredin's Parisian Cafe, and, as the artistic temperament was too impatient to be suited by Jeanne's leisurely methods, it had fallen to Paul to wait upon him. It was to this expert that Paul, emboldened by the geniality of the artist's manner, went for information. How did monsieur sell his pictures? Monsieur said he didn't, except once in a blue moon. But when he did? Oh, he took the thing to the dealers. Paul thanked him. A friend of him, he explained, had painted a picture and wished to sell it.

'Poor devil!' was the artist's comment.

Next day, it happening to be a Thursday, Paul started on his travels. He started buoyantly, but by evening he was as a punctured balloon. Every dealer had the same remark to make—to wit, no room.

'Have you yet sold the picture?' inquired Jeanne, when they met. 'Not yet,' said Paul. 'But they are delicate matters, these negotiations. I use finesse. I proceed with caution.'

He approached the artist again.

'With the dealers,' he said, 'my friend has been a little unfortunate. They say they have no room.'

'*I* know,' said the artist, nodding.

'Is there, perhaps, another way?'

'What sort of a picture is it?' inquired the artist.

Paul became enthusiastic.

'Ah! monsieur, it is beautiful. It is a woodland scene. A beautiful girl—'

'Oh! Then he had better try the magazines. They might use it for a cover.'

Paul thanked him effusively. On the following Thursday he visited divers art editors. The art editors seemed to be in the same unhappy condition as the dealers. 'Overstocked!' was their cry.

'The picture?' said Jeanne, on the Friday morning. 'Is it sold?'

'Not yet,' said Paul, 'but—'

'Always but!'

'My angel!'

'Bah!' said Jeanne, with a toss of her large but shapely head.

By the end of the month Paul was fighting in the last ditch, wandering disconsolately among those who dwell in outer darkness and have grimy thumbs. Seven of these in all he visited on that black Thursday, and each of the seven rubbed the surface of the painting with a grimy thumb, snorted, and dismissed him. Sick and beaten, Paul took the masterpiece back to his skylight room.

All that night he lay awake, thinking. It was a weary bundle of nerves that came to the Parisian Cafe next morning. He was late in arriving, which was good in that it delayed the inevitable question as to the fate of the picture, but bad in every other respect. M. Bredin, squatting behind the cash-desk, grunted fiercely at him; and, worse, Jeanne, who, owing to his absence, had had to be busier than suited her disposition, was distant and haughty. A murky gloom settled upon Paul.

Now it so happened that M. Bredin, when things went well with him, was wont to be filled with a ponderous amiability. It was not often that this took a practical form, though it is on record that in an exuberant moment he once gave a small boy a halfpenny. More frequently it merely led him to soften the porcine austerity of his demeanour. Today, business having been uncommonly good, he felt pleased with the world. He had left his cash-desk and was assailing a bowl of soup at one of the side-tables. Except for a belated luncher at the end of the room the place was empty. It was one of the hours when there was a lull in the proceedings at the Parisian Cafe. Paul was leaning, wrapped in the gloom, against the wall. Jeanne was waiting on the proprietor.

M. Bredin finished his meal and rose. He felt content. All was well with the world. As he lumbered to his desk he passed Jeanne. He stopped. He wheezed a compliment. Then another. Paul, from his place by the wall, watched with jealous fury.

M. Bredin chucked Jeanne under the chin.

As he did so, the belated luncher called 'Waiter!' but Paul was otherwise engaged. His entire nervous system seemed to have been stirred up with a pole. With a hoarse cry he dashed forward. He would destroy this pig who chucked his Jeanne under the chin.

The first intimation M. Bredin had of the declaration of war was the impact of a French roll on his ear. It was one of those nobbly, chunky rolls with sharp corners, almost as deadly as a piece of shrapnel. M. Bredin was incapable of jumping, but he uttered a howl and his vast body quivered like a stricken jelly. A second roll, whizzing by, slapped against the wall. A moment later a cream-bun burst in sticky ruin on the proprietor's left eye.

The belated luncher had been anxious to pay his bill and go, but he came swiftly to the conclusion that this was worth stopping on for. He leaned back in his chair and watched. M. Bredin had entrenched himself behind the cash-desk, peering nervously at Paul through the cream, and Paul, pouring forth abuse in his native tongue, was brandishing a chocolate eclair. The situation looked good to the spectator.

It was spoiled by Jeanne, who seized Paul by the arm and shook him, adding her own voice to the babel. It was enough. The eclair fell to the floor. Paul's voice died away. His face took on again its crushed, hunted expression. The voice of M. Bredin, freed from competition, rose shrill and wrathful.

'The marksman is getting sacked,' mused the onlooker, diagnosing the situation.

He was right. The next moment Paul, limp and depressed, had retired to the kitchen passage, discharged. It was here, after a few minutes, that Jeanne found him.

'Fool! Idiot! Imbecile!' said Jeanne.

Paul stared at her without speaking.

'To throw rolls at the *patron*. Imbecile!'

'He—' began Paul.

'Bah! And what if he did? Must you then attack him like a mad dog? What is it to you?'

Paul was conscious of a dull longing for sympathy, a monstrous sense of oppression. Everything was going wrong. Surely Jeanne must be touched by his heroism? But no. She was scolding furiously. Suppose Andromeda had turned and scolded Perseus after he had slain the sea-monster! Paul mopped his forehead with his napkin. The bottom had dropped out of his world.

'Jeanne!'

'Bah! Do not talk to me, idiot of a little man. Almost you lost me my place also. The *patron* was in two minds. But I coaxed him. A fine thing that would have been, to lose my good place through your foolishness. To throw rolls. My goodness!'

She swept back into the room again, leaving Paul still standing by the kitchen door. Something seemed to have snapped inside him. How long he stood there he did not know, but presently from the dining-room came calls of 'Waiter!' and automatically he fell once more into his work, as an actor takes up his part. A stranger would have noticed nothing remarkable in him. He bustled to and fro with undiminished energy.

At the end of the day M. Bredin paid him his eighteen shillings with a grunt, and Paul walked out of the restaurant a masterless man.

He went to his attic and sat down on the bed. Propped up against the wall was the picture. He looked at it with unseeing eyes. He stared dully before him.

Then thoughts came to him with a rush, leaping and dancing in his mind like imps in Hades. He had a curious sense of detachment. He seemed to be watching himself from a great distance.

This was the end. The little imps danced and leaped; and then one separated itself from the crowd, to grow bigger than, the rest, to pirouette more energetically. He rose. His mind was made up. He would kill himself.

He went downstairs and out into the street. He thought hard as he walked. He would kill himself, but how?

His preoccupation was so great that an automobile, rounding a corner, missed him by inches as he crossed the road. The chauffeur shouted angrily at him as he leapt back.

Paul shook his fist at the retreating lights.

'Pig!' he shouted. 'Assassin! Scoundrel! Villain! Would you kill me? I will take your number, rascal. I will inform the police. Villain!'

A policeman had strolled up and was eyeing him curiously. Paul turned to him, full of his wrongs.

'Officer,' he cried, 'I have a complaint. These pigs of chauffeurs! They are reckless. They drive so recklessly. Hence the great number of accidents.'

'Awful!' said the policeman. 'Pass along, sonny.'

Paul walked on, fuming. It was abominable that these chauffeurs—And then an idea came to him. He had found a way.

It was quiet in the Park. He had chosen the Park because it was dark and there would be none to see and interfere. He waited long in the shadow by the roadside. Presently from the darkness there came the distant drone of powerful engines. Lights appeared, like the blazing eyes of a dragon swooping down to devour its prey.

He ran out into the road with a shout.

It was an error, that shout. He had intended it for an inarticulate farewell to his picture, to Jeanne, to life. It was excusable to the driver of the motor that he misinterpreted it. It seemed to him a cry of warning. There was a great jarring of brakes, a scuttering of locked wheels on the dry road, and the car came to a standstill a full yard from where he stood.

'What the deuce—' said a cool voice from behind the lights.

Paul struck his chest and folded his arms.

'I am here,' he cried. 'Destroy me!'

'Let George do it,' said the voice, in a marked American accent. 'I never murder on a Friday; it's unlucky. If it's not a rude question, which asylum are you from? Halloa!'

The exclamation was one of surprise, for Paul's nerves had finally given way, and he was now in a heap on the road, sobbing.

The man climbed down and came into the light. He was a tall young man with a pleasant, clean-cut face. He stopped and shook Paul.

'Quit that,' he said. 'Maybe it's not true. And if it is, there's always hope. Cut it out. What's the matter? All in?'

Paul sat up, gulping convulsively. He was thoroughly unstrung. The cold, desperate mood had passed. In its place came the old feeling of desolation. He was a child, aching for sympathy. He wanted to tell his troubles. Punctuating his narrative with many gestures and an occasional gulp, he proceeded to do so. The American listened attentively.

'So you can't sell your picture, and you've lost your job, and your girl has shaken you?' he said. 'Pretty bad, but still you've no call to go mingling with automobile wheels. You come along with me to my hotel, and tomorrow we'll see if we can't fix up something.'

There was breakfast at the hotel next morning, a breakfast to put heart into a man. During the meal a messenger dispatched in a cab to Paul's lodgings returned with the canvas. A deferential waiter informed the American that it had been taken with every possible care to his suite.

'Good,' said the young man. 'If you're through, we'll go and have a look at it.'

They went upstairs. There was the picture resting against a chair.

'Why, I call that fine,' said the young man. 'It's a cracker jack.'

Paul's heart gave a sudden leap. Could it be that here was the wealthy connoisseur? He was wealthy, for he drove an automobile and lived in an expensive hotel. He was a connoisseur, for he had said that the picture was a crackerjack.

'Monsieur is kind,' murmured Paul.

'It's a bear-cat,' said the young man, admiringly.

'Monsieur is flattering,' said Paul, dimly perceiving a compliment.

'I've been looking for a picture like that,' said the young man, 'for months.'

Paul's eyes rolled heavenwards.

'If you'll make a few alterations, I'll buy it and ask for more.'

'Alterations, monsieur?'

'One or two small ones.' He pointed to the stooping figure of the shepherd. 'Now, you see this prominent citizen. What's he doing?'

'He is stooping,' said Paul, fervently, 'to bestow upon his loved one a kiss. And she, sleeping, all unconscious, dreaming of him—'

'Never mind about her. Fix your mind on him. Willie is the "star" in this show. You have summed him up accurately. He is stooping. Stooping good. Now, if that fellow was wearing braces and stooped like that, you'd say he'd burst those braces, wouldn't you?'

With a somewhat dazed air Paul said that he thought he would. Till now he had not looked at the figure from just that view-point.

'You'd say he'd bust them?'

'Assuredly, monsieur.'

'No!' said the young man, solemnly, tapping him earnestly on the chest. 'That's where you're wrong. Not if they were Galloway's Tried and Proven. Galloway's Tried and Proven will stand any old strain you care to put on them. See small bills. Wear Galloway's Tried and Proven, and fate cannot touch you. You can take it from me. I'm the company's general manager.'

'Indeed, monsieur!'

'And I'll make a proposition to you. Cut out that mossy bank, and make the girl lying in a hammock. Put Willie in shirt-sleeves instead of a bath-robe, and fix him up with a pair of the Tried and Proven, and I'll give you three thousand dollars for that picture and a retaining fee of four thousand a year to work for us and nobody else for any number of years you care to mention. You've got the goods. You've got just the touch. That happy look on Willie's face, for instance. You can see in a minute why he's so happy. It's because he's wearing the Tried and Proven, and he knows that however far he stoops they won't break. Is that a deal?'

Paul's reply left no room for doubt. Seizing the young man firmly round the waist, he kissed him with extreme fervour on both cheeks.

'Here, break away!' cried the astonished general manager. 'That's no way to sign a business contract.'

It was at about five minutes after one that afternoon that Constable Thomas Parsons, patrolling his beat, was aware of a man motioning to him from the doorway of Bredin's Parisian Cafe and Restaurant. The man looked like a pig. He grunted like a pig. He had the lavish *embonpoint* of a pig. Constable Parsons suspected that he had a porcine soul. Indeed, the thought flitted across Constable Parsons' mind that, if he were to tie a bit of blue ribbon round his neck, he could win prizes with him at a show.

'What's all this?' he inquired, halting.

The stout man talked volubly in French. Constable Parsons shook his head.

'Talk sense,' he advised.

'In dere,' cried the stout man, pointing behind him into the restaurant, 'a man, a—how you say?—yes, sacked. An employe whom I yesterday sacked, today he returns. I say to him, "Cochon, va!"'

'What's that?'

'I say, "Peeg, go!" How you say? Yes, "pop off!" I say, "Peeg, pop off!" But he—no, no; he sits and will not go. Come in, officer, and expel him.'

With massive dignity the policeman entered the restaurant. At one of the tables sat Paul, calm and distrait. From across the room Jeanne stared freezingly.

'What's all this?' inquired Constable Parsons. Paul looked up.

'I too,' he admitted, 'I cannot understand. Figure to yourself, monsieur. I enter this cafe to lunch, and this man here would expel me.'

'He is an employe whom I—I myself—have but yesterday dismissed,' vociferated M. Bredin. 'He has no money to lunch at my restaurant.'

The policeman eyed Paul sternly.

'Eh?' he said. 'That so? You'd better come along.'

Paul's eyebrows rose.

Before the round eyes of M. Bredin he began to produce from his pockets and to lay upon the table bank-notes and sovereigns. The cloth was covered with them.

He picked up a half-sovereign.

'If monsieur,' he said to the policeman, 'would accept this as a slight consolation for the inconvenience which this foolish person here has caused him—'

'Not half,' said Mr Parsons, affably. 'Look here'—he turned to the gaping proprietor—'if you go on like this you'll be getting yourself into trouble. See? You take care another time.'

Paul called for the bill of fare.

It was the inferior person who had succeeded to his place as waiter who attended to his needs during the meal; but when he had lunched it was Jeanne who brought his coffee.

She bent over the table.

'You sold your picture, Paul—yes?' she whispered. 'For much money? How glad I am, dear Paul. Now we will—'

Paul met her glance coolly.

'Will you be so kind,' he said, 'as to bring me also a cigarette, my good girl?'

THE MAN WHO DISLIKED CATS

It was Harold who first made us acquainted, when I was dining one night at the Cafe Britannique, in Soho. It is a peculiarity of the Cafe Britannique that you will always find flies there, even in winter. Snow was falling that night as I turned in at the door, but, glancing about me, I noticed several of the old faces. My old acquaintance, Percy the bluebottle, looking wonderfully fit despite his years, was doing deep breathing exercises on a mutton cutlet, and was too busy to do more than pause for a moment to nod at me; but his cousin, Harold, always active, sighted me and bustled up to do the honours.

He had finished his game of touch-last with my right ear, and was circling slowly in the air while he thought out other ways of entertaining me, when there was a rush of air, a swish of napkin, and no more Harold.

I turned to thank my preserver, whose table adjoined mine. He was a Frenchman, a melancholy-looking man. He had the appearance of one who has searched for the leak in life's gas-pipe with a lighted candle; of one whom the clenched fist of Fate has smitten beneath the temperamental third waistcoat-button.

He waved my thanks aside. 'It was a bagatelle,' he said. We became friendly. He moved to my table, and we fraternized over our coffee.

Suddenly he became agitated. He kicked at something on the floor. His eyes gleamed angrily.

'Ps-s-st!' he hissed. 'Va-t'en!'

I looked round the corner of the table, and perceived the restaurant cat in dignified retreat.

'You do not like cats?' I said.

'I 'ate all animals, monsieur. Cats especially.' He frowned. He seemed to hesitate.

'I will tell you my story,' he said. 'You will sympathize. You have a sympathetic face. It is the story of a man's tragedy. It is the story of a blighted life. It is the story of a woman who would not forgive. It is the story—'

'I've got an appointment at eleven,' I said.

He nodded absently, drew at his cigarette, and began:

I have conceived my 'atred of animals, monsieur, many years ago in Paris. Animals are to me a symbol for the lost dreams of youth, for ambitions foiled, for artistic impulses cruelly stifled. You are astonished. You ask why I say these things. I shall tell you.

I am in Paris, young, ardent, artistic. I wish to paint pictures. I 'ave the genius, the ent'usiasm. I wish to be disciple of the great Bouguereau. But no. I am dependent for support upon an uncle. He is rich. He is proprietor of the great Hotel Jules Priaulx. My name is also Priaulx. He is not sympathetic. I say, 'Uncle, I 'ave the genius, the ent'usiasm. Permit me to paint.' He shakes his head. He say, 'I will give you position in my hotel, and you shall earn your living.' What choice?

I weep, but I kill my dreams, and I become cashier at my uncle's hotel at a salary of thirty-five francs a week. I, the artist, become a machine for the changing of money at dam bad salary. What would you? What choice? I am dependent. I go to the hotel, and there I learn to 'ate all animals. Cats especially.

I will tell you the reason. My uncle's hotel is fashionable hotel. Rich Americans, rich Maharajahs, rich people of every nation come to my uncle's hotel. They come, and with them they have brought their pets. Monsieur, it was the existence of a nightmare. Wherever I have looked there are animals. Listen. There is an Indian prince. He has with him two dromedaries. There is also one other Indian prince. With him is a giraffe. The giraffe drink every day one dozen best champagne to keep his coat good. I, the artist, have my bock, and my coat is not good. There is a guest with a young lion. There is a guest with an alligator. But especially there is a cat. He is fat. His name is Alexander. He belongs to an American woman. She is fat. She exhibits him to me. He is wrapped in a silk and fur creation like an opera cloak. Every day she exhibits him. It is 'Alexander this' and 'Alexander that', till I 'ate Alexander very much. I 'ate all the animals, but especially Alexander.

And so, monsieur, it goes on, day by day, in this hotel that is a Zoological Garden. And every day I 'ate the animals the more. But especially Alexander.

We artists, monsieur, we are martyrs to our nerves. It became insupportable, this thing. Each day it became more insupportable. At night I dream of all the animals, one by one—the giraffe, the two dromedaries, the young lion, the alligator, and Alexander. Especially Alexander. You have 'eard of men who cannot endure the society of a cat—how they cry out and jump in the air if a cat is among those present. *Hein?* Your Lord Roberts? Precisely, monsieur. I have read so much. Listen, then. I am become by degrees almost like 'im. I do not cry out and jump in the air when I see the cat Alexander, but I grind my teeth and I 'ate 'im.

Yes, I am the sleeping volcano, and one morning, monsieur, I have suffered the eruption. It is like this. I shall tell you.

Not only at that time am I the martyr to nerves, but also to toothache. That morning I 'ave 'ad the toothache very bad. I 'ave been in pain the most terrible. I groan as I add up the figures in my book.

As I groan I 'ear a voice.

'Say good morning to M. Priaulx, Alexander.' Conceive my emotions, monsieur, when this fat, beastly cat is placed before me upon my desk!

It put the cover upon it. No, that is not the phrase. The lid. It put the lid upon it. All my smothered 'atred of the animal burst forth. I could no longer conceal my 'atred.

I rose. I was terrible. I seized 'im by the tail. I flung him—I did not know where. I did not care. Not then. Afterwards, yes, but not then.

Your Longfellow has a poem. 'I shot an arrow into the air. It fell to earth, I know not where.' And then he has found it. The arrow in the 'eart of a friend. Am I right? Also was that the tragedy with me. I flung the cat Alexander. My uncle, on whom I am dependent, is passing at the moment. He has received the cat in the middle of his face.

My companion, with the artist's instinct for the 'curtain', paused. He looked round the brightly-lit restaurant. From every side arose the clatter of knife and fork, and the clear, sharp note of those who drank soup. In a distant corner a small waiter with a large voice was calling the cook names through the speaking-tube. It was a cheerful scene, but it brought no cheer to my companion. He sighed heavily and resumed:

I 'urry over that painful scene. There is blooming row. My uncle is 'ot-tempered man. The cat is 'eavy cat. I 'ave thrown 'im very hard, for my nerves and my toothache and my 'atred 'ave given me the giant's strength. Alone is this enough to enrage my 'ot-tempered uncle. I am there in his hotel, you will understand, as cashier, not as cat-thrower. And now, besides all this, I have insulted valuable patron. She 'ave left the hotel that day.

There are no doubts in my mind as to the outcome. With certainty I await my *conge*. And after painful scene I get it. I am to go. At once. He 'ave assured the angry American woman that I go at once.

He has called me into his private office. 'Jean,' he has said to me, at the end of other things, 'you are a fool, dolt, no-good imbecile. I give you good place in my hotel, and you spend your time flinging cats. I will 'ave no more of you. But even now I cannot forget that you are my dear brother's child. I will now give you one thousand francs and never see you again.'

I have thanked him, for to me it is wealth. Not before have I ever had one thousand francs of my own.

I go out of the hotel. I go to a *cafe* and order a bock. I smoke a cigarette. It is necessary that I think out plans. Shall I with my one thousand francs rent a studio in the Quarter and commence my life as artist? No. I have still the genius, the ent'usiasm, but I have not the training. To train myself to paint pictures I must study long, and even one thousand francs will not last for ever. Then what shall I do? I do not know. I order one other bock, and smoke more cigarettes, but still I do not know.

And then I say to myself, 'I will go back to my uncle, and plead with him. I will seize favourable opportunity. I will approach him after dinner when he is in good temper. But for that I must be close at hand. I must be—what's your expression?—"Johnny-on-the-spot".'

My mind is made up. I have my plan.

I have gone back to my uncle's hotel, and I have engaged not too expensive bedroom. My uncle does not know. He still is in his private office. I secure my room.

I dine cheaply that night, but I go to theatre and also to supper after the theatre, for have I not my thousand francs? It is late when I reach my bedroom.

I go to bed. I go to sleep.

But I do not sleep long. I am awakened by a voice.

It is a voice that says, 'Move and I shoot! Move and I shoot!' I lie still. I do not move. I am courageous, but I am unarmed.

And the voice says again, 'Move and I shoot!' Is it robbers? Is it some marauder who has made his way to my room to plunder me?

I do not know. Per'aps I think yes.

'Who are you?' I have asked.

There is no answer.

I take my courage in my 'ands. I leap from my bed. I dash for the door. No pistol has been fire. I have reached the passage, and have shouted for assistance.

Hotel officials run up. Doors open. 'What is it?' voices cry.

'There is in my room an armed robber,' I assure them.

And then I have found—no, I am mistaken. My door, you will understand, is open. And as I have said these words, a large green parrot comes 'opping out. My assassin is nothing but a green parrot.

'Move and I shoot!' it has said to those gathered in the corridor. It then has bitten me in the 'and and passed on.

I am chagrined, monsieur. But only for a moment. Then I forget my chagrin. For a voice from a door that 'as opened says with joy, 'It is my Polly, which I 'ave this evening lost I'

I turn. I gasp for admiration. It is a beautiful lady in a pink dressing-gown which 'ave spoken these words.

She has looked at me. I 'ave looked at her. I forget everything but that she is adorable. I forget those who stand by. I forget that the parrot has bitten me in the 'and. I forget even that I am standing there in pyjamas, with on my feet nothing. I can only gaze at her and worship.

I have found words.

'Mademoiselle,' I have said, 'I am rejoiced that I have been the means of restoring to you your bird.'

She has thanked me with her eyes, and then with words also. I am bewitched. She is divine. I care not that my feet are cold. I could wish to stand there talking all night.

She has given a cry of dismay.

'Your 'and! It is wounded!'

I look at my 'and. Yes, it is bleeding, where the bird 'ave bitten it.

'Tchut, mademoiselle,' I have said. 'It is a bagatelle.'

But no. She is distressed. She is what your poet Scott 'ave said, a ministering angel thou. She 'ave torn her 'andkerchief and is binding up my wound. I am enchanted. Such beauty! Such kindness! 'Ardly can I resist to fall on my knees before 'er and declare my passion.

We are twin souls. She has thanked me again. She has scolded the parrot. She has smiled upon me as she retires to her room. It is enough. Nothing is said, but I am a man of sensibility and discernment, and I understand that she will not be offended if I seek to renew our friendship on a more suitable occasion.

The doors shut. The guests have returned to bed, the hotel servants to their duties. And I go back to my room. But not to sleep. It is very late, but I do not sleep. I lie awake and think of 'er.

You will conceive, Monsieur, with what mixed feelings I descend next morning. On the one 'and, I must keep the sharp look-out for my uncle, for 'im I must avoid till he shall have—what do you say in your idiom? Yes, I have it— simmered down and tucked in his shirt. On the other 'and, I must watch for my lady of the parrot. I count the minutes till we shall meet again.

I avoid my uncle with success, and I see 'er about the hour of *dejeuner*. She is talking to old gentleman. I have bowed. She have smiled and motioned me to approach.

'Father,' she has said, 'this is the gentleman who caught Polly.'

We have shaken hands. He is indulgent papa. He has smiled and thanked me also. We have confided to each other our names. He is English. He owns much land in England. He has been staying in Paris. He is rich. His name is 'Enderson. He addresses his daughter, and call her Marion. In my 'eart I also call her Marion. You will perceive that I am, as you say, pretty far gone.

The hour of *dejeuner* has arrived. I entreat them to be my guests. I can run to it, you understand, for there are still in my pockets plenty of my uncle's francs. They consent. I am in 'eaven.

All is well. Our friendship has progressed with marvellous speed. The old gentleman and I are swiftly the dear old pals. I 'ave confided to 'im my dreams of artistic fame, and he has told me 'ow much he dislikes your Lloyd George. He has mentioned that he and Miss Marion depart for London that day. I am desolate. My face tumbles. He has observed my despair. He has invited me to visit them in London.

Imagine my chagrin. To visit them in London is the one thing I desire to do. But how? I accept gratefully, but I ask myself how it is to be done? I am poor blighter with no profession and nine 'undred francs. He 'as taken it for granted that I am wealthy.

What shall I do? I spend the afternoon trying to form a plan. And then I am resolved. I will go to my uncle and say: 'Uncle, I have the magnificent chance to marry the daughter of wealthy English landowner. Already I 'ave her gratitude. Soon—for I am young, 'andsome, debonair—I shall 'ave her love. Give me one more chance, uncle. Be decent old buck, and put up the money for this affair.'

These words I have resolved to say to my uncle.

I go back to the hotel. I enter his private office. I reveal no secret when I say that he is not cordial.

'Ten thousand devils!' he has cried. 'What do you here?'

I 'asten to tell him all, and plead with him to be decent old buck. He does not believe.

Who is he? he asks. This English landowner? How did I meet him? And where?

I tell him. He is amazed.

'You 'ad the infernal impudence to take room in my hotel?' he has cried.

I am crafty. I am diplomat.

'Where else, dear uncle?' I say. 'In all Paris there is no such 'ome from 'ome. The cuisine—marvellous! The beds—of rose-leaves! The attendance—superb! If only for one night, I have said to myself, I must stay in this of all hotels.'

I 'ave—what do you say?—touched the spot.

'In what you say,' he has said, more calmly, 'there is certainly something. It is a good hotel, this of mine!'

The only hotel, I have assured him. The Meurice? *Chut!* I snap my fingers. The Ritz? Bah! Once again I snap my fingers. 'In all Paris there is no hotel like this.'

He 'as simmered down. His shirt is tucked in. 'Tell me again this plan of yours, Jean.'

When I leave 'im we have come to an understanding. It is agreed between us that I am to 'ave one last chance. He will not spoil this promising ship for the 'a'porth of tar. He will give me money for my purpose. But he has said, as we part, if I fail, his 'ands shall be washed of me. He cannot now forget that I am his dear brother's child; but if I fail to accomplish the conquest of the divine Miss Marion, he thinks he will be able to.

It is well. A week later I follow the 'Endersons to London.

For the next few days, monsieur, I am in Paradise. My 'ost has much nice 'ouse in Eaton Square. He is rich, popular. There is much society. And I—I have the *succes fou.* I am young, 'andsome, debonair. I cannot speak the English very well—not so well as I now speak 'im—but I manage. I get along. I am intelligent, amiable. Everyone loves me.

No, not everyone. Captain Bassett, he does not love me. And why? Because he loves the charming Miss Marion, and observes that already I am succeeding with her like a 'ouse on fire. He is *ami de famille.* He is captain in your Garde Ecossais, and my 'ost told me 'e has distinguished himself as soldier pretty much. It may be so. As soldier, per'aps. But at conversation he is not so good. He is quite nice fellow, you understand—'andsome, yes; distinguished, yes. But he does not sparkle. He has not my *verve,* my *elan.* I—how do you say?—I make the rings round him.

But, *Chut!* At that moment I would have made the rings round the 'ole British Army. Yes, and also the Corps Diplomatique. For I am inspired. Love 'as inspired me. I am conqueror.

But I will not weary you, monsieur, with the details of my wooing. You are sympathetic, but I must not weary you. Let us say that I 'ave in four days or five made progress the most remarkable, and proceed to the tragic end.

Almost could I tell it in four words. In them one would say that it is set forth. There was in London at that time popular a song, a comic, vulgar song of the 'Alls, 'The Cat Came Back'. You 'ave 'eard it? Yes? I 'eard it myself, and without emotion. It had no sinister warning for me. It did not strike me as omen. Yet, in those four words, monsieur, is my tragedy.

How? I shall tell you. Every word is a sword twisted in my 'eart, but I shall tell you.

One afternoon we are at tea. All is well. I am vivacious, gay; Miss Marion, charming, gracious. There is present also an aunt, Mr 'Enderson's sister; but 'er I do not much notice. It is to Marion I speak—both with my lips and also with my eyes.

As we sit, Captain Bassett is announced.

He has entered. We have greeted each other politely but coldly, for we are rivals. There is in his manner also a something which I do not much like—a species of suppressed triumph, of elation.

I am uneasy—but only yet vaguely, you will understand. I have not the foreboding that he is about to speak my death-sentence.

He addresses Miss Marion. There is joy in his voice. 'Miss 'Enderson,' he has said, 'I have for you the bally good news. You will remember, isn't it, the cat belonging to the American woman in the hotel at Paris, of which you have spoken to me? Last night at dinner I have been seated beside her. At first I am not certain is it she. Then I say that there cannot be two Mrs Balderstone Rockmettlers in Europe, so I mention to her the cat. And, to cut the long story short, I have ventured to purchase for you as a little present the cat Alexander.'

I have uttered a cry of horror, but it is not 'eard because of Miss Marion's cry of joy.

'Oh, Captain Bassett,' she has said, 'how very splendid of you! Ever since I first saw him have I loved Alexander. I cannot tell you how grateful I am. But it amazes me that you should have been able to induce her to part with 'im. In Paris she has refused all my offers.'

He has paused, embarrassed.

'The fact is,' he has said, 'there is between her and Alexander a certain coolness. He 'as deceived 'er, and she loves him no more. Immediately upon arrival in London, he had the misfortune to 'ave six fine kittens. 'Owever, out of evil cometh good, and I have thus been able to secure 'im for you. 'E is downstairs in a basket!'

Miss Marion 'as rung the bell and commanded for him to be brought instantly.

I will not describe the meeting, monsieur. You are sympathetic. You will understand my feelings. Let us 'urry on.

Figure yourself, monsieur, to what extent I was now 'arassed. I am artist. I am a man of nerves. I cannot be gay, brilliant, debonair in the presence of a cat. Yet always the cat is there. It is terrible.

I feel that I am falling behind in the race. 'Er gratitude has made her the more gracious to Captain Bassett. She smiles upon him. And, like Chanticleer at the sight of the sun, he flaps his wings and crows. He is no longer the silent listener. It is I who have become the silent listener.

I have said to myself that something must be done.

Chance has shown me the way. One afternoon I am by fortune alone in the 'all. In his cage the parrot Polly is 'opping. I address him through the bars.

'Move and I shoot I' he has cried.

The tears have filled my eyes. 'Ow it has brought the 'ole scene back to me!

As I weep, I perceive the cat Alexander approaching.

I have formed a plan. I have opened the cage-door and released the parrot. The cat, I think, will attack the parrot of which Miss 'Enderson is so fond. She will love him no more. He will be expelled.

He paused. I suppose my face must have lost some of its alleged sympathy as he set forth this fiendish plot. Even Percy the bluebottle seemed shocked. He had settled on the sugar-bowl, but at these words he rose in a marked manner and left the table.

'You do not approve?' he said.

I shrugged my shoulders.

'It's no business of mine,' I said. 'But don't you think yourself it was playing it a bit low down? Didn't the thought present itself to you in a shadowy way that it was rather rough on the bird?'

'It did, monsieur. But what would you? It is necessary to break eggs in order to make an omelette. All is fair, you say, in love and war, and this was both. Moreover, you must understand, I do not dictate his movements to the parrot. He is free agent. I do but open the cage-door. Should he 'op out and proceed to the floor where is the cat, that is his affair. I shall continue, yes?'

Alors! I open the cage-door and disappear discreetly. It is not politic that I remain to witness what shall transpire. It is for me to establish an alibi. I go to the drawing-room, where I remain.

At dinner that night Mr 'Enderson has laughed.

'In the 'all this afternoon,' he has said, 'I have seen by chance the dickens of a funny occurrence. That parrot of yours, Marion, had escaped once again from its cage and was 'aving an argument with that cat which Captain Bassett has given to you.'

'Oh! I hope that Alexander 'as not hurt poor Polly, of whom I am very fond,' she has said.

'The affair did not come to blows,' has said Mr 'Enderson. 'You may trust that bird to take care of himself, my dear. When I came upon the scene the cat was crouching in a corner, with his fur bristling and his back up, while Polly, standing before 'im, was telling 'im not to move or he would shoot. Nor did he move, till I 'ad seized the parrot and replaced him in the cage, when he shot upstairs like a streak of lightning. By sheer force of character that excellent bird 'ad won the bloodless victory. I drink to 'im!'

You can conceive my emotion as I listen to this tale. I am like the poet's mice and men whose best-kid schemes have gone away. I am baffled. I am discouraged. I do not know what I shall do. I must find another plan, but I do not know what.

How shall I remove the cat? Shall I kill 'im? No, for I might be suspect.

Shall I 'ire someone to steal 'im? No, for my accomplice might betray me.

Shall I myself steal 'im? Ah! that is better. That is a very good plan.

Soon I have it perfected, this plan. Listen, monsieur; it is as follows. It is simple, but it is good. I will await my opportunity. I will remove the cat secretly from the 'ouse. I will take him to an office of the District Messenger Boys. I will order a messenger to carry him at once to the Cats' House, and to request M. le Directeur immediately to destroy him. It is a simple plan, but it is good.

I carry it through without a 'itch. It is not so difficult to secure the cat. 'E is asleep in the drawing-room. There is nobody at hand. I have in my bedroom a 'at-box which I have brought from Paris. I have brought it with me to the drawing-room. I have placed in it the cat. I have escaped from the 'ouse. The cat has uttered a cry, but none has 'eard. I have reached the office of the District Messenger Boys. I have 'anded over the cat in its box. The manager is courteous, sympathetic. A messenger has started in a cab for the Cats' House. I have breathed a sigh of relief. I am saved.

That is what I say to myself as I return. My troubles are over, and once more I can be gay, debonair, vivacious with Miss Marion, for no longer will there be present the cat Alexander to 'arass me.

When I have returned there is commotion in the 'ouse. I pass on the stairs domestics calling 'Puss, puss!' The butler is chirruping loudly and poking beneath the furniture with a umbrella. All is confusion and agitation.

In the drawing-room is Miss Marion. She is distressed.

'Nowhere,' she has said, 'can there be found the cat Alexander of whom I am so fond. Nowhere in the 'ouse is he, Where can he be? He is lost.'

I am gentle, sympathetic. I endeavour to console her. I 'int to her that am I not sufficient substitute for a beastly cat? She is, however, inconsolable. I must be patient. I must wait my time.

Captain Bassett is announced. He is informed of what has 'appened. He is distressed. He has the air as if he, too, would endeavour to be gentle, sympathetic. But I am Johnny-on-the-spot. I stay till he 'as gone.

Next day again it is 'Puss, puss!' Again the butler has explored under the furniture with the umbrella. Again Miss Marion is distressed. Again 'ave I endeavoured to console.

This time I think I am not so unsuccessful. I am, you understand, young, 'andsome, sympathetic. In another two ticks I am about to seize 'er 'and and declare my passion.

But, before I can do so, Captain Bassett is announced.

I gaze at him as at unsuccessful rival. I am confident. I am conqueror. Ah, I little know! It is in the moments of our highest 'ope, monsieur, that we are destroyed.

Captain Bassett, he, too, 'as the air of the conqueror.

He has begun to speak.

'Miss 'Enderson,' he has said, 'I have once more the bally good news. I rather fancy that I 'ave tracked down the missing Alexander, do you not know?'

Miss Marion 'as cried cut with joy. But I am calm, for is not Alexander already yesterday destroyed?

'It is like this,' he has resumed. 'I have thought to myself where is lost cat most likely to be? And I have answered, "In the Cats' House." I go this morning to the Cats' House, and there I see a cat which is either lost Alexander or his living image. Exactly is he the same to all appearances as the lost Alexander. But there is, when I try to purchase 'im, some curious 'itch which they do not explain. They must 'ave time, they say, to consider. They cannot at once decide.'

'Why, what nonsense!' Miss Marion 'ave cried. 'If the cat is my cat, surely then must they return 'im to me! Come,' she has said, 'let us all three at once in a taxi-cab go to the Cats' House. If the all three of us identify the lost Alexander, then must they return 'im.'

Monsieur, I am uneasy. I have foreboding. But I go. What choice? We go in a taxi-cab to the Cats' House.

The *directeur* is courteous and sympathetic. He has introduced us to the cat, and my 'eart 'as turned to water, for it is Alexander. Why has he not been destroyed?

The *directeur* is speaking. I 'ear him in a dream.

'If you identify 'im as your cat, miss,' he has said, 'the matter is ended. My 'esitation when you, sir, approached me this morning on the matter was due to the fact that a messenger was sent with instructions that he be destroyed at once.'

'Rather rough, wasn't it, that, on the messenger, yes,' Captain Bassett has said. He is facetious, you understand, for he is conqueror.

I am silent. I am not facetious. For already I feel—how do you say?—my fowl is cooked.

'Not the messenger, sir,' the *directeur* has said. 'You 'ave misunderstood me. It was the cat which was to be destroyed as per instructions of the anonymous sender.'

'Who could have played such a wicked trick?' Miss Marion has asked, indignant.

The *directeur* has stooped, and from behind a table he has brought a 'at-box.

'In this,' he has said, 'the above animal was conveyed. But with it was no accompanying letter. The sender was anonymous.'

'Per'aps,' Captain Bassett has said—and still more in a dream I 'ear him—'per'aps on the 'at-box there is some bally name or other, do you not know—what?'

I clutch at the table. The room is spinning round and round. I have no stomach—only emptiness.

'Why, bless me,' the *directeur* has said, 'you're quite right, sir. So there is. Funny of me not to have before observed it. There is a name, and also an address. It is the name of Jean Priaulx, and the address is the Hotel Jules Priaulx, Paris.'

My companion stopped abruptly. He passed a handkerchief over his forehead. With a quick movement he reached for his glass of liqueur brandy and drained it at a gulp.

'Monsieur,' he said, 'you will not wish me to describe the scene? There is no need for me—*hein?*—to be Zolaesque. You can imagine?'

'She chucked you?' In moments of emotion it is the simplest language that comes to the lips.

He nodded.

'And married Captain Bassett?'

He nodded again.

'And your uncle?' I said. 'How did he take it?'

He sighed.

'There was once more,' he said, 'blooming row, monsieur.'

'He washed his hands of you?'

'Not altogether. He was angry, but he gave me one more chance. I am still 'is dear brother's child, and he cannot forget it. An acquaintance of his, a man of letters, a M. Paul Sartines, was in need of a secretary. The post was not well paid, but it was permanent. My uncle insist that I take it. What choice? I took it. It is the post which I still 'old.'

He ordered another liqueur brandy and gulped it down.

'The name is familiar to you, monsieur? You 'ave 'eard of M. Sartines?'

'I don't think I have. Who is he?'

'He is a man of letters, a *savant*. For five years he has been occupied upon a great work. It is with that that I assist him by collecting facts for 'is use. I 'ave spent this afternoon in the British Museum collecting facts. Tomorrow I go again. And the next day. And again after that. The book will occupy yet another ten years before it is completed. It is his great work.'

'It sounds as if it was,' I said. 'What's it about?'

He signalled to the waiter.

'*Garçon*, one other liqueur brandy. The book, monsieur, is a '*Istory of the Cat in Ancient Egypt*.'

RUTH IN EXILE

The clock struck five—briskly, as if time were money. Ruth Warden got up from her desk and, having put on her hat, emerged into the outer office where M. Gandinot received visitors. M. Gandinot, the ugliest man in Roville-sur-Mer, presided over the local *mont-de-piete*, and Ruth served him, from ten to five, as a sort of secretary-clerk. Her duties, if monotonous, were simple. They consisted of sitting, detached and invisible, behind a ground-glass screen, and entering details of loans in a fat book. She was kept busy as a rule, for Roville possesses two casinos, each offering the attraction of *petits chevaux*, and just round the corner is Monte Carlo. Very brisk was the business done by M. Gandinot, the pawnbroker, and very frequent were the pitying shakes of the head and clicks of the tongue of M. Gandinot, the man; for in his unofficial capacity Ruth's employer had a gentle soul, and winced at the evidences of tragedy which presented themselves before his official eyes.

He blinked up at Ruth as she appeared, and Ruth, as she looked at him, was conscious, as usual, of a lightening of the depression which, nowadays, seemed to have settled permanently upon her. The peculiar quality of M. Gandinot's extraordinary countenance was that it induced mirth—not mocking laughter, but a kind of smiling happiness. It possessed that indefinable quality which characterizes the Billiken, due, perhaps, to the unquenchable optimism which shone through the irregular features; for M. Gandinot, despite his calling, believed in his fellow-man.

'You are going, mademoiselle?'

As Ruth was wearing her hat and making for the door, and as she always left at this hour, a purist might have considered the question superfluous; but M. Gandinot was a man who seized every opportunity of practising his English.

'You will not wait for the good papa who calls so regularly for you?'

'I think I won't today, M. Gandinot. I want to get out into the air. I have rather a headache. Will you tell my father I have gone to the Promenade?'

M. Gandinot sighed as the door closed behind her. Ruth's depression had not escaped his notice. He was sorry for her. And not without cause, for Fate had not dealt too kindly with Ruth.

It would have amazed Mr Eugene Warden, that genial old gentleman, if, on one of those occasions of manly emotion when he was in the habit of observing that he had been nobody's enemy but his own, somebody had hinted that he had spoiled his daughter's life. Such a thought had never entered his head. He was one of those delightful, irresponsible, erratic persons whose heads thoughts of this kind do not enter, and who are about as deadly to those whose lives are bound up with theirs as a Upas tree.

In the memory of his oldest acquaintance, Ruth's father had never done anything but drift amiably through life. There had been a time when he had done his drifting in London, feeding cheerfully from the hand of a long-suffering brother-in-law. But though blood, as he was wont to remark while negotiating his periodical loans, is thicker than water, a brother-in-law's affection has its limits. A day came when Mr Warden observed with pain that his relative responded less nimbly to the touch. And a little while later the other delivered his ultimatum. Mr Warden was to leave England, and to stay away from England, to behave as if England no longer existed on the map, and a small but sufficient allowance would be made to him. If he declined to do this, not another penny of the speaker's money would he receive. He could choose.

He chose. He left England, Ruth with him. They settled in Roville, that haven of the exile who lives upon remittances.

Ruth's connexion with the *mont-de-piete* had come about almost automatically. Very soon after their arrival it became evident that, to a man of Mr Warden's nature, resident a stone's-throw distant from two casinos, the small allowance was not likely to go very far. Even if Ruth had not wished to work, circumstances could have compelled her. As it was, she longed for something to occupy her, and, the vacancy at the *mont-de-piete* occurring, she had snatched at it. There was a certain fitness in her working there. Business transactions with that useful institution had always been conducted by her, it being Mr Warden's theory that Woman can extract in these crises just that extra franc or two which is denied to the mere male. Through constantly going round, running across, stepping over, and popping down to the *mont-de-piete* she had established almost a legal claim on any post that might be vacant there.

And under M. Gandinot's banner she had served ever since.

Five minutes' walk took her to the Promenade des Anglais, that apparently endless thoroughfare which is Roville's pride. The evening was fine and warm. The sun shone gaily on the white-walled houses, the bright Gardens, and the two gleaming casinos. But Ruth walked listlessly, blind to the glitter of it all.

Visitors who go to Roville for a few weeks in the winter are apt to speak of the place, on their return, in a manner that conveys the impression that it is a Paradise on earth, with gambling facilities thrown in. But, then, they are visitors. Their sojourn comes to an end. Ruth's did not.

A voice spoke her name. She turned, and saw her father, dapper as ever, standing beside her.

'What an evening, my dear!' said Mr Warden. 'What an evening! Smell the sea!'

Mr Warden appeared to be in high spirits. He hummed a tune and twirled his cane. He chirruped frequently to Bill, the companion of his walks abroad, a wiry fox-terrier of a demeanour, like his master's, both jaunty and slightly disreputable. An air of gaiety pervaded his bearing.

'I called in at the *mont-de-piete* but you had gone. Gandinot told me you had come here. What an ugly fellow that Gandinot is! But a good sort. I like him. I had a chat with him.'

The high spirits were explained. Ruth knew her father. She guessed, correctly, that M. Gandinot, kindest of pawnbrokers, had obliged, in his unofficial capacity, with a trifling loan.

'Gandinot ought to go on the stage,' went on Mr Warden, pursuing his theme. 'With that face he would make his fortune. You can't help laughing when you see it. One of these days—'

He broke off. Stirring things had begun to occur in the neighbourhood of his ankles, where Bill, the fox-terrier, had encountered an acquaintance, and, to the accompaniment of a loud, gargling noise, was endeavouring to bite his head off. The acquaintance, a gentleman of uncertain breed, equally willing, was chewing Bill's paw with the gusto of a gourmet. An Irish terrier, with no personal bias towards either side, was dancing round and attacking each in turn as he came uppermost. And two poodles leaped madly in and out of the melee, barking encouragement.

It takes a better man than Mr Warden to break up a gathering of this kind. The old gentleman was bewildered. He added his voice to the babel, and twice smote Bill grievously with his cane with blows intended for the acquaintance, but beyond that he effected nothing. It seemed probable that the engagement would last till the combatants had consumed each other, after the fashion of the Kilkenny cats, when there suddenly appeared from nowhere a young man in grey.

The world is divided into those who can stop dog-fights and those who cannot. The young man in grey belonged to the former class. Within a minute from his entrance on the scene the poodles and the Irish terrier had vanished; the dog of doubtful breed was moving off up the hill, yelping, with the dispatch of one who remembers an important appointment, and Bill, miraculously calmed, was seated in the centre of the Promenade, licking honourable wounds.

Mr Warden was disposed to effervesce with gratitude. The scene had shaken him, and there had been moments when he had given his ankles up for lost.

'Don't mention it,' said the young man. 'I enjoy arbitrating in these little disputes. Dogs seem to like me and trust my judgement. I consider myself as a sort of honorary dog.'

'Well, I am bound to say, Mr—?'

'Vince—George Vince.'

'My name is Warden. My daughter.'

Ruth inclined her head, and was conscious of a pair of very penetrating brown eyes looking eagerly into hers in a manner which she thoroughly resented. She was not used to the other sex meeting her gaze and holding it as if confident of a friendly welcome. She made up her mind in that instant that this was a young man who required suppression.

'I've seen you several times out here since I arrived, Miss Warden,' said Mr Vince. 'Four in all,' he added, precisely.

'Really?' said Ruth.

She looked away. Her attitude seemed to suggest that she had finished with him, and would be obliged if somebody would come and sweep him up.

As they approached the casino restlessness crept into Mr Warden's manner. At the door he stopped and looked at Ruth.

'I think, my dear—' he said.

'Going to have a dash at the *petits chevaux?* inquired Mr Vince. 'I was there just now. I have an infallible system.'

Mr Warden started like a war-horse at the sound of the trumpet.

'Only it's infallible the wrong way,' went on the young man. 'Well, I wish you luck. I'll see Miss Warden home.'

'Please don't trouble,' said Ruth, in the haughty manner which had frequently withered unfortunate fellow-exiles in their tracks.

It had no such effect on Mr Vince.

'I shall like it,' he said.

Ruth set her teeth. She would see whether he would like it.

They left Mr Warden, who shot in at the casino door like a homing rabbit, and walked on in silence, which lasted till Ruth, suddenly becoming aware that her companion's eyes were fixed on her face, turned her head, to meet a gaze of complete, not to say loving, admiration. She flushed. She was accustomed to being looked at admiringly, but about this particular look there was a subtle quality that distinguished it from the ordinary—something proprietorial.

Mr Vince appeared to be a young man who wasted no time on conventional conversation-openings.

'Do you believe in affinities, Miss Warden?' he said,

'No,' said Ruth.

'You will before we've done,' said Mr Vince, confidently. 'Why did you try to snub me just now?'

'Did I?'

'You mustn't again. It hurts me. I'm a sensitive man. Diffident. Shy. Miss Warden, will you marry me?'

Ruth had determined that nothing should shake her from her icy detachment, but this did. She stopped with a gasp, and stared at him.

Mr Vince reassured her.

'I don't expect you to say "Yes". That was just a beginning—the shot fired across the bows by way of warning. In you, Miss Warden, I have found my affinity. Have you ever considered this matter of affinities? Affinities are the—the—Wait a moment.'

He paused, reflecting.

'I—' began Ruth.

"Sh!' said the young man, holding up his hand.

Ruth's eyes flashed. She was not used to having "Sh!' said to her by young men, and she resented it.

'I've got it,' he declared, with relief. 'I knew I should, but these good things take time. Affinities are the zero on the roulette-board of life. Just as we select a number on which to stake our money, so do we select a type of girl whom we think we should like to marry. And just as zero pops up instead of the number, so does our affinity come along and upset all our preconceived notions of the type of girl we should like to marry.'

'I—' began Ruth again.

'The analogy is in the rough at present. I haven't had time to condense and polish it. But you see the idea. Take my case, for instance. When I saw you a couple of days ago I knew in an instant that you were my affinity. But for years I had been looking for a woman almost your exact opposite. You are dark. Three days ago I couldn't have imagined myself marrying anyone who was not fair. Your eyes are grey. Three days ago my preference for blue eyes was a byword. You have a shocking temper. Three days ago—'

'Mr Vince!'

'There!' said that philosopher, complacently. 'You stamped. The gentle, blue-eyed blonde whom I was looking for three days ago would have drooped timidly. Three days ago my passion for timid droopers amounted to an obsession.'

Ruth did not reply. It was useless to bandy words with one who gave such clear evidence of being something out of the common run of word-bandiers. No verbal attack could crush this extraordinary young man. She walked on, all silence and stony profile, uncomfortably conscious that her companion was in no way abashed by the former and was regarding the latter with that frank admiration which had made itself so obnoxious to her before, until they reached their destination. Mr Vince, meanwhile, chatted cheerfully, and pointed out objects of interest by the wayside.

At the door Ruth permitted herself a word of farewell.

'Good-bye,' she said.

'Till tomorrow evening,' said Mr Vince. 'I shall be coming to dinner.'

Mr Warden ambled home, very happy and contented, two hours later, with half a franc in his pocket, this comparative wealth being due to the fact that the minimum stake permitted by the Roville casino is just double that sum. He was sorry not to have won, but his mind was too full of rosy dreams to permit of remorse. It was the estimable old gentleman's dearest wish that his daughter should marry some rich, open-handed man who would keep him in affluence for the remainder of his days, and to that end he was in the habit of introducing to her notice any such that came his way. There was no question of coercing Ruth. He was too tender-hearted for that. Besides he couldn't. Ruth was not the sort of girl who is readily coerced. He contented himself with giving her the opportunity to inspect his exhibits. Roville is a sociable place, and it was not unusual for him to make friends at the casino and to bring them home, when made, for a cigar. Up to the present, he was bound to admit, his efforts had not been particularly successful. Ruth, he reflected sadly, was a curious girl. She did not show her best side to these visitors. There was no encouragement in her manner. She was apt to frighten the unfortunate exhibits. But of this young man Vince he had brighter hopes. He was rich. That was proved by the very handsome way in which he had behaved in the matter of a small loan when, looking in at the casino after parting from Ruth, he had found Mr Warden in sore straits for want of a little capital to back a brand-new system which he had conceived through closely observing the run of the play. He was also obviously attracted by Ruth. And, as he was remarkably presentable—indeed, quite an unusually good-looking young man—

there seemed no reason why Ruth should not be equally attracted by him. The world looked good to Mr Warden as he fell asleep that night.

Ruth did not fall asleep so easily. The episode had disturbed her. A new element had entered her life, and one that gave promise of producing strange by-products.

When, on the following evening, Ruth returned from the stroll on the Promenade which she always took after leaving the *mont-de-piete*, with a feeling of irritation towards things in general, this feeling was not diminished by the sight of Mr Vince, very much at his ease, standing against the mantelpiece of the tiny parlour.

'How do you do?' he said. 'By an extraordinary coincidence I happened to be hanging about outside this house just now, when your father came along and invited me in to dinner. Have you ever thought much about coincidences, Miss Warden? To my mind, they may be described as the zero on the roulette-board of life.'

He regarded her fondly.

'For a shy man, conscious that the girl he loves is inspecting him closely and making up her mind about him,' he proceeded, 'these unexpected meetings are very trying ordeals. You must not form your judgement of me too hastily. You see me now, nervous, embarrassed, tongue-tied. But I am not always like this. Beneath this crust of diffidence there is sterling stuff, Miss Warden. People who know me have spoken of me as a little ray of sun—But here is your father.'

Mr Warden was more than usually disappointed with Ruth during dinner. It was the same old story. So far from making herself pleasant to this attractive stranger, she seemed positively to dislike him. She was barely civil to him. With a sigh Mr Warden told himself that he did not understand Ruth, and the rosy dreams he had formed began to fade.

Ruth's ideas on the subject of Mr Vince as the days went by were chaotic. Though she told herself that she thoroughly objected to him, he had nevertheless begun to have an undeniable attraction for her. In what this attraction consisted she could not say. When she tried to analyse it, she came to the conclusion that it was due to the fact that he was the only element in her life that made for excitement. Since his advent the days had certainly passed more swiftly for her. The dead level of monotony had been broken. There was a certain fascination in exerting herself to suppress him, which increased daily as each attempt failed.

Mr Vince put this feeling into words for her. He had a maddening habit of discussing the progress of his courtship in the manner of an impartial lecturer.

'I am making headway,' he observed. 'The fact that we cannot meet without your endeavouring to plant a temperamental left jab on my spiritual solar plexus encourages me to think that you are beginning at last to understand that we are affinities. To persons of spirit like ourselves the only happy marriage is that which is based on a firm foundation of almost incessant quarrelling. The most beautiful line in English poetry, to my mind, is, "We fell out, my wife and I." You would be wretched with a husband who didn't like you to quarrel with him. The position of affairs now is that I have become necessary to you. If I went out of your life now

I should leave an aching void. You would still have that beautiful punch of yours, and there would be nobody to exercise it on. You would pine away. From now on matters should, I think, move rapidly. During the course of the next week I shall endeavour to propitiate you with gifts. Here is the first of them.'

He took a piece of paper from his pocket and handed it her. It was a pencil-sketch, rough and unfinished, but wonderfully clever. Even Ruth could appreciate that—and she was a prejudiced observer, for the sketch was a caricature of herself. It represented her, drawn up to her full height, with enormous, scornful eyes and curling lips, and the artist had managed to combine an excellent likeness while accentuating everything that was marked in what she knew had come to be her normal expression of scorn and discontent.

'I didn't know you were an artist, Mr Vince,' she said, handing it back.

'A poor amateur. Nothing more. You may keep it.'

'I have not the slightest wish to keep it.'

'You haven't?'

'It is not in the least clever, and it is very impertinent of you to show it to me. The drawing is not funny. It is simply rude.'

'A little more,' said Mr Vince, 'and I shall begin to think you don't like it. Are you fond of chocolates?'

Ruth did not answer.

'I am sending you some tomorrow.'

'I shall return them.'

'Then I shall send some more, and some fruit. Gifts!' soliloquized Mr Vince. 'Gifts! That is the secret. Keep sending gifts. If men would only stick to gifts and quarrelling, there would be fewer bachelors.'

On the morrow, as promised, the chocolates arrived, many pounds of them in a lordly box. The bludgeoning of fate had not wholly scotched in Ruth a human weakness for sweets, and it was with a distinct effort that she wrapped the box up again and returned it to the sender. She went off to her work at the *mont-de-piete* with a glow of satisfaction which comes to those who exhibit an iron will in trying circumstances.

And at the *mont-de-piete* there occurred a surprising incident.

Surprising incidents, as Mr Vince would have said, are the zero on the roulette-board of life. They pop up disturbingly when least expected, confusing the mind and altering pre-conceived opinions. And this was a very surprising incident indeed.

Ruth, as has been stated, sat during her hours of work behind a ground-glass screen, unseen and unseeing. To her the patrons of the establishment were mere disembodied voices—wheedling voices, pathetic voices, voices that protested, voices that hectored, voices that whined, moaned, broke, appealed to the saints, and in various other ways endeavoured to instil into M. Gandinot more spacious and princely views on the subject advancing money on property pledged. She was sitting behind her screen this morning, scribbling idly on the blotting-pad, for there had been a lull in the business, when the door opened, and the polite,

'Bonjour, monsieur,' of M. Gandinot announced the arrival of another unfortunate.

And then, shaking her like an electric shock, came a voice that she knew—the pleasant voice of Mr Vince.

The dialogues that took place on the other side of the screen were often protracted and always sordid, but none had seemed to Ruth so interminable, so hideously sordid, as this one.

Round and round its miserable centre—a silver cigarette-case—the dreary argument circled. The young man pleaded; M. Gandinot, adamant in his official role, was immovable.

Ruth could bear it no longer. She pressed her hands over her burning ears, and the voices ceased to trouble her.

And with the silence came thought, and a blaze of understanding that flashed upon her and made all things clear. She understood now why she had closed her ears.

Poverty is an acid which reacts differently on differing natures. It had reduced Mr Eugene Warden's self-respect to a minimum. Ruth's it had reared up to an abnormal growth. Her pride had become a weed that ran riot in her soul, darkening it and choking finer emotions. Perhaps it was her father's naive stratagems for the enmeshing of a wealthy husband that had produced in her at last a morbid antipathy to the idea of playing beggar-maid to any man's King Cophetua. The state of mind is intelligible. The Cophetua legend never has been told from the beggar-maid's point of view, and there must have been moments when, if a woman of spirit, she resented that monarch's somewhat condescending attitude, and felt that, secure in his wealth and magnificence, he had taken her grateful acquiescence very much for granted.

This, she saw now, was what had prejudiced her against George Vince. She had assumed that he was rich. He had conveyed the impression of being rich. And she had been on the defensive against him accordingly. Now, for the first time, she seemed to know him. A barrier had been broken down. The royal robes had proved tinsel, and no longer disguised the man she loved.

A touch on her arm aroused her. M. Gandinot was standing by her side. Terms, apparently had been agreed upon and the interview concluded, for in his hand was a silver cigarette-case.

'Dreaming, mademoiselle? I could not make you hear. The more I call to you, the more you did not answer. It is necessary to enter this loan.'

He recited the details and Ruth entered them in her ledger. This done, M. Gandinot, doffing his official self, sighed.

'It is a place of much sorrow, mademoiselle, this office. How he would not take no for an answer, that young man, recently departed. A fellow-countryman of yours, mademoiselle. You would say, "What does this young man, so well-dressed, in a *mont-de-piete*?" But I know better, I, Gandinot. You have an expression, you English—I heard it in Paris in a cafe, and inquired its meaning— when you say of a man that he swanks. How many young men have I seen here, admirably dressed—rich, you would say. No, no. The *mont-de-piete* permits no secrets. To swank, mademoiselle, what is it? To deceive the world, yes. But not the *mont-de-piete*. Yesterday also, when you had departed, was he here, that young man. Yet here he is once more today. He spends his money quickly, alas! that poor young swanker.'

When Ruth returned home that evening she found her father in the sitting-room, smoking a cigarette. He greeted her with effusion, but with some uneasiness—for the old gentleman had nerved himself to a delicate task. He had made up his mind tonight to speak seriously to Ruth on the subject of her unsatisfactory behaviour to Mr Vince. The more he saw of that young man the more positive was he that this was the human gold-mine for which he had been searching all these weary years. Accordingly, he threw away his cigarette, kissed Ruth on the forehead, and began to speak.

It had long been Mr Warden's opinion that, if his daughter had a fault, it was a tendency towards a quite unnecessary and highly inconvenient frankness. She had not that tact which he would have liked a daughter of his to possess. She would not evade, ignore, agree not to see. She was at times painfully blunt.

This happened now. He was warming to his subject when she interrupted him with a question.

'What makes you think Mr Vince is rich, father?' she asked.

Mr Warden was embarrassed. The subject of Mr Vince's opulence had not entered into his discourse. He had carefully avoided it. The fact that he was thinking of it and that Ruth knew that he was thinking of it, and that he knew that Ruth knew, had nothing to do with the case. The question was not in order, and it embarrassed him.

'I—why—I don't—I never said he was rich, my dear. I have no doubt that he has ample—'

'He is quite poor.'

Mr Warden's jaw fell slightly.

'Poor? But, my dear, that's absurd!' he cried. 'Why, only this evening—'

He broke off abruptly, but it was too late.

'Father, you've been borrowing money from him!'

Mr Warden drew in his breath, preparatory to an indignant denial, but he altered his mind and remained silent. As a borrower of money he had every quality but one. He had come to look on her perspicacity in this matter as a sort of second sight. It had frequently gone far to spoiling for him the triumph of success.

'And he has to pawn things to live!' Her voice trembled. 'He was at the *mont-de-piete* today. And yesterday too. I heard him. He was arguing with M. Gandinot—haggling—'

Her voice broke. She was sobbing helplessly. The memory of it was too raw and vivid.

Mr Warden stood motionless. Many emotions raced through his mind, but chief among them the thought that this revelation had come at a very fortunate time. An exceedingly lucky escape, he felt. He was aware, also, of a certain measure of indignation against this deceitful young man who had fraudulently imitated a gold-mine with what might have been disastrous results.

The door opened and Jeanne, the maid-of-all-work, announced Mr Vince.

He entered the room briskly.

'Good evening!' he said. 'I have brought you some more chocolates, Miss Warden, and some fruit. Great Scott! What's the matter?'

He stopped, but only for an instant. The next he had darted across the room, and, before the horrified eyes of Mr Warden, was holding Ruth in his arms. She clung to him.

Bill, the fox-terrier, over whom Mr Vince had happened to stumble, was the first to speak. Almost simultaneously Mr Warden joined in, and there was a striking similarity between the two voices, for Mr Warden, searching for words, emitted as a preliminary to them a sort of passionate yelp.

Mr Vince removed the hand that was patting Ruth's shoulder and waved it reassuringly at him.

'It's all right,' he said.

'All right! All *right*!'

'Affinities,' explained Mr Vince over his shoulder. 'Two hearts that beat as one. We're going to be married. What's the matter, dear? Don't you worry; you're all right.'

'I refuse!' shouted Mr Warden. 'I absolutely refuse.'

Mr Vince lowered Ruth gently into a chair and, holding her hand, inspected the fermenting old gentleman gravely.

'You refuse?' he said. 'Why, I thought you liked me.'

Mr Warden's frenzy had cooled. It had been something foreign to his nature. He regretted it. These things had to be managed with restraint.

'My personal likes and dislikes,' he said, 'have nothing to do with the matter, Mr Vince. They are beside the point. I have my daughter to consider. I cannot allow her to marry a man without a penny.'

'Quite right,' said Mr Vince, approvingly. 'Don't have anything to do with the fellow. If he tries to butt in, send for the police.'

Mr Warden hesitated. He had always been a little ashamed of Ruth's occupation. But necessity compelled.

'Mr Vince, my daughter is employed at the *mont-de-piete*, and was a witness to all that took place this afternoon.'

Mr Vince was genuinely agitated. He looked at Ruth, his face full of concern.

'You don't mean to say you have been slaving away in that stuffy—Great Scott! I'll have you out of that quick. You mustn't go there again.'

He stooped and kissed her.

'Perhaps you had better let me explain,' he said. 'Explanations, I always think, are the zero on the roulette-board of life. They're always somewhere about, waiting to pop up. Have you ever heard of Vince's Stores, Mr Warden? Perhaps they are since your time. Well, my father is the proprietor. One of our specialities is children's toys, but we haven't picked a real winner for years, and my father when I last saw him seemed so distressed about it that I said I'd see if I couldn't whack out an idea for something. Something on the lines of the Billiken, only better, was what he felt he needed. I'm not used to brain work, and after a spell of it I felt I wanted a rest. I came here to recuperate, and the very first morning I got an inspiration. You may have noticed that the manager of the *mont-de-piete* here isn't strong on conventional good looks. I saw him at the casino, and the thing flashed on me. He thinks his name's Gandinot, but it isn't. It's Uncle Zip, the Hump-Curer, the Man who Makes You Smile.'

He pressed Ruth's hand affectionately.

'I lost track of him, and it was only the day before yesterday that I discovered who he was and where he was to be found. Well, you can't go up to a man and ask him to pose as a model for Uncle Zip, the Hump-Curer. The only way to get sittings was to approach him in the way of business. So I collected what property I had and waded in. That's the whole story. Do I pass?'

Mr Warden's frosty demeanour had gradually thawed during this recital, and now the sun of his smile shone out warmly. He gripped Mr Vince's hand with every evidence of esteem, and after that he did what was certainly the best thing, by passing gently from the room. On his face, as he went, was a look such as Moses might have worn on the summit of Pisgah.

It was some twenty minutes later that Ruth made a remark.

'I want you to promise me something,' she said. 'Promise that you won't go on with that Uncle Zip drawing. I know it means ever so much money, but it might hurt poor M. Gandinot's feelings, and he has been very kind to me.'

'That settles it,' said Mr Vince. 'It's hard on the children of Great Britain, but say no more. No Uncle Zip for them.'

Ruth looked at him, almost with awe.

'You really won't go on with it? In spite of all the money you would make? Are you always going to do just what I ask you, no matter what it costs you?'

He nodded sadly.

'You have sketched out in a few words the whole policy of my married life. I feel an awful fraud. And I had encouraged you to look forward to years of incessant quarrelling. Do you think you can manage without it? I'm afraid it's going to be shockingly dull for you,' said Mr Vince, regretfully.

ARCHIBALD'S BENEFIT

Archibald Mealing was one of those golfers in whom desire outruns performance. Nobody could have been more willing than Archibald. He tried, and tried hard. Every morning before he took his bath he would stand in front of his mirror and practise swings. Every night before he went to bed he would read the golden words of some master on the subject of putting, driving, or approaching. Yet on the links most of his time was spent in retrieving lost balls or replacing America. Whether it was that Archibald pressed too much or pressed too little, whether it was that his club deviated from the dotted line which joined the two points A and B in the illustrated plate of the man making the brassy shot in the *Hints on Golf* book, or whether it was that he was pursued by some malignant fate, I do not know. Archibald rather favoured the last theory.

The important point is that, in his thirty-first year, after six seasons of untiring effort, Archibald went in for a championship, and won it.

Archibald, mark you, whose golf was a kind of blend of hockey, Swedish drill, and buck-and-wing dancing.

I know the ordeal I must face when I make such a statement. I see clearly before me the solid phalanx of men from Missouri, some urging me to tell it to the King of Denmark, others insisting that I produce my Eskimos. Nevertheless, I do not shrink. I state once more that in his thirty-first year Archibald Mealing went in for a golf championship, and won it.

Archibald belonged to a select little golf club, the members of which lived and worked in New York, but played in Jersey. Men of substance, financially as well as physically, they had combined their superfluous cash and with it purchased a strip of land close to the sea. This land had been drained—to the huge discomfort of a colony of mosquitoes which had come to look on the place as their private property—and converted into links, which had become a sort of refuge for incompetent golfers. The members of the Cape Pleasant Club were easygoing refugees from other and more exacting clubs, men who pottered rather than raced round the links; men, in short, who had grown tired of having to stop their game and stand aside in order to allow perspiring experts to whiz past them. The Cape Pleasant golfers did not make themselves slaves to the game. Their language, when they foozled, was gently regretful rather than sulphurous. The moment in the day's play which they enjoyed most was when they were saying: 'Well, here's luck!' in the club-house.

It will, therefore, be readily understood that Archibald's inability to do a hole in single figures did not handicap him at Cape Pleasant as it might have done at St. Andrews. His kindly clubmates took him to their bosoms to a man, and looked on him as a brother. Archibald's was one of those admirable natures which prompt their possessor frequently to remark: 'These are on me!' and his fellow golfers were not slow to appreciate the fact. They all loved Archibald.

Archibald was on the floor of his bedroom one afternoon, picking up the fragments of his mirror—a friend had advised him to practise the Walter J. Travis lofting shot—when the telephone bell rang. He took up the receiver, and was hailed by the comfortable voice of McCay, the club secretary.

'Is that Mealing?' asked McCay. 'Say, Archie, I'm putting your name down for our championship competition. That's right, isn't it?'

'Sure,' said Archibald. 'When does it start?'

'Next Saturday.'

'That's me.'

'Good for you. Oh, Archie.'

'Hello?'

'A man I met today told me you were engaged. Is that a fact?'

'Sure,' murmured Archibald, blushfully.

The wire hummed with McCay's congratulations.

'Thanks,' said Archibald. 'Thanks, old man. What? Oh, yes. Milsom's her name. By the way, her family have taken a cottage at Cape Pleasant for the summer. Some distance from the links. Yes, very convenient, isn't it? Good-bye.'

He hung up the receiver and resumed his task of gathering up the fragments. Now McCay happened to be of a romantic and sentimental nature. He was by profession a chartered accountant, and inclined to be stout; and all rather stout chartered accountants are sentimental. McCay was the sort of man who keeps old ball programmes and bundles of letters tied round with lilac ribbon. At country houses, where they lingered in the porch after dinner to watch the moonlight flooding the quiet garden, it was McCay and his colleague who lingered longest. McCay knew Ella Wheeler Wilcox by heart, and could take Browning without anaesthetics. It is not to be wondered at, therefore, that Archibald's remark about his fiancee coming to live at Cape Pleasant should give him food for thought. It appealed to him.

He reflected on it a good deal during the day, and, running across Sigsbee, a fellow Cape Pleasanter, after dinner that night at the Sybarites' Club, he spoke of the matter to him. It so happened that both had dined excellently, and were looking on the world with a sort of cosy benevolence. They were in the mood when men pat small boys on the head and ask them if they mean to be President when they grow up.

'I called up Archie Mealing today,' said McCay. 'Did you know he was engaged?'

'I did hear something about it. Girl of the name of Wilson, or—'

'Milsom. She's going to spend the summer at Cape Pleasant, Archie tells me.'

'Then she'll have a chance of seeing him play in the championship competition.'

McCay sucked his cigar in silence for a while, watching with dreamy eyes the blue smoke as it curled ceiling-ward. When he spoke his voice was singularly soft.

'Do you know, Sigsbee,' he said, sipping his Maraschino with a gentle melancholy—'do you know, there is something wonderfully pathetic to me in this business. I see the whole thing so clearly. There was a kind of quiver in the poor old chap's voice when he said: "She is coming to Cape Pleasant," which told me more than any words could have done. It is a tragedy in its way, Sigsbee. We may smile at it, think it trivial; but it is none the less a tragedy. That warm-hearted, enthusiastic girl, all eagerness to see the man she loves do well—Archie, poor old Archie, all on fire to prove to her that her trust in him is not misplaced, and the end—Disillusionment—Disappointment—Unhappiness.'

'He ought to keep his eye on the ball,' said the more practical Sigsbee.

'Quite possibly,' continued McCay, 'he has told her that he will win this championship.'

'If Archie's mutt enough to have told her that,' said Sigsbee decidedly, 'he deserves all he gets. Waiter, two Scotch highballs.'

McCay was in no mood to subscribe to this stony-hearted view.

'I tell you,' he said, 'I'm *sorry* for Archie! I'm *sorry* for the poor old chap. And I'm more than sorry for the girl.'

'Well, I don't see what we can do,' said Sigsbee. 'We can hardly be expected to foozle on purpose, just to let Archie show off before his girl.'

McCay paused in the act of lighting his cigar, as one smitten with a great thought.

'Why not?' he said. 'Why not, Sigsbee? Sigsbee, you've hit it.'

'Eh?'

'You have! I tell you, Sigsbee, you've solved the whole thing. Archie's such a bully good fellow, why not give him a benefit? Why not let him win this championship? You aren't going to tell me that you care whether you win a tin medal or not?'

Sigsbee's benevolence was expanding under the influence of the Scotch highball and his cigar. Little acts of kindness on Archie's part, here a cigar, there a lunch, at another time seats for the theatre, began to rise to the surface of his memory like rainbow-coloured bubbles. He wavered.

'Yes, but what about the rest of the men?' he said. 'There will be a dozen or more in for the medal.'

'We can square them,' said McCay confidently. 'We will broach the matter to them at a series of dinners at which we will be joint hosts. They are white men who will be charmed to do a little thing like that for a sport like Archie.'

'How about Gossett?' said Sigsbee.

McCay's face clouded. Gossett was an unpopular subject with members of the Cape Pleasant Golf Club. He was the serpent in their Eden. Nobody seemed quite to know how he had got in, but there, unfortunately, he was. Gossett had introduced into Cape Pleasant golf a cheerless atmosphere of the rigour of the game. It was to enable them to avoid just such golfers as Gossett that the Cape Pleasanters had founded their club. Genial courtesy rather than strict attention to the rules had been the leading characteristics of their play till his arrival. Up to that time it had been looked on as rather bad form to exact a penalty. A cheery give-and-take system had prevailed. Then Gossett had come, full of strange rules, and created about the same stir in the community which a hawk would create in a gathering of middle-aged doves.

'You can't square Gossett,' said Sigsbee.

McCay looked unhappy.

'I forgot him,' he said. 'Of course, nothing will stop him trying to win. I wish we could think of something. I would almost as soon see him lose as Archie win. But, after all, he does have off days sometimes.'

'You need to have a very off day to be as bad as Archie.'

They sat and smoked in silence.

'I've got it,' said Sigsbee suddenly. 'Gossett is a fine golfer, but nervous. If we upset his nerves enough, he will go right off his stroke. Couldn't we think of some way?'

McCay reached out for his glass.

'Yours is a noble nature, Sigsbee,' he said.

'Oh, no,' said the paragon modestly. 'Have another cigar?'

In order that the render may get the mental half-Nelson on the plot of this narrative which is so essential if a short story is to charm, elevate, and instruct, it is necessary now, for the nonce (but only for the nonce), to inspect Archibald's past life.

Archibald, as he had stated to McCay, was engaged to a Miss Milsom—Miss Margaret Milsom. How few men, dear reader, are engaged to girls with *svelte* figures, brown hair, and large blue eyes, now sparkling and vivacious, now dreamy and soulful, but always large and blue! How few, I say. You are, dear reader, and so am I, but who else? Archibald was one of the few who happened to be.

He was happy. It is true that Margaret's mother was not, as it were, wrapped up in him. She exhibited none of that effervescent joy at his appearance which we like to see in our mothers-in-law elect. On the contrary, she generally cried bitterly whenever she saw him, and at the end of ten minutes was apt to retire sobbing to her room, where she remained in a state of semi-coma till an advanced hour. She was by way of being a confirmed invalid, and something about Archibald seemed to get right in among her nerve centres, reducing them for the time being to a complicated hash. She did not like Archibald. She said she liked big, manly men. Behind his back she not infrequently referred to him as a 'gaby'; sometimes even as that 'guffin'.

She did not do this to Margaret, for Margaret, besides being blue-eyed, was also a shade quick-tempered. Whenever she discussed Archibald, it was with her son Stuyvesant. Stuyvesant Milsom, who thought Archibald a bit of an ass, was always ready to sit and listen to his mother on the subject, it being, however, an understood thing that at the conclusion of the seance she yielded one or two saffron-coloured bills towards his racing debts. For Stuyvesant, having developed a habit of backing horses which either did not start at all or else sat down and thought in the middle of the race, could always do with ten dollars or so. His prices for these interviews worked out, as a rule, at about three cents a word.

In these circumstances it was perhaps natural that Archibald and Margaret should prefer to meet, when they did meet, at some other spot than the Milsom home. It suited them both better that they should arrange a secret tryst on these occasions. Archibald preferred it because being in the same room as Mrs Milsom always made him feel like a murderer with particularly large feet; and Margaret preferred it because, as she told Archibald, these secret meetings lent a touch of poetry to what might otherwise have been a commonplace engagement.

Archibald thought this charming; but at the same time he could not conceal from himself the fact that Margaret's passion for the poetic cut, so to speak, both ways. He admired and loved the loftiness of her soul, but, on the other hand, it was a tough job having to live up to it. For Archibald was a very ordinary young man. They had tried to inoculate him with a love of poetry at school, but it had not taken. Until he was thirty he had been satisfied to class all poetry (except that of Mr George Cohan) under the general heading of punk. Then he met Margaret, and the trouble began. On the day he first met her, at a picnic, she had looked so soulful, so aloof from this world, that he had felt instinctively that here was a girl who expected more from a man than a mere statement that the weather was great. It so chanced that he knew just one quotation from the classics, to wit, Tennyson's critique of the Island-Valley of Avilion. He knew this because he had had the passage to write out one hundred and fifty times at school, on the occasion of his being caught smoking by one of the faculty who happened to be a passionate admirer of the 'Idylls of the King'.

A remark of Margaret's that it was a splendid day for a picnic and that the country looked nice gave him his opportunity.

'It reminds me,' he said, 'it reminds me strongly of the Island-Valley of Avilion, where falls not hail, or rain, or any snow, nor ever wind blows loudly; but it lies deep-meadow'd, happy, fair, with orchard lawns....'

He broke off here to squash a hornet; but Margaret had heard enough. 'Are you fond of the poets, Mr Mealing?' she said, with a far-off look.

'Me?' said Archibald fervently. 'Me? Why, I eat 'em alive!'

And that was how all the trouble had started. It had meant unremitting toil for Archibald. He felt that he had set himself a standard from which he must not fall. He bought every new volume of poetry which was praised in the press, and learned the reviews by heart. Every evening he read painfully a portion of the classics. He plodded through the poetry sections of Bartlett's *Familiar Quotations*. Margaret's devotion to the various bards was so enthusiastic, and her reading so wide, that there were times when Archibald wondered if he could endure the strain. But he persevered heroically, and so far had not been found wanting. But the strain was fearful.

The early stages of the Cape Pleasant golf tournament need no detailed description. The rules of match play governed the contests, and Archibald disposed of his first three opponents before the twelfth hole. He had been diffident when he teed off with McCay in the first round, but, finding that he defeated the secretary with ease, he met one Butler in the second round with more confidence. Butler, too, he routed; with the result that, by the time he faced Sigsbee in round three, he was practically the conquering hero. Fortune seemed to be beaming upon him with almost insipid sweetness. When he was trapped in the bunker at the seventh hole, Sigsbee became trapped as well. When he sliced at the sixth tee, Sigsbee pulled. And Archibald, striking a brilliant vein, did the next three holes in eleven, nine, and twelve; and, romping home, qualified for the final.

Gossett, that serpent, meanwhile, had beaten each of his three opponents without much difficulty.

The final was fixed for the following Thursday morning. Gossett, who was a broker, had made some frivolous objection about the difficulty of absenting himself from Wall Street, but had been overruled. When Sigsbee pointed out that he could easily defeat Archibald and get to the city by lunch-time if he wished, and that in any case his partner would be looking after things, he allowed himself to be persuaded, though reluctantly. It was a well-known fact that Gossett was in the midst of some rather sizeable deals at that time.

Thursday morning suited Archibald admirably. It had occurred to him that he could bring off a double event. Margaret had arrived at Cape Pleasant on the previous evening, and he had arranged by telephone to meet her at the end of the board-walk, which was about a mile from the links, at one o'clock, supply her with lunch, and spend the afternoon with her on the water. If he started his match with Gossett at eleven-thirty, he would have plenty of time to have his game and be at the end of the board-walk at the appointed hour. He had no delusions about the respective merits of Gossett and himself as golfers. He knew that Gossett would win the necessary ten holes off the reel. It was saddening, but it was a scientific fact. There was no avoiding it. One simply had to face it.

Having laid these plans, he caught the train on the Thursday morning with the consoling feeling that, however sadly the morning might begin, it was bound to end well.

The day was fine, the sun warm, but tempered with a light breeze. One or two of the club had come to watch the match, among them Sigsbee.

Sigsbee drew Gossett aside.

'You must let me caddie for you, old man,' he said. 'I know your temperament so exactly. I know how little it takes to put you off your stroke. In an ordinary game you might take one of these boys, I know, but on an important occasion like this you must not risk it. A grubby boy, probably with a squint, would almost certainly get on your nerves. He might even make comments on the game, or whistle. But I understand you. You must let me carry your clubs.'

'It's very good of you,' said Gossett.

'Not at all,' said Sigsbee.

Archibald was now preparing to drive off from the first tee. He did this with great care. Everyone who has seen Archibald Mealing play golf knows that his teeing off is one of the most impressive sights ever witnessed on the links. He tilted his cap over his eyes, waggled his club a little, shifted his feet, waggled his club some more, gazed keenly towards the horizon for a moment, waggled his club again, and finally, with the air of a Strong Man lifting a bar of iron, raised it slowly above his head. Then, bringing it down with a sweep, he drove the ball with a lofty slice some fifty yards. It was rarely that he failed either to slice or pull his ball. His progress from hole to hole was generally a majestic zigzag.

Gossett's drive took him well on the way to the green. He holed out in five. Archibald, mournful but not surprised, made his way to the second tee.

The second hole was shorter. Gossett won it in three. The third he took in six, the fourth in four. Archibald began to feel that he might just as well not be there. He was practically a spectator.

At this point he reached in his pocket for his tobacco-pouch, to console himself with smoke. To his dismay he found it was not there. He had had it in the train, but now it had vanished. This added to his gloom, for the pouch had been given to him by Margaret, and he had always thought it one more proof of the way her nature towered over the natures of other girls that she had not woven a monogram on it in forget-me-nots. This record pouch was missing, and Archibald mourned for the loss.

His sorrows were not alleviated by the fact that Gossett won the fifth and sixth holes.

It was now a quarter past twelve, and Archibald reflected with moody satisfaction that the massacre must soon be over, and that he would then be able to forget it in the society of Margaret.

As Gossett was about to drive off from the seventh tee, a telegraph boy approached the little group.

'Mr Gossett,' he said.

Gossett lowered his driver, and wheeled round, but Sigsbee had snatched the envelope from the boy's hand.

'It's all right, old man,' he said. 'Go right ahead. I'll keep it safe for you.'

'Give it to me,' said Gossett anxiously. 'It may be from the office. Something may have happened to the market. I may be needed.'

'No, no,' said Sigsbee, soothingly. 'Don't you worry about it. Better not open it. It might have something in it that would put you off your stroke. Wait till the end of the game.'

'Give it to me. I want to see it.'

Sigsbee was firm.

'No,' he said. 'I'm here to see you win this championship and I won't have you taking any risks. Besides, even if it was important, a few minutes won't make any difference.'

'Well, at any rate, open it and read it.'

'It is probably in cipher,' said Sigsbee. 'I wouldn't understand it. Play on, old man. You've only a few more holes to win.'

Gossett turned and addressed his ball again. Then he swung. The club tipped the ball, and it rolled sluggishly for a couple of feet. Archibald approached the tee. Now there were moments when Archibald could drive quite decently. He always applied a considerable amount of muscular force to his efforts. It was in that direction, as a rule, he erred. On this occasion, whether inspired by his rival's failure or merely favoured by chance, he connected with his ball at precisely the right moment. It flew from the tee, straight, hard, and low, struck the ground near the green, bounded on and finally rocked to within a foot of the hole. No such long ball had been driven on the Cape Pleasant links since their foundation.

That it should have taken him three strokes to hole out from this promising position was unfortunate, but not fatal, for Gossett, who seemed suddenly to have fallen off his game, only reached the green in seven. A moment later a murmur of approval signified the fact that Archibald had won his first hole.

'Mr Gossett,' said a voice.

Those murmuring approval observed that the telegraph boy was once more in their midst. This time he bore two missives. Sigsbee dexterously impounded both.

'No,' he said with decision. 'I absolutely refuse to let you look at them till the game is over. I know your temperament.'

Gossett gesticulated.

'But they must be important. They must come from my office. Where else would I get a stream of telegrams? Something has gone wrong. I am urgently needed.'

Sigsbee nodded gravely.

'That is what I fear,' he said. 'That is why I cannot risk having you upset. Time enough, Gossett, for bad news after the game. Play on, man, and dismiss it from your mind. Besides, you couldn't get back to New York just yet, in any case. There are no trains. Dismiss the whole thing from your mind and just play your usual, and you're sure to win.'

Archibald had driven off during this conversation, but without his previous success. This time he had pulled his ball into some long grass. Gossett's drive was, however, worse; and the subsequent movement of the pair to the hole resembled more than anything else the manoeuvres of two men rolling peanuts with toothpicks as the result of an election bet. Archibald finally took the hole in twelve after Gossett had played his fourteenth.

When Archibald won the next in eleven and the tenth in nine, hope began to flicker feebly in his bosom. But when he won two more holes, bringing the score to like-as-we-lie, it flamed up within him like a beacon.

The ordinary golfer, whose scores per hole seldom exceed those of Colonel Bogey, does not understand the whirl of mixed sensations which the really incompetent performer experiences on the rare occasions when he does strike a winning vein. As stroke follows stroke, and he continues to hold his opponent, a wild exhilaration surges through him, followed by a sort of awe, as if he were doing something wrong, even irreligious. Then all these yeasty emotions subside and are blended into one glorious sensation of grandeur and majesty, as of a giant among pygmies.

By the time that Archibald, putting with the care of one brushing flies off a sleeping Venus, had holed out and won the thirteenth, he was in the full grip of this feeling. And as he walked to the fifteenth tee, after winning the fourteenth, he felt that this was Life, that till now he had been a mere mollusc.

Just at that moment he happened to look at his watch, and the sight was like a douche of cold water. The hands stood at five minutes to one.

Let us pause and ponder on this point for a while. Let us not dismiss it as if it were some mere trivial, everyday difficulty. You, dear reader, play an accurate, scientific game and beat your opponent with ease every time you go the links, and so do I; but Archibald was not like us. This was the first occasion on which he had ever felt that he was playing well enough to give him a chance of defeating a really good man. True, he had beaten McCay, Sigsbee, and Butler in the earlier rounds; but they were ignoble rivals compared with Gossett. To defeat Gossett, however, meant the championship. On the other hand, he was passionately devoted to Margaret Milsom, whom he was due to meet at the end of the board-walk at one sharp. It was now five minutes to one, and the end of the board-walk still a mile away.

The mental struggle was brief but keen. A sharp pang, and his mind was made up. Cost what it might, he must stay on the links. If Margaret broke off the engagement—well, it might be that Time would heal the wound, and that after many years he would find some other girl for whom he might come to care in a wrecked, broken sort of way. But a chance like this could never come again. What is Love compared with holing out before your opponent?

The excitement now had become so intense that a small boy, following with the crowd, swallowed his chewing-gum; for a slight improvement had become noticeable in Gossett's play, and a slight improvement in the play of almost anyone meant that it became vastly superior to Archibald's. At the next hole the improvement was not marked enough to have its full effect, and Archibald contrived to halve. This made him two up and three to play. What the average golfer would consider a commanding lead. But Archibald was no average golfer. A commanding lead for him would have been two up and one to play.

To give the public of his best, your golfer should have his mind cool and intent upon the game. Inasmuch as Gossett was worrying about the telegrams, while Archibald, strive as he might to dismiss it, was haunted by a vision of Margaret standing alone and deserted on the board-walk, play became, as it were, ragged. Fine putting enabled Gossett to do the sixteenth hole in twelve, and when, winning the seventeenth in nine, he brought his score level with Archibald's the match seemed over. But just then—

'Mr Gossett!' said a familiar voice.

Once more was the much-enduring telegraph boy among those present.

'T'ree dis time!' he observed.

Gossett sprang, but again the watchful Sigsbee was too swift.

'Be brave, Gossett—be brave,' he said. 'This is a crisis in the game. Keep your nerve. Play just as if nothing existed outside the links. To look at these telegrams now would be fatal.'

Eye-witnesses of that great encounter will tell the story of the last hole to their dying day. It was one of those Titanic struggles which Time cannot efface from the memory. Archibald was fortunate in getting a good start. He only missed twice before he struck his ball on the tee. Gossett had four strokes ere he achieved the feat. Nor did Archibald's luck desert him in the journey to the green. He was out of the bunker in eleven.

Gossett emerged only after sixteen. Finally, when Archibald's twenty-first stroke sent the ball trickling into the hole, Gossett had played his thirtieth.

The ball had hardly rested on the bottom of the hole before Gossett had begun to tear the telegrams from their envelopes. As he read, his eyes bulged in their sockets.

'Not bad news, I hope,' said a sympathetic bystander.

Sigsbee took the sheaf of telegrams.

The first ran: 'Good luck. Hope you win. McCay.' The second also ran: 'Good luck. Hope you win. McCay.' So, singularly enough, did the third, fourth, fifth, sixth, and seventh.

'Great Scott!' said Sigsbee. 'He seems to have been pretty anxious not to run any risk of missing you, Gossett.'

As he spoke, Archibald, close beside him, was looking at his watch. The hands stood at a quarter to two.

Margaret and her mother were seated in the parlour when Archibald arrived. Mrs Milsom, who had elicited the fact that Archibald had not kept his appointment, had been saying 'I told you so' for some time, and this had not improved Margaret's temper. When, therefore, Archibald, damp and dishevelled, was shown in, the chill in the air nearly gave him frost-bite. Mrs Milsom did her celebrated imitation of the Gorgon, while Margaret, lightly humming an air, picked up a weekly paper and became absorbed in it.

'Margaret, let me explain,' panted Archibald. Mrs Milsom was understood to remark that she dared say. Margaret's attention was riveted by a fashion plate.

'Driving in a taximeter to the ferry this morning,' resumed Archibald, 'I had an accident.'

This was the result of some rather feverish brainwork on the way from the links to the cottage.

The periodical flopped to the floor.

'Oh, Archie, are you hurt?'

'A few scratches, nothing more; but it made me miss my train.'

'What train did you catch?' asked Mrs Milsom sepulchrally.

'The one o'clock. I came straight on here from the station.'

'Why,' said Margaret, 'Stuyvesant was coming home on the one o'clock train. Did you see him?'

Archibald's jaw dropped slightly.

'Er—no,' he said.

'How curious,' said Margaret.

'Very curious,' said Archibald.

'Most curious,' said Mrs Milsom.

They were still reflecting on the singularity of this fact when the door opened, and the son of the house entered in person.

'Thought I should find you here, Mealing,' he said. 'They gave me this at the station to give to you; you dropped it this morning when you got out of the train.'

He handed Archibald the missing pouch.

'Thanks,' said the latter huskily. 'When you say this morning, of course you mean this afternoon, but thanks all the same—thanks—thanks.'

'No, Archibald Mealing, he does *not* mean this afternoon,' said Mrs Milsom. 'Stuyvesant, speak! From what train did that guf—did Mr Mealing alight when he dropped the tobacco-pouch?'

'The ten o'clock, the fellow told me. Said he would have given it back to him then only he sprinted off in the deuce of a hurry.'

Six eyes focused themselves upon Archibald.

'Margaret,' he said, 'I will not try to deceive you—'

'You may try,' observed Mrs Milsom, 'but you will not succeed.'

'Well, Archibald?'

Archibald fingered his collar.

'There was no taximeter accident.'

'Ah!' said Mrs Milsom.

'The fact is, I have been playing in a golf tournament.'

Margaret uttered an exclamation of surprise.

'Playing golf!'

Archibald bowed his head with manly resignation.

'Why didn't you tell me? Why didn't you arrange for us to meet on the links? I should have loved it.'

Archibald was amazed.

'You take an interest in golf, Margaret? You! I thought you scorned it, considered it an unintellectual game. I thought you considered all games unintellectual.'

'Why, I play golf myself. Not very well.'

'Margaret! Why didn't you tell me?'

'I thought you might not like it. You were so spiritual, so poetic. I feared you would despise me.'

Archibald took a step forward. His voice was tense and trembling.

'Margaret,' he said, 'this is no time for misunderstandings. We must be open with one another. Our happiness is at stake. Tell me honestly, do you like poetry really?'

Margaret hesitated, then answered bravely:

'No, Archibald,' she said, 'it is as you suspect. I am not worthy of you. I do *not* like poetry. Ah, you shudder! You turn away! Your face grows hard and scornful!'

'I don't!' yelled Archibald. 'It doesn't! It doesn't do anything of the sort! You've made me another man!'

She stared, wild-eyed, astonished.

'What! Do you mean that you, too—'

'I should just say I do. I tell you I hate the beastly stuff. I only pretended to like it because I thought you did. The hours I've spent learning it up! I wonder I've not got brain fever.'

'Archie! Used you to read it up, too? Oh, if I'd only known!'

'And you forgive me—this morning, I mean?'

'Of course. You couldn't leave a golf tournament. By the way, how did you get on?'

Archibald coughed.

'Rather well,' he said modestly. 'Pretty decently. In fact, not badly. As a matter of fact, I won the championship.'

'The championship!' whispered Margaret. 'Of America?'

'Well, not *absolutely* of America,' said Archibald. 'But all the same, a championship.'

'My hero.'

'You won't be wanting me for a while, I guess?' said Stuyvesant nonchalantly. 'Think I'll smoke a cigarette on the porch.'

And sobs from the stairs told that Mrs Milsom was already on her way to her room.

THE MAN, THE MAID, AND THE MIASMA

Although this story is concerned principally with the Man and the Maid, the Miasma pervades it to such an extent that I feel justified in putting his name on the bills. Webster's Dictionary gives the meaning of the word 'miasma' as 'an infection floating in the air; a deadly exhalation'; and, in the opinion of Mr Robert Ferguson, his late employer, that description, though perhaps a little too flattering, on the whole summed up Master Roland Bean pretty satisfactorily. Until the previous day he had served Mr Ferguson in the capacity of office-boy; but there was that about Master Bean which made it practically impossible for anyone to employ him for long. A syndicate of Galahad, Parsifal, and Marcus Aurelius might have done it, but to an ordinary erring man, conscious of things done which should not have been done, and other things equally numerous left undone, he was too oppressive. One conscience is enough for any man. The employer of Master Bean had to cringe before two. Nobody can last long against an office-boy whose eyes shine with quiet, respectful reproof through gold-rimmed spectacles, whose manner is that of a middle-aged saint, and who obviously knows all the Plod and Punctuality books by heart and orders his life by their precepts. Master Bean was a walking edition of *Stepping-Stones to Success, Millionaires who Have Never Smoked,* and *Young Man, Get up Early.* Galahad, Parsifal, and Marcus Aurelius, as I say, might have remained tranquil in his presence, but Robert Ferguson found the contract too large. After one month he had braced himself up and sacked the Punctual Plodder.

Yet now he was sitting in his office, long after the last clerk had left, long after the hour at which he himself was wont to leave, his mind full of his late employee.

Was this remorse? Was he longing for the touch of the vanished hand, the gleam of the departed spectacles? He was not. His mind was full of Master Bean because Master Bean was waiting for him in the outer office; and he lingered on at his desk, after the day's work was done, for the same reason. Word had been brought to him earlier in the evening, that Master Roland Bean would like to see him. The answer to that was easy: 'Tell him I'm busy.' Master Bean's admirably dignified reply was that he understood how great was the pressure of Mr Ferguson's work, and that he would wait till he was at liberty. Liberty! Talk of the liberty of the treed possum, but do not use the word in connexion with a man bottled up in an office, with Roland Bean guarding the only exit.

Mr Ferguson kicked the waste-paper basket savagely. The unfairness of the thing hurt him. A sacked office-boy ought to stay sacked. He had no business to come popping up again like Banquo's ghost. It was not playing the game.

The reader may wonder what was the trouble—why Mr Ferguson could not stalk out and brusquely dispose of his foe; but then the reader has not employed Master Bean for a month. Mr Ferguson had, and his nerve had broken.

A slight cough penetrated the door between the two offices. Mr Ferguson rose and grabbed his hat. Perhaps a sudden rush—he shot out with the tense

concentration of one moving towards the refreshment-room at a station where
the train stops three minutes.

'Good evening, sir!' was the watcher's view-hallo.

'Ah, Bean,' said Mr Ferguson, flitting rapidly, 'you still here? I thought you
had gone. I'm afraid I cannot stop now. Some other time—'

He was almost through.

'I fear, sir, that you will be unable to get out,' said Master Bean,
sympathetically. 'The building is locked up.'

Men who have been hit by bullets say the first sensation is merely a sort of
dull shock. So it was with Mr Ferguson. He stopped in his tracks and stared.

'The porter closes the door at seven o'clock punctually, sir. It is now nearly
twenty minutes after the hour.'

Mr Ferguson's brain was still in the numbed stage.

'Closes the door?' he said.

'Yes, sir.'

'Then how are we to get out?'

'I fear we cannot get out, sir.'

Mr Ferguson digested this.

'I am no longer in your employment, sir,' said Master Bean, respectfully, 'but I
hope that in the circumstances you will permit me to remain here during the
night.'

'During the night!'

'It would enable me to sleep more comfortably than on the stairs.'

'But we can't stop here all night,' said Mr Ferguson, feebly.

He had anticipated an unpleasant five minutes in Master Bean's company.
Imagination boggled at the thought of an unpleasant thirteen hours.

He collapsed into a chair.

'I called,' said Master Bean, shelving the trivial subject of the prospective vigil,
'in the hope that I might persuade you, sir, to reconsider your decision in regard
to my dismissal. I can assure you, sir, that I am extremely anxious to give
satisfaction. If you would take me back and inform me how I have fallen short, I
would endeavour to improve, I—'

'We can't stop here all night,' interrupted Mr Ferguson, bounding from his
chair and beginning to pace the floor.

'Without presumption, sir, I feel that if you were to give me another chance I
should work to your satisfaction. I should endeavour—'

Mr Ferguson stared at him in dumb horror. He had a momentary vision of a
sleepless night spent in listening to a nicely-polished speech for the defence. He
was seized with a mad desire for flight. He could not leave the building, but he
must get away somewhere and think.

He dashed from the room and raced up the dark stairs. And as he arrived at
the next floor his eye was caught by a thin pencil of light which proceeded from a
door on the left.

No shipwrecked mariner on a desert island could have welcomed the
appearance of a sail with greater enthusiasm. He bounded at the door. He knew

to whom the room belonged. It was the office of one Blaythwayt; and Blaythwayt was not only an acquaintance, but a sportsman. Quite possibly there might be a pack of cards on Blaythwayt's person to help pass the long hours. And if not, at least he would be company and his office a refuge. He flung open the door without going through the formality of knocking. Etiquette is not for the marooned.

'I say, Blaythwayt—' he began, and stopped abruptly.

The only occupant of the room was a girl.

'I beg your pardon,' he said, 'I thought—'

He stopped again. His eyes, dazzled with the light, had not seen clearly. They did so now.

'You!' he cried.

The girl looked at him, first with surprise, then with a cool hostility. There was a long pause. Eighteen months had passed since they had parted, and conversation does not flow easily after eighteen months of silence, especially if the nature of the parting has been bitter and stormy.

He was the first to speak.

'What are you doing here?' he said.

'I thought my doings had ceased to interest you,' she said. 'I am Mr Blaythwayt's secretary, I have been here a fortnight. I have wondered if we should meet. I used to see you sometimes in the street.'

'I never saw you.'

'No?' she said indifferently.

He ran his hand through his hair in a dazed way.

'Do you know we are locked in?' he said.

He had expected wild surprise and dismay. She merely clicked her tongue in an annoyed manner.

'Again!' she said. 'What a nuisance! I was locked in only a week ago.'

He looked at her with unwilling respect, the respect of the novice for the veteran. She was nothing to him now, of course. She had passed out of his life. But he could not help remembering that long ago—eighteen months ago—what he had admired most in her had been this same spirit, this game refusal to be disturbed by Fate's blows. It braced him up.

He sat down and looked curiously at her.

'So you left the stage?' he said.

'I thought we agreed when we parted not to speak to one another,' said she, coldly.

'Did we? I thought it was only to meet as strangers.'

'It's the same thing.'

'Is it? I often talk to strangers.'

'What a bore they must think you!' she said, hiding one-eighth of a yawn with the tips of two fingers. 'I suppose,' she went on, with faint interest, 'you talk to them in trains when they are trying to read their paper?'

'I don't force my conversation on anyone.'

'Don't you?' she said, raising her eyebrows in sweet surprise. 'Only your company—is that it?'

'Are you alluding to the present occasion?'

'Well, you have an office of your own in this building, I believe.'

'I have.'

'Then why—'

'I am at perfect liberty,' he said, with dignity, 'to sit in my friend Blaythwayt's office if I choose. I wish to see Mr Blaythwayt.'

'On business?'

He proved that she had established no corner in raised eyebrows.

'I fear,' he said, 'that I cannot discuss my affairs with Mr Blaythwayt's employees. I must see him personally.'

'Mr Blaythwayt is not here.'

'I will wait.'

'He will not be here for thirteen hours.'

I'll wait.'

'Very well,' she burst out; 'you have brought it on yourself. You've only yourself to blame. If you had been good and had gone back to your office, I would have brought you down some cake and cocoa.'

'Cake and cocoa!' said he, superciliously.

'Yes, cake and cocoa,' she snapped. 'It's all very well for you to turn up your nose at them now, but wait. You've thirteen hours of this in front of you. I know what it is. Last time I had to spend the night here I couldn't get to sleep for hours, and when I did I dreamed that I was chasing chocolate *eclairs* round and round Trafalgar Square. And I never caught them either. Long before the night was finished I would have given *anything* for even a dry biscuit. I made up my mind I'd always keep something here in case I ever got locked in again—yes, smile. You'd better while you can.'

He was smiling, but wanly. Nobody but a professional fasting man could have looked unmoved into the Inferno she had pictured. Then he rallied.

'Cake!' he said, scornfully.

She nodded grimly.

'Cocoa!'

Again that nod, ineffably sinister.

'I'm afraid I don't care for either,' he said.

'If you will excuse me,' she said, indifferently, 'I have a little work that I must finish.'

She turned to her desk, leaving him to his thoughts. They were not exhilarating. He had maintained a brave front, but inwardly he quailed. Reared in the country, he had developed at an early age a fine, healthy appetite. Once, soon after his arrival in London, he had allowed a dangerous fanatic to persuade him that the secret of health was to go without breakfast.

His lunch that day had cost him eight shillings, and only decent shame had kept the figure as low as that. He knew perfectly well that long ere the dawn of day his whole soul would be crying out for cake, squealing frantically for cocoa.

Would it not be better to—no, a thousand times no! Death, but not surrender. His self-respect was at stake. Looking back, he saw that his entire relations with this girl had been a series of battles of will. So far, though he had certainly not won, he had not been defeated. He must not be defeated now.

He crossed his legs and sang a gay air under his breath.

'If you wouldn't mind,' said the girl, looking up.

'I beg your pardon?'

'Your groaning interrupts my work.'

'I was not groaning. I was singing.'

'Oh, I'm sorry!'

'Not at all.'

Eight bars rest.

Mr Ferguson, deprived of the solace of song, filled in the time by gazing at the toiler's back-hair. It set in motion a train of thought—an express train bound for the Land of Yesterday. It recalled days in the woods, evenings on the lawn. It recalled sunshine—storm. Plenty of storm. Minor tempests that burst from a clear sky, apparently without cause, and the great final tornado. There had been cause enough for that. Why was it, mused Mr Ferguson, that every girl in every country town in every county of England who had ever recited 'Curfew shall not ring tonight' well enough to escape lynching at the hands of a rustic audience was seized with the desire to come to London and go on the stage?

He sighed.

'Please don't snort,' said a cold voice, from behind the back-hair.

There was a train-wreck in the Land of Yesterday. Mr Ferguson, the only survivor, limped back into the Present.

The Present had little charm, but at least it was better than the cakeless Future. He fixed his thoughts on it. He wondered how Master Bean was passing the time. Probably doing deep-breathing exercises, or reading a pocket Aristotle.

The girl pushed back her chair and rose.

She went to a small cupboard in the corner of the room, and from it produced in instalments all that goes to make cake and cocoa. She did not speak. Presently, filling Space, there sprang into being an Odour; and as it reached him Mr Ferguson stiffened in his chair, bracing himself as for a fight to the death. It was more than an odour. It was the soul of the cocoa singing to him. His fingers gripped the arms of the chair. This was the test.

The girl separated a section of cake from the parent body. She caught his eye.

'You had better go,' she said. 'If you go now it's just possible that I may—but I forgot, you don't like cocoa.'

'No,' said he, resolutely, 'I don't.'

She seemed now in the mood for conversation.

'I wonder why you came up here at all,' she said.

'There's no reason why you shouldn't know. I came up here because my late office-boy is downstairs.'

'Why should that send you up?'

'You've never met him or you wouldn't ask. Have you ever had to face someone who is simply incarnate Saintliness and Disapproval, who—'

'Are you forgetting that I was engaged to you for several weeks?'

He was too startled to be hurt. The idea of himself as a Roland Bean was too new to be assimilated immediately. It called for meditation.

'Was I like that?' he said at last, almost humbly.

'You know you were. Oh, I'm not thinking only about your views on the stage! It was everything. Whatever I did you were there to disapprove like a—like a—like an aunt,' she concluded triumphantly. 'You were too good for anything. If only you would, just once, have done something wrong. I think I'd have—But you couldn't. You're simply perfect.'

A man will remain cool and composed under many charges. Hint that his tastes are criminal, and he will shrug his shoulders. But accuse him of goodness, and you rouse the lion.

Mr Ferguson's brow darkened.

'As a matter of fact,' he said, haughtily, 'I was to have had supper with a chorus-girl this very night.'

'How very appalling!' said she, languidly.

She sipped her cocoa.

'I suppose you consider that very terrible?' she said.

'For a beginner.'

She crumbled her cake. Suddenly she looked up.

'Who is she?' she demanded, fiercely.

'I beg your pardon?' he said, coming out of a pleasant reverie.

'Who is this girl?'

'She—er—her name—her name is Marie—Marie Templeton.'

She seemed to think for a moment.

'That dear old lady?' she said.' I know her quite well.'

'What!'

'"Mother" we used to call her. Have you met her son?'

'Her son?'

'A rather nice-looking man. He plays heavy parts on tour. He's married and has two of the sweetest children. Their grandmother is devoted to them. Hasn't she ever mentioned them to you?'

She poured herself out another cup of cocoa. Conversation again languished.

'I suppose you're very fond of her?' she said at length.

'I'm devoted to her.' He paused. 'Dear little thing!' he added.

She rose and moved to the door. There was a nasty gleam in her eyes.

'You aren't going?' he said.

'I shall be back in a moment. I'm just going to bring your poor little office-boy up here. He must be missing you.'

He sprang up, but she had gone. Leaning over the banisters, he heard a door open below, then a short conversation, and finally footsteps climbing the stairs.

It was pitch dark on the landing. He stepped aside, and they passed without seeing him. Master Bean was discoursing easily on cocoa, the processes whereby it was manufactured, and the remarkable distances which natives of Mexico had covered with it as their only food. The door opened, flooding the landing with light, and Mr Ferguson, stepping from ambush, began to descend the stairs.

The girl came to the banisters.

'Mr Ferguson!'

He stopped.

'Did you want me?' he asked.

'Are you going back to your office?'

'I am. I hope you will enjoy Bean's society. He has a fund of useful information on all subjects.'

He went on. After a while she returned to the room and closed the door.

Mr Ferguson went into his office and sat down.

There was once a person of the name of Simeon Stylites, who took up a position on top of a pillar and stayed there, having no other engagements, for thirty years. Mr Ferguson, who had read Tennyson's poem on the subject, had until tonight looked upon this as a pretty good thing. Reading the lines:

> ...thrice ten years,
> Thrice multiplied by superhuman pangs,
> In hunger and in thirsts, fevers and colds,
> In coughs, aches, stitches, ulcerous throes, and cramps, ...
> Patient on this tall pillar I have borne.
> Rain, wind, frost, heat, hail, damp, and sleet, and snow,

he had gathered roughly, as it were, that Simeon had not been comfortable. He had pitied him. But now, sitting in his office-chair, he began to wonder what the man had made such a fuss about. He suspected him of having had a touch of the white feather in him. It was not as if he had not had food. He talked about 'hungers and thirsts', but he must have had something to eat, or he could not have stayed the course. Very likely, if the truth were known, there was somebody below who passed him up regular supplies of cake and cocoa.

He began to look on Simeon as an overrated amateur.

Sleep refused to come to him. It got as far as his feet, but no farther. He rose and stamped to restore the circulation.

It was at this point that he definitely condemned Simeon Stylites as a sybaritic fraud.

If this were one of those realistic Zolaesque stories I would describe the crick in the back that—but let us hurry on.

It was about six hours later—he had no watch, but the numbers of aches, stitches, not to mention cramps, that he had experienced could not possibly have been condensed into a shorter period—that his manly spirit snapped. Let us not judge him too harshly. The girl upstairs had broken his heart, ruined his life, and practically compared him to Roland Bean, and his pride should have built up an impassable wall between them, but—she had cake and cocoa. In similar circumstances King Arthur would have grovelled before Guinevere.

He rushed to the door and tore it open. There was a startled exclamation from the darkness outside.

'I hope I didn't disturb you,' said a meek voice.

Mr Ferguson did not answer. His twitching nostrils were drinking in a familiar aroma.

'Were you asleep? May I come in? I've brought you some cake and cocoa.'

He took the rich gifts from her in silence. There are moments in a man's life too sacred for words. The wonder of the thing had struck him dumb. An instant before and he had had but a desperate hope of winning these priceless things from her at the cost of all his dignity and self-respect. He had been prepared to secure them through a shower of biting taunts, a blizzard of razor-like 'I told you so's'. Yet here he was, draining the cup, and still able to hold his head up, look the world in the face, and call himself a man.

His keen eye detected a crumb on his coat-sleeve. This retrieved and consumed, he turned to her, seeking explanation.

She was changed. The battle-gleam had faded from her eyes. She seemed scared and subdued. Her manner was of one craving comfort and protection. 'That awful boy!' she breathed.

'Bean?' said Mr Ferguson, picking a crumb off the carpet.

'He's frightful.'

'I thought you might get a little tired of him! What has he been doing?'

'Talking. I feel battered. He's like one of those awful encyclopedias that give you a sort of dull leaden feeling in your head directly you open them. Do you know how many tons of water go over Niagara Falls every year?'

'No.'

'He does.'

'I told you he had a fund of useful information. The Purpose and Tenacity books insist on it. That's how you Catch your Employer's Eye. One morning the boss suddenly wants to know how many horsehair sofas there are in Brixton, the number of pins that would reach from London Bridge to Waterloo. You tell him, and he takes you into partnership. Later you become a millionaire. But I haven't thanked you for the cocoa. It was fine.'

He waited for the retort, but it did not come. A pleased wonderment filled him. Could these things really be thus?

'And it isn't only what he says,' she went on. 'I know what you mean about him now. It's his accusing manner.'

'I've tried to analyse that manner. I believe it's the spectacles.'

'It's frightful when he looks at you; you think of all the wrong things you have ever done or ever wanted to do.'

'Does he have that effect on you?' he said, excitedly. 'Why, that exactly describes what I feel.'

The affinities looked at one another.

She was the first to speak.

'We always did think alike on most things, didn't we?' she said.

'Of course we did.'

He shifted his chair forward.

'It was all my fault,' he said. 'I mean, what happened.'

'It wasn't. It—'

'Yes, it was. I want to tell you something. I don't know if it will make any difference now, but I should like you to know it. It's this. I've altered a good deal since I came to London. For the better, I think. I'm a pretty poor sort of specimen still, but at least I don't imagine I can measure life with a foot-rule. I don't judge the world any longer by the standards of a country town. London has knocked some of the corners off me. I don't think you would find me the Bean type any longer. I don't disapprove of other people much now. Not as a habit. I find I have enough to do keeping myself up to the mark.'

'I want to tell you something, too,' she said. 'I expect it's too late, but never mind. I want you to hear it. I've altered, too, since I came to London. I used to think the Universe had been invented just to look on and wave its hat while I did great things. London has put a large piece of cold ice against my head, and the swelling has gone down. I'm not the girl with ambitions any longer. I just want to keep employed, and not have too bad a time when the day's work is over.'

He came across to where she sat.

'We said we would meet as strangers, and we do. We never have known each other. Don't you think we had better get acquainted?' he said.

There was a respectful tap at the door.

'Come in?' snapped Mr Ferguson. 'Well?' Behind the gold-rimmed spectacles of Master Bean there shone a softer look than usual, a look rather complacent than disapproving.

'I must apologize, sir, for intruding upon you. I am no longer in your employment, but I do hope that in the circumstances you will forgive my entering your private office. Thinking over our situation just now an idea came to me by means of which I fancy we might be enabled to leave the building.'

'What!'

'It occurred to me, sir, that by telephoning to the nearest police-station—'

'Good heavens!' cried Mr Ferguson.

Two minutes later he replaced the receiver.

'It's all right,' he said. 'I've made them understand the trouble. They're bringing a ladder. I wonder what the time is? It must be about four in the morning.'

Master Bean produced a Waterbury watch.

'The time, sir, is almost exactly half past ten.'

'Half past ten! We must have been here longer than three hours. Your watch is wrong.'

'No, sir, I am very careful to keep it exactly right. I do not wish to run any risk of being unpunctual.'

'Half past ten!' cried Mr Ferguson. 'Why, we're in heaps of time to look in at the Savoy for supper. This is great. I'll phone them to keep a table.'

'Supper! I thought—'

She stopped.

'What's that? Thought what?'

'Hadn't you an engagement for supper?'

He stared at her.

'Whatever gave you that idea? Of course not.'

'I thought you said you were taking Miss Templeton—'

'Miss Temp—Oh!' His face cleared. 'Oh, there isn't such a person. I invented her. I had to when you accused me of being like our friend the Miasma. Legitimate self-defence.'

'I do not wish to interrupt you, sir, when you are busy,' said Master Bean, 'but—'

'Come and see me tomorrow morning,' said Mr Ferguson.

'Bob,' said the girl, as the first threatening mutters from the orchestra heralded an imminent storm of melody, 'when that boy comes tomorrow, what are going to do?'

'Call up the police.'

'No, but you must do something. We shouldn't have been here if it hadn't been for him.'

'That's true!' He pondered. 'I've got it; I'll get him a job with Raikes and Courtenay.'

'Why Raikes and Courtenay?'

'Because I have a pull with them. But principally,' said Mr Ferguson, with a devilish grin, 'because they live in Edinburgh, which, as you are doubtless aware, is a long, long way from London.'

He bent across the table.

'Isn't this like old times?' he said. 'Do you remember the first time I ever ki—'

Just then the orchestra broke out.

THE GOOD ANGEL

Any man under thirty years of age who tells you he is not afraid of an English butler lies. He may not show his fear. Outwardly he may be brave—aggressive even, perhaps to the extent of calling the great man 'Here!' or 'Hi!' But, in his heart, when he meets that, cold, blue, introspective eye, he quakes.

The effect that Keggs, the butler at the Keiths', had on Martin Rossiter was to make him feel as if he had been caught laughing in a cathedral. He fought against the feeling. He asked himself who Keggs was, anyway; and replied defiantly that Keggs was a Menial—and an overfed Menial. But all the while he knew that logic was useless.

When the Keiths had invited him to their country home he had been delighted. They were among his oldest friends. He liked Mr Keith. He liked Mrs Keith. He loved Elsa Keith, and had done so from boyhood.

But things had gone wrong. As he leaned out of his bedroom window at the end of the first week, preparatory to dressing for dinner, he was more than half inclined to make some excuse and get right out of the place next day. The bland dignity of Keggs had taken all the heart out of him.

Nor was it Keggs alone who had driven his thoughts towards flight. Keggs was merely a passive evil, like toothache or a rainy day. What had begun actively to make the place impossible was a perfectly pestilential young man of the name of Barstowe.

The house-party at the Keiths had originally been, from Martin's view-point, almost ideal. The rest of the men were of the speechless, moustache-tugging breed. They had come to shoot, and they shot. When they were not shooting they congregated in the billiard-room and devoted their powerful intellects exclusively to snooker-pool, leaving Martin free to talk undisturbed to Elsa. He had been doing this for five days with great contentment when Aubrey Barstowe arrived. Mrs Keith had developed of late leanings towards culture. In her town house a charge of small-shot, fired in any direction on a Thursday afternoon, could not have failed to bring down a poet, a novelist, or a painter. Aubrey Barstowe, author of *The Soul's Eclipse* and other poems, was a constant member of the crowd. A youth of insinuating manners, he had appealed to Mrs Keith from the start; and unfortunately the virus had extended to Elsa. Many a pleasant, sunshiny Thursday afternoon had been poisoned for Martin by the sight of Aubrey and Elsa together on a distant settee, matching temperaments. The rest is too painful. It was a rout. The poet did not shoot, so that when Martin returned of an evening his rival was about five hours of soul-to-soul talk up and only two to play. And those two, the after-dinner hours, which had once been the hours for which Martin had lived, were pure torture.

So engrossed was he with his thoughts that the first intimation he had that he was not alone in the room was a genteel cough. Behind him, holding a small can, was Keggs.

'Your 'ot water, sir,' said the butler, austerely but not unkindly.

Keggs was a man—one must use that word, though it seems grossly inadequate—of medium height, pigeon-toed at the base, bulgy half-way up, and bald at the apex. His manner was restrained and dignified, his voice soft and grave.

But it was his eye that quelled Martin. That cold, blue, dukes-have-treated-me-as-an-elder-brother eye.

He fixed it upon him now, as he added, placing the can on the floor. 'It is Frederick's duty, but tonight I hundertook it.'

Martin had no answer. He was dazed. Keggs had spoken with the proud humility of an emperor compelled by misfortune to shine shoes.

'Might I have a word with you, sir?'

'Ye-e-ss, yes,' stammered Martin. 'Won't you take a—I mean, yes, certainly.'

'It is perhaps a liberty,' began Keggs. He paused, and raked Martin with the eye that had rested on dining dukes.

'Not at all,' said Martin, hurriedly.

'I should like,' went on Keggs, bowing, 'to speak to you on a somewhat intimate subject—Miss Elsa.'

Martin's eyes and mouth opened slowly.

'You are going the wrong way to work, if you will allow me to say so, sir.'

Martin's jaw dropped another inch.

'Wha-a—'

'Women, sir,' proceeded Keggs, 'young ladies—are peculiar. I have had, if I may say so, certain hopportunities of observing their ways. Miss Elsa reminds me in some respects of Lady Angelica Fendall, whom I had the honour of knowing when I was butler to her father, Lord Stockleigh. Her ladyship was hinclined to be romantic. She was fond of poetry, like Miss Elsa. She would sit by the hour, sir, listening to young Mr Knox reading Tennyson, which was no part of his duties, he being employed by his lordship to teach Lord Bertie Latin and Greek and what not. You may have noticed, sir, that young ladies is often took by Tennyson, hespecially in the summertime. Mr Barstowe was reading Tennyson to Miss Elsa in the 'all when I passed through just now. *The Princess*, if I am not mistaken.'

'I don't know what the thing was,' groaned Martin. 'She seemed to be enjoying it.'

'Lady Angelica was greatly addicted to *The Princess*. Young Mr Knox was reading portions of that poem to her when his lordship come upon them. Most rashly his lordship made a public hexpose and packed Mr Knox off next day. It was not my place to volunteer advice, but I could have told him what would happen. Two days later her ladyship slips away to London early in the morning, and they're married at a registry-office. That is why I say that you are going the wrong way to work with Miss Elsa, sir. With certain types of 'igh spirited young lady hopposition is useless. Now, when Mr Barstowe was reading to Miss Elsa on the occasion to which I 'ave alluded, you were sitting by, trying to engage her attention. It's not the way, sir. You should leave them alone together. Let her see so much of him, and nobody else but him, that she will grow tired of him. Fondness for poetry, sir, is very much like the whisky 'abit. You can't cure a man what has got that by hopposition. Now, if you will permit me to offer a word of advice, sir, I say, let Miss Elsa 'ave all the poetry she wants.'

Martin was conscious of one coherent feeling at the conclusion of this address, and that was one of amazed gratitude. A lesser man who had entered his room and begun to discuss his private affairs would have had reason to retire with some speed; but that Keggs should descend from his pedestal and interest himself in such lowly matters was a different thing altogether.

'I'm very much obliged—' he was stammering, when the butler raised a deprecatory hand.

'My interest in the matter,' he said, smoothly, 'is not entirely haltruistic. For some years back, in fact, since Miss Elsa came out, we have had a matrimonial sweepstake in the servants' hall at each house-party. The names of the gentlemen in the party are placed in a hat and drawn in due course. Should Miss Elsa become engaged to any member of the party, the pool goes to the drawer of his name. Should no engagement occur, the money remains in my charge until the following year, when it is added to the new pool. Hitherto I have 'ad the misfortune to draw nothing but married gentlemen, but on this occasion I have secured you, sir. And I may tell you, sir,' he added, with stately courtesy, 'that, in the opinion of the servants' hall, your chances are 'ighly fancied,—very 'ighly. The pool has now reached considerable proportions and, 'aving had certain losses on the Turf very recent, I am extremely anxious to win it. So I thought, if I might take the liberty, sir, I would place my knowledge of the sex at your disposal. You will find it sound in every respect. That is all. Thank you, sir.'

Martin's feelings had undergone a complete revulsion. In the last few minutes the butler had shed his wings and grown horns, cloven feet, and a forked tail. His rage deprived him of words. He could only gurgle.

'Don't thank me, sir,' said the butler, indulgently. 'I ask no thanks. We are working together for a common hobject, and any little 'elp I can provide is given freely.'

'You old scoundrel!' shouted Martin, his wrath prevailing even against that blue eye. 'You have the insolence to come to me and—'

He stopped. The thought of these hounds, these demons, coolly gossiping and speculating below stairs about Elsa, making her the subject of little sporting flutters to relieve the monotony of country life, choked him.

'I shall tell Mr Keith,' he said.

The butler shook his bald head gravely.

'I shouldn't, sir. It is a 'ighly fantastic story, and I don't think he would believe it.'

'Then I'll—Oh, get out!'

Keggs bowed deferentially.

'If you wish it, sir,' he said, 'I will withdraw. If I may make the suggestion, sir, I think you should commence to dress. Dinner will be served in a few minutes. Thank you, sir.'

He passed softly out of the room.

It was more as a demonstration of defiance against Keggs than because he really hoped that anything would come of it that Martin approached Elsa next morning after breakfast. Elsa was strolling on the terrace in front of the house with the bard, but Martin broke in on the conference with the dogged determination of a steam-drill.

'Coming out with the guns today, Elsa?' he said.

She raised her eyes. There was an absent look in them.

'The guns?' she said. 'Oh, no; I hate watching men shoot.'

'You used to like it.'

'I used to like dolls,' she said, impatiently.

Mr Barstowe gave tongue. He was a slim, tall, sickeningly beautiful young man, with large, dark eyes, full of expression.

'We develop,' he said. 'The years go by, and we develop. Our souls expand—timidly at first, like little, half-fledged birds stealing out from the—'

'I don't know that I'm so set on shooting today, myself,' said Martin. 'Will you come round the links?'

'I am going out in the motor with Mr Barstowe,' said Elsa.

'The motor!' cried Mr Barstowe. 'Ah, Rossiter, that is the very poetry of motion. I never ride in a motor-car without those words of Shakespeare's ringing in my mind: "I'll put a girdle round about the earth in forty minutes."'

'I shouldn't give way to that sort of thing if I were you,' said Martin. 'The police are pretty down on road-hogging in these parts.'

'Mr Barstowe was speaking figuratively,' said Elsa, with disdain.

'Was he?' grunted Martin, whose sorrows were tending to make him every day more like a sulky schoolboy. 'I'm afraid I haven't got a poetic soul.'

'I'm afraid you haven't,' said Elsa.

There was a brief silence. A bird made itself heard in a neighbouring tree.

'"The moan of doves in immemorial elms,"' quoted Mr Barstowe, softly.

'Only it happens to be a crow in a beech,' said Martin, as the bird flew out.

Elsa's chin tilted itself in scorn. Martin turned on his heel and walked away.

'It's the wrong way, sir; it's the wrong way,' said a voice. 'I was hobserving you from a window, sir. It's Lady Angelica over again. Hopposition is useless, believe me, sir.'

Martin faced round, flushed and wrathful. The butler went on unmoved: 'Miss Elsa is going for a ride in the car today, sir.'

'I know that.'

'Uncommonly tricky things, these motor-cars. I was saying so to Roberts, the chauffeur, just as soon as I 'eard Miss Elsa was going out with Mr Barstowe. I said, "Roberts, these cars is tricky; break down when you're twenty miles from hanywhere as soon as look at you. Roberts," I said, slipping him a sovereign, "'ow awful it would be if the car should break down twenty miles from hanywhere today!"'

Martin stared.

'You bribed Roberts to—'

'Sir! I gave Roberts the sovereign because I am sorry for him. He is a poor man, and has a wife and family to support.'

'Very well,' said Martin, sternly; 'I shall go and warn Miss Keith.'

'Warn her, sir!'

'I shall tell her that you have bribed Roberts to make the car break down so that—'

Keggs shook his head.

'I fear she would hardly credit the statement, sir. She might even think that you was trying to keep her from going for your own pussonal ends.'

'I believe you are the devil,' said Martin.

'I 'ope you will come to look on me, sir,' said Keggs, unctuously, 'as your good hangel.'

Martin shot abominably that day, and, coming home in the evening gloomy and savage, went straight to his room, and did not reappear till dinner-time. Elsa had been taken in by one of the moustache-tuggers. Martin found himself seated on her other side. It was so pleasant to be near her, and to feel that the bard was away at the other end of the table, that for the moment his spirits revived.

'Well, how did you like the ride?' he asked, with a smile. 'Did you put that girdle round the world?'

She looked at him—once. The next moment he had an uninterrupted view of her shoulder, and heard the sound of her voice as she prattled gaily to the man on her other side.

His heart gave a sudden bound. He understood now. The demon butler had had his wicked way. Good heavens! She had thought he was taunting her! He must explain at once. He—

'Hock or sherry, sir?'

He looked up into Kegg's expressionless eyes. The butler was wearing his on-duty mask. There was no sign of triumph in his face.

'Oh, sherry. I mean hock. No, sherry. Neither.'

This was awful. He must put this right.

'Elsa,' he said.

She was engrossed in her conversation with her neighbour.

From down the table in a sudden lull in the talk came the voice of Mr Barstowe. He seemed to be in the middle of a narrative.

'Fortunately,' he was saying, 'I had with me a volume of Shelley, and one of my own little efforts. I had read Miss Keith the whole of the latter and much of the former before the chauffeur announced that it was once more possible—'

'Elsa,' said the wretched man, 'I had no idea—you don't think—'

She turned to him.

'I beg your pardon?' she said, very sweetly.

'I swear I didn't know—I mean, I'd forgotten—I mean—'

She wrinkled her forehead.

'I'm really afraid I don't understand.'

'I mean, about the car breaking down.'

'The car? Oh, yes. Yes, it broke down. We were delayed quite a little while. Mr Barstowe read me some of his poems. It was perfectly lovely. I was quite sorry when Roberts told us we could go on again. But do you really mean to tell me, Mr Lambert, that you—'

And once more the world became all shoulder.

When the men trailed into the presence of the ladies for that brief seance on which etiquette insisted before permitting the stampede to the billiard-room, Elsa was not to be seen.

'Elsa?' said Mrs Keith in answer to Martin's question. 'She has gone to bed. The poor child has a headache. I am afraid she had a tiring day.'

There was an early start for the guns next morning, and as Elsa did not appear at breakfast Martin had to leave without seeing her. His shooting was even worse than it had been on the previous day.

It was not until late in the evening that the party returned to the house. Martin, on the way to his room, met Mrs Keith on the stairs. She appeared somewhat agitated.

'Oh, Martin,' she said. 'I'm so glad you're back. Have you seen anything of Elsa?'

'Elsa?'

'Wasn't she with the guns?'

'With the guns' said Martin, puzzled. 'No.'

'I have seen nothing of her all day. I'm getting worried. I can't think what can have happened to her. Are you sure she wasn't with the guns?'

'Absolutely certain. Didn't she come in to lunch?'

'No. Tom,' she said, as Mr Keith came up, 'I'm so worried about Elsa. I haven't seen her all day. I thought she must be out with the guns.'

Mr Keith was a man who had built up a large fortune mainly by consistently refusing to allow anything to agitate him. He carried this policy into private life.

'Wasn't she in at lunch?' he asked, placidly.

'I tell you I haven't seen her all day. She breakfasted in her room—'

'Late?'

'Yes. She was tired, poor girl.'

'If she breakfasted late,' said Mr Keith, 'she wouldn't need any lunch. She's gone for a stroll somewhere.'

'Would you put back dinner, do you think?' inquired Mrs Keith, anxiously.

'I am not good at riddles,' said Mr Keith, comfortably, 'but I can answer that one. I would not put back dinner. I would not put back dinner for the King.'

Elsa did not come back for dinner. Nor was hers the only vacant place. Mr Barstowe had also vanished. Even Mr Keith's calm was momentarily ruffled by this discovery. The poet was not a favourite of his—it was only reluctantly that he had consented to his being invited at all; and the presumption being that when two members of a house-party disappear simultaneously they are likely to be spending the time in each other's society, he was annoyed. Elsa was not the girl to make a fool of herself, of course, but—He was unwontedly silent at dinner.

Mrs Keith's anxiety displayed itself differently. She was frankly worried, and mentioned it. By the time the fish had been reached conversation at the table had fixed itself definitely on the one topic.

'It isn't the car this time, at any rate,' said Mr Keith. 'It hasn't been out today.'

'I can't understand it,' said Mrs Keith for the twentieth time. And that was the farthest point reached in the investigation of the mystery.

By the time dinner was over a spirit of unrest was abroad. The company sat about in uneasy groups. Snooker-pool was, if not forgotten, at any rate shelved. Somebody suggested search-parties, and one or two of the moustache-tuggers wandered rather aimlessly out into the darkness.

Martin was standing in the porch with Mr Keith when Keggs approached. As his eyes lit on him, Martin was conscious of a sudden solidifying of the vague suspicion which had been forming in his mind. And yet that suspicion seemed so wild. How could Keggs, with the worst intentions, have had anything to do with this? He could not forcibly have abducted the missing pair and kept them under lock and key. He could not have stunned them and left them in a ditch. Nevertheless, looking at him standing there in his attitude of deferential dignity, with the light from the open door shining on his bald head, Martin felt perfectly certain that he had in some mysterious fashion engineered the whole thing.

'Might I have a word, sir, if you are at leisure?'

'Well, Keggs?'

'Miss Elsa, sir.'

'Yes?'

Kegg's voice took on a sympathetic softness.

'It was not my place, sir, to make any remark while in the dining-room, but I could not 'elp but hoverhear the conversation. I gathered from remarks that was passed that you was somewhat hat a loss to account for Miss Elsa's non-appearance, sir.'

Mr Keith laughed shortly.

'You gathered that, eh?'

Keggs bowed.

'I think, sir, that possibly I may be hable to throw light on the matter.'

'What!' cried Mr Keith. 'Great Scott, man! then why didn't you say so at the time? Where is she?'

'It was not my place, sir, to henter into the conversation of the dinner-table,' said the butler, with a touch of reproof. 'If I might speak now, sir?'

Mr Keith clutched at his forehead.

'Heavens above! Do you want a signed permit to tell me where my daughter is? Get on, man, get on!'

'I think it 'ighly possible, sir, that Miss Elsa and Mr Barstowe may be on the hisland in the lake, sir.' About half a mile from the house was a picturesque strip of water, some fifteen hundred yards in width and a little less in length, in the centre of which stood a small and densely wooded island. It was a favourite haunt of visitors at the house when there was nothing else to engage their attention, but during the past week, with shooting to fill up the days, it had been neglected.

'On the island?' said Mr Keith. 'What put that idea into your head?'

'I 'appened to be rowing on the lake this morning, sir. I frequently row of a morning, sir, when there are no duties to detain me in the 'ouse. I find the hexercise hadmirable for the 'ealth. I walk briskly to the boat-'ouse, and—'

'Yes, yes. I don't want a schedule of your daily exercises. Cut out the athletic reminiscences and come to the point.'

'As I was rowing on the lake this morning, sir, I 'appened to see a boat 'itched up to a tree on the hisland. I think that possibly Miss Elsa and Mr Barstowe might 'ave taken a row out there. Mr Barstowe would wish to see the hisland, sir, bein' romantic.'

'But you say you saw the boat there this morning?'

'Yes, sir.'

'Well, it doesn't take all day to explore a small island. What's kept them all this while?'

'It is possible, sir, that the rope might not have 'eld. Mr Barstowe, if I might say so, sir, is one of those himpetuous literary pussons, and possibly he homitted to see that the knot was hadequately tied. Or'—his eye, grave and inscrutable, rested for a moment on Martin's—'some party might 'ave come along and huntied it a-puppus.'

'Untied it on purpose?' said Mr Keith. 'What on earth for?'

Keggs shook his head deprecatingly, as one who, realizing his limitations, declines to attempt to probe the hidden sources of human actions.

'I thought it right, sir, to let you know,' he said.

'Right? I should say so. If Elsa has been kept starving all day on that island by that long-haired—Here, come along, Martin.'

He dashed off excitedly into the night. Martin remained for a moment gazing fixedly at the butler.

'I 'ope, sir,' said Keggs, cordially, 'that my hinformation will prove of genuine hassistance.'

'Do you know what I should like to do to you?' said Martin slowly.

'I think I 'ear Mr Keith calling you, sir.'

'I should like to take you by the scruff of your neck and—'

'There, sir! Didn't you 'ear 'im then? Quite distinct it was.'

Martin gave up the struggle with a sense of blank futility. What could you do with a man like this? It was like quarrelling with Westminster Abbey.

'I should 'urry, sir,' suggested Keggs, respectfully. 'I think Mr Keith must have met with some haccident.'

His surmise proved correct. When Martin came up he found his host seated on the ground in evident pain.

'Twisted my ankle in a hole,' he explained, briefly. 'Give me an arm back to the house, there's a good fellow, and then run on down to the lake and see if what Keggs said is true.'

Martin did as he was requested—so far, that is to say, as the first half of the commission was concerned. As regarded the second, he took it upon himself to make certain changes. Having seen Mr Keith to his room, he put the fitting-out of the relief ship into the good hands of a group of his fellow guests whom he discovered in the porch. Elsa's feelings towards her rescuer might be one of unmixed gratitude; but it might, on the other hand, be one of resentment. He did not wish her to connect him in her mind with the episode in any way whatsoever. Martin had once released a dog from a trap, and the dog had bitten him. He had been on an errand of mercy, but the dog had connected him with his sufferings and acted accordingly. It occurred to Martin that Elsa's frame of mind would be uncommonly like that dog's.

The rescue-party set off. Martin lit a cigarette, and waited in the porch.

It seemed a very long time before anything happened, but at last, as he was lighting his fifth cigarette, there came from the darkness the sound of voices. They drew nearer. Someone shouted:

'It's all right. We've found them.'

Martin threw away his cigarette and went indoors.

Elsa Keith sat up as her mother came into the room. Two nights and a day had passed since she had taken to her bed.

'How are you feeling today, dear?'

'Has he gone, mother?'

'Who?'

'Mr Barstowe?'

'Yes, dear. He left this morning. He said he had business with his publisher in London.'

'Then I can get up,' said Elsa, thankfully.

'I think you're a little hard on poor Mr Barstowe, Elsa. It was just an accident, you know. It was not his fault that the boat slipped away.'

'It was, it was, it *was*!' cried Elsa, thumping the pillow malignantly. 'I believe he did it on purpose, so that he could read me his horrid poetry without my having a chance to escape. I believe that's the only way he can get people to listen to it.'

'But you used to like it, darling. You said he had such a musical voice.'

'Musical voice!' The pillow became a shapeless heap. 'Mother, it was like a nightmare! If I had seen him again I should have had hysterics. It was *awful!* If he had been even the least bit upset himself I think I could have borne up. But he *enjoyed* it! He *revelled* in it! He said it was like Omar Khayyam in the Wilderness and Shelley's *Epipsychidion*, whatever that is; and he prattled on and on and read and read till my head began to split. Mother'—her voice sank to a whisper—'I hit him!'

'Elsa!'

'I did!' she went on, defiantly. 'I hit him as hard as I could, and he—he'—she broke off into a little gurgle of laughter—'he tripped over a bush and fell right down; and I wasn't a bit ashamed. I didn't think it unladylike or anything. I was just as proud as I could be. And it stopped him talking.'

'But, Elsa, *dear!* Why?'

'The sun had just gone down; and it was a lovely sunset, and the sky looked like a great, beautiful slice of underdone beef; and I said so to him, and he said, sniffily, that he was afraid he didn't see the resemblance. And I asked him if he wasn't starving. And he said no, because as a rule all that he needed was a little ripe fruit. And that was when I hit him.'

'Elsa!'

'Oh, I know it was awfully wrong, but I just had to. And now I'll get up. It looks lovely out.'

Martin had not gone out with the guns that day. Mrs Keith had assured him that there was nothing wrong with Elsa, that she was only tired, but he was anxious, and had remained at home, where bulletins could reach him. As he was returning from a stroll in the grounds he heard his name called, and saw Elsa lying in the hammock under the trees near the terrace.

'Why, Martin, why aren't you out with the guns?' she said.

'I wanted to be on the spot so that I could hear how you were.'

'How nice of you! Why don't you sit down?'

'May I?'

Elsa fluttered the pages of her magazine.

'You know, you're a very restful person, Martin. You're so big and outdoory. How would you like to read to me for a while? I feel so lazy.'

Martin took the magazine.

'What shall I read? Here's a poem by—'

Elsa shuddered.

'Oh, please, no,' she cried. 'I couldn't bear it. I'll tell you what I should love— the advertisements. There's one about sardines. I started it, and it seemed splendid. It's at the back somewhere.'

'Is this it—Langley and Fielding's sardines?'

'That's it.'

Martin began to read.

'"Langley and Fielding's sardines. When you want the daintiest, most delicious sardines, go to your grocer and say, 'Langley and Fielding's, please!' You will then be sure of having the finest Norwegian smoked sardines, packed in the purest olive oil."'

Elsa was sitting with her eyes closed and a soft smile of pleasure curving her mouth.

'Go on,' she said, dreamily.

'"Nothing nicer."' resumed Martin, with an added touch of eloquence as the theme began to develop, '"for breakfast, lunch, or supper. Probably your grocer stocks them. Ask him. If he does not, write to us. Price fivepence per tin. The best sardines and the best oil!"'

'Isn't it *lovely*?' she murmured.

Her hand, as it swung, touched his. He held it. She opened her eyes.

'Don't stop reading,' she said. 'I never heard anything so soothing.'

'Elsa!'

He bent towards her. She smiled at him. Her eyes were dancing.

'Elsa, I—'

'Mr Keith,' said a quiet voice, 'desired me to say—'

Martin started away. He glared up furiously. Gazing down upon them stood Keggs. The butler's face was shining with a gentle benevolence.

'Mr Keith desired me to say that he would be glad if Miss Elsa would come and sit with him for a while.'

'I'll come at once,' said Elsa, stepping from the hammock.

The butler bowed respectfully and turned away. They stood watching him as he moved across the terrace.

'What a saintly old man Keggs looks,' said Elsa. 'Don't you think so? He looks as if he had never even thought of doing anything he shouldn't. I wonder if he ever has?'

'I wonder!' said Martin.

'He looks like a stout angel. What were you saying, Martin, when he came up?'

POTS O'MONEY

Owen Bentley was feeling embarrassed. He looked at Mr Sheppherd, and with difficulty restrained himself from standing on one leg and twiddling his fingers. At one period of his career, before the influence of his uncle Henry had placed him in the London and Suburban Bank, Owen had been an actor. On the strength of a batting average of thirty-three point nought seven for Middlesex, he had been engaged by the astute musical-comedy impresario to whom the idea first occurred that, if you have got to have young men to chant 'We are merry and gay, tra-la, for this is Bohemia,' in the Artists' Ball scene, you might just as well have young men whose names are known to the public. He had not been an actor long, for loss of form had put him out of first-class cricket, and the impresario had given his place in the next piece to a googly bowler who had done well in the last Varsity match; but he had been one long enough to experience that sinking sensation which is known as stage-fright. And now, as he began to explain to Mr Sheppherd that he wished for his consent to marry his daughter Audrey, he found himself suffering exactly the same symptoms.

From the very start, from the moment when he revealed the fact that his income, salary and private means included, amounted to less than two hundred pounds, he had realized that this was going to be one of his failures. It was the gruesome Early Victorianness of it all that took the heart out of him. Mr Sheppherd had always reminded him of a heavy father out of a three-volume novel, but, compared with his demeanour as he listened now, his attitude hitherto had been light and whimsical. Until this moment Owen had not imagined that this sort of thing ever happened nowadays outside the comic papers. By the end of the second minute he would not have been surprised to find himself sailing through the air, urged by Mr Sheppherd's boot, his transit indicated by a dotted line and a few stars.

Mr Sheppherd's manner was inclined to bleakness.

'This is most unfortunate,' he said. 'Most unfortunate. I have my daughter's happiness to consider. It is my duty as a father.' He paused. 'You say you have no prospects? I should have supposed that your uncle—? Surely, with his influence—?'

'My uncle shot his bolt when he got me into the bank. That finished him, as far as I'm concerned. I'm not his only nephew, you know. There are about a hundred others, all trailing him like bloodhounds.'

Mr Sheppherd coughed the small cough of disapproval. He was feeling more than a little aggrieved.

He had met Owen for the first time at dinner at the house of his uncle Henry, a man of unquestioned substance, whose habit it was to invite each of his eleven nephews to dinner once a year. But Mr Sheppherd did not know this. For all he knew, Owen was in the habit of hobnobbing with the great man every night. He could not say exactly that it was sharp practice on Owen's part to accept his invitation to call, and, having called, to continue calling long enough to make the present deplorable situation possible; but he felt that it would have been in better taste for the young man to have effaced himself and behaved more like a bank-clerk and less like an heir.

'I am exceedingly sorry for this, Mr Bentley,' he said, 'but you will understand that I cannot—It is, of course, out of the question. It would be best, in the circumstances, I think, if you did not see my daughter again—'

'She's waiting in the passage outside,' said Owen, simply.

'—after today. Good-bye.'

Owen left the room. Audrey was hovering in the neighbourhood of the door. She came quickly up to him, and his spirits rose, as they always did, at the sight of her.

'Well?' she said.

He shook his head.

'No good,' he said.

Audrey considered the problem for a moment, and was rewarded with an idea.

'Shall I go in and cry?'

'It wouldn't be of any use.'

'Tell me what happened.'

'He said I mustn't see you again.'

'He didn't mean it.'

'He thinks he did.'

Audrey reflected.

'We shall simply have to keep writing, then. And we can talk on the telephone. That isn't seeing each other. Has your bank a telephone?'

'Yes. But—'

'That's all right, then. I'll ring you up every day.'

'I wish I could make some money,' said Owen, thoughtfully. 'But I seem to be one of those chaps who can't. Nothing I try comes off. I've never drawn anything except a blank in a sweep. I spent about two pounds on sixpenny postal orders when the Limerick craze was on, and didn't win a thing. Once when I was on tour I worked myself to a shadow, dramatizing a novel. Nothing came of that, either.'

'What novel?'

'A thing called *White Roses,* by a woman named Edith Butler.'

Audrey looked up quickly.

'I suppose you knew her very well? Were you great friends?'

'I didn't know her at all. I'd never met her. I just happened to buy the thing at a bookstall, and thought it would make a good play. I expect it was pretty bad rot. Anyhow, she never took the trouble to send it back or even to acknowledge receipt.'

'Perhaps she never got it?'

'I registered it.'

'She was a cat,' said Audrey, decidedly. 'I'm glad of it, though. If another woman had helped you make a lot of money, I should have died of jealousy.'

Routine is death to heroism. For the first few days after his parting with Mr Sheppherd, Owen was in heroic mood, full of vaguely dashing schemes, regarding the world as his oyster, and burning to get at it, sword in hand. But routine, with its ledgers and its copying-ink and its customers, fell like a grey cloud athwart his horizon, blotting out rainbow visions of sudden wealth, dramatically won. Day by day the glow faded and hopelessness grew.

If the glow did not entirely fade it was due to Audrey, who more than fulfilled her promise of ringing him up on the telephone. She rang him up at least once, frequently several times, every day, a fact which was noted and commented upon in a harshly critical spirit by the head of his department, a man with no soul and a strong objection to doing his subordinates' work for them.

As a rule, her conversation, though pleasing, was discursive and lacked central motive, but one morning she had genuine news to impart.

'Owen'—her voice was excited—'have you seen the paper today? Then listen. I'll read it out. Are you listening? This is what it says: "The Piccadilly Theatre will reopen shortly with a dramatized version of Miss Edith Butler's popular novel, *White Roses*, prepared by the authoress herself. A strong cast is being engaged, including—" And then a lot of names. What are you going to do about it, Owen?'

'What am I going to do?'

'Don't you see what's happened? That awful woman has stolen your play. She has waited all these years, hoping you would forget. What are you laughing at?'

'I wasn't laughing.'

'Yes, you were. It tickled my ear. I'll ring off if you do it again. You don't believe me. Well, you wait and see if I'm not—'

'Edith Butler's incapable of such a thing.'

There was a slight pause at the other end of the wire.

'I thought you said you didn't know her,' said Audrey, jealously.

'I don't—I don't,' said Owen, hastily. 'But I've read her books. They're simply chunks of superfatted sentiment. She's a sort of literary onion. She compels tears. A woman like that couldn't steal a play if she tried.'

'You can't judge authors from their books. You must go and see the play when it comes on. Then you'll see I'm right. I'm absolutely certain that woman is trying to swindle you. Don't laugh in that horrid way. Very well, I told you I should ring off, and now I'm going to.'

At the beginning of the next month Owen's annual holiday arrived. The authorities of the London and Suburban Bank were no niggards. They recognized that a man is not a machine. They gave their employees ten days in the year in which to tone up their systems for another twelve months' work.

Owen spent his boyhood in the Shropshire village of which his father had been rector, and thither he went when his holiday came round, to the farm of one Dorman. He was glad of the chance to get to Shropshire. There is something about the country there, with its green fields and miniature rivers, that soothes the wounded spirit and forms a pleasant background for sentimental musings.

It was comfortable at the farm. The household consisted of Mr Dorman, an old acquaintance, his ten-year-old son George, and Mr Dorman's mother, an aged lady with a considerable local reputation as a wise woman. Rumour had it that the future held no mysteries for her, and it was known that she could cure warts, bruised fingers, and even the botts by means of spells.

Except for these, Owen had fancied that he was alone in the house. It seemed not, however. There was a primeval piano in his sitting-room, and on the second morning it suited his mood to sit down at this and sing 'Asthore', the fruity pathos of which ballad appealed to him strongly at this time, accompanying himself by an ingenious arrangement in three chords. He had hardly begun, however, when Mr Dorman appeared, somewhat agitated.

'If you don't mind, Mr Owen,' he said. 'I forgot to tell you. There's a lit'ery gent boarding with me in the room above, and he can't bear to be disturbed.'

A muffled stamping from the ceiling bore out his words.

'Writing a book he is,' continued Mr Dorman. 'He caught young George a clip over the ear-'ole yesterday for blowing his trumpet on the stairs. Gave him sixpence afterwards, and said he'd skin him if he ever did it again. So, if you don't mind—'

'Oh, all right,' said Owen. 'Who is he?'

'Gentleman of the name of Prosser.'

Owen could not recollect having come across any work by anyone of that name; but he was not a wide reader; and, whether the man above was a celebrity or not, he was entitled to quiet.

'I never heard of him,' he said, 'but that's no reason why I should disturb him. Let him rip. I'll cut out the musical effects in future.'

The days passed smoothly by. The literary man remained invisible, though occasionally audible, tramping the floor in the frenzy of composition. Nor, until the last day of his visit, did Owen see old Mrs Dorman.

That she was not unaware of his presence in the house, however, was indicated on the last morning. He was smoking an after-breakfast pipe at the open window and waiting for the dog-cart that was to take him to the station, when George, the son of the house, entered.

George stood in the doorway, grinned, and said:

'Farsezjerligranmatellyerforchbythecards?'

'Eh?' said Owen.

The youth repeated the word.

'Once again.'

On the second repetition light began to creep in. A boyhood spent in the place, added to this ten days' stay, had made Owen something of a linguist.

'Father says would I like grandma to do what?'

'Tell yer forch'n by ther cards.'

'Where is she?'

'Backyarnder.'

Owen followed him into the kitchen, where he found Mr Dorman, the farmer, and, seated at the table, fumbling with a pack of cards, an old woman, whom he remembered well.

'Mother wants to tell your fortune,' said Mr Dorman, in a hoarse aside. 'She always will tell visitors' fortunes. She told Mr Prosser's, and he didn't half like it, because she said he'd be engaged in two months and married inside the year. He said wild horses wouldn't make him do it.'

'She can tell me that if she likes. I shan't object.'

'Mother, here's Mr Owen.'

'I seed him fast enough,' said the old woman, briskly. 'Shuffle, an' cut three times.'

She then performed mysterious manoeuvres with the cards.

'I see pots o' money,' announced the sibyl.

'If she says it, it's there right enough,' said her son.

'She means my bonus,' said Owen. 'But that's only ten pounds. And I lose it if I'm late twice more before Christmas.'

'It'll come sure enough.'

'Pots,' said the old woman, and she was still mumbling the encouraging word when Owen left the kitchen and returned to the sitting-room.

He laughed rather ruefully. At that moment he could have found a use for pots o' money.

He walked to the window, and looked out. It was a glorious morning. The heat-mist was dancing over the meadow beyond the brook, and from the farmyard came the liquid charawks of care-free fowls. It seemed wicked to leave these haunts of peace for London on such a day.

An acute melancholy seized him. Absently, he sat down at the piano. The prejudices of literary Mr Prosser had slipped from his mind. Softly at first, then gathering volume as the spirit of the song gripped him, he began to sing 'Asthore'. He became absorbed.

He had just, for the sixth time, won through to 'Iyam-ah waiting for-er theeee-yass-thorre,' and was doing some intricate three-chord work preparatory to starting over again, when a loaf of bread whizzed past his ear. It missed him by an inch, and crashed against a plaster statuette of the Infant Samuel on the top of the piano.

It was a standard loaf, containing eighty per cent of semolina, and it practically wiped the Infant Samuel out of existence. At the same moment, at his back, there sounded a loud, wrathful snort.

He spun round. The door was open, and at the other side of the table was standing a large, black-bearded, shirt-sleeved man, in an attitude rather reminiscent of Ajax defying the lightning. His hands trembled. His beard bristled. His eyes gleamed ferociously beneath enormous eyebrows. As Owen turned, he gave tongue in a voice like the discharge of a broadside.

'Stop it!'

Owen's mind, wrenched too suddenly from the dreamy future to the vivid present, was not yet completely under control. He gaped.

'Stop—that—infernal—noise!' roared the man.

He shot through the door, banging it after him, and pounded up the stairs.

Owen was annoyed. The artistic temperament was all very well, but there were limits. It was absurd that obscure authors should behave in this way. Prosser! Who on earth was Prosser? Had anyone ever heard of him? No! Yet here he was going about the country clipping small boys over the ear-hole, and flinging loaves of bread at bank-clerks as if he were Henry James or Marie Corelli. Owen reproached himself bitterly for his momentary loss of presence of mind. If he had only kept his head, he could have taken a flying shot at the man with the marmalade-pot. It had been within easy reach. Instead of which, he had merely stood and gaped. Of all sad words of tongue or pen, the saddest are these, 'It might have been.'

His manly regret was interrupted by the entrance of Mr Dorman with the information that the dog-cart was at the door.

Audrey was out of town when Owen arrived in London, but she returned a week later. The sound of her voice through the telephone did much to cure the restlessness from which he had been suffering since the conclusion of his holiday. But the thought that she was so near yet so inaccessible produced in him a meditative melancholy which enveloped him like a cloud that would not lift. His manner became distrait. He lost weight.

If customers were not vaguely pained by his sad, pale face, it was only because the fierce rush of modern commercial life leaves your business man little leisure for observing pallor in bank-clerks. What did pain them was the gentle dreaminess with which he performed his duties. He was in the Inward Bills Department, one of the features of which was the sudden inrush, towards the end of each afternoon, of hatless, energetic young men with leather bags strapped to their left arms, clamouring for mysterious crackling documents, much fastened with pins. Owen had never quite understood what it was that these young men did want, and now his detached mind refused even more emphatically to grapple with the problem. He distributed the documents at random with the air of a preoccupied monarch scattering largess to the mob, and the subsequent chaos had to be handled by a wrathful head of the department in person.

Man's power of endurance is limited. At the end of the second week the overwrought head appealed passionately for relief, and Owen was removed to the Postage Department, where, when he had leisure from answering Audrey's telephone calls, he entered the addresses of letters in a large book and took them to the post. He was supposed also to stamp them, but a man in love cannot think of everything, and he was apt at times to overlook this formality.

One morning, receiving from one of the bank messengers the usual intimation that a lady wished to speak to him on the telephone, he went to the box and took up the receiver.

'Is that you, Owen? Owen, I went to *White Roses* last night. Have you been yet?'

'Not yet.'

'Then you must go tonight. Owen, I'm *certain* you wrote it. It's perfectly lovely. I cried my eyes out. If you don't go tonight, I'll never speak to you again, even on the telephone. Promise.'

'Must I?'

'Yes, you must. Why, suppose it *is* yours! It may mean a fortune. The stalls were simply packed. I'm going to ring up the theatre now and engage a seat for you, and pay for it myself.'

'No—I say—' protested Owen.

'Yes, I shall. I can't trust you to go if I don't. And I'll ring up early tomorrow to hear all about it. Good-bye.'

Owen left the box somewhat depressed. Life was quite gloomy enough as it was, without going out of one's way to cry one's eyes out over sentimental plays.

His depression was increased by the receipt, on his return to his department, of a message from the manager, stating that he would like to see Mr Bentley in his private room for a moment. Owen never enjoyed these little chats with Authority. Out of office hours, in the circle of his friends, he had no doubt the manager was a delightful and entertaining companion; but in his private room his conversation was less enjoyable.

The manager was seated at his table, thoughtfully regarding the ceiling. His resemblance to a stuffed trout, always striking, was subtly accentuated, and Owen, an expert in these matters, felt that his fears had been well founded—there was trouble in the air. Somebody had been complaining of him, and he was now about, as the phrase went, to be 'run-in'.

A large man, seated with his back to the door, turned as he entered, and Owen recognized the well-remembered features of Mr Prosser, the literary loaf-slinger.

Owen regarded him without resentment. Since returning to London he had taken the trouble of looking up his name in *Who's Who* and had found that he was not so undistinguished as he had supposed. He was, it appeared, a Regius Professor and the author of some half-dozen works on sociology—a record, Owen felt, that almost justified loaf-slinging and earhole clipping in moments of irritation.

The manager started to speak, but the man of letters anticipated him.

'Is this the fool?' he roared. 'Young man, I have no wish to be hard on a congenital idiot who is not responsible for his actions, but I must insist on an explanation. I understand that you are in charge of the correspondence in this office. Well, during the last week you have three times sent unstamped letters to my fiancee, Miss Vera Delane, Woodlands, Southbourne, Hants. What's the matter with you? Do you think she likes paying twopence a time, or what is it?'

Owen's mind leaped back at the words. They recalled something to him. Then he remembered.

He was conscious of a not unpleasant thrill. He had not known that he was superstitious, but for some reason he had not been able to get those absurd words of Mr Dorman's mother out of his mind. And here was another prediction of hers, equally improbable, fulfilled to the letter.

'Great Scott!' he cried. 'Are you going to be married?'

Mr Prosser and the manager started simultaneously.

'Mrs Dorman said you would be,' said Owen. 'Don't you remember?'

Mr Prosser looked keenly at him.

'Why, I've seen you before,' he said. 'You're the young turnip-headed scallywag at the farm.'

'That's right,' said Owen.

'I've been wanting to meet you again. I thought the whole thing over, and it struck me,' said Mr Prosser, handsomely, 'that I may have seemed a little abrupt at our last meeting.'

'No, no.'

'The fact is, I was in the middle of an infernally difficult passage of my book that morning, and when you began—'

'It was my fault entirely. I quite understand.'

Mr Prosser produced a card-case.

'We must see more of each other,' he said. 'Come and have a bit of dinner some night. Come tonight.'

'I'm very sorry. I have to go to the theatre tonight.'

'Then come and have a bit of supper afterwards. Excellent. Meet me at the Savoy at eleven-fifteen. I'm glad I didn't hit you with that loaf. Abruptness has been my failing through life. My father was just the same. Eleven-fifteen at the Savoy, then.'

The manager, who had been listening with some restlessness to the conversation, now intervened. He was a man with a sense of fitness of things, and he objected to having his private room made the scene of what appeared to be a reunion of old college chums. He hinted as much.

'Ha! Prrumph!' he observed, disapprovingly. 'Er—Mr Bentley, that is all. You may return to your work—ah'mmm! Kindly be more careful another time in stamping the letters.'

'Yes, by Jove,' said Mr Prosser, suddenly reminded of his wrongs, 'that's right. Exercise a little ordinary care, you ivory-skulled young son of a gun. Do you think Miss Delane is *made* of twopences? Keep an eye on him,' he urged the manager. 'These young fellows nowadays want someone standing over them with a knout all the time. Be more careful another time, young man. Eleven-fifteen, remember. Make a note of it, or you'll go forgetting *that*.'

The seat Audrey had bought for him at the Piccadilly Theatre proved to be in the centre of the sixth row of stalls—practically a death-trap. Whatever his sufferings might be, escape was impossible. He was securely wedged in.

The cheaper parts of the house were sparsely occupied, but the stalls were full. Owen, disapproving of the whole business, refused to buy a programme, and settled himself in his seat prepared for the worst. He had a vivid recollection of *White Roses*, the novel, and he did not anticipate any keen enjoyment from it in its dramatized form. He had long ceased to be a, member of that large public for which Miss Edith Butler catered. The sentimental adventures of governesses in ducal houses—the heroine of *White Roses* was a governess—no longer contented his soul.

There is always a curiously dream-like atmosphere about a play founded on a book. One seems to have seen it all before. During the whole of the first act Owen attributed to this his feeling of familiarity with what was going on on the stage. At the beginning of the second act he found himself anticipating events. But it was not till the third act that the truth sank in.

The third was the only act in which, in his dramatization, he had taken any real liberties with the text of the novel. But in this act he had introduced a character who did not appear in the novel—a creature of his own imagination. And now, with bulging eyes, he observed this creature emerge from the wings, and heard him utter lines which he now clearly remembered having written.

Audrey had been right! Serpent Edith Butler had stolen his play.

His mind, during the remainder of the play, was active. By the time the final curtain fell and he passed out into the open air he had perceived some of the difficulties of the case. To prove oneself the author of an original play is hard, but not impossible. Friends to whom one had sketched the plot may come forward as witnesses. One may have preserved rough notes. But a dramatization of a novel is another matter. All dramatizations of any given novel must necessarily be very much alike.

He started to walk along Piccadilly, and had reached Hyde Park Corner before he recollected that he had an engagement to take supper with Mr Prosser at the Savoy Hotel. He hailed a cab.

'You're late,' boomed the author of sociological treatises, as he appeared. 'You're infernally late. I suppose, in your woollen-headed way, you forgot all about it. Come along. We'll just have time for an olive and a glass of something before they turn the lights out.'

Owen was still thinking deeply as he began his supper. Surely there was some way by which he could prove his claims. What had he done with the original manuscript? He remembered now. He had burnt it. It had seemed mere useless litter then. Probably, he felt bitterly, the woman Butler had counted on this.

Mr Prosser concluded an animated conversation with a waiter on the subject of the wines of France, leaned forward, and, having helped himself briskly to anchovies, began to talk. He talked loudly and rapidly. Owen, his thoughts far away, hardly listened.

Presently the waiter returned with the selected brand. He filled Owen's glass, and Owen drank, and felt better. Finding his glass magically full once more, he emptied it again. And then suddenly he found himself looking across the table at his Host, and feeling a sense of absolute conviction that this was the one man of all others whom he would have selected as a confidant. How kindly, though somewhat misty, his face was! How soothing, if a little indistinct, his voice!

'Prosser,' he said, 'you are a man of the world, and I should like your advice. What would you do in a case like this? I go to a theatre to see a play, and what do I find?'

He paused, and eyed his host impressively.

'What's that tune they're playing?' said Mr Prosser. 'You hear it everywhere. One of these Viennese things, I suppose.'

Owen was annoyed. He began to doubt whether, after all, Mr Prosser's virtues as a confidant were not more apparent than real.

'I find, by Jove,' he continued, 'that I wrote the thing myself.'

'It's not a patch on *The Merry Widow*,' said Mr Prosser.

Owen thumped the table.

'I tell you I find I wrote the thing myself.'

'What thing?'

'This play I'm telling you about. This *White Roses* thing.'

He found that he had at last got his host's ear. Mr Prosser seemed genuinely interested.

'What do you mean?'

Owen plunged on with his story. He started from its dim beginning, from the days when he had bought the novel on his journey from Bath to Cheltenham. He described his methods of work, his registering of the package, his suspense, his growing resignation. He sketched the progress of his life. He spoke of Audrey and gave a crisp character-sketch of Mr Sheppherd. He took his hearer right up to the moment when the truth had come home to him.

Towards the end of his narrative the lights went out, and he finished his story in the hotel courtyard. In the cool air he felt revived. The outlines of Mr Prosser became sharp and distinct again.

The sociologist listened admirably. He appeared absorbed, and did not interrupt once.

'What makes you so certain that this was your version?' he asked, as they passed into the Strand.

Owen told him of the creature of his imagination in Act III.

'But you have lost your manuscript?'

'Yes; I burnt it.'

'Just what one might have expected you to do,' said Mr Prosser, unkindly. 'Young man, I begin to believe that there may be something in this. You haven't got a ghost of a proof that would hold water in a court of law, of course; but still, I'm inclined to believe you. For one thing, you haven't the intelligence to invent such a story.'

Owen thanked him.

'In fact, if you can answer me one question I shall be satisfied.'

It seemed to Owen that Mr Prosser was tending to get a little above himself. As an intelligent listener he had been of service, but that appeared to be no reason why he should constitute himself a sort of judge and master of the ceremonies.

'That's very good of you,' he said; 'but will Edith Butler be satisfied? That's more to the point.'

'I *am* Edith Butler,' said Mr Prosser.

Owen stopped. 'You?'

'You need not babble it from the house-tops. You are the only person besides my agent who knows it, and I wouldn't have told you if I could have helped it. It isn't a thing I want known. Great Scott, man, don't goggle at me like a fish! Haven't you heard of pseudonyms before?'

'Yes, but—'

'Well, never mind. Take it from me that I *am* Edith Butler. Now listen to me. That manuscript reached me when I was in the country. There was no name on it. That in itself points strongly to the fact that you were its author. It was precisely the chuckle-headed sort of thing you would have done, to put no name on the thing.'

'I enclosed a letter, anyhow.'

'There was a letter enclosed. I opened the parcel out of doors. There was a fresh breeze blowing at the time. It caught the letter, and that was the last I saw of it. I had read as far as "Dear Madam". But one thing I do remember about it, and that was that it was sent from some hotel in Cheltenham, and I could remember it if I heard it. Now, then?'

'I can tell it you. It was Wilbraham's. I was stopping there.'

'You pass,' said Mr Prosser. 'It was Wilbraham's.'

Owen's heart gave a jump. For a moment he walked on air.

'Then do you mean to say that it's all right—that you believe—'

'I do,' said Mr Prosser. 'By the way,' he said, 'the notice of *White Roses* went up last night.'

Owen's heart turned to lead.

'But—but—' he stammered. 'But tonight the house was packed.'

'It was. Packed with paper. All the merry dead-heads in London were there. It has been the worst failure this season. And, by George,' he cried, with sudden vehemence, 'serve 'em right. If I told them once it would fail in England, I told them a hundred times. The London public won't stand that sort of blithering twaddle.'

Owen stopped and looked round. A cab was standing across the road. He signalled to it. He felt incapable of walking home. No physical blow could have unmanned him more completely than this hideous disappointment just when, by a miracle, everything seemed to be running his way.

'Sooner ride than walk,' said Mr Prosser, pushing his head through the open window. 'Laziness—slackness—that's the curse of the modern young man. Where shall I tell him to drive to?'

Owen mentioned his address. It struck him that he had not thanked his host for his hospitality.

'It was awfully good of you to give me supper, Mr Prosser,' he said. 'I've enjoyed it tremendously.'

'Come again,' said Mr Prosser. 'I'm afraid you're disappointed about the play?'

Owen forced a smile.

'Oh, no, that's all right,' he said. 'It can't be helped.'

Mr Prosser half turned, then thrust his head through the window again.

'I knew there was something I had forgotten to say,' he said. 'I ought to have told you that the play was produced in America before it came to London. It ran two seasons in New York and one in Chicago, and there are three companies playing it still on the road. Here's my card. Come round and see me tomorrow. I can't tell you the actual figures off-hand, but you'll be all right. You'll have pots o' money.'

OUT OF SCHOOL

Mark you, I am not defending James Datchett. I hold no brief for James. On the contrary, I am very decidedly of the opinion that he should not have done it. I merely say that there were extenuating circumstances. Just that. Ext. circ. Nothing more.

Let us review the matter calmly and judicially, not condemning James offhand, but rather probing the whole affair to its core, to see if we can confirm my view that it is possible to find excuses for him.

We will begin at the time when the subject of the Colonies first showed a tendency to creep menacingly into the daily chit-chat of his Uncle Frederick.

James's Uncle Frederick was always talking more or less about the Colonies, having made a substantial fortune out in Western Australia, but it was only when James came down from Oxford that the thing became really menacing. Up to that time the uncle had merely spoken of the Colonies *as* Colonies. Now he began to speak of them with sinister reference to his nephew. He starred James. It became a case of 'Frederick Knott presents James Datchett in "The Colonies",' and there seemed every prospect that the production would be an early one; for if there was one section of the public which Mr Knott disliked more than another, it was Young Men Who Ought To Be Out Earning Their Livings Instead Of Idling At Home. He expressed his views on the subject with some eloquence whenever he visited his sister's house. Mrs Datchett was a widow, and since her husband's death had been in the habit of accepting every utterance of her brother Frederick as a piece of genuine all-wool wisdom; though, as a matter of fact, James's uncle had just about enough brain to make a jay-bird fly crooked, and no more. He had made his money through keeping sheep. And any fool can keep sheep. However, he had this reputation for wisdom, and what he said went. It was not long, therefore, before it was evident that the ranks of the Y.M.W.O.T.B.O.E.T.L.I. O.I.A.H. were about to lose a member.

James, for his part, was all against the Colonies. As a setting for his career, that is to say. He was no Little Englander. He had no earthly objection to Great Britain *having Colonies*. By all means have Colonies. They could rely on him for moral support. But when it came to legging it out to West Australia to act as a sort of valet to Uncle Frederick's beastly sheep—no. Not for James. For him the literary life. Yes, that was James's dream—to have a stab at the literary life. At Oxford he had contributed to the *Isis*, and since coming down had been endeavouring to do the same to the papers of the Metropolis. He had had no success so far. But some inward voice seemed to tell him—(Read on. Read on. This is no story about the young beginner's struggles in London. We do not get within fifty miles of Fleet Street.)

A temporary compromise was effected between the two parties by the securing for James of a post as assistant-master at Harrow House, the private school of one Blatherwick, M.A., the understanding being that if he could hold the job he could remain in England and write, if it pleased him, in his spare time. But if he fell short in any way as a handler of small boys he was to descend a step in the animal kingdom and be matched against the West Australian sheep. There was to be no second chance in the event of failure. From the way Uncle Frederick talked James almost got the idea that he attached a spiritual importance to a connexion with sheep. He seemed to strive with a sort of religious frenzy to convert James to West Australia. So James went to Harrow House with much the same emotions that the Old Guard must have felt on their way up the hill at Waterloo.

Harrow House was a grim mansion on the outskirts of Dover. It is better, of course, to be on the outskirts of Dover than actually in it, but when you have said that you have said everything. James's impressions of that portion of his life were made up almost entirely of chalk. Chalk in the school-room, chalk all over the country-side, chalk in the milk. In this universe of chalk he taught bored boys the rudiments of Latin, geography, and arithmetic, and in the evenings, after a stately cup of coffee with Mr Blatherwick in his study, went to his room and wrote stories. The life had the advantage of offering few distractions. Except for Mr Blatherwick and a weird freak who came up from Dover on Tuesdays and Fridays to teach French, he saw nobody.

It was about five weeks from the beginning of term that the river of life at Harrow House became ruffled for the new assistant-master.

I want you to follow me very closely here. As far as the excusing of James's conduct is concerned, it is now or never. If I fail at this point to touch you, I have shot my bolt.

Let us marshal the facts.

In the first place it was a perfectly ripping morning.

Moreover he had received at breakfast a letter from the editor of a monthly magazine accepting a short story.

This had never happened to him before.

He was twenty-two.

And, just as he rounded the angle of the house, he came upon Violet, taking the air like himself.

Violet was one of the housemaids, a trim, energetic little person with round blue eyes and a friendly smile. She smiled at James now. James halted.

'Good morning, sir,' said Violet.

From my list of contributory causes I find that I have omitted one item—viz., that there did not appear to be anybody else about.

James looked meditatively at Violet. Violet looked smilingly at James. The morning was just as ripping as it had been a moment before. James was still twenty-two. And the editor's letter had not ceased to crackle in his breast-pocket.

Consequently James stooped, and—in a purely brotherly way—kissed Violet.

This, of course, was wrong. It was no part of James's duties as assistant-master at Harrow House to wander about bestowing brotherly kisses on housemaids. On the other hand, there was no great harm done. In the circles in which Violet moved the kiss was equivalent to the hand-shake of loftier society. Everybody who came to the back door kissed Violet. The carrier did; so did the grocer, the baker, the butcher, the gardener, the postman, the policeman, and the fishmonger. They were men of widely differing views on most points. On religion, politics, and the prospects of the entrants for the three o'clock race their opinions clashed. But in one respect they were unanimous. Whenever they came to the back door of Harrow House they all kissed Violet.

'I've had a story accepted by the *Universal Magazine*,' said James, casually.

'Have you, sir?' said Violet.

'It's a pretty good magazine. I shall probably do a great deal for it from time to time. The editor seems a decent chap.'

'Does he, sir?'

'I shan't tie myself up in any way, of course, unless I get very good terms. But I shall certainly let him see a good lot of my stuff. Jolly morning, isn't it?'

He strolled on; and Violet, having sniffed the air for a few more minutes with her tip-tilted nose, went indoors to attend to her work.

Five minutes later James, back in the atmosphere of chalk, was writing on the blackboard certain sentences for his class to turn into Latin prose. A somewhat topical note ran through them. As thus:

'The uncle of Balbus wished him to tend sheep in the Colonies (*Provincia*).'

'Balbus said that England was good enough for him (*placeo*).'

'Balbus sent a story (versus) to Maecenas, who replied that he hoped to use it in due course.'

His mind floated away from the classroom when a shrill voice brought him back.

'Sir, please, sir, what does "due course" mean?'

James reflected. 'Alter it to "immediately,"' he said.

'Balbus is a great man,' he wrote on the blackboard.

Two minutes later he was in the office of an important magazine, and there was a look of relief on the editor's face, for James had practically promised to do a series of twelve short stories for him.

It has been well observed that when a writer has a story rejected he should send that story to another editor, but that when he has one accepted he should send another story to that editor. Acting on this excellent plan, James, being off duty for an hour after tea, smoked a pipe in his bedroom and settled down to work on a second effort for the Universal.

He was getting on rather well when his flow of ideas was broken by a knock on the door.

'Come in,' yelled James. (Your author is notoriously irritable.)

The new-comer was Adolf. Adolf was one of that numerous band of Swiss and German youths who come to this country prepared to give their services ridiculously cheap in exchange for the opportunity of learning the English language. Mr Blatherwick held the view that for a private school a male front-door opener was superior to a female, arguing that the parents of prospective pupils would be impressed by the sight of a man in livery. He would have liked something a bit more imposing than Adolf, but the latter was the showiest thing that could be got for the money, so he made the best of it, and engaged him. After all, an astigmatic parent, seeing Adolf in a dim light, might be impressed by him. You never could tell.

'Well?' said James, glaring.

'Anysing vrom dze fillage, sare?'

The bulk of Adolf's perquisites consisted of the tips he received for going to the general store down the road for tobacco, stamps, and so on. 'No. Get out,' growled James, turning to his work.

He was surprised to find that Adolf, so far from getting out, came in and shut the door.

'Zst!' said Adolf, with a finger on his lips.

James stared.

'In dze garten zis morning,' proceeded his visitor, grinning like a gargoyle, 'I did zee you giss Violed. Zo!'

James's heart missed a beat. Considered purely as a situation, his present position was not ideal. He had to work hard, and there was not much money attached to the job. But it was what the situation stood for that counted. It was his little rock of safety in the midst of a surging ocean of West Australian sheep. Once let him lose his grip on it, and there was no chance for him. He would be swept away beyond hope of return.

'What do you mean?' he said hoarsely.

'In dze garten. I you vrom a window did zee. You und Violed. Zo!' And Adolf, in the worst taste, gave a realistic imitation of the scene, himself sustaining the role of James.

James said nothing. The whole world seemed to be filled with a vast baa-ing, as of countless flocks.

'Lizzun!' said Adolf. 'Berhaps I Herr Blazzervig dell. Berhaps not I do. Zo!'

James roused himself. At all costs he must placate this worm. Mr Blatherwick was an austere man. He would not overlook such a crime.

He appealed to the other's chivalry.

'What about Violet?' he said. 'Surely you don't want to lose the poor girl her job? They'd be bound to sack her, too.'

Adolf's eyes gleamed.

'Zo? Lizzun! When I do gom virst here, I myself do to giss Violed vunce vish. But she do push dze zide of my face, and my lof is durned to hate.'

James listened attentively to this tabloid tragedy, but made no comment.

'Anysing vrom dze fillage, sare?'

Adolf's voice was meaning. James produced a half-crown.

'Here you are, then. Get me half a dozen stamps and keep the change.'

'Zdamps? Yes, sare. At vunce.'

James's last impression of the departing one was of a vast and greasy grin, stretching most of the way across his face.

Adolf, as blackmailer, in which role he now showed himself, differed in some respects from the conventional blackmailer of fiction. It may be that he was doubtful as to how much James would stand, or it may be that his soul as a general rule was above money. At any rate, in actual specie he took very little from his victim. He seemed to wish to be sent to the village oftener than before, but that was all. Half a crown a week would have covered James's financial loss.

But he asserted himself in another way. In his most light-hearted moments Adolf never forgot the reason which had brought him to England. He had come to the country to learn the language, and he meant to do it. The difficulty which had always handicapped him hitherto—namely, the poverty of the vocabularies of those in the servants' quarters—was now removed. He appointed James tutor-in-chief of the English language to himself, and saw that he entered upon his duties at once.

The first time that he accosted James in the passage outside the classroom, and desired him to explain certain difficult words in a leading article of yesterday's paper, James was pleased. Adolf, he thought, regarded the painful episode as closed. He had accepted the half-crown as the full price of silence, and was now endeavouring to be friendly in order to make amends.

This right-minded conduct gratified James. He felt genially disposed toward Adolf. He read the leading article, and proceeded to give a full and kindly explanation of the hard words. He took trouble over it. He went into the derivations of the words. He touched on certain rather tricky sub-meanings of the same. Adolf went away with any doubts he might have had of James's capabilities as a teacher of English definitely scattered. He felt that he had got hold of the right man.

There was a shade less geniality in James's manner when the same thing happened on the following morning. But he did not refuse to help the untutored foreigner. The lecture was less exhaustive than that of the previous morning, but we must suppose that it satisfied Adolf, for he came again next day, his faith in his teacher undiminished.

James was trying to write a story. He turned on the student.

'Get out!' he howled. 'And take that beastly paper away. Can't you see I'm busy? Do you think I can spend all my time teaching you to read? Get out!'

'Dere some hard vord vos,' said Adolf, patiently, 'of which I gannot dze meaning.'

James briefly cursed the hard word.

'But,' proceeded Adolf, 'of one vord, of dze vord "giss", I dze meaning know. Zo!'

James looked at him. There was a pause.

Two minutes later the English lesson was in full swing.

All that James had ever heard or read about the wonderful devotion to study of the modern German young man came home to him during the next two weeks. Our English youth fritters away its time in idleness and pleasure-seeking. The German concentrates. Adolf concentrated like a porous plaster. Every day after breakfast, just when the success of James's literary career depended on absolute seclusion, he would come trotting up for his lesson. James's writing practically ceased.

This sort of thing cannot last. There is a limit, and Adolf reached it when he attempted to add night-classes to the existing curriculum.

James, as had been said, was in the habit of taking coffee with Mr Blatherwick in his study after seeing the boys into bed. It was while he was on his way to keep this appointment, a fortnight after his first interview with Adolf, that the young student waylaid him with the evening paper.

Something should have warned Adolf that the moment was not well chosen. To begin with, James had a headache, the result of a hard day with the boys. Then that morning's English lesson had caused him to forget entirely an idea which had promised to be the nucleus of an excellent plot. And, lastly, passing through the hall but an instant before, he had met Violet, carrying the coffee and the evening post to the study, and she had given him two long envelopes addressed in his own handwriting. He was brooding over these, preparatory to opening them, at the very moment when Adolf addressed him.

'Eggscuse,' said Adolf, opening the paper.

James's eyes gleamed ominously.

'Zere are here,' continued Adolf, unseeing, 'some beyond-gombarison hard vords vich I do nod onderstand. For eggsample—'

It was at this point that James kicked him.

Adolf leaped like a stricken chamois.

'Vot iss?' he cried.

With these long envelopes in his hand James cared for nothing. He kicked Adolf again.

'Zo!' said the student, having bounded away. He added a few words in his native tongue, and proceeded. 'Vait! Lizzun! I zay to you, vait! Brezendly, ven I haf dze zilver bolished und my odder dudies zo numerous berformed, I do Herr Blazzervig vil vith von liddle szdory vich you do know go. Zo!'

He shot off to his lair.

James turned away and went down the passage to restore his nervous tissues with coffee.

Meanwhile, in the study, leaning against the mantelpiece in moody reflection, Mr Blatherwick was musing sadly on the hardships of the schoolmaster's life. The proprietor of Harrow House was a long, grave man, one of the last to hold out against the anti-whisker crusade. He had expressionless hazel eyes, and a general air of being present in body but absent in spirit. Mothers who visited the school to introduce their sons put his vagueness down to activity of mind. 'That busy brain,' they thought, 'is never at rest. Even while he is talking to us some abstruse point in the classics is occupying his mind.'

What was occupying his mind at the present moment was the thoroughly unsatisfactory conduct of his wife's brother, Bertie Baxter. The more tensely he brooded over the salient points in the life-history of his wife's brother, Bertie Baxter, the deeper did the iron become embedded in his soul. Bertie was one of Nature's touchers. This is the age of the specialist, Bertie's speciality was borrowing money. He was a man of almost eerie versatility in this direction. Time could not wither nor custom stale his infinite variety. He could borrow with a breezy bluffness which made the thing practically a hold-up. And anon, when his victim had steeled himself against this method, he could extract another five-pound note from his little hoard with the delicacy of one playing spillikins. Mr Blatherwick had been a gold-mine to him for years. As a rule, the proprietor of Harrow House unbelted without complaint, for Bertie, as every good borrower should, had that knack of making his victim feel during the actual moment of paying over, as if he had just made a rather good investment. But released from the spell of his brother-in-law's personal magnetism, Mr Blatherwick was apt to brood. He was brooding now. Why, he was asking himself morosely, should he be harassed by this Bertie? It was not as if Bertie was penniless. He had a little income of his own. No, it was pure lack of consideration. Who was Bertie that he—

At this point in his meditations Violet entered with the after-dinner coffee and the evening post.

Mr Blatherwick took the letters. There were two of them, and one he saw, with a rush of indignation, was in the handwriting of his brother-in-law. Mr Blatherwick's blood simmered. So the fellow thought he could borrow by post, did he? Not even trouble to pay a visit, eh? He tore the letter open, and the first thing he saw was a cheque for five pounds.

Mr Blatherwick was astounded. That a letter from his brother-in-law should not contain a request for money was surprising; that it should contain a cheque, even for five pounds, was miraculous.

He opened the second letter. It was short, but full of the finest, noblest sentiments; to wit, that the writer, Charles J. Pickersgill, having heard the school so highly spoken of by his friend, Mr Herbert Baxter, would be glad if Mr Blatherwick could take in his three sons, aged seven, nine, and eleven respectively, at the earliest convenient date.

Mr Blatherwick's first feeling was one of remorse that even in thought he should have been harsh to the golden-hearted Bertie. His next was one of elation.

Violet, meanwhile, stood patiently before him with the coffee. Mr Blatherwick helped himself. His eye fell on Violet.

Violet was a friendly, warm-hearted little thing. She saw that Mr Blatherwick had had good news; and, as the bearer of the letters which had contained it, she felt almost responsible. She smiled kindly up at Mr Blatherwick.

Mr Blatherwick's dreamy hazel eye rested pensively upon her. The major portion of his mind was far away in the future, dealing with visions of a school grown to colossal proportions, and patronized by millionaires. The section of it which still worked in the present was just large enough to enable him to understand that he felt kindly, and even almost grateful, to Violet. Unfortunately it was too small to make him see how wrong it was to kiss her in a vague, fatherly way across the coffee tray just as James Datchett walked into the room.

James paused. Mr Blatherwick coughed. Violet, absolutely unmoved, supplied James with coffee, and bustled out of the room.

She left behind her a somewhat massive silence.

Mr Blatherwick coughed again.

'It looks like rain,' said James, carelessly.

'Ah?' said Mr Blatherwick.

'Very like rain,' said James.

'Indeed!' said Mr Blatherwick.

A pause.

'Pity if it rains,' said James.

'True,' said Mr Blatherwick.

Another pause.

'Er—Datchett,' said Mr Blatherwick.

'Yes,' said James.

'I—er—feel that perhaps—'

James waited attentively.

'Have you sugar?'

'Plenty, thanks,' said James.

'I shall be sorry if it rains,' said Mr Blatherwick.

Conversation languished.

James laid his cup down.

'I have some writing to do,' he said. 'I think I'll be going upstairs now.'

'Er—just so,' said Mr Blatherwick, with relief. 'Just so. An excellent idea.'

'Er—Datchett,' said Mr Blatherwick next day, after breakfast.

'Yes?' said James.

A feeling of content was over him this morning. The sun had broken through the clouds. One of the long envelopes which he had received on the previous night had turned out, on examination, to contain a letter from the editor accepting the story if he would reconstruct certain passages indicated in the margin.

'I have—ah—unfortunately been compelled to dismiss Adolf,' said Mr Blatherwick.

'Yes?' said James. He had missed Adolf's shining morning face.

'Yes. After you had left me last night he came to my study with a malicious—er—fabrication respecting yourself which I need not—ah—particularize.'

James looked pained. Awful thing it is, this nourishing vipers in one's bosom.

'Why, I've been giving Adolf English lessons nearly every day lately. No sense of gratitude, these foreigners,' he said, sadly.

'So I was compelled,' proceeded Mr Blatherwick, 'to—in fact, just so.'

James nodded sympathetically.

'Do you know anything about West Australia?' he asked, changing the subject. 'It's a fine country, I believe. I had thought of going there at one time.'

'Indeed?' said Mr Blatherwick.

'But I've given up the idea now,' said James.

THREE FROM DUNSTERVILLE

Once upon a time there was erected in Longacre Square, New York, a large white statue, labelled 'Our City', the figure of a woman in Grecian robes holding aloft a shield. Critical citizens objected to it for various reasons, but its real fault was that its symbolism was faulty. The sculptor should have represented New York as a conjuror in evening dress, smiling blandly as he changed a rabbit into a bowl of goldfish. For that, above all else, is New York's speciality. It changes.

Between 1 May, when she stepped off the train, and 16 May, when she received Eddy Moore's letter containing the information that he had found her a post as stenographer in the office of Joe Rendal, it had changed Mary Hill quite remarkably.

Mary was from Dunsterville, which is in Canada. Emigrations from Dunsterville were rare. It is a somnolent town; and, as a rule, young men born there follow in their father's footsteps, working on the paternal farm or helping in the paternal store. Occasionally a daring spirit will break away, but seldom farther than Montreal. Two only of the younger generation, Joe Rendal and Eddy Moore, had set out to make their fortunes in New York; and both, despite the gloomy prophecies of the village sages, had prospered.

Mary, third and last emigrant, did not aspire to such heights. All she demanded from New York for the present was that it should pay her a living wage, and to that end, having studied by stealth typewriting and shorthand, she had taken the plunge, thrilling with excitement and the romance of things; and New York had looked at her, raised its eyebrows, and looked away again. If every city has a voice, New York's at that moment had said 'Huh!' This had damped Mary. She saw that there were going to be obstacles. For one thing, she had depended so greatly on Eddy Moore, and he had failed her. Three years before, at a church festival, he had stated specifically that he would die for her. Perhaps he was still willing to do that—she had not inquired—but, at any rate, he did not see his way to employing her as a secretary. He had been very nice about it. He had smiled kindly, taken her address, and said he would do what he could, and had then hurried off to meet a man at lunch. But he had not given her a position. And as the days went by and she found no employment, and her little stock of money dwindled, and no word came from Eddy, New York got to work and changed her outlook on things wonderfully. What had seemed romantic became merely frightening. What had been exciting gave her a feeling of dazed helplessness.

But it was not until Eddy's letter came that she realized the completeness of the change. On 1 May she would have thanked Eddy politely for his trouble, adding, however, that she would really prefer not to meet poor Joe again. On 16 May she welcomed him as something Heaven-sent. The fact that she was to be employed outweighed a thousand-fold the fact that her employer was to be Joe.

It was not that she disliked Joe. She was sorry for him.

She remembered Joe, a silent, shambling youth, all hands, feet, and shyness, who had spent most of his spare time twisting his fingers and staring adoringly at her from afar. The opinion of those in the social whirl of Dunsterville had been that it was his hopeless passion for her that had made him fly to New York. It would be embarrassing meeting him again. It would require tact to discourage his silent worshipping without wounding him more deeply. She hated hurting people.

But, even at the cost of that, she must accept the post. To refuse meant ignominious retreat to Dunsterville, and from that her pride revolted. She must revisit Dunsterville in triumph or not at all.

Joe Rendal's office was in the heart of the financial district, situated about half-way up a building that, to Mary, reared amidst the less impressive architecture of her home-town, seemed to reach nearly to the sky. A proud-looking office-boy, apparently baffled and mortified by the information that she had an appointment, took her name, and she sat down, filled with a fine mixed assortment of emotions, to wait.

For the first time since her arrival in New York she felt almost easy in her mind. New York, with its shoving, jostling, hurrying crowds; a giant fowl-run, full of human fowls scurrying to and fro; clucking, ever on the look-out for some desired morsel, and ever ready to swoop down and snatch it from its temporary possessor, had numbed her. But now she felt a slackening of the strain. New York might be too much for her, but she could cope with Joe.

The haughty boy returned. Mr Rendal was disengaged. She rose and went into an inner room, where a big man was seated at a desk.

It was Joe. There was no doubt about that. But it was not the Joe she remembered, he of the twisted ringers and silent stare. In his case, New York had conjured effectively. He was better-looking, better-dressed, improved in every respect. In the old days one had noticed the hands and feet and deduced the presence of Joe somewhere in the background. Now they were merely adjuncts. It was with a rush of indignation that Mary found herself bucolic and awkward. Awkward with Joe! It was an outrage.

His manner heightened the feeling. If he had given the least sign of embarrassment she might have softened towards him. He showed no embarrassment whatever. He was very much at his ease. He was cheerful. He was even flippant.

'Welcome to our beautiful little city,' he said.

Mary was filled with a helpless anger. What right had he to ignore the past in this way, to behave as if her presence had never reduced him to pulp?

'Won't you sit down?' he went on. 'It's splendid, seeing you again, Mary. You're looking very well. How long have you been in New York? Eddy tells me you want to be taken on as a secretary. As it happens, there is a vacancy for just that in this office. A big, wide vacancy, left by a lady who departed yester-day in a shower of burning words and hairpins. She said she would never return, and between ourselves, that was the right guess. Would you mind letting me see what you can do? Will you take this letter down?'

Certainly there was something compelling about this new Joe. Mary took the pencil and pad which he offered—and she took them meekly. Until this moment she had always been astonished by the reports which filtered through to Dunsterville of his success in the big city. Of course, nobody had ever doubted his perseverance; but it takes something more than perseverance to fight New York fairly and squarely, and win. And Joe had that something. He had force. He was sure of himself.

'Read it please,' he said, when he had finished dictating. 'Yes, that's all right. You'll do.'

For a moment Mary was on the point of refusing. A mad desire gripped her to assert herself, to make plain her resentment at this revolt of the serf. Then she thought of those scuttling, clucking crowds, and her heart failed her.

'Thank you,' she said, in a small voice.

As she spoke the door opened.

'Well, well, well!' said Joe. 'Here we all are! Come in, Eddy. Mary has just been showing me what she can do.'

If time had done much for Joe, it had done more for his fellow-emigrant, Eddy Moore. He had always been good-looking and—according to local standards—presentable. Tall, slim, with dark eyes that made you catch your breath when they looked into yours, and a ready flow of speech, he had been Dunsterville's prize exhibit. And here he was with all his excellence heightened and accentuated by the polish of the city. He had filled out. His clothes were wonderful. And his voice, when he spoke, had just that same musical quality.

'So you and Joe have fixed it up? Capital! Shall we all go and lunch somewhere?'

'Got an appointment,' said Joe. 'I'm late already. Be here at two sharp, Mary.' He took up his hat and went out.

The effect of Eddy's suavity had been to make Mary forget the position in which she now stood to Joe. Eddy had created for the moment quite an old-time atmosphere of good fellowship. She hated Joe for shattering this and reminding her that she was his employee. Her quick flush was not lost on Eddy.

'Dear old Joe is a little abrupt sometimes,' he said. 'But—'

'He's a pig!' said Mary, defiantly.

'But you mustn't mind it. New York makes men like that.'

'It hasn't made you—not to me, at any rate. Oh, Eddy,' she cried, impulsively, 'I'm frightened. I wish I had never come here. You're the only thing in this whole city that isn't hateful.'

'Poor little girl!' he said. 'Never mind. Let me take you and give you some lunch. Come along.'

Eddy was soothing. There was no doubt of that. He stayed her with minced chicken and comforted her with soft shelled crab. His voice was a lullaby, lulling her Joe-harassed nerves to rest.

They discussed the dear old days. A carper might have said that Eddy was the least bit vague on the subject of the dear old days. A carper might have pointed out that the discussion of the dear old days, when you came to analyse it, was practically a monologue on Mary's part, punctuated with musical 'Yes, yes's' from her companion. But who cares what carpers think? Mary herself had no fault to find. In the roar of New York Dunsterville had suddenly become very dear to her, and she found in Eddy a sympathetic soul to whom she could open her heart.

'Do you remember the old school, Eddy, and how you and I used to walk there together, you carrying my dinner-basket and helping me over the fences?'

'Yes, yes.'

'And we'd gather hickory-nuts and persimmons?'

'Persimmons, yes,' murmured Eddy.

'Do you remember the prizes the teacher gave the one who got best marks in the spelling class? And the treats at Christmas, when we all got twelve sticks of striped peppermint candy? And drawing the water out of the well in that old wooden bucket in the winter, and pouring it out in the playground and skating on it when it froze? And wasn't it cold in the winter, too! Do you remember the stove in the schoolroom? How we used to crowd round it!'

'The stove, yes,' said Eddy, dreamily. 'Ah, yes, the stove. Yes, yes. Those were the dear old days!' Mary leaned her elbows on the table and her chin on her hands, and looked across at him with sparkling eyes.

'Oh, Eddy,' she said, 'you don't know how nice it is to meet someone who remembers all about those old times! I felt a hundred million miles from Dunsterville before I saw you, and I was homesick. But now it's all different.'

'Poor little Mary!'

'Do you remember—?'

He glanced at his watch with some haste.

'It's two o'clock,' he said. 'I think we should be going.'

Mary's face fell.

'Back to that pig, Joe! I hate him. And I'll show him that I do!'

Eddy looked almost alarmed.

'I—I shouldn't do that,' he said. 'I don't think I should do that. It's only his manner at first. You'll get to like him better. He's an awfully good fellow really, Joe. And if you—er—quarrelled with him you might find it hard—what I mean is, it's not so easy to pick up jobs in New York, I shouldn't like to think of you, Mary,' he added, tenderly, 'hunting for a job—tired—perhaps hungry—'

Mary's eyes filled with tears.

'How good you are, Eddy!' she said. 'And I'm horrid, grumbling when I ought to be thanking you for getting me the place. I'll be nice to him—if I can—as nice as I can.'

'That's right. Do try. And we shall be seeing quite a lot of each other. We must often lunch together.'

Mary re-entered the office not without some trepidation. Two hours ago it would have seemed absurd to be frightened of Joe, but Eddy had brought it home to her again how completely she was dependent on her former serf's good-will. And he had told her to be back at two sharp, and it was now nearly a quarter past.

The outer office was empty. She went on into the inner room.

She had speculated as she went on Joe's probable attitude. She had pictured him as annoyed, even rude. What she was not prepared for was to find him on all fours, grunting and rooting about in a pile of papers. She stopped short.

'What *are* you doing?' she gasped.

'I can't think what you meant,' he said. 'There must be some mistake. I'm not even a passable pig. I couldn't deceive a novice.'

He rose and dusted his knees.

'Yet you seemed absolutely certain in the restaurant just now. Did you notice that you were sitting near to a sort of jungle of potted palms? I was lunching immediately on the other side of the forest.'

Mary drew herself up and fixed him with an eye that shone with rage and scorn.

'Eavesdropper!' she cried.

'Not guilty,' he said, cheerfully. 'I hadn't a notion that you were there till you shouted, "That pig Joe, I hate him!" and almost directly afterwards I left.'

'I did not shout.'

'My dear girl, you cracked a wine-glass at my table. The man I was lunching with jumped clean out of his seat and swallowed his cigar. You ought to be more careful!'

Mary bit her lip.

'And now, I suppose, you are going to dismiss me?'

'Dismiss you? Not much. The thing has simply confirmed my high opinion of your qualifications. The ideal secretary must have two qualities: she must be able to sec. and she must think her employer a pig. You fill the bill. Would you mind taking down this letter?'

Life was very swift and stimulating for Mary during the early days of her professional career. The inner workings of a busy broker's office are always interesting to the stranger. She had never understood how business men made their money, and she did not understand now; but it did not take her long to see that if they were all like Joe Rendal they earned it. There were days of comparative calm. There were days that were busy. And there were days that packed into the space of a few hours the concentrated essence of a music-hall knock-about sketch, an earthquake, a football scrummage, and the rush-hour on the Tube; when the office was full of shouting men, when strange figures dived in and out and banged doors like characters in an old farce, and Harold, the proud office-boy, lost his air of being on the point of lunching with a duke at the club and perspired like one of the proletariat. On these occasions you could not help admiring Joe, even if you hated him. When a man is doing his own job well, it is impossible not to admire him. And Joe did his job well, superlatively well. He was everywhere. Where others trotted, he sprang. Where others raised their voices, he yelled. Where others were in two places at once, he was in three and moving towards a fourth.

These upheavals had the effect on Mary of making her feel curiously linked to the firm. On ordinary days work was work, but on these occasions of storm and stress it was a fight, and she looked on every member of the little band grouped under the banner of J. Rendal as a brother-in-arms. For Joe, while the battle raged, she would have done anything. Her resentment at being under his orders vanished completely. He was her captain, and she a mere unit in the firing line. It was a privilege to do what she was told. And if the order came sharp and abrupt, that only meant that the fighting was fierce and that she was all the more fortunate in being in a position to be of service.

The reaction would come with the end of the fight. Her private hostilities began when the firm's ceased. She became an ordinary individual again, and so did Joe. And to Joe, as an ordinary individual, she objected. There was an indefinable something in his manner which jarred on her. She came to the conclusion that it was principally his insufferable good-humour. If only he would lose his temper with her now and then, she felt he would be bearable. He lost it with others. Why not with her? Because, she told herself bitterly, he wanted to show her that she mattered so little to him that it was not worth while quarrelling with her; because he wanted to put her in the wrong, to be superior. She had a perfect right to hate a man who treated her in that way.

She compared him, to his disadvantage, with Eddy. Eddy, during these days, continued to be more and more of a comfort. It rather surprised her that he found so much time to devote to her. When she had first called on him, on her arrival in the city, he had given her the impression—more, she admitted, by his manner than his words—that she was not wanted. He had shown no disposition to seek her company. But now he seemed always to be on hand. To take her out to lunch appeared to be his chief hobby.

One afternoon Joe commented on it, with that air of suppressing an indulgent smile which Mary found so trying.

'I saw you and Eddy at Stephano's just now,' he said, between sentences of a letter which he was dictating. 'You're seeing a great deal of Eddy, aren't you?'

'Yes,' said Mary. 'He's very kind. He knows I'm lonely.' She paused. '*He* hasn't forgotten the old days,' she said, defiantly.

Joe nodded.

'Good old Eddy!' he said.

There was nothing in the words to make Mary fire up, but much in the way they were spoken, and she fired up accordingly.

'What do you mean?' she cried.

'Mean?' queried Joe.

'You're hinting at something. If you have anything to say against Eddy, why don't you say it straight out?'

'It's a good working rule in life never to say anything straight out. Speaking in parables, I will observe that, if America was a monarchy instead of a republic and people here had titles, Eddy would be a certainty for first Earl of Pearl Street.'

Dignity fought with curiosity in Mary for a moment. The latter won.

'I don't know what you mean! Why Pearl Street?'

'Go and have a look at it.'

Dignity recovered its ground. Mary tossed her head.

'We are wasting a great deal of time,' she said, coldly. 'Shall I take down the rest of this letter?'

'Great idea!' said Joe, indulgently. 'Do.'

A policeman, brooding on life in the neighbourhood of City Hall Park and Broadway that evening, awoke with a start from his meditations to find himself being addressed by a young lady. The young lady had large grey eyes and a slim figure. She appealed to the aesthetic taste of the policeman.

'Hold to me, lady,' he said, with gallant alacrity. 'I'll see yez acrost.'

'Thank you, I don't want to cross,' she said. 'Officer!'

The policeman rather liked being called 'Officer'.

'Ma'am?' he beamed.

'Officer, do you know a street called Pearl Street?'

'I do that, ma'am.'

She hesitated. 'What sort of street is it?'

The policeman searched in his mind for a neat definition.

'Darned crooked, miss,' he said.

He then proceeded to point the way, but the lady had gone.

It was a bomb in a blue dress that Joe found waiting for him at the office next morning. He surveyed it in silence, then raised his hands over his head,

'Don't shoot,' he said. 'What's the matter?'

'What right had you to say that about Eddy? You know what I mean—about Pearl Street.'

Joe laughed.

'Did you take a look at Pearl Street?'

Mary's anger blazed out.

'I didn't think you could be so mean and cowardly,' she cried. 'You ought to be ashamed to talk about people behind their backs, when—when—besides, if he's what you say, how did it happen that you engaged me on his recommendation?'

He looked at her for an instant without replying. 'I'd have engaged you,' he said, 'on the recommendation of a syndicate of forgers and three-card-trick men.'

He stood fingering a pile of papers on the desk.

'Eddy isn't the only person who remembers the old days, Mary,' he said slowly.

She looked at him, surprised. There was a note in his voice that she had not heard before. She was conscious of a curious embarrassment and a subtler feeling which she could not analyse. But before she could speak, Harold, the office-boy, entered the room with a card, and the conversation was swept away on a tidal wave of work.

Joe made no attempt to resume it. That morning happened to be one of the earthquake, knock-about-sketch mornings, and conversation, what there was of it, consisted of brief, strenuous remarks of a purely business nature.

But at intervals during the day Mary found herself returning to his words. Their effect on her mind puzzled her. It seemed to her that somehow they caused things to alter their perspective. In some way Joe had become more human. She still refused to believe that Eddy was not all that was chivalrous and noble, but her anger against Joe for his insinuations had given way to a feeling of regret that he should have made them. She ceased to look on him as something wantonly malevolent, a Thersites recklessly slandering his betters. She felt that there must have been a misunderstanding somewhere and was sorry for it.

Thinking it over, she made up her mind that it was for her to remove this misunderstanding. The days which followed strengthened the decision; for the improvement in Joe was steadily maintained. The indefinable something in his manner which had so irritated her had vanished. It had been, when it had existed, so nebulous that words were not needed to eliminate it. Indeed, even now she could not say exactly in what it had consisted. She only knew that the atmosphere had changed. Without a word spoken on either side it seemed that peace had been established between them, and it amazed her what a difference it made. She was soothed and happy, and kindly disposed to all men, and every day felt more strongly the necessity of convincing Joe and Eddy of each other's merits, or, rather, of convincing Joe, for Eddy, she admitted, always spoke most generously of the other.

For a week Eddy did not appear at the office. On the eighth day, however, he rang her up on the telephone, and invited her to lunch.

Later in the morning Joe happened to ask her out to lunch.

'I'm so sorry,' said Mary; 'I've just promised Eddy. He wants me to meet him at Stephano's, but—' She hesitated. 'Why shouldn't we all lunch together?' she went on, impulsively.

She hurried on. This was her opening, but she felt nervous. The subject of Eddy had not come up between them since that memorable conversation a week before, and she was uncertain of her ground.

'I wish you liked Eddy, Joe,' she said. 'He's very fond of you, and it seems such a shame that—I mean—we're all from the same old town, and—oh, I know I put it badly, but—'

'I think you put it very well,' said Joe; 'and if I could like a man to order I'd do it to oblige you. But—well, I'm not going to keep harping on it. Perhaps you'll see through Eddy yourself one of these days.'

A sense of the hopelessness of her task oppressed Mary. She put on her hat without replying, and turned to go.

At the door some impulse caused her to glance back, and as she did so she met his eye, and stood staring. He was looking at her as she had so often seen him look three years before in Dunsterville—humbly, appealingly, hungrily.

He took a step forward. A sort of panic seized her. Her fingers were on the door-handle. She turned it, and the next moment was outside.

She walked slowly down the street. She felt shaken. She had believed so thoroughly that his love for her had vanished with his shyness and awkwardness in the struggle for success in New York. His words, his manner—everything had pointed to that. And now—it was as if those three years had not been. Nothing had altered, unless it were—herself.

Had she altered? Her mind was in a whirl. This thing had affected her like some physical shock. The crowds and noises of the street bewildered her. If only she could get away from them and think quietly—

And then she heard her name spoken, and looked round, to see Eddy.

'Glad you could come,' he said. 'I've something I want to talk to you about. It'll be quiet at Stephano's.'

She noticed, almost unconsciously, that he seemed nervous. He was unwontedly silent. She was glad of it. It helped her to think.

He gave the waiter an order, and became silent again, drumming with his fingers on the cloth. He hardly spoke till the meal was over and the coffee was on the table. Then he leant forward.

'Mary,' he said, 'we've always been pretty good friends, haven't we?'

His dark eyes were looking into hers. There was an expression in them that was strange to her. He smiled, but it seemed to Mary that there was effort behind the smile.

'Of course we have, Eddy,' she said. He touched her hand.

'Dear little Mary!' he said, softly.

He paused for a moment.

'Mary,' he went on, 'you would like to do me a good turn? You would, wouldn't you, Mary?'

'Why, Eddy, of course!'

He touched her hand again. This time, somehow, the action grated on her. Before, it had seemed impulsive, a mere spontaneous evidence of friendship. Now there was a suggestion of artificiality,—of calculation. She drew back a little in her chair. Deep down in her some watchful instinct had sounded an alarm. She was on guard.

He drew in a quick breath.

'It's nothing much. Nothing at all. It's only this. I—I—Joe will be writing a letter to a man called Weston on Thursday—Thursday remember. There won't be anything in it—nothing of importance—nothing private—but—I—I want you to mail me a copy of it, Mary. A—a copy of—'

She was looking at him open-eyed. Her face was white and shocked.

'For goodness' sake,' he said, irritably, 'don't look like that. I'm not asking you to commit murder. What's the matter with you? Look here, Mary; you'll admit you owe me something, I suppose? I'm the only man in New York that's ever done anything for you. Didn't I get you your job? Well, then, it's not as if I were asking you to do anything dangerous, or difficult, or—'

She tried to speak, but could not. He went on rapidly. He did not look at her. His eyes wandered past her, shifting restlessly.

'Look here,' he said; 'I'll be square with you. You're in New York to make money. Well, you aren't going to make it hammering a typewriter. I'm giving you your chance. I'm going to be square with you. Let me see that letter, and—'

His voice died away abruptly. The expression on his face changed. He smiled, and this time the effort was obvious.

'Halloa, Joe!' he said.

Mary turned. Joe was standing at her side. He looked very large and wholesome and restful.

'I don't want to intrude,' he said; 'but I wanted to see you, Eddy, and I thought I should catch you here. I wrote a letter to Jack Weston yesterday—after I got home from the office—and one to you; and somehow I managed to post them in the wrong envelopes. It doesn't matter much, because they both said the same thing.'

'The same thing?'

'Yes; I told you I should be writing to you again on Thursday, to tip you something good that I was expecting from old Longwood. Jack Weston has just rung me up on the 'phone to say that he got a letter that doesn't belong to him. I explained to him and thought I'd drop in here and explain to you. Why, what's your hurry, Eddy?'

Eddy had risen from his seat.

'I'm due back at the office,' he said, hoarsely.

'Busy man! I'm having a slack day. Well, good-bye. I'll see Mary back.'

Joe seated himself in the vacant chair.

'You're looking tired,' he said. 'Did Eddy talk too much?'

'Yes, he did ... Joe, you were right.'

'Ah—Mary!' Joe chuckled. 'I'll tell you something I didn't tell Eddy. It wasn't entirely through carelessness that I posted those letters in the wrong envelopes. In fact, to be absolutely frank, it wasn't through carelessness at all. There's an old gentleman in Pittsburgh by the name of John Longwood, who occasionally is good enough to inform me of some of his intended doings on the market a day or so before the rest of the world knows them, and Eddy has always shown a strong desire to get early information too. Do you remember my telling you that your predecessor at the office left a little abruptly? There was a reason. I engaged her as a confidential secretary, and she overdid it. She confided in Eddy. From the look on your face as I came in I gathered that he had just been proposing that you should perform a similar act of Christian charity. Had he?'

Mary clenched her hands.

'It's this awful New York!' she cried. 'Eddy was never like that in Dunsterville.'

'Dunsterville does not offer quite the same scope,' said Joe.

'New York changes everything,' Mary returned. 'It has changed Eddy—it has changed you.'

He bent towards her and lowered his voice.

'Not altogether,' he said. 'I'm just the same in one way. I've tried to pretend I had altered, but it's no use. I give it up. I'm still just the same poor fool who used to hang round staring at you in Dunsterville.'

A waiter was approaching the table with the air, which waiters cultivate, of just happening by chance to be going in that direction. Joe leaned farther forward, speaking quickly.

'And for whom,' he said, 'you didn't care a single, solitary snap of your fingers, Mary.'

She looked up at him. The waiter hovered, poising for his swoop. Suddenly she smiled.

'New York has changed me too, Joe,' she said.

'Mary!' he cried.

'Ze pill, sare,' observed the waiter.

Joe turned.

'Ze what!' he exclaimed. 'Well, I'm hanged! Eddy's gone off and left me to pay for his lunch! That man's a wonder! When it comes to brain-work, he's in a class by himself.' He paused. 'But I have the luck,' he said.

THE TUPPENNY MILLIONAIRE

In the crowd that strolled on the Promenade des Etrangers, enjoying the morning sunshine, there were some who had come to Roville for their health, others who wished to avoid the rigours of the English spring, and many more who liked the place because it was cheap and close to Monte Carlo.

None of these motives had brought George Albert Balmer. He was there because, three weeks before, Harold Flower had called him a vegetable.

What is it that makes men do perilous deeds? Why does a man go over Niagara Falls in a barrel? Not for his health. Half an hour with a skipping-rope would be equally beneficial to his liver. No; in nine cases out of ten he does it to prove to his friends and relations that he is not the mild, steady-going person they have always thought him. Observe the music-hall acrobat as he prepares to swing from the roof by his eyelids. His gaze sweeps the house. 'It isn't true,' it seems to say. 'I'm not a jelly-fish.'

It was so with George Balmer.

In London at the present moment there exist some thousands of respectable, neatly-dressed, mechanical, unenterprising young men, employed at modest salaries by various banks, corporations, stores, shops, and business firms. They are put to work when young, and they stay put. They are mussels. Each has his special place on the rock, and remains glued to it all his life.

To these thousands George Albert Balmer belonged. He differed in no detail from the rest of the great army. He was as respectable, as neatly-dressed, as mechanical, and as unenterprising. His life was bounded, east, west, north, and south, by the Planet Insurance Company, which employed him; and that there were other ways in which a man might fulfil himself than by giving daily imitations behind a counter of a mechanical figure walking in its sleep had never seriously crossed his mind.

On George, at the age of twenty-four, there descended, out of a dear sky, a legacy of a thousand pounds.

Physically, he remained unchanged beneath the shock. No trace of hauteur crept into his bearing. When the head of his department, calling his attention to a technical flaw in his work of the previous afternoon, addressed him as 'Here, you—young what's-your-confounded-name!' he did not point out that this was no way to speak to a gentleman of property. You would have said that the sudden smile of Fortune had failed to unsettle him.

But all the while his mind, knocked head over heels, was lying in a limp heap, wondering what had struck it.

To him, in his dazed state, came Harold Flower. Harold, messenger to the Planet Insurance Company and one of the most assiduous money-borrowers in London, had listened to the office gossip about the legacy as if to the strains of some grand, sweet anthem. He was a bibulous individual of uncertain age, who, in the intervals of creeping about his duties, kept an eye open for possible additions to his staff of creditors. Most of the clerks at the Planet had been laid under contribution by him in their time, for Harold had a way with him that was good for threepence any pay-day, and it seemed to him that things had come to a sorry pass if he could not extract something special from Plutocrat Balmer in his hour of rejoicing.

Throughout the day he shadowed George, and, shortly before closing-time, backed him into a corner, tapped him on the chest, and requested the temporary loan of a sovereign.

In the same breath he told him that he was a gentleman, that a messenger's life was practically that of a blanky slave, and that a young man of spirit who wished to add to his already large fortune would have a bit on Giant Gooseberry for the City and Suburban. He then paused for a reply.

Now, all through the day George had been assailed by a steady stream of determined ear-biters. Again and again he had been staked out as an ore-producing claim by men whom it would have been impolitic to rebuff. He was tired of lending, and in a mood to resent unauthorized demands. Harold Flower's struck him as particularly unauthorized. He said so.

It took some little time to convince Mr Flower that he really meant it, but, realizing at last the grim truth, he drew a long breath and spoke.

'Ho!' he said. 'Afraid you can't spare it, can't you? A gentleman comes and asks you with tack and civility for a temp'y loan of about 'arf nothing, and all you do is to curse and swear at him. Do you know what I call you—you and your thousand quid? A tuppenny millionaire, that's what I call you. Keep your blooming money. That's all I ask. *Keep* it. Much good you'll get out of it. I know your sort. You'll never have any pleasure of it. Not you. You're the careful sort. You'll put it into Consols, *you* will, and draw your three-ha'pence a year. Money wasn't meant for your kind. It don't *mean* nothing to you. You ain't got the go in you to appreciate it. A vegetable—that's all you are. A blanky little vegetable. A blanky little gor-blimey vegetable. I seen turnips with more spirit in 'em that what you've got. And Brussels sprouts. Yes, *and* parsnips.'

It is difficult to walk away with dignity when a man with a hoarse voice and a watery eye is comparing you to your disadvantage with a parsnip, and George did not come anywhere near achieving the feat. But he extricated himself somehow, and went home brooding.

Mr Flower's remarks rankled particularly because it so happened that Consols were the identical investment on which he had decided. His Uncle Robert, with whom he lived as a paying guest, had strongly advocated them. Also they had suggested themselves to him independently.

But Harold Flower's words gave him pause. They made him think. For two weeks and some days he thought, flushing uncomfortably whenever he met that watery but contemptuous eye. And then came the day of his annual vacation, and with it inspiration. He sought out the messenger, whom till now he had carefully avoided.

'Er—Flower,' he said.

'Me lord?'

'I am taking my holiday tomorrow. Will you forward my letters? I will wire you the address. I have not settled on my hotel yet. I am popping over'—he paused—'I am popping over,' he resumed, carelessly, 'to Monte.'

'To who?' inquired Mr Flower.

'To Monte. Monte Carlo, you know.'

Mr Flower blinked twice rapidly, then pulled himself together.

'Yus, I *don't* think!' he said.

And that settled it.

The George who strolled that pleasant morning on the Promenade des Strangers differed both externally and internally from the George who had fallen out with Harold Flower in the offices of the Planet Insurance Company. For a day after his arrival he had clung to the garb of middle-class England. On the second he had discovered that this was unpleasantly warm and, worse, conspicuous. At the Casino Municipale that evening he had observed a man wearing an arrangement in bright yellow velvet without attracting attention. The sight had impressed him. Next morning he had emerged from his hotel in a flannel suit so light that it had been unanimously condemned as impossible by his Uncle Robert, his Aunt Louisa, his Cousins Percy, Eva, and Geraldine, and his Aunt Louisa's mother, and at a shop in the Rue Lasalle had spent twenty francs on a Homburg hat. And Roville had taken it without blinking.

Internally his alteration had been even more considerable. Roville was not Monte Carlo (in which gay spot he had remained only long enough to send a picture post-card to Harold Flower before retiring down the coast to find something cheaper), but it had been a revelation to him. For the first time in his life he was seeing colour, and it intoxicated him. The silky blueness of the sea was startling. The pure white of the great hotels along the promenade and the Casino Municipale fascinated him. He was dazzled. At the Casino the pillars were crimson and cream, the tables sky-blue and pink. Seated on a green-and-white striped chair he watched a *revue*, of which from start to finish he understood but one word—'out', to wit—absorbed in the doings of a red-moustached gentleman in blue who wrangled in rapid French with a black-moustached gentleman in yellow, while a snow-white *commere* and a *compere* in a mauve flannel suit looked on at the brawl.

It was during that evening that there flitted across his mind the first suspicion he had ever had that his Uncle Robert's mental outlook was a little limited.

And now, as he paced the promenade, watching the stir and bustle of the crowd, he definitely condemned his absent relative as a narrow-minded chump.

If the brown boots which he had polished so assiduously in his bedroom that morning with the inside of a banana-skin, and which now gleamed for the first time on his feet, had a fault, it was that they were a shade tight. To promenade with the gay crowd, therefore, for any length of time was injudicious; and George, warned by a red-hot shooting sensation that the moment had arrived for rest, sank down gracefully on a seat, to rise at once on discovering that between him and it was something oblong with sharp corners.

It was a book—a fat new novel. George drew it out and inspected it. There was a name inside—Julia Waveney.

George, from boyhood up, had been raised in that school of thought whose watchword is 'Findings are keepings', and, having ascertained that there was no address attached to the name, he was on the point, I regret to say, of pouching the volume, which already he looked upon as his own, when a figure detached itself from the crowd, and he found himself gazing into a pair of grey and, to his startled conscience, accusing eyes.

'Oh, thank you! I was afraid it was lost.'

She was breathing quickly, and there was a slight flush on her face. She took the book from George's unresisting hand and rewarded him with a smile.

'I missed it, and I couldn't think where I could have left it. Then I remembered that I had been sitting here. Thank you so much.'

She smiled again, turned, and walked away, leaving George to reckon up all the social solecisms he had contrived to commit in the space of a single moment. He had remained seated, he reminded himself, throughout the interview; one. He had not raised his hat, that fascinating Homburg simply made to be raised with a debonair swish under such conditions; two. Call it three, because he ought to have raised it twice. He had gaped like a fool; four. And, five, he had not uttered a single word of acknowledgement in reply to her thanks.

Five vast bloomers in under a minute ! What could she have thought of him? The sun ceased to shine. What sort of an utter outsider could she have considered him? An east wind sprang up. What kind of a Cockney bounder and cad could she have taken him for? The sea turned to an oily grey; and George, rising, strode back in the direction of his hotel in a mood that made him forget that he had brown boots on at all.

His mind was active. Several times since he had come to Roville he had been conscious of a sensation which he could not understand, a vague, yearning sensation, a feeling that, splendid as everything was in this paradise of colour, there was nevertheless something lacking. Now he understood. You had to be in love to get the full flavour of these vivid whites and blues. He was getting it now. His mood of dejection had passed swiftly, to be succeeded by an exhilaration such as he had only felt once in his life before, about half-way through a dinner given to the Planet staff on a princely scale by a retiring general manager.

He was exalted. Nothing seemed impossible to him. He would meet the girl again on the promenade, he told himself, dashingly renew the acquaintance, show her that he was not the gaping idiot he had appeared. His imagination donned its seven-league boots. He saw himself proposing—eloquently—accepted, married, living happily ever after.

It occurred to him that an excellent first move would be to find out where she was staying. He bought a paper and turned to the list of visitors. Miss Waveney. Where was it. He ran his eye down the column.

And then, with a crash, down came his air-castles in hideous ruin.

'Hotel Cercle de la Mediterranee. Lord Frederick Weston. The Countess of Southborne and the Hon. Adelaide Liss. Lady Julia Waveney—'

He dropped the paper and hobbled on to his hotel. His boots had begun to hurt him again, for he no longer walked on air.

At Roville there are several institutions provided by the municipality for the purpose of enabling visitors temporarily to kill thought. Chief among these is the Casino Municipale, where, for a price, the sorrowful may obtain oblivion by means of the ingenious game of *boule*. Disappointed lovers at Roville take to *boule* as in other places they might take to drink. It is a fascinating game. A wooden-faced high priest flicks a red india-rubber ball into a polished oaken bowl, at the bottom of which are holes, each bearing a number up to nine. The ball swings round and round like a planet, slows down, stumbles among the holes, rests for a moment in the one which you have backed, then hops into the next one, and you lose. If ever there was a pastime calculated to place young Adam Cupid in the background, this is it.

To the *boule* tables that night fled George with his hopeless passion. From the instant when he read the fatal words in the paper he had recognized its hopelessness. All other obstacles he had been prepared to overcome, but a title—no. He had no illusions as to his place in the social scale. The Lady Julias of this world did not marry insurance clerks, even if their late mother's cousin had left them a thousand pounds. That day-dream was definitely ended. It was a thing of the past—all over except the heartache.

By way of a preliminary sip of the waters of Lethe, before beginning the full draught, he placed a franc on number seven and lost. Another franc on six suffered the same fate. He threw a five-franc cart-wheel recklessly on evens. It won.

It was enough. Thrusting his hat on the back of his head and wedging himself firmly against the table, he settled down to make a night of it.

There is nothing like *boule* for absorbing the mind. It was some time before George became aware that a hand was prodding him in the ribs. He turned, irritated. Immediately behind him, filling the landscape, were two stout Frenchmen. But, even as he searched his brain for words that would convey to them in their native tongue his disapproval of this jostling, he perceived that they, though stout and in a general way offensive, were in this particular respect guiltless. The prodding hand belonged to somebody invisible behind them. It was small and gloved, a woman's hand. It held a five-franc piece.

Then in a gap, caused by a movement in the crowd, he saw the face of Lady Julia Waveney.

She smiled at him.

'On eight, please, would you mind?' he heard her say, and then the crowd shifted again and she disappeared, leaving him holding the coin, his mind in a whirl.

The game of *boule* demands undivided attention from its devotees. To play with a mind full of other matters is a mistake. This mistake George made. Hardly conscious of what he was doing, he flung the coin on the board. She had asked him to place it on eight, and he thought that he had placed it on eight. That, in reality, blinded by emotion, he had placed it on three was a fact which came home to him neither then nor later.

Consequently, when the ball ceased to roll and a sepulchral voice croaked the news that eight was the winning number, he fixed on the croupier a gaze that began by being joyful and expectant and ended, the croupier remaining entirely unresponsive, by being wrathful.

He leaned towards him.

'Monsieur,' he said. *'Moi! J'ai jete cinq francs sur huit!'*

The croupier was a man with a pointed moustache and an air of having seen all the sorrow and wickedness that there had ever been in the world. He twisted the former and permitted a faint smile to deepen the melancholy of the latter, but he did not speak.

George moved to his side. The two stout Frenchmen had strolled off, leaving elbow-room behind them.

He tapped the croupier on the shoulder.

'I say,' he said. 'What's the game? *J'ai jete cinq francs sur huit,* I tell you, *moi!*

A forgotten idiom from the days of boyhood and French exercises came to him.

'Moi qui parle,' he added.

'Messieurs, faites vos jeux,' crooned the croupier, in a detached manner.

To the normal George, as to most Englishmen of his age, the one cardinal rule in life was at all costs to avoid rendering himself conspicuous in public. Than George normal, no violet that ever hid itself in a mossy bank could have had a greater distaste for scenes. But tonight he was not normal. Roville and its colour had wrought a sort of fever in his brain. *Boule* had increased it. And love had caused it to rage. If this had been entirely his own affair it is probable that the croupier's frigid calm would have quelled him and he would have retired, fermenting but baffled. But it was not his own affair. He was fighting the cause of the only girl in the world. She had trusted him. Could he fail her? No, he was dashed if he could. He would show her what he was made of. His heart swelled within him. A thrill permeated his entire being, starting at his head and running out at his heels. He felt tremendous—a sort of blend of Oliver Cromwell, a Berserk warrior, and Sir Galahad.

'Monsieur,' he said again. 'Hi! What about it?'

This time the croupier did speak.

'C'est fini,' he said; and print cannot convey the pensive scorn of his voice. It stung George, in his exalted mood, like a blow. Finished, was it? All right, now he would show them. They had asked for it, and now they should get it. How much did it come to? Five francs the stake had been, and you got seven times your stake. And you got your stake back. He was nearly forgetting that. Forty francs in all, then. Two of those gold what-d'you-call'ems, in fact. Very well, then.

He leaned forward quickly across the croupier, snatched the lid off the gold tray, and removed two louis.

It is a remarkable fact in life that the scenes which we have rehearsed in our minds never happen as we have pictured them happening. In the present case, for instance, it had been George's intention to handle the subsequent stages of this little dispute with an easy dignity. He had proposed, the money obtained, to hand it over to its rightful owner, raise his hat, and retire with an air, a gallant champion of the oppressed. It was probably about one-sixteenth of a second after his hand had closed on the coins that he realized in the most vivid manner that these were not the lines on which the incident was to develop, and, with all his heart, he congratulated himself on having discarded those brown boots in favour of a worn but roomy pair of gent's Oxfords.

For a moment there was a pause and a silence of utter astonishment, while the minds of those who had witnessed the affair adjusted themselves to the marvel, and then the world became full of starting eyes, yelling throats, and clutching hands. From all over the casino fresh units swarmed like bees to swell the crowd at the centre of things. Promenaders ceased to promenade, waiters to wait. Elderly gentlemen sprang on to tables.

But in that momentary pause George had got off the mark. The table at which he had been standing was the one nearest to the door, and he had been on the door side of it. As the first eyes began to start, the first throats to yell, and the first hands to clutch, he was passing the counter of the money-changer. He charged the swing-door at full speed, and, true to its mission, it swung. He had a vague glimpse from the corner of his eye of the hat-and-cloak counter, and then he was in the square with the cold night breeze blowing on his forehead and the stars winking down from the blue sky.

A paper-seller on the pavement, ever the man of business, stepped forward and offered him the Paris edition of the *Daily Mail*, and, being in the direct line of transit, shot swiftly into the road and fell into a heap, while George, shaken but going well, turned off to the left, where there seemed to be rather more darkness than anywhere else.

And then the casino disgorged the pursuers.

To George, looking hastily over his shoulder, there seemed a thousand of them. The square rang with their cries. He could not understand them, but gathered that they were uncomplimentary. At any rate, they stimulated a little man in evening dress strolling along the pavement towards him, to become suddenly animated and to leap from side to side with outstretched arms.

Panic makes Harlequin three-quarters of us all. For one who had never played Rugby football George handled the situation well. He drew the defence with a feint to the left, then, swerving to the right, shot past into the friendly darkness. From behind came the ringing of feet and an evergrowing din.

It is one of the few compensations a fugitive pursued by a crowd enjoys that, while he has space for his manoeuvres, those who pursue are hampered by their numbers. In the little regiment that pounded at his heels it is probable that there were many faster runners than George. On the other hand, there were many slower, and in the early stages of the chase these impeded their swifter brethren.

At the end of the first half-minute, therefore, George, not sparing himself, had drawn well ahead, and for the first time found leisure for connected thought.

His brain became preternaturally alert, so that when, rounding a corner, he perceived entering the main road from a side-street in front of him a small knot of pedestrians, he did not waver, but was seized with a keen spasm of presence of mind. Without pausing in his stride, he pointed excitedly before him, and at the same moment shouted the words, '*La! La! Vite! Vite!*'

His stock of French was small, but it ran to that, and for his purpose it was ample. The French temperament is not stolid. When the French temperament sees a man running rapidly and pointing into the middle distance and hears him shouting, '*La! La! Vite! Vite!*' it does not stop to make formal inquiries. It sprints like a mustang. It did so now, with the happy result that a moment later George was racing down the road, the centre and recognized leader of an enthusiastic band of six, which, in the next twenty yards, swelled to eleven.

Five minutes later, in a wine-shop near the harbour, he was sipping the first glass of a bottle of cheap but comforting *vin ordinaire* while he explained to the interested proprietor, by means of a mixture of English, broken French, and gestures that he had been helping to chase a thief, but had been forced by fatigue to retire prematurely for refreshment. The proprietor gathered, however, that he had every confidence in the zeal of his still active colleagues.

It is convincing evidence of the extent to which love had triumphed over prudence in George's soul that the advisability of lying hid in his hotel on the following day did not even cross his mind. Immediately after breakfast, or what passed for it at Roville, he set out for the Hotel Cercle de la Mediterranee to hand over the two louis to their owner.

Lady Julia, he was informed on arrival, was out. The porter, politely genial, advised monsieur to seek her on the Promenade des Etrangers.

She was there, on the same seat where she had left the book.

'Good morning,' he said.

She had not seen him coming, and she started at his voice. The flush was back on her face as she turned to him. There was a look of astonishment in the grey eyes.

He held out the two louis.

'I couldn't give them to you last night,' he said.

A horrible idea seized him. It had not occurred to him before.

'I say,' he stammered—'I say, I hope you don't think I had run off with your winnings for good! The croupier wouldn't give them up, you know, so I had to grab them and run. They came to exactly two louis. You put on five francs, you know, and you get seven times your stake. I—'

An elderly lady seated on the bench, who had loomed from behind a parasol towards the middle of these remarks, broke abruptly into speech.

'Who is this young man?'

George looked at her, startled. He had hardly been aware of her presence till now. Rapidly he diagnosed her as a mother—or aunt. She looked more like an aunt. Of course, it must seem odd to her, his charging in like this, a perfect stranger, and beginning to chat with her daughter, or niece, or whatever it was. He began to justify himself.

'I met your—this young lady'—something told him that was not the proper way to put it, but hang it, what else could he say?—'at the casino last night.'

He stopped. The effect of his words on the elderly lady was remarkable. Her face seemed to turn to stone and become all sharp points. She stared at the girl.

'So you were gambling at the casino last night?' she said.

She rose from the seat, a frozen statue of displeasure.

'I shall return to the hotel. When you have arranged your financial transactions with your—friend, I should like to speak to you. You will find me in my room.'

George looked after her dumbly.

The girl spoke, in a curiously strained voice, as if she were speaking to herself.

'I don't care,' she said. 'I'm glad.'

George was concerned.

'I'm afraid your mother is offended, Lady Julia.'

There was a puzzled look in her grey eyes as they met his. Then they lit up. She leaned back in the seat and began to laugh, softly at first, and then with a note that jarred on George. Whatever the humour of the situation—and he had not detected it at present—this mirth, he felt, was unnatural and excessive.

She checked herself at length, and a flush crept over her face.

'I don't know why I did that,' she said, abruptly. 'I'm sorry. There was nothing funny in what you said. But I'm not Lady Julia, and I have no mother. That was Lady Julia who has just gone, and I am nothing more important than her companion.'

'Her companion!'

'I had better say her late companion. It will soon be that. I had strict orders, you see, not to go near the casino without her—and I went.'

'Then—then I've lost you your job—I mean, your position! If it hadn't been for me she wouldn't have known. I—'

'You have done me a great service,' she said. 'You have cut the painter for me when I have been trying for months to muster up the courage to cut it for myself. I don't suppose you know what it is to get into a groove and long to get out of it and not have the pluck. My brother has been writing to me for a long time to join him in Canada. And I hadn't the courage, or the energy, or whatever it is that takes people out of grooves. I knew I was wasting my life, but I was fairly happy—at least, not unhappy; so—well, there it was. I suppose women are like that.'

'And now—?'

'And now you have jerked me out of the groove. I shall go out to Bob by the first boat.'

He scratched the concrete thoughtfully with his stick.

'It's a hard life out there,' he said.

'But it *is* a life.'

He looked at the strollers on the promenade. They seemed very far away—in another world.

'Look here,' he said, hoarsely, and stopped. 'May I sit down?' he asked, abruptly. 'I've got something to say, and I can't say it when I'm looking at you.'

He sat down, and fastened his gaze on a yacht that swayed at anchor against the cloudless sky.

'Look here,' he said. 'Will you marry me?'

He heard her turn quickly, and felt her eyes upon him. He went on doggedly.

'I know,' he said, 'we only met yesterday. You probably think I'm mad.'

'I don't think you're mad,' she said, quietly. 'I only think you're too quixotic. You're sorry for me and you are letting a kind impulse carry you away, as you did last night at the casino. It's like you.'

For the first time he turned towards her.

'I don't know what you suppose I am,' he said, 'but I'll tell you. I'm a clerk in an insurance office. I get a hundred a year and ten days' holiday. Did you take me for a millionaire? If I am, I'm only a tuppenny one. Somebody left me a thousand pounds a few weeks ago. That's how I come to be here. Now you know all about me. I don't know anything about you except that I shall never love anybody else. Marry me, and we'll go to Canada together. You say I've helped you out of your groove. Well, I've only one chance of getting out of mine, and that's through you. If you won't help me, I don't care if I get out of it or not. Will you pull me out?'

She did not speak. She sat looking out to sea, past the many-coloured crowd.

He watched her face, but her hat shaded her eyes and he could read nothing in it.

And then, suddenly, without quite knowing how it had got there, he found that her hand was in his, and he was clutching it as a drowning man clutches a rope.

He could see her eyes now, and there was a message in them that set his heart racing. A great content filled him. She was so companionable, such a friend. It seemed incredible to him that it was only yesterday that they had met for the first time.

'And now,' she said, 'would you mind telling me your name?'

The little waves murmured as they rolled lazily up the beach. Somewhere behind the trees in the gardens a band had begun to play. The breeze, blowing in from the blue Mediterranean, was charged with salt and happiness. And from a seat on the promenade, a young man swept the crowd with a defiant gaze.

'It isn't true,' it seemed to say. 'I'm not a jelly-fish.'

AHEAD OF SCHEDULE

It was to Wilson, his valet, with whom he frequently chatted in airy fashion before rising of a morning, that Rollo Finch first disclosed his great idea. Wilson was a man of silent habit, and men of silent habit rarely escaped Rollo's confidences.

'Wilson,' he said one morning from the recesses of his bed, as the valet entered with his shaving-water, 'have you ever been in love?'

'Yes, sir,' said the valet, unperturbed.

One would hardly have expected the answer to be in the affirmative. Like most valets and all chauffeurs, Wilson gave the impression of being above the softer emotions.

'What happened?' inquired Rollo.

'It came to nothing, sir,' said Wilson, beginning to strop the razor with no appearance of concern.

'Ah!' said Rollo. 'And I bet I know why. You didn't go the right way to work.'

'No, sir?'

'Not one fellow in a hundred does. I know. I've thought it out. I've been thinking the deuce of a lot about it lately. It's dashed tricky, this making love. Most fellows haven't a notion how to work it. No system. No system, Wilson, old scout.'

'No, sir?'

'Now, I *have* a system. And I'll tell it you. It may do you a bit of good next time you feel that impulse. You're not dead yet. Now, my system is simply to go to it gradually, by degrees. Work by schedule. See what I mean?'

'Not entirely, sir.'

'Well, I'll give you the details. First thing, you want to find the girl.'

'Just so, sir.'

'Well, when you've found her, what do you do? You just look at her. See what I mean?'

'Not entirely, sir.'

'Look at her, my boy. That's just the start—the foundation. You develop from that. But you keep away. That's the point. I've thought this thing out. Mind you, I don't claim absolutely all the credit for the idea myself. It's by way of being based on Christian Science. Absent treatment, and all that. But most of it's mine. All the fine work.'

'Yes, sir?'

'Yes. Absolutely all the fine work. Here's the thing in a nutshell. You find the girl. Right. Of course, you've got to meet her once, just to establish the connexion. Then you get busy. First week, looks. Just look at her. Second week, letters. Write to her every day. Third week, flowers. Send her some every afternoon. Fourth week, presents with a bit more class about them. Bit of jewellery now and then. See what I mean? Fifth week,—lunches and suppers and things. Sixth week, propose, though you can do it in the fifth week if you see a chance. You've got to leave that to the fellow's judgement. Well, there you are. See what I mean?'

Wilson stropped his master's razor thoughtfully.

'A trifle elaborate, sir, is it not?' he said.

Rollo thumped the counterpane.

'I knew you'd say that. That's what nine fellows out of ten *would* say. They'd want to rush it. I tell you, Wilson, old scout, you *can't* rush it.'

Wilson brooded awhile, his mind back in the passionate past.

'In Market Bumpstead, sir—'

'What the deuce is Market Bumpstead?'

'A village, sir, where I lived until I came to London.'

'Well?'

'In Market Bumpstead, sir, the prevailing custom was to escort the young lady home from church, buy her some little present—some ribbons, possibly—next day, take her for a walk, and kiss her, sir.'

Wilson's voice, as he unfolded these devices of the dashing youth of Market Bumpstead, had taken on an animation quite unsuitable to a conscientious valet. He gave the impression of a man who does not depend on idle rumour for his facts. His eye gleamed unprofessionally for a moment before resuming its habitual expression of quiet introspection.

Rollo shook his head.

'That sort of thing might work in a village,' he said, 'but you want something better for London.'

Rollo Finch—in the present unsatisfactory state of the law parents may still christen a child Rollo—was a youth to whom Nature had given a cheerful disposition not marred by any superfluity of brain. Everyone liked Rollo—the great majority on sight, the rest as soon as they heard that he would be a millionaire on the death of his Uncle Andrew. There is a subtle something, a sort of nebulous charm, as it were, about young men who will be millionaires on the death of their Uncle Andrew which softens the ruggedest misanthrope.

Rollo's mother had been a Miss Galloway, of Pittsburgh, Pennsylvania, U.S.A.; and Andrew Galloway, the world-famous Braces King, the inventor and proprietor of the inimitable 'Tried and Proven', was her brother. His braces had penetrated to every corner of the earth. Wherever civilization reigned you would find men wearing Galloway's 'Tried and Proven'.

Between Rollo and this human benefactor there had always existed friendly relations, and it was an open secret that, unless his uncle were to marry and supply the world with little Galloways as well as braces, the young man would come into his money.

So Rollo moved on his way through life, popular and happy. Always merry and bright. That was Rollo.

Or nearly always. For there were moments—we all have our greyer moments—when he could have wished that Mr Galloway had been a trifle older or a trifle less robust. The Braces potentate was at present passing, in excellent health, through the Indian summer of life. He was, moreover, as has been stated, by birth and residence a Pittsburgh man. And the tendency of middle-aged Pittsburgh millionaires to marry chorus-girls is notoriously like the homing instinct of pigeons. Something—it may be the smoke—seems to work on them like a charm.

In the case of Andrew Galloway, Nature had been thwarted up till now by the accident of an unfortunate attachment in early life. The facts were not fully known, but it was generally understood that his fiancee had exercised Woman's prerogative and changed her mind. Also, that she had done this on the actual wedding-day, causing annoyance to all, and had clinched the matter by eloping to Jersey City with the prospective bridegroom's own coachman. Whatever the facts, there was no doubt about their result. Mr Galloway, having abjured woman utterly, had flung himself with moody energy into the manufacture and propagation of his 'Tried and Proven' Braces, and had found consolation in it ever since. He would be strong, he told himself, like his braces. Hearts might snap beneath a sudden strain. Not so the 'Tried and Proven'. Love might tug and tug again, but never more should the trousers of passion break away from the tough, masterful braces of self-control.

As Mr Galloway had been in this frame of mind for a matter of eleven years, it seemed to Rollo not unreasonable to hope that he might continue in it permanently. He had the very strongest objection to his uncle marrying a chorus-girl; and, as the years went on and the disaster did not happen, his hopes of playing the role of heir till the fall of the curtain grew stronger and stronger. He was one of those young men who must be heirs or nothing. This is the age of the specialist, and years ago Rollo had settled on his career. Even as a boy, hardly capable of connected thought, he had been convinced that his speciality, the one thing he could do really well, was to inherit money. All he wanted was a chance. It would be bitter if Fate should withhold it from him.

He did not object on principle to men marrying chorus-girls. On the contrary, he wanted to marry one himself.

It was this fact which had given that turn to his thoughts which had finally resulted in the schedule.

The first intimation that Wilson had that the schedule was actually to be put into practical operation was when his employer, one Monday evening, requested him to buy a medium-sized bunch of the best red roses and deliver them personally, with a note, to Miss Marguerite Parker at the stage-door of the Duke of Cornwall's Theatre.

Wilson received the order in his customary gravely deferential manner, and was turning to go; but Rollo had more to add.

'Flowers, Wilson,' he said, significantly.

'So I understood you to say, sir. I will see to it at once.'

'See what I mean? Third week, Wilson.'

'Indeed, sir?'

Rollo remained for a moment in what he would have called thought.

'Charming girl, Wilson.'

'Indeed, sir?'

'Seen the show?'

'Not yet, sir.'

'You should,' said Rollo, earnestly. 'Take my advice, old scout, and see it first chance you get. It's topping. I've had the same seat in the middle of the front row of the stalls for two weeks.'

'Indeed, sir?'

'Looks, Wilson! The good old schedule.'

'Have you noticed any satisfactory results, sir?'

'It's working. On Saturday night she looked at me five times. She's a delightful girl, Wilson. Nice, quiet girl—not the usual sort. I met her first at a lunch at Oddy's. She's the last girl on the O.P. side. I'm sure you'd like her, Wilson.'

'I have every confidence in your taste, sir.'

'You'll see her for yourself this evening. Don't let the fellow at the stage-door put you off. Slip him half a crown or a couple of quid or something, and say you must see her personally. Are you a close observer, Wilson?'

'I think so, sir.'

'Because I want you to notice particularly how she takes it. See that she reads the note in your presence. I've taken a good deal of trouble over that note, Wilson. It's a good note. Well expressed. Watch her face while she's reading it.'

'Very good, sir. Excuse me, sir.'

'Eh?'

'I had almost forgotten to mention it. Mr Galloway rang up on the telephone shortly before you came in.'

'What! Is he in England?'

Mr Galloway was in the habit of taking occasional trips to Great Britain to confer with the general manager of his London branch. Rollo had grown accustomed to receiving no notice of these visits.

'He arrived two days ago on the *Baltic*, sir. He left a message that he was in London for a week, and would be glad if you would dine with him tomorrow at his club.'

Rollo nodded. On these occasions it was his practice to hold himself unreservedly at Mr Galloway's disposal. The latter's invitations were royal commands. Rollo was glad that the visit had happened now. In another two weeks it might have been disastrous to the schedule.

The club to which the Braces King belonged was a richly but gloomily furnished building in Pall Mall, a place of soft carpets, shaded lights, and whispers. Grave, elderly men moved noiselessly to and fro, or sat in meditative silence in deep arm-chairs. Sometimes the visitor felt that he was in a cathedral, sometimes in a Turkish bath; while now and then there was a suggestion of the waiting-room of a more than usually prosperous dentist. It was magnificent, but not exhilarating.

Rollo was shown into the smoking-room, where his uncle received him. There was a good deal of Mr Andrew Galloway. Grief, gnawing at his heart, had not sagged his ample waistcoat, which preceded him as he moved in much the same manner as Birnam Woods preceded the army of Macduff. A well-nourished hand crept round the corner of the edifice and enveloped Rollo's in a powerful grip.

'Ah, my boy!' bellowed Mr Galloway cheerfully. His voice was always loud. 'Glad you've come.'

It would be absurd to say that Rollo looked at his uncle keenly. He was not capable of looking keenly at anyone. But certainly a puzzled expression came into his face. Whether it was the heartiness of the other's handshake or the unusual cheeriness of his voice, he could not say; but something gave him the impression that a curious change had come over the Braces King. When they had met before during the last few years Mr Galloway had been practically sixteen stone five of blood and iron—one of those stern, soured men. His attitude had been that of one for whom Life's music had ceased. Had he then inserted another record? His manner conveyed that idea.

Sustained thought always gave Rollo a headache. He ceased to speculate.

'Still got the same *chef* here, uncle?' he said. 'Deuced brainy fellow. I always like dining here.'

'Here!' Mr Galloway surveyed the somnolent occupants of the room with spirited scorn. 'We aren't going to dine in this forsaken old mausoleum. I've sent in my resignation today. If I find myself wanting this sort of thing at any time, I'll go to Paris and hunt up the Morgue. Bunch of old dead-beats! Bah! I've engaged a table at Romano's. That's more in my line. Get your coat, and let's be going.'

In the cab Rollo risked the headache. At whatever cost this thing must be pondered over. His uncle prattled gaily throughout the journey. Once he whooped—some weird, forgotten college yell, dragged from the misty depths of the past. It was passing strange. And in this unusual manner the two rolled into the Strand, and drew up at Romano's door.

Mr Galloway was a good trencherman. At a very early date he had realized that a man who wishes to make satisfactory braces must keep his strength up. He wanted a good deal here below, and he wanted it warm and well cooked. It was, therefore, not immediately that his dinner with Rollo became a feast of reason and a flow of soul. Indeed, the two revellers had lighted their cigars before the elder gave forth any remark that was not purely gastronomic.

When he did jerk the conversation up on to a higher plane, he jerked it hard. He sent it shooting into the realms of the soulful with a whiz.

'Rollo,' he said, blowing a smoke-ring, 'do you believe in affinities?'

Rollo, in the act of sipping a liqueur brandy, lowered his glass in surprise. His head was singing slightly as the result of some rather spirited Bollinger (extra sec), and he wondered if he had heard aright.

Mr Galloway continued, his voice rising as he spoke.

'My boy,' he said, 'I feel young tonight for the first time in years. And, hang it, I'm not so old! Men have married at twice my age.'

Strictly speaking, this was incorrect, unless one counted Methuselah; but perhaps Mr Galloway spoke figuratively.

'Three times my age,' he proceeded, leaning back and blowing smoke, thereby missing his nephew's agitated start. 'Four times my age. Five times my age. Six—'

He pulled himself together in some confusion. A generous wine, that Bollinger. He must be careful.

He coughed.

'Are you—you aren't—are you—' Rollo paused. 'Are you thinking of getting married, uncle?'

Mr Galloway's gaze was still on the ceiling.

'A great deal of nonsense,' he yelled severely, 'is talked about men lowering themselves by marrying actresses. I was a guest at a supper-party last night at which an actress was present. And a more charming, sensible girl I never wish to meet. Not one of your silly, brainless chits who don't know the difference between lobster Newburg and canvas-back duck, and who prefer sweet champagne to dry. No, sir! Not one of your mincing, affected kind who pretend they never touch anything except a spoonful of cold *consomme*. No, sir! Good, healthy appetite. Enjoyed her food, and knew why she was enjoying it. I give you my word, my boy, until I met her I didn't know a woman existed who could talk so damned sensibly about a *bavaroise au rhum*.'

He suspended his striking tribute in order to relight his cigar.

'She can use a chafing-dish,' he resumed, his voice vibrating with emotion. 'She told me so. She said she could fix chicken so that a man would leave home for it.' He paused, momentarily overcome. '*And* Welsh rarebits,' he added reverently.

He puffed hard at his cigar.

'Yes,' he said. 'Welsh rarebits, too. And because,' he shouted wrathfully, 'because, forsooth, she earns an honest living by singing in the chorus of a comic opera, a whole bunch of snivelling idiots will say I have made a fool of myself. Let them!' he bellowed, sitting up and glaring at Rollo. 'I say, let them! I'll show them that Andrew Galloway is not the man to—to—is not the man—' He stopped. 'Well, anyway, I'll show them,' he concluded rather lamely.

Rollo eyed him with fallen jaw. His liqueur had turned to wormwood. He had been fearing this for years. You may drive out Nature with a pitchfork, but she will return. Blood will tell. Once a Pittsburgh millionaire, always a Pittsburgh millionaire. For eleven years his uncle had fought against his natural propensities, with apparent success; but Nature had won in the end. His words could have no other meaning. Andrew Galloway was going to marry a chorus-girl.

Mr Galloway rapped on the table, and ordered another kummel.

'Marguerite Parker!' he roared dreamily, rolling the words round his tongue, like port.

'Marguerite Parker!' exclaimed Rollo, bounding in his chair.

His uncle met his eye sternly.

'That was the name I said. You seem to know it. Perhaps you have something to say against the lady. Eh? Have you? Have you? I warn you to be careful. What do you know of Miss Parker? Speak!'

'Er—no, no. Oh, no! I just know the name, that's all. I—I rather think I met her once at lunch. Or it may have been somebody else. I know it was someone.'

He plunged at his glass. His uncle's gaze relaxed its austerity.

'I hope you will meet her many more times at lunch, my boy. I hope you will come to look upon her as a second mother.'

This was where Rollo asked if he might have a little more brandy.

When the restorative came he drank it at a gulp; then looked across at his uncle. The great man still mused.

'Er—when is it to be?' asked Rollo. 'The wedding, and all that?'

'Hardly before the Fall, I think. No, not before the Fall. I shall be busy till then. I have taken no steps in the matter yet.'

'No steps? You mean—? Haven't you—haven't you proposed?'

'I have had no time. Be reasonable, my boy; be reasonable.'

'Oh!' said Rollo.

He breathed a long breath. A suspicion of silver lining had become visible through the clouds.

'I doubt,' said Mr Galloway, meditatively, 'if I shall be able to find time till the end of the week. I am very busy. Let me see. Tomorrow? No. Meeting of the shareholders. Thursday? Friday? No. No, it will have to stand over till Saturday. After Saturday's matinee. That will do excellently.'

There is a dramatic spectacle to be observed every day in this land of ours, which, though deserving of recognition, no artist has yet pictured on canvas. We allude to the suburban season-ticket holder's sudden flash of speed. Everyone must have seen at one time or another a happy, bright-faced season-ticket holder strolling placidly towards the station, humming, perhaps, in his light-heartedness, some gay air. He feels secure. Fate cannot touch him, for he has left himself for once plenty of time to catch that 8.50, for which he has so often sprinted like the gazelle of the prairie. As he strolls, suddenly his eye falls on the church clock. The next moment with a passionate cry he is endeavouring to lower his record for the fifty-yard dash. All the while his watch has been fifteen minutes slow.

In just such a case was Rollo Finch. He had fancied that he had plenty of time. And now, in an instant, the fact was borne in upon him that he must hurry.

For the greater part of the night of his uncle's dinner he lay sleepless, vainly endeavouring to find a way out of the difficulty. It was not till early morning that he faced the inevitable. He hated to abandon the schedule. To do so meant changing a well-ordered advance into a forlorn hope. But circumstances compelled it. There are moments when speed alone can save love's season-ticket holder.

On the following afternoon he acted. It was no occasion for stint. He had to condense into one day the carefully considered movements of two weeks, and to the best of his ability he did so. He bought three bouquets, a bracelet, and a gold Billiken with ruby eyes, and sent them to the theatre by messenger-boy. With them went an invitation to supper.

Then, with the feeling that he had done all that was possible, he returned to his flat and waited for the hour.

He dressed with more than usual care that night. Your wise general never throws away a move. He was particular about his tie. As a rule, Wilson selected one for him. But there had been times when Wilson had made mistakes. One could not rely absolutely on Wilson's taste in ties. He did not blame him. Better men than Wilson had gone wrong over an evening tie. But tonight there must be no taking of chances.

'Where do we keep our ties, Wilson?' he asked.

'The closet to the right of the door, sir. The first twelve shallow shelves, counting from the top, sir. They contain a fair selection of our various cravats. Replicas in bulk are to be found in the third nest of drawers in your dressing-room, sir.'

'I only want one, my good man. I'm not a regiment. Ah! I stake all on this one. Not a word, Wilson. No discussion. This is the tie I wear. What's the time?'

'Eight minutes to eleven, sir.'

'I must be off. I shall be late. I shan't want you any more tonight. Don't wait for me.'

'Very good, sir.'

Rollo left the room, pale but determined, and hailed a taxi.

It is a pleasant spot, the vestibule of the Carlton Hotel. Glare—glitter—distant music—fair women—brave men. But one can have too much of it, and as the moments pass, and she does not arrive, a chill seems to creep into the atmosphere. We wait on, hoping against hope, and at last, just as waiters and commissionaires are beginning to eye us with suspicion, we face the truth. She is not coming. Then out we crawl into cold, callous Pall Mall, and so home. You have been through it, dear reader, and so have I.

And so, at eleven forty-five that evening, had Rollo. For a full three-quarters of an hour he waited, scanning the face of each new arrival with the anxious scrutiny of a lost dog seeking its master; but at fourteen minutes to twelve the last faint flicker of hope had died away. A girl may be a quarter of an hour late for supper. She may be half an hour late. But there is a limit, and to Rollo's mind forty-five minutes passed it. At ten minutes to twelve a uniformed official outside the Carlton signalled to a taxi-cab, and there entered it a young man whose faith in Woman was dead.

Rollo meditated bitterly as he drove home. It was not so much the fact that she had not come that stirred him. Many things may keep a girl from supper. It was the calm way in which she had ignored the invitation. When you send a girl three bouquets, a bracelet, and a gold Billiken with ruby eyes, you do not expect an entire absence of recognition. Even a penny-in-the-slot machine treats you better than that. It may give you hairpins when you want matches but at least it takes some notice of you.

He was still deep in gloomy thought when he inserted his latchkey and opened the door of his flat.

He was roused from his reflections by a laugh from the sitting-room. He started. It was a pleasant laugh, and musical, but it sent Rollo diving, outraged, for the handle of the door. What was a woman doing in his sitting-room at this hour? Was his flat an hotel?

The advent of an unbidden guest rarely fails to produce a certain *gene*. The sudden appearance of Rollo caused a dead silence.

It was broken by the fall of a chair on the carpet as Wilson rose hurriedly to his feet.

Rollo stood in the doorway, an impressive statue of restrained indignation. He could see the outlying portions of a girl in blue at the further end of the table, but Wilson obscured his vision.

'Didn't expect you back, sir,' said Wilson.

For the first time in the history of their acquaintance his accustomed calm seemed somewhat ruffled.

'So I should think,' said Rollo. 'I believe you, by George!'

'You had better explain, Jim,' said a dispassionate voice from the end of the table.

Wilson stepped aside.

'My wife, sir,' he said, apologetically, but with pride.

'Your wife!'

'We were married this morning, sir.'

The lady nodded cheerfully at Rollo. She was small and slight, with an impudent nose and a mass of brown hair.

'Awfully glad to meet you,' she said, cracking a walnut.

Rollo gaped.

She looked at him again.

'We've met, haven't we? Oh yes, I remember. We met at lunch once. And you sent me some flowers. It was ever so kind of you,' she said, beaming.

She cracked another nut. She seemed to consider that the introductions were complete and that formality could now be dispensed with once more. She appeared at peace with all men.

The situation was slipping from Rollo's grip. He continued to gape.

Then he remembered his grievance.

'I think you might have let me know you weren't coming to supper.'

'Supper?'

'I sent a note to the theatre this afternoon.'

'I haven't been to the theatre today. They let me off because I was going to be married. I'm so sorry. I hope you didn't wait long.'

Rollo's resentment melted before the friendliness of her smile.

'Hardly any time,' he said, untruthfully.

'If I might explain, sir,' said Wilson.

'By George! If you can, you'll save me from a brainstorm. Cut loose, and don't be afraid you'll bore me. You won't.'

'Mrs Wilson and I are old friends, sir. We come from the same town. In fact—'

Rollo's face cleared.

'By George! Market what's-its-name! Why, of course. Then she—'

'Just so, sir. If you recollect, you asked me once if I had ever been in love, and I replied in the affirmative.'

'And it was—'

'Mrs Wilson and I were engaged to be married before either of us came to London. There was a misunderstanding, which was entirely my—'

'Jim! It was mine.'

'No, it was all through my being a fool.'

'It was not. You know it wasn't!'

Rollo intervened.

'Well?'

'And when you sent me with the flowers, sir—well, we talked it over again, and—that was how it came about, sir.'

The bride looked up from her walnuts.

'You aren't angry?' she smiled up at Rollo.

'Angry?' He reflected. Of course, it was only reasonable that he should be a little—well, not exactly angry, but—And then for the first time it came to him that the situation was not entirely without its compensations. Until that moment he had completely forgotten Mr Galloway.

'Angry?' he said. 'Great Scott, no! Jolly glad I came back in time to get a bit of the wedding-breakfast. I want it, I can tell you. I'm hungry. Here we all are, eh? Let's enjoy ourselves. Wilson, old scout, bustle about and give us your imitation of a bridegroom mixing a "B. and S." for the best man. Mrs Wilson, if you'll look in at the theatre tomorrow you'll find one or two small wedding presents waiting for you. Three bouquets—they'll be a bit withered, I'm afraid—a bracelet, and a gold Billiken with ruby eyes. I hope he'll bring you luck. Oh, Wilson!'

'Sir?'

'Touching this little business—don't answer if it's a delicate question, but I *should* like to know—I suppose you didn't try the schedule. What? More the Market Thingummy method, eh? The one you described to me?'

'Market Bumpstead, sir?' said Wilson. 'On those lines.'

Rollo nodded thoughtfully.

'It seems to me,' he said, 'they know a thing or two down in Market Bumpstead.'

'A very rising little place, sir,' assented Wilson.

SIR AGRAVAINE

A TALE OF KING ARTHUR'S ROUND TABLE

Some time ago, when spending a delightful week-end at the ancestral castle of my dear old friend, the Duke of Weatherstonhope (pronounced Wop), I came across an old black-letter MS. It is on this that the story which follows is based.

I have found it necessary to touch the thing up a little here and there, for writers in those days were weak in construction. Their idea of telling a story was to take a long breath and start droning away without any stops or dialogue till the thing was over.

I have also condensed the title. In the original it ran, '"How it came about that ye good Knight Sir Agravaine ye Dolorous of ye Table Round did fare forth to succour a damsel in distress and after divers journeyings and perils by flood and by field did win her for his bride and right happily did they twain live ever afterwards," by Ambrose ye monk.'

It was a pretty snappy title for those days, but we have such a high standard in titles nowadays that I have felt compelled to omit a few yards of it.

We may now proceed to the story.

The great tournament was in full swing. All through the afternoon boiler-plated knights on mettlesome chargers had hurled themselves on each other's spears, to the vast contentment of all. Bright eyes shone; handkerchiefs fluttered; musical voices urged chosen champions to knock the cover off their brawny adversaries. The cheap seats had long since become hoarse with emotion. All round the arena rose the cries of itinerant merchants: 'Iced malvoisie,' 'Score-cards; ye cannot tell the jousters without a score-card.' All was revelry and excitement.

A hush fell on the throng. From either end of the arena a mounted knight in armour had entered.

The herald raised his hand.

'Ladeez'n gemmen! Battling Galahad and Agravaine the Dolorous. Galahad on my right, Agravaine on my left. Squires out of the ring. Time!'

A speculator among the crowd offered six to one on Galahad, but found no takers. Nor was the public's caution without reason.

A moment later the two had met in a cloud of dust, and Agravaine, shooting over his horse's crupper, had fallen with a metallic clang.

He picked himself up, and limped slowly from the arena. He was not unused to this sort of thing. Indeed, nothing else had happened to him in his whole jousting career.

The truth was that Sir Agravaine the Dolorous was out of his element at King Arthur's court, and he knew it. It was this knowledge that had given him that settled air of melancholy from which he derived his title.

Until I came upon this black-letter MS. I had been under the impression, like, I presume, everybody else, that every Knight of the Round Table was a model of physical strength and beauty. Malory says nothing to suggest the contrary. Nor does Tennyson. But apparently there were exceptions, of whom Sir Agravaine the Dolorous must have been the chief.

There was, it seems, nothing to mitigate this unfortunate man's physical deficiencies. There is a place in the world for the strong, ugly man, and there is a place for the weak, handsome man. But to fall short both in features and in muscle is to stake your all on brain. And in the days of King Arthur you did not find the populace turning out to do homage to brain. It was a drug on the market. Agravaine was a good deal better equipped than his contemporaries with grey matter, but his height in his socks was but five feet four; and his muscles, though he had taken three correspondence courses in physical culture, remained distressingly flaccid. His eyes were pale and mild, his nose snub, and his chin receded sharply from his lower lip, as if Nature, designing him, had had to leave off in a hurry and finish the job anyhow. The upper teeth, protruding, completed the resemblance to a nervous rabbit.

Handicapped in this manner, it is no wonder that he should feel sad and lonely in King Arthur's court. At heart he ached for romance; but romance passed him by. The ladies of the court ignored his existence, while, as for those wandering damsels who came periodically to Camelot to complain of the behaviour of dragons, giants, and the like, and to ask permission of the king to take a knight back with them to fight their cause (just as, nowadays, one goes out and calls a policeman), he simply had no chance. The choice always fell on Lancelot or some other popular favourite.

The tournament was followed by a feast. In those brave days almost everything was followed by a feast. The scene was gay and animated. Fair ladies, brave knights, churls, varlets, squires, scurvy knaves, men-at-arms, malapert rogues—all were merry. All save Agravaine. He sat silent and moody. To the jests of Dagonet he turned a deaf ear. And when his neighbour, Sir Kay, arguing with Sir Percivale on current form, appealed to him to back up his statement that Sir Gawain, though a workman-like middle-weight, lacked the punch, he did not answer, though the subject was one on which he held strong views. He sat on, brooding.

As he sat there, a man-at-arms entered the hall.

'Your majesty,' he cried, 'a damsel in distress waits without.'

There was a murmur of excitement and interest.

'Show her in,' said the king, beaming.

The man-at-arms retired. Around the table the knights were struggling into an upright position in their seats and twirling their moustaches. Agravaine alone made no movement. He had been through this sort of thing so often. What were distressed damsels to him? His whole demeanour said, as plainly as if he had spoken the words, 'What's the use?'

The crowd at the door parted, and through the opening came a figure at the sight of whom the expectant faces of the knights turned pale with consternation. For the new-comer was quite the plainest girl those stately halls had ever seen. Possibly the only plain girl they had ever seen, for no instance is recorded in our authorities of the existence at that period of any such.

The knights gazed at her blankly. Those were the grand old days of chivalry, when a thousand swords would leap from their scabbards to protect defenceless woman, if she were beautiful. The present seemed something in the nature of a special case, and nobody was quite certain as to the correct procedure.

An awkward silence was broken by the king.

'Er—yes?' he said.

The damsel halted.

'Your majesty,' she cried, 'I am in distress. I crave help!'

'Just so,' said the king, uneasily, flashing an apprehensive glance at the rows of perturbed faces before him. 'Just *so*. What—er—what is the exact nature of the—ah—trouble? Any assistance these gallant knights can render will, I am sure, be—ah—eagerly rendered.'

He looked imploringly at the silent warriors. As a rule, this speech was the signal for roars of applause. But now there was not even a murmur.

'I may say enthusiastically,' he added.

Not a sound.

'Precisely,' said the king, ever tactful. 'And now—you were saying?'

'I am Yvonne, the daughter of Earl Dorm of the Hills,' said the damsel, 'and my father has sent me to ask protection from a gallant knight against a fiery dragon that ravages the country-side.'

'A dragon, gentlemen,' said the king, aside. It was usually a safe draw. Nothing pleased the knight of that time more than a brisk bout with a dragon. But now the tempting word was received in silence.

'Fiery,' said the king.

Some more silence.

The king had recourse to the direct appeal. 'Sir Gawain, this Court would be greatly indebted to you if—'

Sir Gawain said he had strained a muscle at the last tournament.

'Sir Pelleas.'

The king's voice was growing flat with consternation. The situation was unprecedented.

Sir Pelleas said he had an ingrowing toe-nail.

The king's eye rolled in anguish around the table. Suddenly it stopped. It brightened. His look of dismay changed to one of relief.

A knight had risen to his feet. It was Agravaine.

'Ah!' said the king, drawing a deep breath.

Sir Agravaine gulped. He was feeling more nervous than he had ever felt in his life. Never before had he risen to volunteer his services in a matter of this kind, and his state of mind was that of a small boy about to recite his first piece of poetry.

It was not only the consciousness that every eye, except one of Sir Balin's which had been closed in the tournament that afternoon, was upon him. What made him feel like a mild gentleman in a post-office who has asked the lady assistant if she will have time to attend to him soon and has caught her eye, was the fact that he thought he had observed the damsel Yvonne frown as he rose. He groaned in spirit. This damsel, he felt, wanted the proper goods or none at all. She might not be able to get Sir Lancelot or Sir Galahad; but she was not going to be satisfied with a half-portion.

The fact was that Sir Agravaine had fallen in love at first sight. The moment he had caught a glimpse of the damsel Yvonne, he loved her devotedly. To others she seemed plain and unattractive. To him she was a Queen of Beauty. He was amazed at the inexplicable attitude of the knights around him. He had expected them to rise in a body to clamour for the chance of assisting this radiant vision. He could hardly believe, even now, that he was positively the only starter.

'This is Sir Agravaine the Dolorous,' said the king to the damsel. 'Will you take him as your champion?'

Agravaine held his breath. But all was well. The damsel bowed.

'Then, Sir Agravaine,' said the king, 'perhaps you had better have your charger sent round at once. I imagine that the matter is pressing—time and—er—dragons wait for no man.'

Ten minutes later Agravaine, still dazed, was jogging along to the hills, with the damsel by his side.

It was some time before either of them spoke. The damsel seemed preoccupied, and Agravaine's mind was a welter of confused thoughts, the most prominent of which and the one to which he kept returning being the startling reflection that he, who had pined for romance so long, had got it now in full measure.

A dragon! Fiery withal. Was he absolutely certain that he was capable of handling an argument with a fiery dragon? He would have given much for a little previous experience of this sort of thing. It was too late now, but he wished he had had the forethought to get Merlin to put up a magic prescription for him, rendering him immune to dragon-bites. But did dragons bite? Or did they whack at you with their tails? Or just blow fire?

There were a dozen such points that he would have liked to have settled before starting. It was silly to start out on a venture of this sort without special knowledge. He had half a mind to plead a forgotten engagement and go straight back.

Then he looked at the damsel, and his mind was made up. What did death matter if he could serve her?

He coughed. She came out of her reverie with a start.

'This dragon, now?' said Agravaine.

For a moment the damsel did not reply. 'A fearsome worm, Sir Knight,' she said at length. 'It raveneth by day and by night. It breathes fire from its nostrils.'

'Does it!' said Agravaine. '*Does* it! I You couldn't give some idea what it looks like, what kind of *size* it is?'

'Its body is as thick as ten stout trees, and its head touches the clouds.'

'Does it!' said Agravaine thoughtfully. '*Does* it!'

'Oh, Sir Knight, I pray you have a care.'

'I will,' said Agravaine. And he had seldom said anything more fervently. The future looked about as bad as it could be. Any hopes he may have entertained that this dragon might turn out to be comparatively small and inoffensive were dissipated. This was plainly no debilitated wreck of a dragon, its growth stunted by excessive-fire-breathing. A body as thick as ten stout trees! He would not even have the melancholy satisfaction of giving the creature indigestion. For all the impression he was likely to make on that vast interior, he might as well be a salted almond.

As they were speaking, a dim mass on the skyline began to take shape.

'Behold!' said the damsel. 'My father's castle.' And presently they were riding across the drawbridge and through the great gate, which shut behind them with a clang.

As they dismounted a man came out through a door at the farther end of the courtyard.

'Father,' said Yvonne, 'this is the gallant knight Sir Agravaine, who has come to—' it seemed to Agravaine that she hesitated for a moment.

'To tackle our dragon?' said the father. 'Excellent. Come right in.'

Earl Dorm of the Hills, was a small, elderly man, with what Agravaine considered a distinctly furtive air about him. His eyes were too close together, and he was over-lavish with a weak, cunning smile Even Agravaine, who was in the mood to like the whole family, if possible, for Yvonne's sake, could not help feeling that appearances were against this particular exhibit. He might have a heart of gold beneath the outward aspect of a confidence-trick expert whose hobby was dog-stealing, but there was no doubt that his exterior did not inspire a genial glow of confidence.

'Very good of you to come,' said the earl.

'It's a pleasure,' said Agravaine. 'I have been hearing all about the dragon.'

'A great scourge,' agreed his host. 'We must have a long talk about it after dinner.'

It was the custom in those days in the stately homes of England for the whole strength of the company to take their meals together. The guests sat at the upper table, the ladies in a gallery above them, while the usual drove of men-at-arms, archers, malapert rogues, varlets, scurvy knaves, scullions, and plug-uglies attached to all medieval households, squashed in near the door, wherever they could find room.

The retinue of Earl Dorm was not strong numerically—the household being, to judge from appearances, one that had seen better days; but it struck Agravaine that what it lacked in numbers it made up in toughness. Among all those at the bottom of the room there was not one whom it would have been agreeable to meet alone in a dark alley. Of all those foreheads not one achieved a height of more than one point nought four inches. A sinister collection, indeed, and one which, Agravaine felt, should have been capable of handling without his assistance any dragon that ever came into the world to stimulate the asbestos industry.

He was roused from his reflections by the voice of his host.

'I hope you are not tired after your journey, Sir Agravaine? My little girl did not bore you, I trust? We are very quiet folk here. Country mice. But we must try to make your visit interesting.'

Agravaine felt that the dragon might be counted upon to do that. He said as much.

'Ah, yes, the dragon,' said Earl Dorm, 'I was forgetting the dragon. I want to have a long talk with you about that dragon. Not now. Later on.'

His eye caught Agravaine's, and he smiled that weak, cunning smile of his. And for the first time the knight was conscious of a curious feeling that all was not square and aboveboard in this castle. A conviction began to steal over him that in some way he was being played with, that some game was afoot which he did not understand, that—in a word—there was dirty work at the cross-roads.

There was a touch of mystery in the atmosphere which made him vaguely uneasy. When a fiery dragon is ravaging the countryside to such an extent that the S.O.S. call has been sent out to the Round Table, a knight has a right to expect the monster to be the main theme of conversation. The tendency on his host's part was apparently to avoid touching on the subject at all. He was vague and elusive; and the one topic on which an honest man is not vague and elusive is that of fiery dragons. It was not right. It was as if one should phone for the police and engage them, on arrival, in a discussion on the day's football results.

A wave of distrust swept over Agravaine. He had heard stories of robber chiefs who lured strangers into their strongholds and then held them prisoners while the public nervously dodged their anxious friends who had formed subscription lists to make up the ransom. Could this be such a case? The man certainly had an evasive manner and a smile which would have justified any jury in returning a verdict without leaving the box. On the other hand, there was Yvonne. His reason revolted against the idea of that sweet girl being a party to any such conspiracy.

No, probably it was only the Earl's unfortunate manner. Perhaps he suffered from some muscular weakness of the face which made him smile like that.

Nevertheless, he certainly wished that he had not allowed himself to be deprived of his sword and armour. At the time it had seemed to him that the Earl's remark that the latter needed polishing and the former stropping betrayed only a kindly consideration for his guest's well-being. Now, it had the aspect of being part of a carefully-constructed plot.

On the other hand—here philosophy came to his rescue—if anybody did mean to start anything, his sword and armour might just as well not be there. Any one of those mammoth low-brows at the door could eat him, armour and all.

He resumed his meal, uneasy but resigned.

Dinner at Earl Dorm's was no lunch-counter scuffle. It started early and finished late. It was not till an advanced hour that Agravaine was conducted to his room.

The room which had been allotted to him was high up in the eastern tower. It was a nice room, but to one in Agravaine's state of suppressed suspicion a trifle too solidly upholstered. The door was of the thickest oak, studded with iron nails. Iron bars formed a neat pattern across the only window.

Hardly had Agravaine observed these things when the door opened, and before him stood the damsel Yvonne, pale of face and panting for breath.

She leaned against the doorpost and gulped.

'Fly!' she whispered.

Reader, if you had come to spend the night in the lonely castle of a perfect stranger with a shifty eye and a rogues' gallery smile, and on retiring to your room had found the door kick-proof and the window barred, and if, immediately after your discovery of these phenomena, a white-faced young lady had plunged in upon you and urged you to immediate flight, wouldn't that jar you?

It jarred Agravaine.

'Eh?' he cried.

'Fly! Fly, Sir Knight.'

Another footstep sounded in the passage. The damsel gave a startled look over her shoulder.

'And what's all this?'

Earl Dorm appeared in the dim-lit corridor. His voice had a nasty tinkle in it.

'Your—your daughter,' said Agravaine, hurriedly, 'was just telling me that breakfast would—'

The sentence remained unfinished. A sudden movement of the earl's hand, and the great door banged in his face. There came the sound of a bolt shooting into its socket. A key turned in the lock. He was trapped.

Outside, the earl had seized his daughter by the wrist and was administering a paternal cross-examination.

'What were you saying to him?'

Yvonne did not flinch.

'I was bidding him fly.'

'If he wants to leave this castle,' said the earl, grimly, 'he'll have to.'

'Father,' said Yvonne,' I can't.'

'Can't what?'

'I can't.'

His grip on her wrist tightened. From the other side of the door came the muffled sound of blows on the solid oak. 'Oh?' said Earl Dorm. 'You can't, eh? Well, listen to me. You've got to. Do you understand? I admit he might be better-looking, but—'

'Father, I love him.'

He released her wrist, and stared at her in the uncertain light.

'You love him!'

'Yes.'

'Then what—? Why? Well, I never did understand women,' he said at last, and stumped off down the passage.

While this cryptic conversation was in progress, Agravaine, his worst apprehensions realized, was trying to batter down the door. After a few moments, however, he realized the futility of his efforts, and sat down on the bed to think.

At the risk of forfeiting the reader's respect, it must be admitted that his first emotion was one of profound relief. If he was locked up like this, it must mean that that dragon story was fictitious, and that all danger was at an end of having to pit his inexperience against a ravening monster who had spent a lifetime devouring knights. He had never liked the prospect, though he had been prepared to go through with it, and to feel that it was definitely cancelled made up for a good deal.

His mind next turned to his immediate future. What were they going to do with him? On this point he felt tolerably comfortable. This imprisonment could mean nothing more than that he would be compelled to disgorge a ransom. This did not trouble him. He was rich, and, now that the situation had been switched to a purely business basis, he felt that he could handle it.

In any case, there was nothing to be gained by sitting up, so he went to bed, like a good philosopher.

The sun was pouring through the barred window when he was awoken by the entrance of a gigantic figure bearing food and drink.

He recognized him as one of the scurvy knaves who had dined at the bottom of the room the night before—a vast, beetle-browed fellow with a squint, a mop of red hair, and a genius for silence. To Agravaine's attempts to engage him in conversation he replied only with grunts, and in a short time left the room, closing and locking the door behind him.

He was succeeded at dusk by another of about the same size and ugliness, and with even less conversational *elan*. This one did not even grunt.

Small-talk, it seemed, was not an art cultivated in any great measure by the lower orders in the employment of Earl Dorm.

The next day passed without incident. In the morning the strabismic plug-ugly with the red hair brought him food and drink, while in the evening the non-grunter did the honours. It was a peaceful life, but tending towards monotony, and Agravaine was soon in the frame of mind which welcomes any break in the daily round.

He was fortunate enough to get it.

He had composed himself for sleep that night, and was just dropping comfortably off, when from the other side of the door he heard the sound of angry voices.

It was enough to arouse him. On the previous night silence had reigned. Evidently something out of the ordinary was taking place.

He listened intently and distinguished words.

'Who was it I did see thee coming down the road with?'

'Who was it thou didst see me coming down the road with?'

'Aye, who was it I did see thee coming down the road with?'

'Who dost thou think thou art?'

'Who do I think that I am?'

'Aye, who dost thou think thou art?'

Agravaine could make nothing of it. As a matter of fact, he was hearing the first genuine cross-talk that had ever occurred in those dim, pre-music-hall days. In years to come dialogue on these lines was to be popular throughout the length and breadth of Great Britain. But till then it had been unknown.

The voices grew angrier. To an initiated listener it would have been plain that in a short while words would be found inadequate and the dagger, that medieval forerunner of the slap-stick, brought into play. But to Agravaine, all inexperienced, it came as a surprise when suddenly with a muffled thud two bodies fell against the door. There was a scuffling noise, some groans, and then silence.

And then with amazement he heard the bolt shoot back and a key grate in the keyhole.

The door swung open. It was dark outside, but Agravaine could distinguish a female form, and, beyond, a shapeless mass which he took correctly to be the remains of the two plug-uglies.

'It is I, Yvonne,' said a voice.

'What is it? What has been happening?'

'It was I. I set them against each other. They both loved one of the kitchen-maids. I made them jealous. I told Walt privily that she had favoured Dickon, and Dickon privily that she loved Walt. And now—'

She glanced at the shapeless heap, and shuddered. Agravaine nodded.

'No wedding-bells for her,' he said, reverently.

'And I don't care. I did it to save you. But come! We are wasting time. Come! I will help you to escape.'

A man who has been shut up for two days in a small room is seldom slow off the mark when a chance presents itself of taking exercise. Agravaine followed without a word, and together they crept down the dark staircase until they had reached the main hall. From somewhere in the distance came the rhythmic snores of scurvy knaves getting their eight hours.

Softly Yvonne unbolted a small door, and, passing through it, Agravaine found himself looking up at the stars, while the great walls of the castle towered above him.

'Good-bye,' said Yvonne.

There was a pause. For the first time Agravaine found himself examining the exact position of affairs. After his sojourn in the guarded room, freedom looked very good to him. But freedom meant parting from Yvonne.

He looked at the sky and he looked at the castle walls, and he took a step back towards the door.

'I'm not so sure I want to go,' he said.

'Oh, fly! Fly, Sir Knight!' she cried.

'You don't understand,' said Agravaine. 'I don't want to seem to be saying anything that might be interpreted as in the least derogatory to your father in any way whatever, but without prejudice, surely he is just a plain, ordinary brigand? I mean it's only a question of a ransom? And I don't in the least object—'

'No, no, no.' Her voice trembled. 'He would ask no ransom.'

'Don't tell me he kidnaps people just as a hobby!'

'You don't understand. He—No, I cannot tell you. Fly!'

'What don't I understand?'

She was silent. Then she began to speak rapidly. 'Very well. I will tell you. Listen. My father had six children, all daughters. We were poor. We had to stay buried in this out-of-the-way spot. We saw no one. It seemed impossible that any of us should ever marry. My father was in despair. Then he said, "If we cannot get to town, the town must come to us." So he sent my sister Yseult to Camelot to ask the king to let us have a knight to protect us against a giant with three heads. There was no giant, but she got the knight. It was Sir Sagramore. Perhaps you knew him?'

Agravaine nodded. He began to see daylight.

'My sister Yseult was very beautiful. After the first day Sir Sagramore forgot all about the giant, and seemed to want to do nothing else except have Yseult show him how to play cat's cradle. They were married two months later, and my father sent my sister Elaine to Camelot to ask for a knight to protect us against a wild unicorn.'

'And who bit?' asked Agravaine, deeply interested.

'Sir Malibran of Devon. They were married within three weeks, and my father—I can't go on. You understand now.'

'I understand the main idea,' said Agravaine. 'But in my case—'

'You were to marry me,' said Yvonne. Her voice was quiet and cold, but she was quivering.

Agravaine was conscious of a dull, heavy weight pressing on his heart. He had known his love was hopeless, but even hopelessness is the better for being indefinite. He understood now.

'And you naturally want to get rid of me before it can happen,' he said. 'I don't wonder. I'm not vain... Well, I'll go. I knew I had no chance. Good-bye.'

He turned. She stopped him with a sharp cry.

'What do you mean? You cannot wish to stay now? I am saving you.'

'Saving me! I have loved you since the moment you entered the Hall at Camelot,' said Agravaine.

She drew in her breath.

'You—you love me!'

They looked at each other in the starlight. She held out her hands.

'Agravaine!'

She drooped towards him, and he gathered her into his arms. For a novice, he did it uncommonly well.

It was about six months later that Agravaine, having ridden into the forest, called upon a Wise Man at his cell.

In those days almost anyone who was not a perfect bonehead could set up as a Wise Man and get away with it. All you had to do was to live in a forest and grow a white beard. This particular Wise Man, for a wonder, had a certain amount of rude sagacity. He listened carefully to what the knight had to say.

'It has puzzled me to such an extent,' said Agravaine, 'that I felt that I must consult a specialist. You see me. Take a good look at me. What do you think of my personal appearance? You needn't hesitate. It's worse than that. I am the ugliest man in England.'

'Would you go as far as that?' said the Wise Man, politely.

'Farther. And everybody else thinks so. Everybody except my wife. She tells me that I am a model of manly beauty. You know Lancelot? Well, she says I have Lancelot whipped to a custard. What do you make of that? And here's another thing. It is perfectly obvious to me that my wife is one of the most beautiful creatures in existence. I have seen them all, and I tell you that she stands alone. She is literally marooned in Class A, all by herself. Yet she insists that she is plain. What do you make of it?'

The Wise Man stroked his beard.

'My son,' he said, 'the matter is simple. True love takes no account of looks.'

'No?' said Agravaine.

'You two are affinities. Therefore, to you the outward aspect is nothing. Put it like this. Love is a thingummybob who what-d'you-call-its.'

'I'm beginning to see,' said Agravaine.

'What I meant was this. Love is a wizard greater than Merlin. He plays odd tricks with the eyesight.'

'Yes,' said Agravaine.

'Or, put it another way. Love is a sculptor greater than Praxiteles. He takes an unsightly piece of clay and moulds it into a thing divine.'

'I get you,' said Agravaine.

The Wise Man began to warm to his work.

'Or shall we say—'

'I think I must be going,' said Agravaine. 'I promised my wife I would be back early.'

'We might put it—' began the Wise Man perseveringly.

'I understand,' said Agravaine, hurriedly. 'I quite see now. Good-bye.'

The Wise Man sighed resignedly.

'Good-bye, Sir Knight,' he said. 'Good-bye. Pay at ye desk.'

And Agravaine rode on his way marvelling.

THE GOAL-KEEPER AND THE PLUTOCRAT

The main difficulty in writing a story is to convey to the reader clearly yet tersely the natures and dispositions of one's leading characters. Brevity, brevity—that is the cry. Perhaps, after all, the play-bill style is the best. In this drama of love, football (Association code), and politics, then, the principals are as follows, in their order of entry:

ISABEL RACKSTRAW (an angel).

THE HON. CLARENCE TRESILLIAN (a Greek god).

LADY RUNNYMEDE (a proud old aristocrat).

MR RACKSTRAW (a multi-millionaire City man and Radical politician).

More about Clarence later. For the moment let him go as a Greek god. There were other sides, too, to Mr Rackstraw's character, but for the moment let him go as a multi-millionaire City man and Radical politician. Not that it is satisfactory; it is too mild. The Radical politics of other Radical politicians were as skim-milk to the Radical politics of Radical Politician Rackstraw. Where Mr Lloyd George referred to the House of Lords as blithering backwoodsmen and asinine anachronisms, Mr Rackstraw scorned to be so guarded in his speech. He did not mince his words. His attitude towards a member of the peerage was that of the terrier to the perambulating cat.

It was at a charity bazaar that Isabel and Clarence first met. Isabel was presiding over the Billiken, Teddy—bear, and Fancy Goods stall. There she stood, that slim, radiant girl, bouncing Ardent Youth out of its father's hard—earned with a smile that alone was nearly worth the money, when she observed, approaching, the handsomest man she had ever seen. It was—this is not one of those mystery stories—it was Clarence Tresillian. Over the heads of the bevy of gilded youths who clustered round the stall their eyes met. A thrill ran through Isabel. She dropped her eyes. The next moment Clarence had made his spring; the gilded youths had shredded away like a mist, and he was leaning towards her, opening negotiations for the purchase of a yellow Teddy-bear at sixteen times its face value.

He returned at intervals during the afternoon. Over the second Teddy-bear they became friendly, over the third intimate. He proposed as she was wrapping up the fourth golliwog, and she gave him her heart and the parcel simultaneously. At six o'clock, carrying four Teddy-bears, seven photograph frames, five golliwogs, and a billiken, Clarence went home to tell the news to his parents.

Clarence, when not at the University, lived with his father and mother in Belgrave Square. His mother had been a Miss Trotter, of Chicago, and it was on her dowry that the Runnymedes contrived to make both ends meet. For a noble family they were in somewhat straitened circumstances financially. They lived, simply and without envy of their rich fellow-citizens, on their hundred thousand pounds a year. They asked no more. It enabled them to entertain on a modest scale. Clarence had been able to go to Oxford; his elder brother, Lord Staines, into the Guards. The girls could buy an occasional new frock. On the whole, they were a thoroughly happy, contented English family of the best sort. Mr Trotter, it is true, was something of a drawback. He was a rugged old tainted millionaire of the old school, with a fondness for shirt-sleeves and a tendency to give undue publicity to toothpicks. But he had been made to understand at an early date that the dead-line for him was the farther shore of the Atlantic Ocean, and he now gave little trouble.

Having dressed for dinner, Clarence proceeded to the library, where he found his mother in hysterics and his father in a state of collapse on the sofa. Clarence was too well-bred to make any comment. A true Runnymede, he affected to notice nothing, and, picking up the evening paper, began to read. The announcement of his engagement could be postponed to a more suitable time.

'Clarence!' whispered a voice from the sofa.

'Yes, father?'

The silver-haired old man gasped for utterance.

'I've lost my little veto,' he said, brokenly, at length.

'Where did you see it last?' asked Clarence, ever practical.

'It's that fellow Rackstraw!' cried the old man, in feeble rage. 'That bounder Rackstraw! He's the man behind it all. The robber!'

'Clarence!'

It was his mother who spoke. Her voice seemed to rip the air into a million shreds and stamp on them. There are few things more terrible than a Chicago voice raised in excitement or anguish.

'Mother?'

'Never mind your pop and his old veto. He didn't know he had one till the paper said he'd lost it. You listen to me. Clarence, we are ruined.'

Clarence looked at her inquiringly.

'Ruined much?' he asked.

'Bed-rock,' said his mother. 'If we have sixty thousand dollars a year after this, it's all we shall have.'

A low howl escaped from the stricken old man on the sofa.

Clarence betrayed no emotion.

'Ah,' he said, calmly. 'How did it happen?'

'I've just had a cable from Chicago, from your grand-pop. He's been trying to corner wheat. He always was an impulsive old gazook.'

'But surely,' said Clarence, a dim recollection of something he had heard or read somewhere coming to him, 'isn't cornering wheat a rather profitable process?'

'Sure,' said his mother. 'Sure it is. I guess dad's try at cornering wheat was about the most profitable thing that ever happened—to the other fellows. It seems like they got busy and clubbed fifty-seven varieties of Hades out of your old grand-pop. He's got to give up a lot of his expensive habits, and one of them is sending money to us. That's how it is.'

'And on top of that, mind you,' moaned Lord Runnymede, 'I lose my little veto. It's bitter—bitter.'

Clarence lit a cigarette and drew at it thoughtfully. 'I don't see how we're going to manage on twelve thousand quid a year,' he said.

His mother crisply revised his pronouns.

'We aren't,' she said. 'You've got to get out and hustle.'

Clarence looked at her blankly.

'Me?'

'You.'

'Work?'

'Work.'

Clarence drew a deep breath.

'Work? Well, of course, mind you, fellows *do* work,' he went on, thoughtfully. 'I was lunching with a man at the Bachelor's only yesterday who swore he knew a fellow who had met a man whose cousin worked. But I don't see what I could do, don't you know.'

His father raised himself on the sofa.

'Haven't I given you the education of an English gentleman?'

'That's the difficulty,' said Clarence.

'Can't you do *anything*?' asked his mother.

'Well, I can play footer. By Jove, I'll sign on as a pro. I'll take a new name. I'll call myself Jones. I can get signed on in a minute. Any club will jump at me.'

This was no idle boast. Since early childhood Clarence had concentrated his energies on becoming a footballer, and was now an exceedingly fine goal-keeper. It was a pleasing sight to see him, poised on one foot in the attitude of a Salome dancer, with one eye on the man with the ball, the other gazing coldly on the rest of the opposition forward line, uncurl abruptly like the main-spring of a watch and stop a hot one. Clarence in goal was the nearest approach to an india-rubber acrobat and society contortionist to be seen off the music-hall stage. He was, in brief, hot stuff. He had the goods.

Scarcely had he uttered these momentous words when the butler entered with the announcement that he was wanted by a lady on the telephone.

It was Isabel, disturbed and fearful.

'Oh, Clarence,' she cried, 'my precious angel wonder-child, I don't know how to begin.'

'Begin just like that,' said Clarence, approvingly. 'It's topping. You can't beat it.'

'Clarence, a terrible thing has happened. I told papa of our engagement, and he wouldn't hear of it. He c-called you a a p-p-p—'

'A what?'

'A pr-pr-pr—'

'He's wrong. I'm nothing of the sort. He must be thinking of someone else.'

'A preposterous excrescence on the social cosmos. He doesn't like your father being an earl.'

'A man may be an earl and still a gentleman,' said Clarence, not without a touch of coldness in his voice.

'I forgot to tell him that. But I don't think it would make any difference. He says I shall only marry a man who works.'

'I am going to work, dearest,' said Clarence. 'I am going to work like a horse. Something—I know not what—tells me I shall be rather good at work. And one day when I—'

'Good-bye,' said Isabel, hastily. 'I hear papa coming.'

Clarence, as he had predicted, found no difficulty in obtaining employment. He was signed on at once, under the name of Jones, by Houndsditch Wednesday, the premier metropolitan club, and embarked at once on his new career.

The season during which Clarence Tresillian kept goal for Houndsditch Wednesday is destined to live long in the memory of followers of professional football. Probably never in the history of the game has there been such persistent and widespread mortality among the more distant relatives of office-boys and junior clerks. Statisticians have estimated that if all the grandmothers alone who perished between the months of September and April that season could have been placed end to end, they would have reached from Hyde Park Corner to the outskirts of Manchester. And it was Clarence who was responsible for this holocaust. Previous to the opening of the season sceptics had shaken their heads over the Wednesday's chances in the First League. Other clubs had bought up the best men in the market, leaving only a mixed assortment of inferior Scotsmen, Irishmen, and Northcountrymen to uphold the honour of the London club.

And then, like a meteor, Clarence Tresillian had flashed upon the world of football. In the opening game he had behaved in the goal-mouth like a Chinese cracker, and exhibited an absolutely impassable defence; and from then onward, except for an occasional check, Houndsditch Wednesday had never looked back.

Among the spectators who flocked to the Houndsditch ground to watch Clarence perform there appeared week after week a little, grey, dried-up man, insignificant except for a certain happy choice of language in moments of emotion and an enthusiasm far surpassing that of the ordinary spectator. To the trained eye there are subtle distinctions between football enthusiasts. This man belonged to the comparatively small class of those who have football on the cerebrum.

Fate had made Daniel Rackstraw a millionaire and a Radical, but at heart he was a spectator of football. He never missed a match. His library of football literature was the finest in the country. His football museum had but one equal, that of Mr Jacob Dodson, of Manchester. Between them the two had cornered, at enormous expense, the curio market of the game. It was Rackstraw who had secured the authentic pair of boots in which Bloomer had first played for England; but it was Dodson who possessed the painted india-rubber ball used by Meredith when a boy—probably the first thing except a nurse ever kicked by that talented foot. The two men were friends, as far as rival connoisseurs can be friends; and Mr Dodson, when at leisure, would frequently pay a visit to Mr Rackstraw's country house, where he would spend hours gazing wistfully at the Bloomer boots, buoyed up only by the thoughts of the Meredith ball at home.

Isabel saw little of Clarence during the winter months, except from a distance. She contented herself with clipping photographs of him from the sporting papers. Each was a little more unlike him than the last, and this lent variety to the collection. Her father marked her new-born enthusiasm for the game with approval. It had been secretly a great grief to the old gentleman that his only child did not know the difference between a linesman and an inside right, and, more, did not seem to care to know. He felt himself drawn closer to her. An understanding, as pleasant as it was new and strange, began to spring up between parent and child.

As for Clarence, how easy it would be to haul up one's slacks to practically an unlimited extent on the subject of his emotions at this time. One can figure him, after the game is over and the gay throng has dispersed, creeping moodily—but what's the use? Brevity—that is the cry. Brevity. Let us on.

The months sped by; the Cup-ties began, and soon it was evident that the Final must be fought out between Houndsditch Wednesday and Mr Jacob Dodson's pet team, Manchester United. With each match the Wednesday seemed to improve. Clarence was a Gibraltar among goal-keepers.

Those were delirious days for Daniel Rackstraw. Long before the fourth round his voice had dwindled to a husky whisper. Deep lines appeared on his forehead; for it is an awful thing for a football enthusiast to be compelled to applaud, in the very middle of the Cup-ties, purely by means of facial expression. In this time of affliction he found Isabel an ever-increasing comfort to him. Side by side they would sit, and the old man's face would lose its drawn look, and light up, as her clear young soprano pealed out over the din, urging this player to shoot, that to kick some opponent in the face; or describing the referee in no uncertain terms as a reincarnation of the late Mr Dick Turpin.

And now the day of the Final at the Crystal Palace approached, and all England was alert, confident of a record-breaking contest. But alas! How truly does Epictetus observe: 'We know not what awaiteth us round the corner, and the hand that counteth its chickens ere they be hatched oft-times doth but step on the banana-skin.' The prophets who anticipated a struggle keener than any in football history were destined to be proved false.

It was not that their judgement of form was at fault. On the run of the season's play Houndsditch Wednesday *v.* Manchester United should have been the two most evenly-matched teams in the history of the game. Forward, the latter held a slight superiority; but this was balanced by the inspired goal-keeping of Clarence Tresillian. Even the keenest supporters of either side were not confident. They argued at length, figuring out the odds with the aid of stubs of pencils and the backs of envelopes, but they were not confident. Out of all those frenzied millions two men alone had no doubts. Mr Daniel Rackstraw said that he did not desire to be unfair to Manchester United. He wished it to be clearly understood that in their own class Manchester United might quite possibly show to considerable advantage. In some rural league, for instance, he did not deny that they might sweep all before them. But when it came to competing with Houndsditch Wednesday—here words failed Mr Rackstraw.

Mr Jacob Dodson, interviewed by the *Manchester Weekly Football Boot*, stated that his decision, arrived at after a close and careful study of the work of both teams, was that Houndsditch Wednesday had rather less chance in the forthcoming tourney than a stuffed rat in the Battersea Dogs' Home. It was his carefully-considered opinion that in a contest with the second eleven of a village Church Lads' Brigade, Houndsditch Wednesday might, with an effort (conceding them that slice of luck which so often turns the tide of a game), scrape home. But when it was a question of meeting a team like Manchester United—here Mr Dodson, shrugging his shoulders despairingly, sank back in his chair, and watchful secretaries brought him round with oxygen.

Throughout the whole country nothing but the approaching match was discussed. Wherever civilization reigned, and in portions of Liverpool, one question alone was on every lip: Who would win? Octogenarians mumbled it. Infants lisped it. Tired City men, trampled under foot in the rush for their tram, asked it of the ambulance attendants who carried them to the hospital.

And then, one bright, clear morning, when the birds sang and all Nature seemed fair and gay, Clarence Tresillian developed mumps.

London was in a ferment. I could have wished to go into details, to describe in crisp, burning sentences the panic that swept like a tornado through a million homes. A little encouragement, the slightest softening of the editorial austerity and the thing would have been done. But no. Brevity. That was the cry. Brevity. Let us on.

Houndsditch Wednesday met Manchester United at the Crystal Palace, and for nearly two hours the sweat of agony trickled unceasingly down the corrugated foreheads of the patriots in the stands. The men from Manchester, freed from the fear of Clarence, smiled grim smiles and proceeded to pile up points. It was in vain that the Houndsditch backs and halfbacks skimmed like swallows about the field. They could not keep the score down. From start to finish Houndsditch were a beaten side.

London during that black period was a desert. Gloom gripped the City. In distant Brixton red-eyed wives faced silently-scowling husbands at the evening meal, and the children were sent early to bed. Newsboys called the extras in a whisper.

Few took the tragedy more nearly to heart than Daniel Rackstraw. Leaving the ground with the air of a father mourning over some prodigal son, he encountered Mr Jacob Dodson, of Manchester.

Now, Mr Dodson was perhaps the slightest bit shy on the finer feelings. He should have respected the grief of a fallen foe. He should have abstained from exulting. But he was in too exhilarated a condition to be magnanimous. Sighting Mr Rackstraw, he addressed himself joyously to the task of rubbing the thing in. Mr Rackstraw listened in silent anguish.

'If we had had Jones—' he said at length.

'That's what they all say,' whooped Mr Dodson, 'Jones! Who's Jones?'

'If we had had Jones, we should have—' He paused. An idea had flashed upon his overwrought mind. 'Dodson,' he said, 'look here. Wait till Jones is well again, and let us play this thing off again for anything you like a side in my private park.'

Mr Dodson reflected.

'You're on,' he said. 'What side bet? A million? Two million? Three?'

Mr Rackstraw shook his head scornfully.

'A million? Who wants a million? I'll put up my Bloomer boot against your Meredith ball. Does that go?'

'I should say it did,' said Mr Dodson, joyfully. 'I've been wanting that boot for years. It's like finding it in one's Christmas stocking.'

'Very well,' said Mr Rackstraw. 'Then let's get it fixed up.'

Honestly, it is but a dog's life, that of the short-story writer. I particularly wished at this point to introduce a description of Mr Rackstraw's country house and estate, featuring the private football ground with its fringe of noble trees. It would have served a double purpose, not only charming the lover of nature, but acting as a fine stimulus to the youth of the country, showing them the sort of home they would be able to buy some day if they worked hard and saved their money. But no. You shall have three guesses as to what was the cry. You give it up? It was Brevity—brevity! Let us on.

The two teams arrived at Mr Rackstraw's house in time for lunch. Clarence, his features once more reduced to their customary finely-chiselled proportions, alighted from the automobile with a swelling heart. Presently he found an opportunity to slip away and meet Isabel. I will pass lightly over the meeting of the two lovers. I will not describe the dewy softness of their eyes, the catching of their breath, their murmured endearments. I could, mind you. It is at just such descriptions that I am particularly happy. But I have grown discouraged. My spirit is broken. It is enough to say that Clarence had reached a level of emotional eloquence rarely met with among goal-keepers of the First League, when Isabel broke from him with a startled exclamation, and vanished; and, looking over his shoulder, Clarence observed Mr Daniel Rackstraw moving towards him.

It was evident from the millionaire's demeanour that he had seen nothing. The look on his face was anxious, but not wrathful. He sighted Clarence, and hurried up to him.

'Jones,' he said, 'I've been looking for you. I want a word with you.'

'A thousand, if you wish it,' said Clarence, courteously.

'Now, look here,' said Mr Rackstraw. 'I want to explain to you just what this game means to me. Don't run away with the idea I've had you fellows down to play an exhibition game just to keep me merry and bright. If Houndsditch wins today, K means that I shall be able to hold up my head again and look my fellow-man in the face, instead of crawling round on my stomach and feeling like a black-beetle under a steam-roller. Do you get that?'

'I do,' replied Clarence.

'And not only that,' went on the millionaire. 'There's more. I have put up my Bloomer boot against Mr Dodson's Meredith hall as a side bet. You understand what that means? It means that either you win or my life is soured for ever. See?'

'I have got you,' said Clarence.

'Good. Then what I wanted to say was this. Today is your day for keeping goal as you've never kept goal before. Everything depends on you. With you keeping goal like mother used to make it, Houndsditch are safe. Otherwise they are completely in the bouillon. It's one thing or the other. It's all up to you. Win, and there's four thousand pounds waiting for you above what you share with the others.'

Clarence waved his hand deprecatingly.

'Mr Rackstraw,' he said, 'keep your dross. I care nothing for money. All I ask of you,' proceeded Clarence, 'is your consent to my engagement to your daughter.'

Mr Rackstraw looked sharply at him.

'Repeat that,' he said. 'I don't think I quite got it.'

'All I ask is your consent to my engagement to your daughter.'

'Young man,' said Mr Rackstraw, not without a touch of admiration, 'I admire cheek. But there is a limit. That limit you have passed so far that you'd need to look for it with a telescope.'

'You refuse your consent?'

'I never said you weren't a clever guesser.'

'Why?'

Mr Rackstraw laughed. One of those nasty, sharp, metallic laughs that hit you like a bullet.

'How would you support my daughter?'

'I was thinking that you would help to some extent.'

'You were, were you?'

'I was.'

'Oh?'

Mr Rackstraw emitted another of those laughs.

'Well,' he said, 'it's off. You can take that as coming from an authoritative source. No wedding-bells for you.'

Clarence drew himself up, fire flashing from his eyes and a bitter smile curving his expressive lips.

'And no Meredith ball for you!' he cried.

Mr Rackstraw started as if some strong hand had plunged an auger into him.

'What?' he shouted.

Clarence shrugged his superbly-modelled shoulders in silence.

'Come, come,' said Mr Rackstraw, 'you wouldn't let a little private difference like that influence you in a really important thing like this football match, would you?'

'I would.'

'You would practically blackmail the father of the girl you love?'

'Every time.'

'Her white-haired old father?'

'The colour of his hair would not affect me.'

'Nothing would move you?'

'Nothing.'

'Then, by George, you're just the son-in-law I want. You shall marry Isabel; and I'll take you into partnership in my business this very day. I've been looking for a good able-bodied bandit like you for years. You make Captain Kidd look like a preliminary three-round bout. My boy, we'll be the greatest combination, you and I, that the City has ever seen. Shake hands.'

For a moment Clarence hesitated. Then his better nature prevailed, and he spoke.

'Mr Rackstraw,' he said, 'I cannot deceive you.'

'That won't matter,' said the enthusiastic old man. 'I bet you'll be able to deceive everybody else. I see it in your eye. My boy, we'll be the greatest—'

'My name is not Jones.'

'Nor is mine. What does that matter?'

'My name is Tresillian. The Hon. Tresillian. I am the younger son of the Earl of Runnymede. To a man of your political views—'

'Nonsense, nonsense,' said Mr Rackstraw. 'What are political views compared with the chance of getting a goal-keeper like you into the family? I remember Isabel saying something to me about you, but I didn't know who you were then.'

'I am a preposterous excrescence on the social cosmos,' said Clarence, eyeing him doubtfully.

'Then I'll be one too,' cried Mr Rackstraw. 'I own I've set my face against it hitherto, but circumstances alter cases. I'll ring up the Prime Minister on the phone tomorrow, and buy a title myself.'

Clarence's last scruple was removed. Silently he gripped the old man's hand, outstretched to meet his.

Little remains to be said, but I am going to say it, if it snows. I am at my best in these tender scenes of idyllic domesticity.

Four years have passed. Once more we are in the Rackstraw home. A lady is coming down the stairs, leading by the hand her little son. It is Isabel. The years have dealt lightly with her. She is still the same stately, beautiful creature whom I would have described in detail long ago if I had been given half a chance. At the foot of the stairs the child stops and points at a small, round object in a glass case.

'Wah?' he says.

'That?' said Isabel. 'That is the ball Mr Meredith used to play with when he was a little boy.'

She looks at a door on the left of the hall, and puts a finger to her lip.

'Hush!' she says. 'We must be quiet. Daddy and grandpa are busy in there cornering wheat.'

And softly mother and child go out into the sunlit garden.

IN ALCALA

In Alcala, as in most of New York's apartment houses, the schedule of prices is like a badly rolled cigarette—thick in the middle and thin at both ends. The rooms half-way up are expensive; some of them almost as expensive as if Fashion, instead of being gone for ever, were still lingering. The top rooms are cheap, the ground-floor rooms cheaper still.

Cheapest of all was the hall-bedroom. Its furniture was of the simplest. It consisted of a chair, another chair, a worn carpet, and a folding-bed. The folding-bed had an air of depression and baffled hopes. For years it had been trying to look like a bookcase in the daytime, and now it looked more like a folding-bed than ever. There was also a plain deal table, much stained with ink. At this, night after night, sometimes far into the morning, Rutherford Maxwell would sit and write stories. Now and then it happened that one would be a good story, and find a market.

Rutherford Maxwell was an Englishman, and the younger son of an Englishman; and his lot was the lot of the younger sons all the world over. He was by profession one of the numerous employees of the New Asiatic Bank, which has its branches all over the world. It is a sound, trustworthy institution, and steady-going relatives would assure Rutherford that he was lucky to have got a berth in it. Rutherford did not agree with them. However sound and trustworthy, it was not exactly romantic. Nor did it err on the side of over-lavishness to those who served it. Rutherford's salary was small. So were his prospects—if he remained in the bank. At a very early date he had registered a vow that he would not. And the road that led out of it for him was the uphill road of literature.

He was thankful for small mercies. Fate had not been over-kind up to the present, but at least she had dispatched him to New York, the centre of things, where he would have the chance to try, instead of to some spot off the map. Whether he won or lost, at any rate he was in the ring, and could fight. So every night he sat in Alcala, and wrote. Sometimes he would only try to write, and that was torture.

There is never an hour of the day or night when Alcala is wholly asleep. The middle of the house is a sort of chorus-girl belt, while in the upper rooms there are reporters and other nightbirds. Long after he had gone to bed, Rutherford would hear footsteps passing his door and the sound of voices in the passage. He grew to welcome them. They seemed to connect him with the outer world. But for them he was alone after he had left the office, utterly alone, as it is possible to be only in the heart of a great city. Some nights he would hear scraps of conversations, at rare intervals a name. He used to build up in his mind identities for the owners of the names. One in particular, Peggy, gave him much food for thought. He pictured her as bright and vivacious. This was because she sang sometimes as she passed his door. She had been singing when he first heard her name. 'Oh, cut it out, Peggy,' a girl's voice had said. 'Don't you get enough of that tune at the theatre?' He felt that he would like to meet Peggy.

June came, and July, making an oven of New York, bringing close, scorching days and nights when the pen seemed made of lead; and still Rutherford worked on, sipping ice-water, in his shirt-sleeves, and filling the sheets of paper slowly, but with a dogged persistence which the weather could not kill. Despite the heat, he was cheerful. Things were beginning to run his way a little now. A novelette, an airy trifle, conceived in days when the thermometer was lower and it was possible to think, and worked out almost mechanically, had been accepted by a magazine of a higher standing than those which hitherto had shown him hospitality. He began to dream of a holiday in the woods. The holiday spirit was abroad. Alcala was emptying itself. It would not be long before he too would be able to get away.

He was so deep in his thoughts that at first he did not hear the knocking at the door. But it was a sharp, insistent knocking, and forced itself upon his attention. He got up and turned the handle.

Outside in the passage was standing a girl, tall and sleepy-eyed. She wore a picture-hat and a costume the keynote of which was a certain aggressive attractiveness. There was no room for doubt as to which particular brand of scent was her favourite at the moment.

She gazed at Rutherford dully. Like Banquo's ghost, she had no speculation in her eyes. Rutherford looked at her inquiringly, somewhat conscious of his shirt-sleeves.

'Did you knock?' he said, opening, as a man must do, with the inevitable foolish question.

The apparition spoke.

'Say,' she said, 'got a cigarette?'

'I'm afraid I haven't,' said Rutherford, apologetically. 'I've been smoking a pipe. I'm very sorry.'

'What?' said the apparition.

'I'm afraid I haven't.'

'Oh!' A pause. 'Say, got a cigarette?'

The intellectual pressure of the conversation was beginning to be a little too much for Rutherford. Combined with the heat of the night it made his head swim.

His visitor advanced into the room. Arriving at the table, she began fiddling with its contents. The pen seemed to fascinate her. She picked it up and inspected it closely.

'Say, what d'you call this?' she said.

'That's a pen,' said Rutherford, soothingly. 'A fountain-pen.'

'Oh!' A pause. 'Say, got a cigarette?'

Rutherford clutched a chair with one hand, and his forehead with the other. He was in sore straits.

At this moment Rescue arrived, not before it was needed. A brisk sound of footsteps in the passage, and there appeared in the doorway a second girl.

'What do you think you're doing, Gladys?' demanded the new-comer. 'You mustn't come butting into folks' rooms this way. Who's your friend?'

'My name is Maxwell,' began Rutherford eagerly.

'What say, Peggy?' said the seeker after cigarettes, dropping a sheet of manuscript to the floor.

Rutherford looked at the girl in the doorway with interest. So this was Peggy. She was little, and trim of figure. That was how he had always imagined her. Her dress was simpler than the other's. The face beneath the picture-hat was small and well-shaped, the nose delicately tip-tilted, the chin determined, the mouth a little wide and suggesting good-humour. A pair of grey eyes looked steadily into his before transferring themselves to the statuesque being at the table.

'Don't monkey with the man's inkwell, Gladys. Come along up to bed.'

'What? Say, got a cigarette?'

'There's plenty upstairs. Come along.'

The other went with perfect docility. At the door she paused, and inspected Rutherford with a grave stare.

'Good night, boy!' she said, with haughty condescension.

'Good night!' said Rutherford.

'Pleased to have met you. Good night.'

'Good night!' said Rutherford.

'Good night!'

'Come along, Gladys,' said Peggy, firmly.

Gladys went.

Rutherford sat down and dabbed his forehead with his handkerchief, feeling a little weak. He was not used to visitors.

2

He had lit his pipe, and was re-reading his night's work preparatory to turning in, when there was another knock at the door. This time there was no waiting. He was in the state of mind when one hears the smallest noise.

'Come in!' he cried.

It was Peggy.

Rutherford jumped to his feet.

'Won't you—' he began, pushing the chair forward.

She seated herself with composure on the table. She no longer wore the picture-hat, and Rutherford, looking at her, came to the conclusion that the change was an improvement.

'This'll do for me,' she said. 'Thought I'd just look in. I'm sorry about Gladys. She isn't often like that. It's the hot weather.'

'It is hot,' said Rutherford.

'You've noticed it? Bully for you! Back to the bench for Sherlock Holmes. Did Gladys try to shoot herself?'

'Good heavens, no! Why?'

'She did once. But I stole her gun, and I suppose she hasn't thought to get another. She's a good girl really, only she gets like that sometimes in the hot weather.' She looked round the room for a moment, then gazed unwinkingly at Rutherford. 'What did you say your name was?' she asked.

'Rutherford Maxwell.'

'Gee! That's going some, isn't it? Wants amputation, a name like that. I call it mean to give a poor, defenceless kid a cuss-word like—what's it? Rutherford? I got it—to go through the world with. Haven't you got something shorter—Tom, or Charles or something?'

'I'm afraid not.'

The round, grey eyes fixed him again.

'I shall call you George,' she decided at last.

'Thanks, I wish you would,' said Rutherford.

'George it is, then. You can call me Peggy. Peggy Norton's my name.'

'Thanks, I will.'

'Say, you're English, aren't you?' she said.

'Yes. How did you know?'

'You're so strong on the gratitude thing. It's "Thanks, thanks," all the time. Not that I mind it, George.'

'Thanks. Sorry. I should say, "Oh, you Peggy!"'

She looked at him curiously.

'How d'you like New York, George?'

'Fine—tonight.'

'Been to Coney?'

'Not yet.'

'You should. Say, what do you do, George?'

'What do I do?'

'Cut it out, George! Don't answer back as though we were a vaudeville team doing a cross-talk act. What do you do? When your boss crowds your envelope on to you Saturdays, what's it for?'

'I'm in a bank.'

'Like it?'

'Hate it!'

'Why don't you quit, then?'

'Can't afford to. There's money in being in a bank. Not much, it's true, but what there is of it is good.'

'What are you doing out of bed at this time of night? They don't work you all day, do they?'

'No; they'd like to, but they don't. I have been writing.'

'Writing what? Say, you don't mind my putting you on the witness-stand, do you? If you do, say so, and I'll cut out the District Attorney act and talk about the weather.'

'Not a bit, really, I assure you. Please ask as many questions as you like.'

'Guess there's no doubt about your being English, George. We don't have time over here to shoot it off like that. If you'd have just said "Sure!" I'd have got a line on your meaning. You don't mind me doing school-marm, George, do you? It's all for your good.'

'Sure,' said Rutherford, with a grin.

She smiled approvingly.

'That's better! You're Little Willie, the Apt Pupil, all right. What were we talking about before we switched off on to the educational rail? I know—about your writing. What were you writing?'

'A story.'

'For a paper?'

'For a magazine.'

'What! One of the fiction stories about the Gibson hero and the girl whose life he saved, like you read?'

'That's the idea.'

She looked at him with a new interest.

'Gee, George, who'd have thought it! Fancy you being one of the high-brows! You ought to hang out a sign. You look just ordinary.'

'Thanks!'

'I mean as far as the grey matter goes. I didn't mean you were a bad looker. You're not. You've got nice eyes, George.'

'Thanks.'

'I like the shape of your nose, too.'

'I say, thanks!'

'And your hair's just lovely!'

'I say, really. Thanks awfully!'

She eyed him in silence for a moment. Then she burst out:

'You say you don't like the bank?'

'I certainly don't.'

'And you'd like to strike some paying line of business?'

'Sure.'

'Then why don't you make your fortune by hiring yourself out to a museum as the biggest human clam in captivity? That's what you are. You sit there just saying "Thanks," and "Bai Jawve, thanks awf'lly," while a girl's telling you nice things about your eyes and hair, and you don't do a thing!'

Rutherford threw back his head and roared with laughter.

'I'm sorry!' he said. 'Slowness is our national failing, you know.'

'I believe you.'

'Tell me about yourself. You know all about me, by now. What do you do besides brightening up the dull evenings of poor devils of bank-clerks?'

'Give you three guesses.'

'Stage?'

'Gee! You're the human sleuth all right, all right! It's a home-run every time when you get your deductive theories unlimbered. Yes, George; the stage it is. I'm an actorine—one of the pony ballet in *The Island of Girls* at the Melody. Seen our show?'

'Not yet. I'll go tomorrow.'

'Great! I'll let them know, so that they can have the awning out and the red carpet down. It's a cute little piece.'

'So I've heard.'

'Well, if I see you in front tomorrow, I'll give you half a smile, so that you shan't feel you haven't got your money's worth. Good night, George!'

'Good night, Peggy!'

She jumped down from the table. Her eye was caught by the photographs on the mantelpiece. She began to examine them.

'Who are these Willies?' she said, picking up a group.

'That is the football team of my old school. The lout with the sheepish smirk, holding the ball, is myself as I was before the cares of the world soured me.'

Her eye wandered along the mantelpiece, and she swooped down on a cabinet photograph of a girl.

'And who's *this*, George?' she cried.

He took the photograph from her, and replaced it, with a curious blend of shyness and defiance, in the very centre of the mantelpiece. For a moment he stood looking intently at it, his elbows resting on the imitation marble.

'Who is it?' asked Peggy. 'Wake up, George. Who's this?'

Rutherford started.

'Sorry,' he said. 'I was thinking about something.'

'I bet you were. You looked like it. Well, who is she?'

'Eh! Oh, that's a girl.'

Peggy laughed satirically.

'Thanks awf'lly, as you would say. I've got eyes, George.'

'I noticed that,' said Rutherford, smiling. 'Charming ones, too.'

'Gee! What would she say if she heard you talking like that!'

She came a step nearer, looking up at him. Their eyes met.

'She would say,' said Rutherford, slowly: '"I know you love me, and I know I can trust you, and I haven't the slightest objection to your telling Miss Norton the truth about her eyes. Miss Norton is a dear, good little sort, one of the best, in fact, and I hope you'll be great pals!"'

There was a silence.

'She'd say that, would she?' said Peggy, at last.

'She would.'

Peggy looked at the photograph, and back again at Rutherford.

'You're pretty fond of her, George, I guess, aren't you?'

'I am,' said Rutherford, quietly.

'George.'

'Yes?'

'George, she's a pretty good long way away, isn't she?'

She looked up at him with a curious light in her grey eyes. Rutherford met her glance steadily.

'Not to me,' he said. 'She's here now, and all the time.'

He stepped away and picked up the sheaf of papers which he had dropped at Peggy's entrance. Peggy laughed.

'Good night, Georgie boy,' she said. 'I mustn't keep you up any more, or you'll be late in the morning. And what would the bank do then? Smash or something, I guess. Good night, Georgie! See you again one of these old evenings.'

'Good night, Peggy!'

The door closed behind her. He heard her footsteps hesitate, stop, and then move quickly on once more.

3

He saw much of her after this first visit. Gradually it became an understood thing between them that she should look in on her return from the theatre. He grew to expect her, and to feel restless when she was late. Once she brought the cigarette-loving Gladys with her, but the experiment was not a success. Gladys was languid and rather overpoweringly refined, and conversation became forced. After that, Peggy came alone.

Generally she found him working. His industry amazed her.

'Gee, George,' she said one night, sitting in her favourite place on the table, from which he had moved a little pile of manuscript to make room for her. 'Don't you ever let up for a second? Seems to me you write all the time.'

Rutherford laughed.

'I'll take a rest,' he said, 'when there's a bit more demand for my stuff than there is at present. When I'm in the twenty-cents-a-word class I'll write once a month, and spend the rest of my time travelling.'

Peggy shook her head.

'No travelling for mine,' she said. 'Seems to me it's just cussedness that makes people go away from Broadway when they've got plunks enough to stay there and enjoy themselves.'

'Do you like Broadway, Peggy?'

'Do I like Broadway? Does a kid like candy? Why, don't you?'

'It's all right for the time. It's not my ideal.'

'Oh, and what particular sort of little old Paradise do *you* hanker after?'

He puffed at his pipe, and looked dreamily at her through the smoke.

'Way over in England, Peggy, there's a county called Worcestershire. And somewhere near the edge of that there's a grey house with gables, and there's a lawn and a meadow and a shrubbery, and an orchard and a rose-garden, and a big cedar on the terrace before you get to the rose-garden. And if you climb to the top of that cedar, you can see the river through the apple trees in the orchard. And in the distance there are hills. And—'

'Of all the rube joints!' exclaimed Peggy, in deep disgust. 'Why, a day of that would be about twenty-three hours and a bit too long for me. Broadway for mine! Put me where I can touch Forty-Second Street without over-balancing, and then you can leave me. I never thought you were such a hayseed, George.'

'Don't worry, Peggy. It'll be a long time, I expect, before I go there. I've got to make my fortune first.'

'Getting anywhere near the John D. class yet?'

'I've still some way to go. But things are moving, I think. Do you know, Peggy, you remind me of a little Billiken, sitting on that table?'

'Thank *you*, George. I always knew my mouth was rather wide, but I did think I had Billiken to the bad. Do you do that sort of Candid Friend stunt with *her*?' She pointed to the photograph on the mantelpiece. It was the first time since the night when they had met that she had made any allusion to it. By silent agreement the subject had been ruled out between them. 'By the way, you never told me her name.'

'Halliday,' said Rutherford, shortly.

'What else?'

'Alice.'

'Don't bite at me, George! I'm not hurting you. Tell me about her. I'm interested. Does she live in the grey house with the pigs and chickens and all them roses, and the rest of the rube outfit?'

'No.'

'Be chummy, George. What's the matter with you?'

'I'm sorry, Peggy,' he said. 'I'm a fool. It's only that it all seems so damned hopeless! Here am I, earning about half a dollar a year, and—Still, it's no use kicking, is it? Besides, I may make a home-run with my writing one of these days. That's what I meant when I said you were a Billiken, Peggy. Do you know, you've brought me luck. Ever since I met you, I've been doing twice as well. You're my mascot.'

'Bully for me! We've all got our uses in the world, haven't we? I wonder if it would help any if I was to kiss you, George?'

'Don't you do it. One mustn't work a mascot too hard.'

She jumped down, and came across the room to where he sat, looking down at him with the round, grey eyes that always reminded him of a kitten's.

'George!'

'Yes?'

'Oh, nothing!'

She turned away to the mantelpiece, and stood gazing at the photograph, her back towards him.

'George!'

'Hullo?'

'Say, what colour eyes has she got?'

'Grey.'

'Like mine?'

'Darker than yours.'

'Nicer than mine?'

'Don't you think we might talk about something else?'

She swung round, her fists clenched, her face blazing.

'I hate you!' she cried. 'I do! I wish I'd never seen you! I wish—'

She leaned on the mantelpiece, burying her face in her arms, and burst into a passion of sobs. Rutherford leaped up, shocked and helpless. He sprang to her, and placed a hand gently on her shoulder.

'Peggy, old girl—'

She broke from him.

'Don't you touch me! Don't you do it! Gee, I wish I'd never seen you!'

She ran to the door, darted through, and banged it behind her.

Rutherford remained where he stood, motionless. Then, almost mechanically, he felt in his pocket for matches, and relit his pipe.

Half an hour passed. Then the door opened slowly. Peggy came in. She was pale, and her eyes were red. She smiled—a pathetic little smile.

'Peggy!'

He took a step towards her.

She held out her hand.

'I'm sorry, George. I feel mean.'

'Dear old girl, what rot!'

'I do. You don't know how mean I feel. You've been real nice to me, George. Thought I'd look in and say I was sorry. Good night, George!'

On the following night he waited, but she did not come. The nights went by, and still she did not come. And one morning, reading his paper, he saw that *The Island of Girls* had gone west to Chicago.

4

Things were not running well for Rutherford. He had had his vacation, a golden fortnight of fresh air and sunshine in the Catskills, and was back in Alcala, trying with poor success, to pick up the threads of his work. But though the Indian Summer had begun, and there was energy in the air, night after night he sat idle in his room; night after night went wearily to bed, oppressed with a dull sense of failure. He could not work. He was restless. His thoughts would not concentrate themselves. Something was wrong; and he knew what it was, though he fought against admitting it to himself. It was the absence of Peggy that had brought about the change. Not till now had he realized to the full how greatly her visits had stimulated him. He had called her laughingly his mascot; but the thing was no joke. It was true. Her absence was robbing him of the power to write.

He was lonely. For the first time since he had come to New York he was really lonely. Solitude had not hurt him till now. In his black moments it had been enough for him to look up at the photograph on the mantelpiece, and instantly he was alone no longer. But now the photograph had lost its magic. It could not hold him. Always his mind would wander back to the little, black-haired ghost that sat on the table, smiling at him, and questioning him with its grey eyes.

And the days went by, unvarying in their monotony. And always the ghost sat on the table, smiling at him.

With the Fall came the reopening of the theatres. One by one the electric signs blazed out along Broadway, spreading the message that the dull days were over, and New York was itself again. At the Melody, where ages ago *The Island of Girls* had run its light-hearted course, a new musical piece was in rehearsal. Alcala was full once more. The nightly snatches of conversation outside his door had recommenced. He listened for her voice, but he never heard it.

He sat up, waiting, into the small hours, but she did not come. Once he had been trying to write, and had fallen, as usual, to brooding—there was a soft knock at the door. In an instant he had bounded from his chair, and turned the handle. It was one of the reporters from upstairs, who had run out of matches. Rutherford gave him a handful. The reporter went out, wondering what the man had laughed at.

There is balm in Broadway, especially by night. Depression vanishes before the cheerfulness of the great white way when the lights are lit and the human tide is in full flood. Rutherford had developed of late a habit of patrolling the neighbourhood of Forty-Second Street at theatre-time. He found it did him good. There is a gaiety, a bonhomie, in the atmosphere of the New York streets. Rutherford loved to stand on the sidewalk and watch the passers-by, weaving stories round them.

One night his wanderings had brought him to Herald Square. The theatres were just emptying themselves. This was the time he liked best. He drew to one side to watch, and as he moved he saw Peggy.

She was standing at the corner, buttoning a glove. He was by her side in an instant.

'Peggy!' he cried.

She was looking pale and tired, but the colour came back to her cheeks as she held out her hand. There was no trace of embarrassment in her manner; only a frank pleasure at seeing him again.

'Where have you been?' he said. 'I couldn't think what had become of you.'

She looked at him curiously.

'Did you miss me, George?'

'Miss you? Of course I did. My work's been going all to pieces since you went away.'

'I only came back last night. I'm in the new piece at the Madison. Gee, I'm tired, George! We've been rehearsing all day.'

He took her by the arm.

'Come along and have some supper. You look worn out. By Jove, Peggy, it's good seeing you again! Can you walk as far as Rector's, or shall I carry you?'

'Guess I can walk that far. But Rector's? Has your rich uncle died and left you a fortune, George?'

'Don't you worry, Peggy. This is an occasion. I thought I was never going to see you again. I'll buy you the whole hotel, if you like.'

'Just supper'll do, I guess. You're getting quite the rounder, George.'

'You bet I am. There are all sorts of sides to my character you've never so much as dreamed of.'

They seemed to know Peggy at Rector's. Paul, the head waiter, beamed upon her paternally. One or two men turned and looked after her as she passed. The waiters smiled slight but friendly smiles. Rutherford, intent on her, noticed none of these things.

Despite her protests, he ordered an elaborate and expensive supper. He was particular about the wine. The waiter, who had been doubtful about him, was won over, and went off to execute the order, reflecting that it was never safe to judge a man by his clothes, and that Rutherford was probably one of these eccentric young millionaires who didn't care how they dressed.

'Well?' said Peggy, when he had finished.

'Well?' said Rutherford.

'You're looking brown, George.'

'I've been away in the Catskills.'

'Still as strong on the rube proposition as ever?'

'Yes. But Broadway has its points, too.'

'Oh, you're beginning to see that? Gee, I'm glad to be back. I've had enough of the Wild West. If anybody ever tries to steer you west of Eleventh Avenue, George, don't you go. There's nothing doing. How have you been making out at your writing stunt?'

'Pretty well. But I wanted you. I was lost without my mascot. I've got a story in this month's *Wilson's*. A long story, and paid accordingly. That's why I'm able to go about giving suppers to great actresses.'

'I read it on the train,' said Peggy. 'It's dandy. Do you know what you ought to do, George? You ought to turn it into a play. There's a heap of money in plays.'

'I know. But who wants a play by an unknown man?'

'I know who would want *Willie in the Wilderness*, if you made it into a play, and that's Winfield Knight. Ever seen him?'

'I saw him in *The Outsider*. He's clever.'

'He's It, if he gets a part to suit him. If he doesn't, he don't amount to a row of beans. It's just a gamble. This thing he's in now is no good. The part doesn't begin to fit him. In a month he'll be squealing for another play, so's you can hear him in Connecticut.'

'He shall not squeal in vain,' said Rutherford. 'If he wants my work, who am I that I should stand in the way of his simple pleasures? I'll start on the thing tomorrow.'

'I can help you some too, I guess. I used to know Winfield Knight. I can put you wise on lots of things about him that'll help you work up Willie's character so's it'll fit him like a glove.'

Rutherford raised his glass.

'Peggy,' he said, 'you're more than a mascot. You ought to be drawing a big commission on everything I write. It beats me how any of these other fellows ever write anything without you there to help them. I wonder what's the most expensive cigar they keep here? I must have it, whatever it is. *Noblesse oblige*. We popular playwrights mustn't be seen in public smoking any cheap stuff.'

It was Rutherford's artistic temperament which, when they left the restaurant, made him hail a taxi-cab. Taxi-cabs are not for young men drawing infinitesimal salaries in banks, even if those salaries are supplemented at rare intervals by a short story in a magazine. Peggy was for returning to Alcala by car, but Rutherford refused to countenance such an anti-climax.

Peggy nestled into the corner of the cab, with a tired sigh, and there was silence as they moved smoothly up Broadway.

He peered at her in the dim light. She looked very small and wistful and fragile. Suddenly an intense desire surged over him to pick her up and crush her to him. He fought against it. He tried to fix his thoughts on the girl at home, to tell himself that he was a man of honour. His fingers, gripping the edge of the seat, tightened till every muscle of his arm was rigid.

The cab, crossing a rough piece of road, jolted Peggy from her corner. Her hand fell on his.

'Peggy!' he cried, hoarsely.

Her grey eyes were wet. He could see them glisten. And then his arms were round her, and he was covering her upturned face with kisses.

The cab drew up at the entrance to Alcala. They alighted in silence, and without a word made their way through into the hall. From force of habit, Rutherford glanced at the letter-rack on the wall at the foot of the stairs. There was one letter in his pigeon-hole.

Mechanically he drew it out; and, as his eyes fell on the handwriting, something seemed to snap inside him.

He looked at Peggy, standing on the bottom stair, and back again at the envelope in his hand. His mood was changing with a violence that left him physically weak. He felt dazed, as if he had wakened out of a trance.

With a strong effort he mastered himself. Peggy had mounted a few steps, and was looking back at him over her shoulder. He could read the meaning now in the grey eyes.

'Good night, Peggy,' he said in a low voice. She turned, facing him, and for a moment neither moved.

'Good night!' said Rutherford again.

Her lips parted, as if she were about to speak, but she said nothing.

Then she turned again, and began to walk slowly upstairs.

He stood watching her till she had reached the top of the long flight. She did not look back.

5

Peggy's nightly visits began afresh after this, and the ghost on the table troubled Rutherford no more. His restlessness left him. He began to write with a new vigour and success. In after years he wrote many plays, most of them good, clear-cut pieces of work, but none that came from him with the utter absence of labour which made the writing of *Willie in the Wilderness* a joy. He wrote easily, without effort. And always Peggy was there, helping, stimulating, encouraging.

Sometimes, when he came in after dinner to settle down to work, he would find a piece of paper on his table covered with her schoolgirl scrawl. It would run somewhat as follows:

'He is proud of his arms. They are skinny, but he thinks them the limit. Better put in a shirt-sleeve scene for Willie somewhere.'

'He thinks he has a beautiful profile. Couldn't you make one of the girls say something about Willie having the goods in that line?'

'He is crazy about golf.'

'He is proud of his French accent. Couldn't you make Willie speak a little piece in French?'

'He' being Winfield Knight.

And so, little by little, the character of Willie grew, till it ceased to be the Willie of the magazine story, and became Winfield Knight himself, with improvements. The task began to fascinate Rutherford. It was like planning a pleasant surprise for a child. 'He'll like that,' he would say to himself, as he wrote in some speech enabling Willie to display one of the accomplishments, real or imagined, of the absent actor. Peggy read it, and approved. It was she who suggested the big speech in the second act where Willie described the progress of his love affair in terms of the golf-links. From her, too, came information as to little traits in the man's character which the stranger would not have suspected.

As the play progressed Rutherford was amazed at the completeness of the character he had built. It lived. Willie in the magazine story might have been anyone. He fitted into the story, but you could not see him. He had no real individuality. But Willie in the play! He felt that he would recognize him in the street. There was all the difference between the two that there is between a nameless figure in some cheap picture and a portrait by Sargent. There were times when the story of the play seemed thin to him, and the other characters wooden, but in his blackest moods he was sure of Willie. All the contradictions in the character rang true: the humour, the pathos, the surface vanity covering a real diffidence, the strength and weakness fighting one another.

'You're alive, my son,' said Rutherford, admiringly, as he read the sheets. 'But you don't belong to me.'

At last there came the day when the play was finished, when the last line was written, and the last possible alteration made; and later, the day when Rutherford, bearing the brown-paper-covered package under his arm, called at the Players' Club to keep an appointment with Winfield Knight.

Almost from the first Rutherford had a feeling that he had met the man before, that he knew him. As their acquaintance progressed—the actor was in an expansive mood, and talked much before coming to business—the feeling grew. Then he understood. This was Willie, and no other. The likeness was extraordinary. Little turns of thought, little expressions—they were all in the play.

The actor paused in a description of how he had almost beaten a champion at golf, and looked at the parcel.

'Is that the play?' he said.

'Yes,' said Rutherford. 'Shall I read it?'

'Guess I'll just look through it myself. Where's Act I? Here we are! Have a cigar while you're waiting?'

Rutherford settled himself in his chair, and watched the other's face. For the first few pages, which contained some tame dialogue between minor characters, it was blank.

'"Enter Willie,"' he said. 'Am I Willie?'

'I hope so,' said Rutherford, with a smile. 'It's the star part.'

'H'm.'

He went on reading. Rutherford watched him with furtive keenness. There was a line coming at the bottom of the page which he was then reading which ought to hit him, an epigram on golf, a whimsical thought put almost exactly as he had put it himself five minutes back when telling his golf story.

The shot did not miss fire. The chuckle from the actor and the sigh of relief from Rutherford were almost simultaneous. Winfield Knight turned to him.

'That's a dandy line about golf,' said he.

Rutherford puffed complacently at his cigar.

'There's lots more of them in the piece,' he said.

'Bully for you,' said the actor. And went on reading.

Three-quarters of an hour passed before he spoke again. Then he looked up.

'It's me,' he said; 'it's me all the time. I wish I'd seen this before I put on the punk I'm doing now. This is me from the drive off the tee. It's great! Say, what'll you have?'

Rutherford leaned back in his chair, his mind in a whirl. He had arrived at last. His struggles were over. He would not admit of the possibility of the play being a failure. He was a made man. He could go where he pleased, and do as he pleased.

It gave him something of a shock to find how persistently his thoughts refused to remain in England. Try as he might to keep them there, they kept flitting back to Alcala.

6

Willie in the Wilderness was not a failure. It was a triumph. Principally, it is true, a personal triumph for Winfield Knight. Everyone was agreed that he had never had a part that suited him so well. Critics forgave the blunders of the piece for the sake of its principal character. The play was a curiously amateurish thing. It was only later that Rutherford learned craft and caution. When he wrote *Willie* he was a colt, rambling unchecked through the field of play-writing, ignorant of its pitfalls. But, with all its faults, *Willie in the Wilderness* was a success. It might, as one critic pointed out, be more of a monologue act for Winfield Knight than a play, but that did not affect Rutherford.

It was late on the opening night when he returned to Alcala. He had tried to get away earlier. He wanted to see Peggy. But Winfield Knight, flushed with success, was in his most expansive mood. He seized upon Rutherford and would not let him go. There was supper, a gay, uproarious supper, at which everybody seemed to be congratulating everybody else. Men he had never met before shook him warmly by the hand. Somebody made a speech, despite the efforts of the rest of the company to prevent him. Rutherford sat there, dazed, out of touch with the mood of the party. He wanted Peggy. He was tired of all this excitement and noise. He had had enough of it. All he asked was to be allowed to slip away quietly and go home. He wanted to think, to try and realize what all this meant to him.

At length the party broke up in one last explosion of handshaking and congratulations; and, eluding Winfield Knight, who proposed to take him off to his club, he started to walk up Broadway.

It was late when he reached Alcala. There was a light in his room. Peggy had waited up to hear the news.

She jumped off the table as he came in.

'Well?' she cried.

Rutherford sat down and stretched out his legs.

'It's a success,' he said. 'A tremendous success!'

Peggy clapped her hands.

'Bully for you, George! I knew it would be. Tell me all about it. Was Winfield good?'

'He was the whole piece. There was nothing in it but him.' He rose and placed his hands on her shoulders. 'Peggy, old girl, I don't know what to say. You know as well as I do that it's all owing to you that the piece has been a success. If I hadn't had your help—'

Peggy laughed.

'Oh, beat it, George!' she said. 'Don't you come jollying me. I look like a high-brow playwright, don't I! No; I'm real glad you've made a hit, George, but don't start handing out any story about it's not being your own. I didn't do a thing.'

'You did. You did everything.'

'I didn't. But, say, don't let's start quarrelling. Tell me more about it. How many calls did you take.'

He told her all that had happened. When he had finished, there was a silence.

'I guess you'll be quitting soon, George?' said Peggy, at last. 'Now that you've made a home-run. You'll be going back to that rube joint, with the cows and hens—isn't that it?'

Rutherford did not reply. He was staring thoughtfully at the floor. He did not seem to have heard.

'I guess that girl'll be glad to see you,' she went on. 'Shall you cable tomorrow, George? And then you'll get married and go and live in the rube house, and become a regular hayseed and—' She broke off suddenly, with a catch in her voice. 'Gee,' she whispered, halt to herself, 'I'll be sorry when you go, George.'

He sprang up.

'Peggy!'

He seized her by the arm. He heard the quick intake of her breath.

'Peggy, listen!' He gripped her till she winced with pain. 'I'm not going back. I'm never going back. I'm a cad, I'm a hound! I know I am. But I'm not going back. I'm going to stay here with you. I want you, Peggy. Do you hear? I want you!'

She tried to draw herself away, but he held her.

'I love you, Peggy! Peggy, will you be my wife?'

There was utter astonishment in her grey eyes. Her face was very white.

'Will you, Peggy?'

He dropped her arm.

'Will you, Peggy?'

'No!' she cried.

He drew back.

'No!' she cried sharply, as if it hurt her to speak. 'I wouldn't play you such a mean trick. I'm too fond of you, George. There's never been anybody just like you. You've been mighty good to me. I've never met a man who treated me like you. You're the only real white man that's ever happened to me, and I guess I'm not going to play you a low-down trick like spoiling your life. George, I thought you knew. Honest, I thought you knew. How did you think I lived in a swell place like this, if you didn't know? How did you suppose everyone knew me at Rector's? How did you think I'd managed to find out so much about Winfield Knight? Can't you guess?'

She drew a long breath.

'I—'

He interrupted her hoarsely.

'Is there anyone now, Peggy?'

'Yes,' she said, 'there is.'

'You don't love him, Peggy, do you?'

'Love him?' She laughed bitterly. 'No; I don't love him.'

'Then come to me, dear,' he said.

She shook her head in silence. Rutherford sat down, his chin resting in his hands. She came across to him, and smoothed his hair.

'It wouldn't do, George,' she said. 'Honest, it wouldn't do. Listen. When we first met, I—I rather liked you, George, and I was mad at you for being so fond of the other girl and taking no notice of me—not in the way I wanted, and I tried—Gee, I feel mean. It was all my fault. I didn't think it would matter. There didn't seem no chance then of your being able to go back and have the sort of good time you wanted; and I thought you'd just stay here and we'd be pals and— but now you can go back, it's all different. I couldn't keep you. It would be too mean. You see, you don't really want to stop. You think you do, but you don't!'

'I love you,' he muttered.

'You'll forget me. It's all just a Broadway dream, George. Think of it like that. Broadway's got you now, but you don't really belong. You're not like me. It's not in your blood, so's you can't get it out. It's the chickens and roses you want really.

Just a Broadway dream. That's what it is. George, when I was a kid, I remember crying and crying for a lump of candy in the window of a store till one of my brothers up and bought it for me just to stop the racket. Gee! For about a minute I was the busiest thing that ever happened, eating away. And then it didn't seem to interest me no more. Broadway's like that for you, George. You go back to the girl and the cows and all of it. It'll hurt some, I guess, but I reckon you'll be glad you did.'

She stooped swiftly, and kissed him on the forehead.

'I'll miss you, dear,' she said, softly, and was gone.

Rutherford sat on, motionless. Outside, the blackness changed to grey, and the grey to white. He got up. He felt very stiff and cold.

'A Broadway dream!' he muttered.

He went to the mantelpiece and took up the photograph. He carried it to the window where he could see it better.

A shaft of sunlight pierced the curtains and fell upon it.

Available from the Echo Library (USA only)
Wodehouse, P. G. (Pelham Grenville), 1881-1975

The Adventures of Sally
The Clicking of Cuthbert
The Coming of Bill
A Damsel in Distress
Death at the Excelsior
And Other Stories
The Gem Collector
The Gold Bat
A Head of Kay's
Indiscretions of Archie
The Intrusion of Jimmy
The Little Nugget
Little Warrior
Love Among the Chickens
A Man of Means
The Man Upstairs and Other Stories
Man with Two Left Feet, The And Other Stories
Mike
Mike and Psmith
My Man Jeeves
Not George Washington — an Autobiographical Novel
Piccadilly Jim
The Politeness of Princes
and Other School Stories
The Pothunters
A Prefect's Uncle
The Prince and Betty
Psmith in the City
Psmith, Journalist
Right Ho, Jeeves
Something New
The Swoop
Tales of St. Austin's
Three Men and a Maid
Uneasy Money
The White Feather
William Tell Told Again
A Wodehouse Miscellany Articles & Stories (English)

Printed in the United States
56565LVS00004B/59